One kiss . . .

Abigail Mercer was breathless with anticipation at being reunited with Spencer Law, whom she met once and later married by proxy. But now the dashing Viscount Ravenswood denies all knowledge of their union! Far too many witnesses have made it impossible for the secretive Spencer to reject his "bride" without causing a scandal. So he has proposed a marriage in-name-only until they can locate his mysteriously absent younger brother—who is responsible for everything!—and untangle this messy affair.

Abigail is incensed, irate . . . and irresistibly attracted to this handsome, infuriating man who hides his smoldering passion behind a proper exterior. So the lady will agree to his terms on one condition: Spencer must seal their bargain with a kiss—one deep, lingering, unforgettable kiss meant to stoke the sensuous flames of love . . . one kiss to melt the icy, resisting heart of the only husband Abigail has ever desired.

P9-EMH-614

Avon Books by
Sabrina Jeffries

ATTENTION: ORGANIZATIONS AND CORPORATIONS
Most Avon Books paperbacks are available at special quantity
discounts for bulk purchases for sales promotions, premiums, or
fund-raising. For information, please call or write:

**Special Markets Department, HarperCollins Publishers Inc.
10 East 53rd Street, New York, New York 10022-5299.
Telephone: (212) 207-7528.   Fax: (212) 207-7222.**

SABRINA JEFFRIES

Married to the Viscount

An Avon Romantic Treasure

AVON BOOKS
An Imprint of HarperCollinsPublishers

AVON BOOKS
An Imprint of HarperCollins*Publishers*
10 East 53rd Street
New York, New York 10022-5299

Copyright © 2004 by Deborah Martin
ISBN: 0-06-009214-9
www.avonromance.com

First Avon Books paperback printing: January 2004

Avon Trademark Reg. U.S. Pat. Off. and in Other Countries, Marca Registrada, Hecho en U.S.A.
HarperCollins® is a registered trademark of HarperCollins Publishers Inc.

Printed in the U.S.A.

10 9 8 7 6 5 4

Prologue

Philadelphia
Early December 1821

Spencer Law, the fifth Viscount Ravenswood, drained yet another redware mug of hard cider. It didn't help. He could still remember what he'd come to the noisy American tavern with his younger brother to forget.

He was going back to England in the morning. Back to the disordered Parliament and disgruntled populace. Back to his demanding duties as undersecretary to the Home Office in his country's time of turmoil. The weight of his responsibilities, which had miraculously eased during his sojourn in America, already began settling heavily upon his shoulders again.

What he needed was more hard cider.

When he called for it, a laugh erupted from Nat, who lounged on a wooden bench across the table from him. "Perhaps you should slow down, old fellow. You're getting foxed."

1

SABRINA JEFFRIES

2

"That's the general idea."

"The great Ravenswood drowning his sorrows in strong drink? Astonishing! Usually you're too busy running England to overindulge. And too dignified." Nat planted his elbows on the sturdy oak table. "Though I must admit you haven't been yourself since we arrived two weeks ago." He cocked his head to examine his brother. "It's Dr. Mercer's daughter, isn't it? She's the one making you act so strangely."

Spencer barely mustered one of his steely-eyed glances. "Don't be absurd."

But just that quickly his mind conjured up the image of Abigail Mercer, whom her father called "my wild rose." A fitting appellation for a woman with leaf-green eyes and petal-soft golden skin and a glorious scarlet bud of a mouth . . .

"You hummed an aria for her yesterday," Nat pointed out.

"I told her about seeing *The Marriage of Figaro* this year, and she wanted to hear some of it. What's your point?"

"I've never heard you hum anything in your life."

"I never had occasion to do so."

"You never felt the urge to do so," Nat said dryly. "Until you met Miss Mercer, that is. Now you spend all your time conversing with a pretty colonial lass—"

"What else is there to do while you discuss business with her ailing father?" Spencer stared down into his empty mug.

"True. And she does seem easy to talk to."

Exactly. Easy to talk to and artless and utterly American. Unlike all those English misses raised to worship a title and an estate, Miss Mercer treated him as if he were her equal in station.

The woman even had the audacity to tease him whenever he grew too serious. No Englishwoman had ever done that. They were too aware of his position—or too cowed by his sober manner—to be at ease in his presence.

Nor did Englishwomen debate him about politics and such. But Miss Mercer plunged right into every argument with all the fervent optimism of her fellow countrymen. It was maddening.

It was fascinating.

"Mind you," Nat went on, "I'm delighted that you and Miss Mercer are friendly. It can't help but soften her father toward my proposal." He steadied his shoulders. "And speaking of that, have you thought any more about advancing me those funds?"

Since his own mug was empty, Spencer reached across to steal his brother's. He wasn't foxed enough yet to deal with this. "You mean, so you can pursue your foolish plan to become a partner in Dr. Mercer's enterprise?"

"It's not foolish," Nat protested. "I know you had reservations about the Mercer Medicinal Company, but you've seen the doctor's records on how well his tonic sold seven years ago—you must admit the numbers are phenomenal. If he hadn't taken ill, he'd be rich by now instead of hounded by creditors. All he needs is someone like me to rejuvenate the company while he's incapacitated."

"Not incapacitated," Spencer corrected. "Dying. The man's dying, Nat."

"But that's precisely why he might sell to me. I already own the shares I won in that card game. And even you must have thought the business a promising investment or you would never have accompanied me to America for a look."

Spencer slumped against the wall behind his hard bench. "You said you'd go without me. Couldn't let you do that, given your past record with other occupations."

Nat bristled. "Must you always throw my failures up at me? Never mind that I was only doing what you wanted. I told you I'd be no good at the law, but you insisted I study for it, so I did."

"Apparently not very hard, since you failed your exams. And let's not forget the navy. After that fiasco, even my influence couldn't keep you in."

Nat winced. "I wasn't cut out to be a navy man. I can't even steer a carriage straight. I only agreed to try because you went to all that trouble to gain me the berth." He leaned forward, his voice growing fierce. "The thing is, I *know* I can do this. I'm good at numbers. That's why I've always won so much at the gaming tables."

"Always?" Spencer finished off the cider in Nat's mug. Where the bloody hell was that tavern maid?

"All right, so I got cocky one night. And you had to pay for it."

"Quite a lot of money, as I recall."

"I know, I know. But this is different. The old man is in a bind—he won't leave the Mercer Company entirely to his daughter, because he thinks she lacks the business sense to pull it out of debt. But if he doesn't find someone to be her partner, he'll have to leave it to some relative he hates. So I can step right in."

The sour-faced tavern maid plunked down two freshly filled redware mugs, and Spencer seized his with a vengeance. Now he had something else to drown out—the unsettling image of Miss Mercer working with his brother.

He mustn't think of that, mustn't think of the mischievous smile she'd be flashing at Nat instead of Spencer. It wasn't as if Spencer could stay here while his brother tried out his fool scheme. A summons from the Home Office mustn't be ignored, and with the sudden resignation of the old home secretary, Spencer was badly needed at home. So like it or not, he had to accept that his pleasant idyll in America was over.

Not that anything could ever come of Spencer's association with Miss Mercer anyway, no matter how cheerful and appealing he found her.

He scowled. Half the women in England would happily settle for a position as Spencer's mistress, yet none of them tempted him. No, his idiotic mind had to seize on the respectable Miss Mercer for its lusty thoughts, a woman who'd take nothing less than marriage. So since he couldn't marry her or anyone else, it was probably just as well he was leaving tomorrow and would never see her again.

Bloody hell.

He drank deeply of his cider, then set the mug down. "How does Evelina feel about all this? Or have you even bothered to tell your future wife about your plan to partner a business halfway around the world with the beautiful Abby Mercer?"

Nat eyed his brother speculatively. "Evelina will understand. It's only temporary. Once the old man dies, I'll buy his daughter out. Miss Mercer will have enough money to support herself, and I'll own Mercer Medicinal."

"You don't know how to run a business."

"You didn't know how to be a soldier all those years ago when Father bought you a commission in the army, but you learned. You're good at that sort of thing."

"I had to be," he growled, resenting his brother's freedom to do as he pleased. Spencer had lost that freedom when their eldest brother died unexpectedly.

"And I have to be good at this. What's left for me? The church?"

They groaned in unison. Even Spencer could see that would never work.

"Besides, I'm not going to run it," Nat went on. "I'll hire a manager for that. I just want to own it."

The growing buzz in Spencer's head hadn't turned him into a complete idiot. "And you want me to give you the money for it."

Nat had the good grace to flush. "Not all of the money. I've kept some of my allowance aside. And in the past two years, I've lived responsibly. I won't need much."

With a roll of his eyes, Spencer reached for his mug again, but Nat stayed his hand. "Soon I'll be married, which is why I want to do something useful with myself, something *I* want to do, not something you choose for me." A wan smile crossed Nat's face. "I know I can make a go of this. So what do you say? If I get Mercer to agree to my plan and I need money, will you send it to me?"

Spencer was still trying to forget Miss Mercer's kissable lips. The ones he would never, could never kiss, even if he wasn't leaving. He drained his mug. "Write to me in London, and I'll do what I can."

Nat's face lit up. "Capital, old fellow, capital! I knew you'd come through for me." Done with his business, Nat attacked his own cider. While he drank, he watched his brother through narrowed eyes. "So you find Miss Mercer beautiful?"

The buzzing in Spencer's head formed the words, " 'She walks in beauty like the night/Of cloudless climes and starry skies.' "

"My God, now you're quoting poetry."

Had he said that aloud? Bloody hell. Spencer brandished his empty mug at his brother. "I always quote verse when I'm foxed."

"You must be very foxed to quote that idiot Byron. Or very impressed by Miss Mercer's looks."

"Who wouldn't be?" And exactly when had he started slurring his words?

Nat fiddled with his mug. "Some men might find her coloring too dark."

"Some men are idiots." Spencer lifted his mug, remembered it was empty, and frowned.

With a chuckle, Nat pushed his own over. "I'm just saying I'm surprised that her being half Indian hasn't put off the great Ravenswood."

"Stop calling me that." Accepting his brother's full mug, Spencer ignored Nat's intent stare. "Besides, half Indian or no, she's of good stock. Her father's family is prominent in Philadelphia, and her mother's father was chief of his tribe. The Seneca, I believe."

"Where did you hear that?"

"She told me herself."

"Ah, yes. During all those conversations. And is that *all* you did? Talk?"

"I don't know what you mean." A burst of raucous laughter from a nearby table made Spencer's head pound, and he rubbed his suddenly throbbing temples.

"Yes, you do. You lust after the woman—admit it. You get that look in your eyes whenever she enters a room, as if you'd like nothing more than to sheathe your sword in her scabbard."

"Don't talk nonsense." And devil take the scoundrel for noticing so much.

Nat watched him closely. "Considering her background and the likelihood that she'll never marry, perhaps you should coax her into becoming your mistress."

Spencer managed a laugh. "That determined American optimism of hers would drive me mad inside a month." He stared down into the dregs of his cider, only to see Abby Mercer as his mistress. All that cheerful eagerness focused on pleasing him and wanting him and writhing about with him naked in his bed . . .

Ridiculous thought. Gently bred women did not agree to be mistresses. Anyway, he was done with having a mistress. Being a woman's protector was too much a parody of the marriage he couldn't have. Better to have the occasional random liaison when he had the time for it. Which wasn't often these days.

"So I suppose marrying her is out of the question," Nat said smoothly.

"Absolutely."

"She seemed well-bred to me, but I suppose she's not refined enough for you."

"Got nothing to do with it. Even if I wanted, I couldn't marry her."

"Because you have your eye on somebody else?" his brother probed.

"Certainly not." Spencer lowered his voice. His head thundered when he spoke too loudly. "Can't marry her, can't marry anyone."

"Of course you can. You have to marry someone. And soon, too. You're already thirty-seven. You ought to settle down with a wife."

"Can't." Damned nuisance to have his words coming out all fuzzy. "No marriage for me." He caught Nat's scowl and added, "That ought to make you happy—you or your son will inherit it all."

"I don't want to inherit it all." Nat sounded panicked. "Evelina and I will be perfectly content with whatever you settle on us, so don't think you'll get out of siring an heir. I've no desire to gain the title and be responsible for tenants and houses and all that rot. I ran a ship aground while I was in the navy—what do you think I'd do to an estate?"

"But you can run a business?"

"Own it, not run it. I told you." Nat scowled. "All right, so perhaps I just don't want to run an estate. It doesn't interest me."

"Didn't interest me, either. But a man does his duty. Yours will be siring an heir."

"By God, you're serious. You really don't intend to marry."

Spencer nodded, feeling rather wobbly. "Plan to be a bachelor till I die."

"Why? It's got nothing to do with Dora, I hope. Just because Father and our stepmother made a hash of their marriage is no reason to think you will."

There was more to it than that, but Spencer dared not explain. Instead he gazed morosely into the glazed red hollow of his empty mug. Nat called for more cider, and Spencer lifted his reeling head. "Shouldn't have any more, you know. I'm foxed."

"Not foxed enough." Nat flashed him a grim smile. "Let

me enjoy the novelty of my perfect brother's exhibiting the same weaknesses we mere mortals possess."

"Not perfect," Spencer muttered. "Not a'tall. That's the trouble, you see."

"No, I don't see." Two mugs magically appeared, and Nat shoved both at Spencer. "Perhaps it's time you explain it to me."

Chapter 1

Even the finest butler may blunder when announcing a surprise guest, but he should use the occasion to learn the correct styling. One never knows when a surprise guest may become important in his employer's household.

Suggestions for the Stoic Servant,
by the Butler to a Very Important Gentleman

London
April 15, 1822

The bride-to-be was here. The groom-to-be was two hours late. As betrothal dinners went, this one qualified for fiasco of the season.

Spencer, reluctant host of the fiasco, surveyed the immaculately appointed dining table in his London town house and sighed. How soon could he call an end to this painful ordeal and retreat to his study and his cognac? Probably not for at least another hour. Anything less would rouse suspicion among his twenty-six guests.

Thanks to his quick thinking and talent for lying, they didn't even know the dinner was a fiasco. And until he found out why Nat had disappeared, he had no intention of letting them in on the secret.

He glanced over at Lady Evelina, the bride-to-be. Thank God she'd apparently accepted his far-fetched tale. Like a china doll, she perched on her chair in cultivated perfection, blond ringlets framing her flawless brow, her cheeks pink but not rouged, and her gown the ideal hue for her porcelain skin. Only her sparkling eyes hinted at the sweet-natured girl Nat and Spencer had teased while she was growing up.

Catching his eye, Evelina dabbed daintily at her cupidbow lips with a damask napkin. "I do hope they don't detain poor Nathaniel at the police offices all night. Did his note say how long it might be?"

That damned fictitious note. "No, but they'll probably keep him awhile," Spencer lied with all the practiced ease of a former spymaster. "He'll have to give testimony against the ruffian he caught snatching that woman's reticule."

"It was so brave of him to run off after the villain all alone," she said. "And then to insist on carrying that man to the police himself—how noble of him!"

"Yes, Nat is nothing if not noble." That lie came harder in the face of young Evelina's starry-eyed loyalty.

Not that Spencer had any other choice. Engaging in a manly pursuit of justice was an acceptable excuse for not attending one's betrothal dinner; abandoning one's bride-to-be was not. Until Spencer knew the reason for Nat's apparent defection, he had to keep lying. Otherwise, Evelina and her widowed mother, Lady Tyndale, would suffer public humiliation. Which Spencer refused to allow.

Where the hell was he? When Spencer had last seen Nat an hour before dinner, his brother hadn't mentioned any plans to dash out. And although Spencer's butler McFee had seen Nat receive a message shortly after that, no one had seen the man leave. But no one could find him, either, not in the house or at any of his favorite London haunts.

Nat had simply vanished, and it looked deliberate. After all, how much trouble could one man get into in only a few hours?

Spencer sighed. Nat had acted strangely ever since his return from America a month ago—he was inordinately inter-

ested in the mail, came and went at all hours, had mysterious
meetings, and in general acted like a man still sowing wild
oats instead of preparing to marry.

Now this. For God's sake, where was he?

"Well, I for one am surprised Nathaniel even had the presence of mind to send a note at all," Evelina's mother commented. "But the man is always so considerate."

"And noble, too," the woman sitting next to her added with
a hint of sarcasm. "Let's not forget 'noble.' "

Wonderful. Now Lady Brumley was putting her nose in it.
Why in hell had Evelina's mother invited a woman popularly
known as the Galleon of Gossip? He should have paid closer
attention to the guest list.

But with England's chaotic political situation occupying
him, he'd had no time to plan the betrothal dinner Lady
Tyndale had expected him to host. So he'd unwisely given
that to her, his designated hostess for the evening. Somehow the intimate little affair he'd suggested had exploded
into this assembly of London society's most prestigious—
and chatty—members. That's what he got for trusting a
woman with the intelligence of a pea.

And there was still a betrothal ball to get through two
nights from now. Fortunately, Lady Tyndale was hosting
that at her home. Spencer shuddered to think what sort of
production it would be. She'd probably invited half the *ton*
to her ball.

If there was a ball. Given Nat's disappearance tonight, that
was no longer certain.

He scowled. He wanted to see Nat settled, damn it.
Twenty-nine was a good age for marrying, and twenty-year-
old Evelina was perfect for him. Insane as it seemed, she'd
apparently been in love with the idiot from girlhood, which
was all a man could ask for.

"That note from your brother," Lady Brumley commented.

"Might we see it for ourselves, Ravenswood? I shall have to write about the event for the paper, and I want all the details of Mr. Law's noble act."

What the nosy woman wanted was to uncover scandal. Clearly she hadn't believed his tale. Just what he needed—the shrewd Lady Brumley voicing her suspicions in that infamous column of hers.

"I thought you had your own sources." Spencer sipped his claret with a carefully cultivated air of boredom. "Or have you grown tired of checking your facts?"

The woman answered his sarcasm in kind. "I suspect that if I wait until tomorrow for that, I'll hear only the official story. Since the London magistrates report directly to you at the Home Office, I don't imagine they'll tell me anything more than you'll allow."

"True." He set down his glass. "But I've already told you all there is to tell."

Spencer cast a surreptitious glance at the clock and barely suppressed his groan. Two hours and thirteen minutes. Perhaps this *was* something other than mere defection. Could Nat have landed in trouble? But how? And with whom?

"I should still like to see the note—" Lady Brumley began.

"You know, my lord," Evelina broke in, "Nathaniel told me and Mama all about his recent visit to America, but we haven't heard a word from *you* about it."

Spencer regarded the girl with surprise. The polite Evelina rarely interrupted anyone, much less a woman of Lady Brumley's standing. Perhaps she wasn't as oblivious to the situation as he'd thought.

When everyone else turned their attention to her, Evelina flushed, but kept her eyes on Spencer. "I know you didn't spend as much time there as Nathaniel, but how did you like it? He seemed to enjoy it quite a lot. He spoke highly of the Mercers and was very impressed with Dr. Mercer's Medicinal Mead." She smiled at her listeners. "That's the doctor's tonic for indigestion and other ailments. Dr. Mercer's company produces it."

"Never heard of it," Lady Brumley put in. "And you can be sure I know all the tonics for indigestion."

"It sells only in America right now, my lady." Evelina served herself asparagus with shaky hands. "But Nathaniel thinks it could sell quite well here. So in exchange for part ownership in the company, Nathaniel is promoting the tonic in England."

Spencer hadn't known what Nat was planning. What else had his brother not told him?

Lady Brumley shot Spencer a reproachful look. "Have you gone mad, my lord? Why would you allow your brother to pursue some wild scheme—"

"But it's not," Evelina put in hastily. "Nathaniel believes this Mercer fellow's enterprise is a worthy one. His lordship does, too—he's agreed to invest in it himself."

"Really, Ravenswood?" Lady Brumley asked. "You're encouraging this idiocy?"

"I'm always eager for a good investment." But Nat hadn't actually asked him for any money yet, and Spencer only half remembered the drunken night when he'd agreed to invest. "In the brief time I had to observe Mercer's company, it seemed sound."

"Nathaniel is determined to make a go of it," Evelina said. "He has his own stake in the firm, you see."

Yes. Nat had apparently done the impossible, because upon his return to England he'd assured Spencer that old Josiah had relented and made him a partner.

"Of course," Evelina went on, "he does have to share the company with the physician's daughter. But that's all right, since Miss Mercer is the one who concocts all the medicines. So he needs her anyway."

Abigail Mercer. Damn, Spencer might have forgotten the

American woman for a few hours, but he'd needed only a mention of her to summon Miss Mercer's image anew—her bright flash of a smile, teasing green eyes, sun-kissed skin. Why couldn't he suppress that picture? He'd known her only two weeks, yet she'd plagued his thoughts for months since.

"So Nat . . . er . . . told you about Miss Mercer?" Spencer ate a forkful of squab pie. What could Nat possibly have said that wouldn't have made Evelina jealous?

"Oh, yes," Evelina answered. "Poor thing, to lose her mother so young, then have to face losing her father, too. And still unmarried at twenty-six! She's unlikely to find a husband even after her father dies. Nathaniel says she's dark and plain as a crow."

Spencer nearly choked. When had Nat become as adept at lying as his older brother? "I believe that Miss Mercer's spinsterhood wasn't the result so much of her looks as of her situation."

"Oh?" Evelina said with interest.

"Her father was ill for many years. As she is his only child, his care fell to her, which allowed her little time for the usual courting." Not to mention that some gentlemen probably objected to her mixed blood. "But I expect she'll find a husband eventually. She's an amiable woman with a good—"

He stopped short. All the women at the table were eyeing him now with rampant curiosity. Bloody hell. He usually knew not to say anything that set matchmaking females to speculating. But Nat's mysterious disappearance had put him off his game. Too late to undo the damage, judging from the shrewd gleam in Lady Brumley's eye.

"You seem to know a great deal about Miss Mercer," the gossip said. "Perhaps she wasn't as dark and plain as your brother claims. What did *you* think of her looks, Ravenswood?"

Thankfully, he was spared answering when the door to the dining room opened to admit his butler. When McFee approached the table and bent close enough to reveal an unnat-

ural pallor beneath his ruddy Scottish skin, Spencer knew
something was wrong.

"What is it?" Spencer asked in a low tone.

"I must speak to you privately, my lord."

McFee probably had news of Nat. Spencer rose and faced
his guests. "I beg your indulgence, but I must step into the
hall a moment."

Amid murmurs of polite assent, Spencer strode out of the
dining room with McFee at his heels, only waiting until he'd
shut the door to ask, "What's happened?"

"There is a female waiting to see you."

Spencer scowled. McFee only used the term "female"
with certain sorts of women. By God, if Nat had sent some
tart with a message . . . "What does she want?"

"To speak to you."

"About my brother?"

"No, my lord."

Relief flooded Spencer. "Then tell her to return tomorrow.
I have no time for this tonight."

"She was most insistent. And I believe you should probably speak to her."

Spencer raised one eyebrow at his butler's presumption.
"Why? Who is she?"

"You see . . . well . . . that is . . ."

"For God's sake, spit it out," Spencer said impatiently. "I
don't have all night."

McFee drew himself up with wounded dignity. "She
claims to be Lady Ravenswood. Your wife."

"My what?!"

The cry echoed down the hall to the magnificent high-
ceilinged foyer where Abigail Mercer waited with her servant, Mrs. Graham. Abby pricked up her ears. "I think his
lordship has been informed of our arrival."

"Thank the good Lord." Mrs. Graham scowled. "That Mr. La-Di-Da of a butler was acting so strange I wondered if he would even announce us."

Abby bit back a smile. Mrs. Graham had been with the Mercer family for an eternity, first as Abby's nursemaid and later as general family servant. Though the aging widow could be a grouse at times, Abby couldn't imagine doing without her. "Well, *I* feared we had the wrong house, especially with all the carriages in front. His lordship must be having guests for dinner, though why he'd do that on the night of our arrival—"

"I just want to know why he didn't have nobody at the docks to fetch us. Didn't you tell him what ship we was coming on, milady?"

"I certainly did. And how odd that his lordship wasn't more solicitous of our comfort. I thought we should never find a hired coach to carry us here."

A commotion at the other end of the hall, doors opening and closing and the murmur of various voices, drew Abby's attention. Lord Ravenswood was probably explaining to his guests why he was being called away.

Mrs. Graham frowned. "His lordship sure sounded surprised to hear of our arrival. But I think, milady—"

Abby burst into laughter. "Heavens, would you stop calling me that? Bad enough that you insisted I wear this ridiculous corset. But the 'milady' you drop into every sentence is really overdoing it. I keep looking around to see whom you mean."

Mrs. Graham sniffed. "Better get used to it. You're a viscountess now."

"I don't feel like a viscountess. I can hardly even think of Lord Ravenswood as a viscount. In America, he was more like a country gentleman. He always made me feel at ease."

"I say it's about time some man treated you like the fine

lass you are. But I didn't like that proxy wedding business, and poor Mr. Nathaniel Law having to stand in for his brother—"

"I didn't mind it so much. This isn't a love match, you know. I can hardly expect romantic behavior from his lordship."

Then again, the way he'd looked at her sometimes during his two weeks in America . . . Just remembering it sent a shiver of delightful anticipation down her spine.

Forcibly she reminded herself of the practical nature of their agreement.

"His letters said he was marrying me because he had 'feelings of respect and admiration.' But that's all right. I have them for him, too." And his admiration could grow into love in time, couldn't it?

He might even now have warmer feelings for her than he would reveal in an impersonal letter. Why else would he have gone so far as to marry an American spinster of mixed blood? Seeing his grand house only confirmed her suspicion that the handsome, clever, and amiable Lord Ravenswood could have any English lady he wanted.

But he'd chosen her. Just thinking of it fairly started her heart to pounding.

A door opened and closed again, but this time the murmurs at the other end of the hall were followed by footsteps. "I think he's coming."

"Lord have mercy!" Mrs. Graham patted down a stray curl of her graying red hair. "Quick, milady, give me some of that Mead for my breath."

"Good idea." Although the Mead was intended for medicinal use, it also made a perfect breath sweetener. Removing her personal vial from the kerseymere reticule that dangled from a cord on her wrist, she handed it to her servant.

Opening it, Mrs. Graham swigged some, winced, and returned it to Abby. "Lordy, that sure is nasty-tasting stuff."

"But the scent makes up for it, don't you think?" Abby lifted the bottle to her lips, the heady aroma of rosemary and neroli oil wafting to her as she sipped. She swished it around in her mouth, then swallowed the bitter tonic as she closed up the vial.

The footsteps had stopped halfway down the hall, and more murmuring could be heard. Abby returned the bottle swiftly to her reticule. Why didn't he just come on?

"How do I look?" Glancing down at her wrinkled traveling gown, Abby groaned. "Oh, I look awful. I hate for him to see me like this."

"Can't be helped. Considering you've been hauled from pillar to post to get here, you look pretty enough." Mrs. Graham stepped in front of her, lifted her black bombazine skirt, and rearranged it to drape more naturally. "You should have let me lace your corset tighter. This gown needs tight lacing to fall proper."

Abby snorted. "If you lace it any tighter, I'll explode out either end."

Mrs. Graham clucked her tongue. "You're just not used to wearing it is all. Your mother, God rest her, shouldn't have let her strange notions keep you from dressing proper."

"Strange notions" was Mrs. Graham's polite term for any of Mama's Senecan beliefs. "Mama was right about corsets being unhealthy."

"But refined ladies must wear 'em, especially in England. You don't want these English thinking you're some country girl not fit to be a viscountess, do you?"

"What is the meaning of this?" rumbled a voice from just beyond Mrs. Graham.

With a squeak, Mrs. Graham whirled around and Abby jumped. Rounding the staircase with that stuffy Mr. McFee at his side was the viscount himself.

My husband, she reminded herself. And heavenly day, what a man. She'd never seen him dressed so formally, his broad shoulders filling out a double-breasted tailcoat and his muscular thighs straining against the fabric of form-fitting breeches.

And all of it jet-black except his shirt. His black attire, silvery eyes, and rapidly clouding brow made her think of Hino, the thunder god of Mama's Senecan tales, thunder and lightning and storm all rolled into one.

Then he strode up to tower over her, and she swallowed hard. She'd forgotten his imposing height. And why did he look so sternly upon her? He'd never done so before. "My lord, it seems we've taken you by surprise, but—"

"You certainly have." His clipped words cast a chill over her. Then his gaze flicked down. "You're in mourning."

She nodded. "Papa passed away two months ago."

The stormy brow softened. "I'm sorry. You have my deepest sympathies."

"Thank you. It was expected, of course, but I still . . . miss him."

"Of course you do," he said, his voice husky with concern.

Thank God. For a moment there, she'd thought him a stranger and not at all the considerate gentleman she'd known in America.

He stepped nearer, swamping her with his familiar spicy scent, thick with bergamot and soap and essence of male. "Death is never expected, my dear, no matter how much one tries to prepare."

His kindness brought tears to her eyes. She brushed them away, and his face softened even more.

Removing his handkerchief, he pressed it into her hand. "Now I understand why you're here. You've come to England to work out the terms of your partnership with my brother, haven't you?" When she stopped blotting her eyes to gape at him, he smiled. "Forgive me, Miss Mercer, if I seemed a bit short at first, but my butler erred in announcing you. He said my *wife* was out here, and I—"

"He didn't err." Her fingers tightened convulsively on his handkerchief. He'd called her Miss Mercer. Dear heaven, surely he wasn't denying . . . "You know perfectly well that we're married."

His smile vanished. "I know no such thing."

Abby glanced to Mrs. Graham for confirmation, but the woman just stood there gawking at him, apparently struck dumb by his outrageous denial.

Reminding herself she was a descendant of a great Seneca chief, she squared her shoulders. "Then perhaps you'd better explain what you meant in your letters when you said you wished to marry me."

The clouds rolled back over his brow. "I didn't write any letters to you."

"But I have them right here!" Now truly alarmed, she hunted through her reticule until she found them, then thrust them at him. "You see? These are yours."

He took the letters and scanned them swiftly. When he lifted his gaze to her, his eyes flashed lightning. "I have never seen these before in my life, madam."

She could hardly breathe, and not just because of the blessed corset either. "But that's your signature on them!"

"No, it's not. It's a very good forgery, I'll warrant you, but a forgery nonetheless. Besides, it doesn't even match the writing on the letters."

His thunderous stare made it clear that he expected *her* to offer the explanations that ought to be forthcoming from *him*.

"Of course it doesn't. Your brother said your secretary wrote the letters, and you only signed them. But Nathaniel insisted that you dictated them yourself and—"

"Nat gave these to you?"

"Yes. They were included with packages he said he received from you."

He scanned the letters again, and the color drained from his features. "That's Nat's handwriting, all right."

Panic gripped Abby's chest. "You mean he wrote them? Why would he— I demand to speak to your brother."

"You'll have to wait your turn," he bit out. "He's not here. He conveniently disappeared a few hours ago, and we've been looking for him ever since."

Dear heaven. Now it all made sense. Nathaniel had been the one to broker the marriage in exchange for part ownership of Papa's company. He'd been the one to convince her and Papa that Lord Ravenswood was eager for the match. And it was Nathaniel who'd taken her dowry.

Numbly Abby searched for the more official-looking piece of paper in her reticule. When she found it, she held it out with a wavering hand. "I guess that means you didn't know about this, either."

Warily, Lord Ravenswood took the paper and examined it. When he lifted his head again, his mouth formed a pained line. "I am so sorry, Miss Mercer—"

"No," she whispered, backing away from the truth in his eyes. "No, it can't be. You can't be saying—"

"I swear I did not authorize my brother to arrange any marriage. I can't imagine why he'd do so. I'll admit that he has forged my name a time or two in the past as a joke, but I never dreamed he would do something like this."

"Oh, Lordy," Mrs. Graham muttered, fanning herself with the frantic movements of someone watching her dreams disintegrate before her very eyes.

As Abby was watching her own dreams die. Lord Ravenswood had never meant to marry her. The fanciful feelings she'd attributed to him, the sweet fantasies she'd conjured up of their future life together . . . they were figments of her own imagination. Figments that Nathaniel had used to his advantage.

The complete humiliation of it seeped into the marrow of her bones. She was here in England, having spent nearly all the meager funds left to her, with her dowry and her father's business stolen—

Spots formed behind her eyes. She tried to breathe, but the blessed corset wouldn't let her, and suddenly the room spun and the spots joined to form one giant spot blotting her vision, and she sank down into blackness . . .

Chapter 2

Do not allow rude servants from other households to provoke you into bad behavior. Your employer will reward your forbearance, and those other servants will only succeed in annoying their own employers.

Suggestions for the Stoic Servant

When Spencer saw Miss Mercer's usually rosy complexion pale to the color of milk, he feared the worst. So when her eyes glazed over and her knees buckled, he dropped the papers and lunged for her. He barely caught her in time to prevent her collapse on the floor.

As he lifted her limp body in his arms, her head wobbled back lifelessly. She looked very ill, and it was all his fault.

"Now see what you've done, you . . . you Englishman you!" Mrs. Graham cried, wielding the vile insult "Englishman" like a club. "How dare you act this way to my sweet mistress, who never done a body wrong in her life?"

His concern increasing by the moment, he examined Miss Mercer's usually vibrant face, which now seemed drained of life. Damn it, she should be rousing by now.

"You changed your mind, is that it?" the angry servant went on. "Or you drummed up some scheme with your brother to steal her dowry—"

"There's a dowry?" he muttered. This was a nightmare.

"You know very well there's a dowry!"

24

"I had no idea. But apparently my brother knew." Was that why Nat had done this fool thing? For some dowry?

"Aye, he knew all right." Mrs. Graham's voice grew shrill. "Your brother ain't nothing but a common thief, I tell you! And if you think I'll stand by and watch while you rob my mistress blind, then you—"

"Good heavens, what is all the commotion about?" came a voice from behind him.

Lady Tyndale. Bloody, bloody hell. His nightmare worsened by the moment.

"Has Nathaniel arrived?" asked another younger voice.

Spencer glanced back to see both Lady Tyndale and Evelina staring at him and his armful of woman. "No. Go back in the dining room."

"Who is that woman?" Evelina asked.

"His lordship's wife," Mrs. Graham offered with a determined glint in her eyes, "newly arrived from America." She picked up the papers Spencer had dropped, then handed them to Evelina.

Torn between caring for the still alarmingly unconscious Miss Mercer and making explanations he didn't know how to make, he opted for the more immediate problem.

"McFee," he barked, "you and Mrs. Graham see that the ladies' bags are brought in. The rest of you return to the dining room, if you please. This is a private matter. I'll be there as soon as I can."

He stalked down the hall. He had to get Miss Mercer somewhere warm to revive her—he couldn't do it in this drafty foyer built more for intimidation than for comfort. But his study was close by, and the fire would be burning.

Thank God. Her shallow breathing and the sickly cast of her generally healthy complexion worried him. He'd never made a woman faint in his life. And to have it be this particular woman, who'd always seemed so robust and happy in America, turned his stomach.

But damn it, she'd taken him by surprise. Forged letters? A marriage license? A stolen dowry? What in bloody hell had come over his brother?

The answer came to him in a flash. It must have something to do with Nat's determination to gain that partnership. Why else had the scoundrel vanished earlier? He must have heard about Miss Mercer's arrival in England and scurried off to hide.

As well he should. When the idiot eventually showed up, Spencer was going to thrash him within an inch of his life.

As Spencer entered the haven of his study, he heard Mrs. Graham explaining to anyone who would listen about how he'd married Miss Mercer by proxy. Good God, what a mess.

Still, his first concern must be Miss Mercer. He carried her motionless body over to a chaise longue. But when he laid her on it and she didn't even moan, his concern exploded into alarm.

Smelling salts. He needed smelling salts, but where was he to find them in a bachelor household? He could call for his housekeeper . . . No, there wasn't enough time.

Then he spied Miss Mercer's reticule, miraculously still attached to her wrist by its cord. Jerking it open, he was relieved to find a bottle inside. He twisted off the cap, then waved the bottle under her nose.

Just as a sweet herbal scent wafted to him, making him wonder if this was smelling salts after all, she gasped and her fragile eyelids fluttered open. Thank God. He set the bottle on the floor, then chafed her hands in his, alarmed by how frigid her fingers were.

"Miss Mercer," he said in a low voice, "are you all right?"

"Wh-what happened?"

Her voice sounded far too reedy and weak to him. "You fainted. What can I do to make you more comfortable? Fetch you some wine? Or brandy perhaps?"

"C-corset," she whispered, licking her lips.

Good God, had she lost her wits when she'd lost consciousness? "What?"

"Can't breathe," she rasped. "This . . . corset. Not used to . . . wearing one."

When she unhooked the fastenings at the front of her gown, he realized what she was trying to tell him. He watched speechlessly as she unhooked her gown, then wriggled out of the restrictive bodice, shoving it down to her waist so she could reach the laces of the corset tied at the back. For a moment, all he could do was gape at the golden female flesh that showed above the lace of her chemise.

Then she glanced up at him as she struggled to catch her breath. "H-help me," she pleaded.

That spurred him into action. First he closed the door to the study, then returned to shift her onto her side. But when he started on the laces, he found them knotted.

"Just cut them," she whispered. "Get it loose!"

Grimly he drew out his penknife, but cutting through the too tight laces of her corset wasn't all that easy. No wonder she couldn't breathe. He had to work his knife into the fabric just to get under the strings. Even then it took some sawing before the annoying thing gave way.

With a satisfied "Ahhh," Miss Mercer relaxed and dragged in several deep breaths.

"I cannot fathom why you women wear such torture devices," he muttered as he pocketed his knife.

"I don't generally." She rolled onto her back again, her bodice now crumpled down about her waist and her corset loosely covering her chemise. "But Mrs. Graham insisted that a viscountess should wear a corset, so—" She took a shuddering breath. "Anyway, she thought it appropriate."

For a viscountess. A pang of guilt shot through him. Nat might have deceived her about Spencer's desire to marry her, but she'd had good reason to believe him. The American

courts would consider both the letters and the marriage certificate valid until Spencer proved otherwise. Now what the
hell was he to do about it?

He felt rather than heard someone enter the room behind
him.

"Is she all right?" Evelina asked timidly.

Lady Brumley's arch voice answered, "She looks more
than all right to me."

Spencer groaned. Lady Brumley had intruded into his
study, too? Damn, the last thing he needed was that sharp-
tongued creature in here, stirring the pot.

"Really, Lord Ravenswood," the Galleon of Gossip went
on, "you could have waited until your guests were gone
to . . . er . . . exert your husbandly rights."

Bloody hell. He hadn't thought how it might look with his
"wife" lying here prone, her gown half undone, her corset
unfastened, and him hovering over her like some lecher. He
jumped to his feet.

"His lordship was merely trying to make me comfortable,"
Miss Mercer explained.

"I'm sure he was." Lady Brumley stooped to pick up the
bottle Spencer had left on the floor. "What's this? Something
to enhance your . . . er . . . comfort?"

"It's smelling salts," Spencer snapped as Miss Mercer
said, "It's the Mead."

Then Mrs. Graham burst into the room. "Oh, my lady, are
you all right?" She caught sight of her mistress's state of undress and cast Spencer a horrified glance. "What has this
monster been doing to you?"

"Out!" He'd had enough of this farce. "All of you, out! I
need a moment with Miss . . . with my . . . Just get out, will
you? And give a man some privacy."

"My lord, you must let me explain to them—" Miss Mercer began as she sat up.

Then her corset fell completely off, revealing a chemise so sheer that the dark buds of her nipples showed through it with startling clarity.

For a moment they all stood frozen, Spencer included. He couldn't tear his eyes from the astounding picture of Miss Mercer bursting free of her corset like a bachelor's erotic fantasy.

Then Lady Tyndale cried, "My dear, your clothes!" and that snapped him out of his shock.

Stepping in front of the chaise longue to block Abby from their view, Spencer whirled to face the growing audience crowding into his study. "Get out now! All of you! You, too, Mrs. Graham. I'll tend to your mistress."

Reluctantly, the servant retreated, as did the others, who looked thoroughly scandalized. Even that nosy Lady Brumley, after casting a sly glance at Spencer, pocketed the bottle she'd been examining and walked out.

A blessed silence descended on his study. Then a small voice behind him broke it. "I-I can't make it work."

He turned to find Miss Mercer sitting up. She'd tossed the corset aside, had wriggled her arms through the sleeves of her gown, and was now futilely attempting to refasten it.

"Without the corset, I can't bring the bodice together over my . . . well . . ."

Struggling to keep his eyes off the twin endowments preventing her from fastening her gown, he quickly removed his coat and draped it over the front of her. He got a whiff of that same herbal scent, but this time it came from her—sweet, lilting, sensual . . .

Good God, he must stop thinking of her like this.

"Thank you, my lord," she murmured. "I was beginning to feel . . . exposed."

"That's my fault. I shouldn't have cut up your corset."

She cast him a wry smile. "If you hadn't, I'd have expired

on the spot." Then her smile faded, and she dropped her head. "I feel very stupid. I've never fainted before."

With a sigh, he sat down beside her on the settee. "Under the circumstances, it was understandable. My brother has much to answer for."

"You mean, because he arranged a marriage to a man who doesn't want me?" she burst out. Throwing her legs over the edge of the chaise longue, she arranged her skirts. "How stupid I was to believe all his claims. I should have known that men like you do not marry American nobodies, but your brother was so very convincing—"

"Yes, Nat can be quite convincing when he wants." He should correct her assumption about her suitability as a wife. But that would mean telling her that he never intended to marry at all, thus inviting the usual questions. Since he had no answer but the truth—which he refused to reveal to anyone—it was better not to raise the subject.

Besides, it would only muddy the waters. The woman had come halfway around the world because she wanted this marriage. If he even hinted at how appealing he found her, she would dig in her heels when he attempted to extricate them from this mess.

No, he couldn't tell her. But he must figure out exactly how legally entangled he was. And that meant getting answers from her.

He examined her face, but her color seemed much improved and she didn't look as if she might faint again. Now was as good a time as any to probe the matter. "Mrs. Graham mentioned a dowry. Is it true that my brother took it?"

She met his gaze evenly. "Yes."

Bloody hell. He'd hoped that was just the babbling of an outraged family retainer. "How can that be possible? Surely your father would have made the bank draft out to me. And Nat couldn't cash it without my cooperation."

She winced. "Unfortunately, my dowry was in gold coins that Papa had saved up. If anything happened to the business, he didn't want his creditors to be able to touch it. So he kept the money secreted away at home until I married."

Spencer scrubbed his hands over his face. Could this night possibly get any worse? "I'm almost afraid to ask, but how much were these coins worth?"

"Papa had it assessed in English pounds for your brother, and I believe it was five thousand pounds, give or take a few."

Yes, the night could get infinitely worse. Five thousand pounds was certainly enough blunt to tempt a man whose yearly allowance was nowhere near that. "Miss Mercer, perhaps you'd better explain how this . . . er . . . marriage came to be."

"All right." Though she held herself rigid, he glimpsed her vulnerability in the trembling of her chin. "After you left Philadelphia, Nathaniel was very attentive to Papa."

His brother's Christian name on her lips inexplicably sparked his temper. "And to you, too, apparently. You speak of him quite informally."

She thrust out her chin. "He asked me to. Because I was soon to be his sister."

Spencer sighed. "Right. Go on then."

"Papa had always planned to leave half his business to my husband, whoever that ended up being. He hoped your brother would marry me, but Nathaniel claimed that his affections lay elsewhere." Her pretty eyes flashed. "I suppose that was another lie."

Devil take Nat for making this perfect creature doubt her attractions for even a second. "Actually, that was true. His fiancée is here tonight, as a matter of fact. She was the one who first entered the study a few minutes ago."

"Oh." She stared down at her gloved hands. "The elegant young blond woman."

"They've been intending to marry for some time." He rose to pace the room, too restless to sit still. "Tonight was their betrothal dinner, but Nat never showed up."

A delicate frown creased her lovely brow. "Could he have heard somehow of my arrival in England?" She thought a moment. "Oh, of course—I wrote a letter to you giving all the details of our expected arrival. He must have intercepted it."

"That would certainly explain his recent obsession with the mail. How many letters did you write me?"

"Two. One after we first married and the one about the ship. There was no time for more." She winced. "But I sent the first one with him when he returned."

"Ah. And once he confiscated the second letter, he must have posted somebody at the docks to watch for your ship, then notify him." He swore a low oath. "Which would explain the note he received just before he disappeared."

The intricacy and thorough planning of this scheme alarmed him. What purpose could Nat have had? To steal her dowry and the company? Nat had done some foolish things in his life, but he'd never been a thief.

Spencer sat down at his desk and steepled his fingers. "You were telling me about our proxy marriage . . ."

"Oh, yes. When Nathaniel realized Papa would only leave the business to my uncle or my husband on my behalf, he tried changing Papa's mind." A bitterness crept into her voice. "I could have told him that wouldn't work. Papa has always been set on my marrying well. He was determined to show his family that my Senecan blood didn't matter. He hired me tutors and dance masters and bought me guides to deportment . . ."

She sighed. "But since Nathaniel wouldn't marry me, Papa insisted on sticking to his plan to leave the business to his own brother. So to gain any part of my inheritance, I'd have had to go live with my uncle."

"Not an appealing notion, I presume."

A bleak look shadowed her dark eyes. "Papa's family disowned him years ago for marrying Mama. I'm sure my uncle would take me in just to have my help with Mercer Medicinal, but I would be treated like . . . well—"

"A poor relation. Or worse."

She nodded. "Papa didn't really want that, but he didn't think I could run the business on my own, either. That's why he was so eager to see me marry."

"So when Nat couldn't assuage him, I was offered up as the sacrificial lamb."

"You could look at it that way, I suppose," she said testily. "Anyway, two months after you left, Nathaniel claimed to have received a letter from you in which you sang my praises." Fiddling with his coat, she added in a soft voice, "I suppose I shouldn't have believed him, but . . . well . . . you and I did have some pleasant conversations, you must admit. And I thought . . . that is . . ."

"Yes, I can see how you would have." Though he'd never made romantic overtures to her, he'd certainly been friendly enough to give credence to Nat's tales.

"Of course, there was also that time when you teased me about how my 'naive American optimism' might one day lead me into ruin." She glanced away, a faint flush staining her cheeks. "It appears you were right. Congratulations."

"I assure you I don't like being right in this instance, Miss Mercer. Especially when my brother was the instrument of your ruin."

With a dismissive wave of her hand, she went on. "Anyway, Nathaniel told Papa that in exchange for half ownership in the company—with the other half to be yours as my husband—he would arrange our marriage. But the wedding would have to take place by proxy, given Papa's dire illness and your difficulty with leaving England."

"Your father agreed to such an odd proposal?"

"Apparently he, too, suffered from a 'naive American optimism.' " When Spencer scowled at her sarcasm, her tone softened. "I suspect he felt he had no choice. He was determined to see me taken care of before he died. And he approved of you."

"I'm sure he did," he said tightly. "I suspect you don't get many wealthy viscounts passing through Philadelphia."

She gazed at him with the betrayed look of a wounded doe. "I thought you knew us better than that, but apparently not." She tilted her chin up at him. "I'm not a fortune hunter, my lord. I do have a dowry . . . or I did until your brother took it." The longer she talked, the higher that proud chin of hers rose. "Papa was less interested in your title and wealth than in your character. He approved of you because he *thought* you were a nice man. Little did he know. I'm sure if he had realized—"

"I am suitably chastened, Miss Mercer," he said, faintly amused. "Pray continue."

Giving a little sniff, she hesitated. When she finally went on, she wouldn't look at him. "We had the proxy wedding, and your brother stood in for you."

"Nobody questioned it?"

Her head shot up, and fire sparked in her eyes. "Why should they? Everybody had met you. There were the letters proposing marriage. Your own brother championed the match. What was there to question?"

"I see your point."

Only slightly mollified, she pulled his rapidly slipping coat back up to her chin. It occurred to Spencer that she might be cold. He rose and went to stoke up the waning fire.

"Shortly after the wedding," she went on, "your brother said he was leaving, that he'd been away from his intended too long. He said that Mrs. Graham and I should follow him as soon as Papa passed on. Then he took the coins and left."

Spencer turned from the fire to stare at her. "Your father didn't find *that* suspicious?"

"He didn't know." She gave a thin smile. "By then he was very ill and I didn't want to worry him. He died shortly after your brother left." Her voice grew choked. "I think Papa only hung on until he saw me settled. He was stubborn that way."

"Many parents are." Spencer glanced over to the massive desk that had once belonged to his own stubborn father. After Spencer's eldest brother, Theo, had died, their father had contracted pneumonia. But the old man had clung to life as long as he could, hoping to see Spencer return from the war to take Theo's place as heir. Unfortunately, Spencer had already become a spy—by the time anyone could notify him of his brother's death and his father's illness, his father was dead.

Without ever hearing of Spencer's inadequacy to be the heir.

"After Papa passed on," Miss Mercer continued, dragging him from his somber reflections, "I arranged for the burial, disposed of our goods, and closed up the house, which Papa had left to my uncle. I wrote you a letter about all this. Then we came here."

Her tale explained a great deal, but not everything. "I see why your father agreed to the match, but why did you? What made you leap willingly into a proxy marriage with a man you barely knew?"

With a sigh, she dragged his coat back up to her chin. "Did you happen to read those letters I handed you, my lord?"

"No." He patted his pockets for them, then remembered dropping them on the floor. Bloody hell. No doubt the harpies in the hall were having a fine time poring over them. "Why? What did they say?"

"You'll be pleased to know you were very convincing in explaining why I'd be better off married to you than living like a cast-off at my uncle's."

"Ah. A practical decision, was it?"

She kept her eyes on the carpet, which she dug at with the

toe of one dainty boot. "Um . . . not entirely. Your brother is a particularly talented liar, you see, and wrote some very . . . nice things about me. I should have caught on when he actually waxed poetic in one letter—writing that I 'walked in beauty like the night of starry climes and cloudy skies.' " Light from the now leaping fire shown on her pained smile. "But I'm unused to such extravagant compliments, so I suppose I wanted to believe him."

Spencer caught his breath. Devil take Nat for remembering what Spencer had half forgotten from the night they were drunk. "Actually, I did . . . er . . . quote that line of poetry to him in reference to you."

Her gaze shot to his. "Oh?"

Bloody hell, he probably shouldn't have revealed that little tidbit. "I was making a point about how other gentlemen might regard you."

Her eyes glinted with humor. "I see. And you used poetry to do so?"

"I was foxed, all right?" he grumbled. "It was my last night in Philadelphia, and Nat and I were drinking. Men often speak nonsense when they're foxed. But apparently my brother decided to use my nonsense to further his own ends."

Her amusement faded. "You mean, to steal my dowry and Papa's company?"

"I suppose." Spencer shook his head. "Though this seems an extreme method for gaining funds, not to mention doomed to failure. He must have realized you would come here and expose him eventually."

"Of course he did. He's the one who paid for our passage to England."

Chapter 3

The wise servant puts his employer's needs first, for when the master prospers, the servant prospers.

Suggestions for the Stoic Servant

Judging from how he gaped at her, Abby had shocked his lordship yet again. It was becoming a habit. Well, he deserved it. He'd certainly done his share of shocking *her* tonight.

"My brother paid for your passage?" Lord Ravenswood echoed.

"How do you think we got here? Papa left me little money—he thought I was married, remember? And he didn't have much to leave anyway. So after I paid for the funeral and settled his debts, there was barely enough left to buy essentials for the trip."

"But why would Nat pay your passage here after stealing your dowry?"

"How should I know?" She dragged his coat back up to her chin, trying not to notice that it smelled thickly of him. "Maybe he had a crisis of conscience. Maybe he hoped you'd make up for my loss. He's *your* brother—why do *you* think he did it?"

"I have no earthly idea." Lord Ravenswood marched back

and forth across the costly Turkish carpet with his hands clasped behind his back in a decidedly military stance. "I can't even begin to fathom my brother's twisted logic."

"Are we being unfair to him by assuming the worst? Maybe he had good intentions. Maybe he wanted to rescue me from my dire situation."

"By encouraging you to marry a man who didn't want to marry you?"

She flinched. "Are you sure he knew? Lord knows I was too dense to see it."

His lordship halted to snap, "That's because you were too busy listening to my idiot brother build fanciful castles for you and me in the air."

Whenever she started to remember why she'd liked him initially, he up and said something annoying like that. "I had no reason to think your brother was making this up. Amazing as it may be for you to believe, I actually thought you liked me."

His heavy sigh contained a lifetime of exasperation. "I did. I do. I just don't want to marry you."

"Which you've made extremely clear. Several times, as a matter of fact."

Eyes like cool summer rain flicked over her. "I'm sorry, Miss Mercer, this has taken me by surprise. I assure you my grumbling has naught to do with you personally. You're an amiable woman whom any man would be delighted to marry, but—"

"You're not just 'any man,' are you? Don't worry—I understand." Now that she'd seen him in his own environment, she understood only too well. "You're a viscount of great social standing and political power. Marriage to an American physician's daughter wouldn't exactly enhance your position."

"That has nothing to do with it." Walking back to his imposing desk of carved mahogany, he stood there arranging papers and replacing a quill pen in its holder. "This is a crucial time in my career, that's all. The government is in an uproar, and I'm much needed at the Home Office. I can't be bothered with a wife at present."

"Since when is a wife a bother?"

"Since when is my reason for not marrying any of your concern?" he countered.

She didn't need his forbidding glare to get his point. She had no business prying into his affairs. She didn't belong here and never would. They both knew it.

Not for one minute did she believe all that hogwash about his career. It was only his polite way of saying she lacked the proper background, class, and connections to be a viscount's wife. She would have realized it sooner, except that the amiable gentleman she'd known in America hadn't seemed to care about such things. But clearly this officious viscount—the one who accused her of being a fortune hunter and lived in a costly mansion—cared very much.

And there was nothing she could do about that. Except maybe curse herself for not realizing that his kindly manner in America was only a façade.

Tamping down her disappointment, she curled her fingers into the supple leather of the chaise longue. "Forgive me for being nosy. It's a bad habit of mine." She ventured another comment. "But maybe your brother wasn't happy about your reluctance to marry. Could that have made him marry you off without your knowledge, to sort of force you into it? I understand that the English insist on the eldest son doing his duty to marry and produce an heir."

He gave a terse nod. "That's because the eldest inherits everything. Which means younger sons are more likely to thwart their elder brothers in marrying than to help them. If the eldest doesn't sire an heir, the next in line inherits. So younger sons resent the eldest, they stage petty rebellions against them, and in extreme cases they try to eliminate them. But they don't help them to acquire wives."

"Then I'm stumped. If he wanted to steal the dowry and the company, he shouldn't have paid for our passage here. But if he had some noble motive, he shouldn't have stolen the dowry and the company. It makes no sense to me, none of it. Only he can explain why he did it."

"And he's not around," Lord Ravenswood said dryly.

A discreet knock at the study door jolted them both. Lord Ravenswood strode to the door and opened it enough to reveal the butler standing there.

"My lord, your dinner guests are . . . er . . ."

"Growing restless. Yes, I imagine they are. Give me a moment, McFee."

"Very good, my lord." The butler started to leave, then held out a sheaf of papers. "Oh, and I relieved Lady Evelina of these. I thought you might prefer to have them in your own possession."

Even from where she sat, Abby recognized the letters and the marriage certificate. Lord Ravenswood took them with a grim nod. "Thank you, McFee. Good work."

After the butler left and his lordship closed the door, he tossed the papers on the leather-lined top of a nearby library table. He stared at them a long moment, then lifted his gaze to her. "We can't unravel this tangle tonight. I have to get rid of my guests, and you and your servant probably need a meal and a good night's sleep."

"Now that you mention it, that does sound wonderful."

"You'll stay here, of course, and in the morning we'll figure out how to proceed. By then I may have located my brother."

Though tempted by hunger and sheer exhaustion to simply acquiesce to his will, she felt obliged to say, "If you'd prefer that we go to a hotel, we will." Then, remembering that his brother had stolen her dowry, she added tartly, "But you'll have to pay for it, since your brother left me with little money."

A muscle ticked in his jaw. "I'm truly sorry about that. I assure you that no matter what happens, you'll be compensated for your financial loss." He ran his finger over the marriage certificate and added dryly, "This wouldn't be the first time I've paid my brother's debts, I assure you."

Now she was a "debt." Wonderful. But given his generosity, she shouldn't complain. The warm and friendly gentleman she'd thought she was marrying wouldn't have left her destitute, but who knew what a great English lord might do if he chose to be nasty? "I don't want to burden you. If you'll simply advance me some funds for my lodgings—"

"Nonsense, giving you a place to stay is the least I can do." He smiled ruefully. "Besides, if I send my 'wife' to a hotel, the gossips will never stop squawking about it."

She shot him a startled glance. "Do you plan to continue this farce?"

"To be honest, Miss Mercer, I don't know what my plans are. Thanks to your chatty servant, the twenty-six people in my dining room have undoubtedly been discussing my new wife for the past half hour. I can hardly put *that* cat back in the bag."

"So what will you tell them? The truth?" And what did he mean, her "chatty servant"? What exactly had Mrs. Graham said during Abby's mortifying faint?

"No, certainly not the truth. But I'll come up with something to buy time until I decide what to do." He arched one eyebrow. "I can be a 'particularly talented liar' myself when necessary."

"Then it runs in the family," she said sweetly.

For the first time since her arrival, he laughed. "Apparently." Opening the door, he beckoned to his hoity-toity butler. "McFee, show our guest to her room and have trays sent up for her and her servant. And have baths drawn, too."

"Thank you," Abigail breathed.

His warm smile fleetingly reminded her of the man she'd

so easily agreed to marry. It made her chest hurt with the loss of him.

"Well then," he said, "I'll see you in the morning."

When he started to walk out in only his shirtsleeves and waistcoat, she leaped up from the chaise longue. "Lord Ravenswood!"

He stopped to look back. "Yes?"

"You'll need this." Holding together the gaping edges of her bodice with one hand, she held his coat out with the other.

Walking up to her, he reached for it. When his hand brushed hers, the frisson of heat that sparked between them so flustered her that she lost hold of the bodice she'd been holding closed.

His gaze dropped down to her exposed chemise, and his breath quickened until it matched the frenzied pace of her own breathing. For a moment, the dark intensity of his stare made her think he might actually kiss her.

Then he seemed to shake himself, and his gaze jerked back to her face. "I believe, Miss Mercer, you had better keep the coat," he said in a throaty murmur that resounded low inside her. He circled around behind her. "After everything that has gone on in this house tonight, the last thing my guests will care about is my missing coat."

Demurring, she let him put it on her. But every whisper of his hand along her shoulder stirred up butterflies in her belly, and every accidental brush of his fingers against her hair resonated to the farthest ends of her silly, besotted heart. Her pulse stumbled the whole time he stood close, swamping her with his delicious scent.

Heavenly day, she had to stop these reactions. He might smell the same as he did in America, and he might occasionally be as kind as he'd been then, but he wasn't the friendly and fascinating gentleman she'd been so eager to marry. He was a viscount very aware of his own consequence. And she'd best remember that.

By the time he stepped away, she had herself under control, despite the tang of bergamot and wine that clung to his coat and bombarded her senses.

Hastily she fastened up the buttons. At least his coat would hide her open bodice, even if it did look comical. When she faced him to find his lips twitching from the effort not to smile, that small politeness made her wonder if she'd been too hasty in her assumptions about his character.

"Can you manage alone now?" he asked.

His gentle tone brought a lump to her throat. "Yes."

Dear heaven, she could handle this mess so much easier when he was being officious and viscountlike. Whenever these vestiges of the man she'd known before appeared, they made her long for what she knew she couldn't have.

She gazed up at him, wishing she had the right to smooth that tendril of dusky brown hair back over his ear or straighten his starch-scented cravat where it had been knocked slightly awry. "I believe I was wrong earlier. You are a nice man after all."

He looked nonplussed. Then a cynical smile curved up his lips. "Do keep that opinion under your hat. Otherwise, I'll never be able to lift my head in Parliament."

She couldn't suppress a laugh. "Don't worry—my lips are sealed."

"Thank God," he said evenly, but his gaze dropped to her lips as if actually checking for a seal.

Or something else entirely, for as his eyes fixed on her mouth, they turned molten, provoking an odd heat to rise deep in her belly.

By the time he tipped his head and murmured, "Until tomorrow then," she'd forgotten what they'd been talking about. And after he was gone, she could only stare after him in complete confusion. She would never understand that man and his intense looks.

Nor did the stiff-lipped butler enlighten her any about his

master as he led the way to her quarters. She did try to get him talking as they climbed a grand staircase whose massive steps were all of white marble—marble, for heaven's sake! But conversing with guests about his employer was apparently not something an English butler condescended to do, and Mr. McFee's one-word replies soon discouraged her from continuing.

Instead she tried to get a good look inside the rooms they passed, but it was too dark. A profusion of expensive beeswax candles in the staircases and halls, however, illuminated gilded mirrors hanging on the hall walls and polished rosewood console tables bordering massive mahogany doors. Velvet-cushioned chairs that looked fit for only the most refined of bottoms dotted the stair landings. Then there were the ornate cornices, medallions in relief, delicately ornamented fanlights, and . . .

Heavenly day. In her youth, when they'd had money, Papa's house had been considered fairly grand by Philadelphia standards. Compared to this, it had been a hovel.

It was almost a relief to reach the end of a fourth-floor hall and have Mr. McFee usher her into a spacious but simply furnished bedchamber where she wasn't reminded of her own foolishness in not realizing from the beginning what a vast gulf lay between her and his lordship.

Mrs. Graham faced off against the stalwart Mr. McFee as soon as they entered. "You sneaky Scot, how dare you put her ladyship in the top of the house like she was a governess. I demand you give us a room in the family quarters. This is his lordship's wife, I'll have you know!"

"Mrs. Graham, please—" Abby began.

"Until his lordship informs me otherwise," Mr. McFee broke in, "you are his guests and belong in a guest bedchamber. Since his lordship keeps late hours when Parliament is in session, I thought it might be more comfortable for you to have a floor to yourself so his comings and goings would not disturb you."

"How very considerate," Abby said hastily. Mrs. Graham wasn't taking this whole change of plan very well. "Thank you for seeing to our comfort, sir."

Mrs. Graham merely sniffed. "You think you're better than us, don't you? But for all your lofty airs, you're still a Scot no better than me. You got no right to look down your nose at either of us."

"I am not a Scot, madam. I am a butler. If, however, the only way I can silence your wagging tongue is to be a Scot . . ." He paused to fix her with a fierce glance. "I'm braw enow to handle any sharp-tongued American lass, so dinna cross me, ye ken?"

The brogue was so flawless that Abby burst into laughter while Mrs. Graham stood there, mouth agape.

Mr. McFee continued, but without the Scottish accent. "Now I shall leave you to your own duties, madam." He scanned the room, then fixed his contemptuous glance on the closed trunks. "I believe they include unpacking your mistress's belongings."

That snapped Mrs. Graham from her daze. "Why, you . . . you . . ." she sputtered, but it was too late. Mr. McFee had already left and closed the door.

"How dare you try to tell *me* how to do my duty, you highfalutin prig, you!" Mrs. Graham shouted at the door.

"He can't hear you, so you might as well give it up."

" 'Dinna cross me' indeed." Mrs. Graham harrumphed. "I still say he should give us a room in the family quarters."

"For heaven's sake, this room is fine. It's twice the size of my bedchamber in Philadelphia." Crossing to a window, she looked out across the moonlit street to the hulking shapes of trees that signaled a park. "And I suspect it's got a lovely view."

"Aye, but it ain't the mistress's bedchamber."

Abby shot her servant a stern glance. "Stop talking that way. You know I'm not the mistress." Determined not to dwell on that depressing thought, she strode to the largest trunk and lifted the lid, checking to be sure that all her precious dried herbs, roots, and seeds had arrived unscathed. She might need them if Lord Ravenswood changed his mind about believing her claims. "His lordship's brother forged the signature, so the wedding can hardly be legal."

Mrs. Graham snorted. "Is that what the man told you while he had you trapped in that room? I suppose he denies there was a dowry, too. I suppose he thinks to throw us out in the street soon as he makes sure we don't got no legal recourse. I suppose he—"

"Actually, he was embarrassed by his brother's actions." Abby opened a satin bag and brought it closer to the candle. Ah, her black haw and boneset seeds had escaped mold entirely. At least *something* had gone right. "He promised to compensate me for the dowry, and he intends to find his brother and set things right. So stop fretting. If you'll remember, he was a perfectly respectable gentleman when he visited us in Philadelphia, and he certainly hasn't changed into a monster now that he's in England."

But he *had* changed into a man she hardly knew and thus a man whose actions she couldn't predict. Firmly, she thrust that unsettling realization from her mind. For the moment, they were safe, and she must take comfort from that.

"I don't trust these English lords, I tell you," Mrs. Graham went on, clearly not as optimistic about the future as Abby was determined to be.

"You certainly trusted them when you thought I was married to one."

"That's different. And what are we to do now he's leaving you out in the cold—"

"This is hardly 'out in the cold,' Mrs. Graham." Swallowing her own apprehension for her servant's benefit, Abby swept her hand to encompass the room. "And if the dinner he told his butler to send up is anything like the one I could smell from the foyer earlier, we'll be eating well, too."

Mention of food perked Mrs. Graham right up. "Why? What were they having?"

"Roast beef, asparagus, at least one kind of meat pie—"

"Lordy, you and your nose! Never seen a body with such a clever one. You could pick a lilac out of a bed of roses, I expect."

"It's not hard to distinguish the smell of roast beef and asparagus, especially when you're hungry." She forced a game smile. "Anyway, my point is we're being cared for quite well."

"But for how long?" Mrs. Graham asked.

"It doesn't matter. As long as his lordship returns my dowry, I don't care how long we stay. Because after we have the money, we're free. We can do anything we want." She held up a packet of seeds and struggled to maintain her cheery façade. "We can return to America, buy a little cottage, start up the business again, and live as comfortably as we please. This could prove to be the best thing that ever happened to us."

Mrs. Graham eyed her mistress skeptically. "I'll believe it when I see it. But mark my words, this ain't gonna be no easy matter, not with the English involved. You'd best not get your heart set on having that money just yet."

"I think you're wrong," Abby said with false bravado. "It'll all be fine, I'm sure."

Yes, perfectly fine. She'd be a woman of property. She'd be free. She could marry whomever she wished.

Tears stung her eyes. A pity then that his lordship was the only man she'd ever wanted to marry.

*   *   *

Evelina waited anxiously in the entrance hall for her future brother-in-law to finish speaking with his last guest. Her mother had gone ahead to the carriage once Evelina had promised to be along shortly. Now if only that pesky Lady Brumley would leave.

"I see that you absolutely refuse to explain how you had a wife show up on your doorstep this evening," the marchioness remarked.

"As I said at dinner," Spence answered, strained smile in place, "I'll soon be making a public announcement about my guest. Until then I'd prefer not to discuss it."

"Then I shall have to give my readers the only version of the story that I have."

"I wouldn't do that if I were you."

Lady Brumley raised an eyebrow and opened her mouth, probably to protest, but Spence's look shut it. Even the Galleon of Gossip wasn't immune to his dire glance.

Evelina shivered. She could never bear to have him look at *her* like that. Thank goodness Nathaniel had no such black stare, or she'd be terrified to marry him.

Spence went on. "However, since you aren't the only gossiping female in town, I am prepared to make you an offer."

"I don't take money to quash stories, Ravenswood," Lady Brumley retorted.

He smiled thinly. "Of course not. But I daresay you'd love to hear all the details directly from the horse's mouth."

Her ladyship cocked her head, setting the ship's bells on her nautical-themed headdress to ringing. "What sort of offer do you have in mind?"

"I promise to relate my tangled tale only to you. As long as you wait a few days to write anything."

"I suppose I could manage that." She regarded him shrewdly. "But I'll hold you to it. No trying to evade me or duck out whenever you see me coming."

"Of course not."

"And I'll give you only one day. Tomorrow I'll be back for my story."

His face gave away nothing. "All right, come tomorrow at four-thirty."

"Four. I need time to write it and get it to the paper for the next day's press."

"Very well, I'll see you then."

Evelina waited impatiently while they finished their good-byes and Lady Brumley left. At last Spence turned to her, looking a trifle easier than before. "And why are you hanging behind, poppet?"

She nearly burst into tears right then to hear him call her by the pet name he'd given her when she was only a girl and he'd come home on leave from the army, bearing French sweets and painted dolls. She'd always thought of him as the older brother she'd never had. "That tale you told us about Nathaniel helping to catch a footpad—that was all a lie, wasn't it?"

He regarded her with his usual earnest attention. "What makes you think that?"

"Because I know you—if you'd thought Nathaniel might be hurt or have trouble with the police, you'd have left the dinner immediately."

"I couldn't leave you and your mother to—"

"It's all perfectly clear to me. Nathaniel doesn't wish to marry me, that's all." The hurt rose in her throat, threatening to squeeze out all her breath. "That woman who came tonight—she's Nathaniel's lady friend, isn't she?" She'd overheard the ladies in the retiring room saying that, though she didn't dare tell Spence. He disapproved of gossip. "She came from America to put a stop to Nathaniel's betrothal, and that's why he isn't here and why you pretended she was your wife. To keep it from me."

"Good God, what a lot of nonsense," Spence said firmly. "I

assure you that the woman's appearance has nothing to do with you."

"He told me she was plain, b-but . . ." All her determination to be strong crumbled as her tears started to flow. "She's pr-pretty. He probably married *her* while he was in America."

"Don't be absurd." Gently Spence drew her into his arms. "You saw that marriage certificate—the name on it was mine."

"I didn't really h-have a chance to look at it," she choked out through her sobs. "Mr. McFee snatched it away too quickly. But N-Nathaniel's name was on it—I saw it!"

"It was there only to show Nat as my representative. That's how it's done for a proxy marriage." He rubbed her back soothingly as he fumbled in his pocket. Mr. McFee stepped forward to hand a handkerchief discreetly to Spence, who then offered it to her. "Come now, don't cry. My brother loves you to distraction—I'm sure of it."

"Then why wasn't he here?" She blew her nose on McFee's handkerchief, wishing she didn't have to look so unladylike in front of Spence.

He tipped up her chin. "I told you, poppet. He was involved in some little mess with a footpad."

"You're not going to tell me what really happened, are you?"

"There's nothing to tell. You're worrying yourself for no reason."

Swallowing her tears, she tried to regain control of herself. She wanted to believe his tale about the footpad. But it just seemed so unlikely.

Unfortunately, Spence would never take her into his confidence. He thought he had to protect her from the truth.

"All right, whatever you say." She stared down at her feet. "But if he does come here for her, you'll tell me, won't you? You won't let me go on thinking he loves me?"

"I promise you it's nothing like—"

"Just say you'll tell me if he does."

He sighed. "Yes, I'll tell you. Now you'd best go on. Your mother is waiting."

Dabbing at her eyes with his handkerchief, she nodded, then hurried out to the waiting carriage.

The ride home was interminable. Mama kept babbling about Spence's new wife and was too oblivious to connect Nat's mysterious disappearance with Miss Mercer's mysterious appearance. But Evelina was nearly certain the two were related.

And now that she and Nathaniel had already . . . Oh, the possibility that he might not love her was too awful to consider.

Mama was still chattering away when they reached home, which was probably why she didn't notice the footman press a note into Evelina's palm as he helped her out of her coat.

A quick glance revealed only one line: *Meet me in the garden as soon as you can.* It lacked a signature, but there was no need for one. Evelina would recognize Nat's fine hand anywhere.

Her heart began to pound. "Mama, I believe I shall take a turn in the garden before I go up." When her mother eyed her curiously, she added, "I had a bit too much wine at dinner. I need to clear my head before I can sleep."

Thankfully, that explanation sufficed, for her mother shrugged and said, "Go on if you must. But don't stay out too long. That chill air will give you a headache."

"I'll be quick," she said in a rush, already halfway down the hall to the back entrance. When she went out, she saw nothing at first. What if he'd come and gone already? Who knew how long ago he'd given that note to the footman— what if he'd tired of waiting for her?

Suddenly a hand pulled her behind a tree, and she was in Nat's arms, being kissed so thoroughly it made her forget everything but him. Until his kiss grew ardent and his hands began to roam, bringing her to her senses.

She pushed him away in high dudgeon. "How dare you show up here as if nothing has happened? How *dare* you?"

Nat held up his hands. "I know, I know, my love. I've behaved very badly. But I had no chance to warn you. By the time my man notified me of Miss Mercer's arrival—"

"I knew this had something to do with that woman!" Evelina's stomach twisted into a knot as she wagged her finger in his face. "She's your mistress, isn't she? And you think you can bring her here under my very nose—"

"My mistress!" he said, laughing. "Miss Mercer? You must be joking. Why would you think she was my mistress?"

Pouting, Evelina crossed her arms over her chest. "You told me she was plain, and she's not. She shows up at our betrothal dinner, and you don't. It's pretty clear to me what's going on."

"That was purely coincidental, I swear. She was supposed to arrive next week. If I'd dreamed she would show up today, I'd have convinced your mother to schedule our dinner sooner."

"You mean you *knew* Miss Mercer was coming?"

"Of course I knew. It's part of my plan."

Evelina's eyes narrowed. "For what? If you don't explain this instant why she's here, Nathaniel Law, I'll call a footman to come throw you out of this garden!" With a pained look he reached for her, but she was having none of that. "Explain yourself first. Then I'll decide if I can forgive you. At the moment, it's not at all certain."

He grimaced. "All right, all right. But let me reassure you of one thing. I love you. I've always loved you. We'll be married as soon as I can manage it. But you'll have to be patient, my darling. Because like it or not, Miss Mercer is here now, and if my plan is to work, I have to disappear for a while."

"Oh, really?" She crossed her arms over her chest. "Then this explanation of yours had better be very, very good."

Chapter 4

If an American should visit your employer, do not expect him to behave like the average Englishman. Americans are a breed unto themselves and must be treated with caution.

Suggestions for the Stoic Servant

The morning after the dinner fiasco, Spencer sat at the breakfast table, waiting for the servants to fetch Miss Mercer. The *Times* sat at his elbow, his coffee was hot and strong, and his buttered eggs were perfectly cooked, yet all he could think of was that bloody female and how she might react to the proposition he meant to put to her this morning.

Surely she would be relieved to have her financial situation so well settled. Then again, the woman was not like an Englishwoman. She had a decided streak of American independence in her.

But he'd considered every other way out of their current predicament, and nothing else sufficed. Evelina had already jumped to strange conclusions. Soon others would, too. So he must act quickly to avoid a scandal.

Whatever happened, the truth must not come out. It would harm too many people—Evelina, her mother, Miss Mercer, him. Nat, too, of course, but at present Spencer didn't much care what that rascal suffered. Especially since the idiot had vanished, leaving Spencer to pick up the pieces.

Fortunately, Spencer excelled at that. And his solution to this dilemma was eminently workable.

So it was a pity that he hated it. He could only hope she didn't hate it, too.

McFee entered the breakfast room, his composure ruffled for a change. Worst of all, he was alone.

"Well?" Spencer demanded. "Where's Miss Mercer?"

"I beg your pardon, my lord, but . . . you see . . . we don't know where she is."

A kernel of unease sprouted in Spencer's gut. "What do you mean—you don't know?"

"The lady is not in her chambers. And that harridan she calls a servant will not say where she's gone or even *if* she's gone."

He rose from his seat. "But you're sure she's not in the house. You've checked all the rooms, searched the kitchens, looked in the street."

"The search is currently under way, my lord. I merely thought I should inform you that we are having trouble locating her."

Devil take it, now what? Surely Miss Mercer wasn't the sort to strike out on her own to look for his brother. And even if she did, would she leave her servant behind? He thought it unlikely.

"If you don't mind my saying so," McFee went on, "American women are a great deal more independent than Englishwomen. Perhaps she went for a morning walk."

"Alone, in the streets of a city she doesn't even know? She better not have done such an idiot thing. I won't have it." Refusing to wait for his staff to find her, he strode for the doorway, only to be nearly knocked over when a footman rushed in.

"We found her!" the young man cried, then paled when he saw his master. "Begging your pardon, my lord. We . . . um . . . found your guest. She's in the garden."

Of course. Where else would a wild American rose go?

"Thank you," he said as he hurried off in that direction. Now he felt foolish for worrying. But the thought of Miss Mercer wandering London alone with no money . . .

He was being absurd. She'd never do such a silly thing. She might be naive and overly optimistic about life's prospects, but she wasn't an idiot.

Thank God. Because if she accepted his proposition, the two of them would be in each other's pockets for some weeks, and he couldn't tolerate stupidity.

When he strode out into the garden, he didn't see her at first. He'd paid a great deal of money for the luxury of gardens that were more substantial than those of the average London house. But as he stalked the pebble paths, glancing under trees and down pleasure walks, he was startled to come upon her where he least expected—in the portion of the garden reserved for the kitchen.

Bonnetless and still clothed in that ghastly black, she bent over a patch of greenery, tenderly moving stalks of plants aside in a methodical manner. Sunlight glinted off her jet hair, and her cheeks looked as satiny pink as rose petals, but it was her uptilted derriere that most tempted him. He had to tamp down a violent urge to lift her skirts and see if her other cheeks were as soft and pink as rose petals.

"What the devil are you doing?" he snapped, annoyed at the effect she always had on him.

When she looked up and saw him there, she straightened, a smile breaking over her face. "I'm looking for rosemary."

"Who's Rosemary?"

She chuckled. "It's a plant, my lord. You know—like thyme and borage?"

"Ah, yes. A plant. And why are you looking for a plant in my gardens at this time of the morning, pray tell?"

Mischief glinted in her eyes. "Where would *you* suggest I look for a plant? Maybe in your study? Or your dining room? Though I suppose—"

"Miss Mercer," he said sternly, "you know what I meant."

He regretted his sharp words when the light died in her face. "Yes." She brushed dirt off her gloved hands, her tone turning practical. "I need rosemary for the Mead. My personal vial of it went missing last night after you used it on me. I have only one other bottle, so I need to mix up some more. I brought all the ingredients for it with me, but the rosemary is best if it's fresh, so I decided to see if your kitchen garden had some."

"And you didn't think to ask one of the servants?"

"To be honest, I wasn't sure if you wanted me talking to the servants. So I figured I'd find the rosemary myself and avoid bothering them."

He couldn't suppress a smile. "You'd have been better off talking to them, considering that they've been searching for you for the past half hour."

A tiny frown graced her eloquent brow. "Whyever for?"

"Because I wanted to speak with you." He gestured to the garden path. "Come, walk with me. After we've had our discussion, I'll tell Cook to get you all the rosemary you require. All right?"

Removing her soiled gloves, she stuffed them into one apron pocket. "As long as you don't mind if I eat breakfast while we talk."

"Breakfast?"

She drew a pear out of her other apron pocket and brandished it before him. "I stole this from your breakfast room. I hope you don't mind."

"Of course not. You're my guest, and hosts generally do feed their guests, you know."

Her natural ebullience returning, she flashed him an impish smile. "Even when their guests have landed them in a most delicate predicament?"

"Especially then. Well-fed guests make less trouble."

Biting into the pear, she walked off down the path. "Do

you get a lot of guests trying to make trouble for you?"

He followed beside her. *None as fetching as you.* "Not recently. And about our particular trouble—"

"Before you say any more, let me assure you that I'm not going to fight you over dissolving a clearly nonexistent marriage. I want nothing from you but the money your brother took." She stopped to pluck a lilac from the shrubs lining the path, then tucked it behind her ear. "You don't have to pay it all right away, but if you could give me a little now, I can wait for the rest until you find your brother."

Giving her money and watching her trot off God knew where was not in his plan. But he was curious to know what was in hers. "And what will you do with the money?"

"Why, I'll produce the Mead, of course, and sell it." Lifting the pear, she bit into it again with such gusto that his pulse quickened at the sight. By God, she was a piece of work—fearless and impetuous and so bloody American she fairly glowed with it.

He forced himself to ignore her winsome charms. "So you mean to take over your father's business."

"Oh, no, I can't." She cast him an arch look. "Technically, you're still my husband, so my half belongs to you. All the papers have your name on them."

"What papers?"

"The ones Nathaniel has, of course, that deal with the business. He took them for you to 'review.'"

One more little surprise, courtesy of his brother. "Nat certainly thought of everything, didn't he?"

"It seems that way. Lying must not be the only thing that runs in your family."

"What's that supposed to mean?" He gritted his teeth. "Surely you don't think I had anything to do with this . . . this fraud."

She sighed. "I suppose not. But you're both profiting from

it. He gained my dowry and now you own half my father's business. With your brother owning the other half."

"I don't want your father's business, I assure you. I'll happily sign it back over to you when I get my hands on the papers."

One of her dark eyebrows lifted a fraction. "And when will that be?"

"I don't know." Staring at the not yet blooming rose bushes lining the garden walls, he thought how sad they looked compared to wild ones. "I sent two of my most discreet investigators out looking for Nat, and what they learned was little help. Except to confirm that he did have somebody at the docks." Spencer began walking again. "They questioned the lad, but he knew only that he'd been paid to watch for your ship and send a message here. He had no idea where Nat might have gone."

Abby kept pace easily with him despite his longer strides. "You don't think anything horrible happened to him, do you?"

Her concern for the rascal after how he'd treated her amazed Spencer. "No. More and more it appears that he left town, taking your dowry and those papers with him. Apparently he grew tired of frittering away his own allowance and has started working on *your* money."

When she halted abruptly, he did, too. She looked ashenfaced, holding her half-eaten pear poised in the air.

He eyed her in alarm. "You're not going to faint again, are you?"

She shook herself, then dropped her hand to her side. "I-I . . . no, of course not. I don't usually faint, you know. It was just the tight corset, that's all."

"Right," he murmured, though he stayed close all the same. "My men will find him, I assure you. But it may take some time."

"Enough time for him to spend all my money." She stared up at him accusingly. "You can't possibly expect me to wait here penniless until he's found."

"You can't gain the business free and clear until we find him."

"I don't need it free and clear," she protested. "Just advance me enough to pay for my return to America, simple lodgings, and a few supplies. Then I'll produce the Mead myself. I'll call it . . . Miss Mercer's Medicinal Mead or something."

"There's more to running a business than producing the product."

"I'm not an idiot, my lord. I realize it won't be easy. But I knew many of Papa's customers and all of his suppliers of ingredients. Though it might take me a while to get things going again, I'm sure I can manage." With an air of defiance, she lifted her pear again and bit into it.

"Running a business is difficult even for a man, much less a woman. How do you know your father's business associates will deal with you? They might decide that Miss Mercer's Medicinal Mead can't possibly be as effective. They'll wonder why you changed its name. They might even assume—and rightly so—that your father didn't support your efforts."

She thrust out her chin. "I'll convince them they're wrong. I'll explain what happened and win them over. I don't see why I can't."

When she wiped pear juice from her lush lips with her bare fingers, the blood beat savagely in his temples . . . and lower. He cursed his uncontrolled reaction. Time to stop dallying, before he changed his mind. "I have a better suggestion." He gestured to a nearby bench. "Come, let's sit a moment."

A decidedly suspicious expression crossed her face, but she did as he asked.

He sat down beside her. "What if I offered to give you double the money Nat stole?"

"Why?" She arched one pretty brow. "Out of the kindness of your heart?"

"I'm afraid not. I'd want something in exchange." When she looked stricken, he realized what she must think. Hastily he added, "I'd want you to continue here in London as my wife. At least for a while."

"But I'm not your wife. Not legally or morally. Those papers are a farce. And since you didn't authorize them—"

"Unfortunately, no one knows that. Several people, including a very persistent writer of gossip for the papers, have already heard you or your servant claim that you're my wife. To deny it would mean either inventing another reason for your claim—and I haven't found a plausible one—or telling the truth."

"Then tell the truth," she snapped.

"It's out of the question. It would embroil my brother in a scandal that would tarnish not only him but his fiancée and her family. Not to mention ruin my own reputation. I can't risk that. Besides, severing the marriage legally would require a trip to America, which I can't make while Parliament is in session. It would also require countless meetings with solicitors, one whiff of which would also cause a scandal."

"For a man who generally does as he pleases, you seem overly concerned about causing 'a scandal,' " she said, mimicking his accent with amazing accuracy.

He wasn't amused. "I told you, the government is in great turmoil. The home secretary recently resigned when people protested certain actions he'd taken." Actions Spencer had rightfully opposed. "The new home secretary has everyone behind him, but a scandal involving his undersecretary and the defrauding of an American innocent would surely change that. I cannot risk it."

She regarded him with surprise. "You're so devoted to your country that you'd remain married to a woman you don't want?"

"I'm not suggesting we continue this state of affairs forever. What I require is a temporary pretend marriage. You remain here as my wife while I locate my brother. Then you can go to my estate until Parliament is no longer in session and I'm free to leave England. We'll tell everyone we're returning to your home to settle your late father's affairs. While in America, we'll legally dissolve the marriage, and we'll be free again."

"Aren't you worried about *that* causing a scandal?"

He shrugged. "It's not as if anyone here would find out about a discreet legal maneuver taking place in America."

"But how will you explain when you return here without your wife?"

"I'll say you were so happy to be home that you chose to stay. You'll be my estranged wife. It's more common than you think and less likely to cause comment."

"I guess so," she said archly. "After being astonished by your marrying a vulgar American, your friends won't be surprised when you want to get rid of her."

"That's not what I meant."

Anger flared in her eyes. "You can wax on at dinner parties about how happy you are to have your highly unsuitable wife out of your hair."

"I'd never say anything of the sort. And if I found you so unsuitable, why in God's name would I suggest maintaining the marriage at all, even temporarily?"

"Because you have no choice. Apparently you prefer the scandal of having a common American wife to the scandal of having a thief and a fraud for a brother. Especially when the wife can be disposed of once she's outlived her usefulness."

The bloody wench insisted on viewing this as something that helped only him. "You'll benefit from this arrangement, too. When it's over, you'll own your father's business—

which I might point out was never possible before—and have plenty of money to run it. And you'll still be able to marry. I don't know why you're complaining."

Her anger faded to sadness. "No, I guess you don't." Biting off more pear, she chewed it mechanically, her eyes staring blindly ahead. "Let me see if I understand you correctly—after our 'marriage' is severed, I'll be free. But you'll be married, at least in society's eyes."

"Exactly."

"And that doesn't bother you?"

"Not at the moment, no."

He could reveal that he never planned to marry, but then she'd plague him with questions he still refused to answer. Or worse, she might regard his determination never to marry as a challenge.

No, better to stick to his story about his busy career. Surely not even Abby would attempt to entice a man into continuing a marriage that might damage his future.

"But eventually you'll want to marry," she said, tossing her pear core into the daisies behind them. "What then?"

He thought fast. "I'll tell everyone that you died. Who would know?"

"They could find out easily enough."

"You let me worry about that. Since there's no prospective Lady Ravenswood on the horizon at the moment, my first concern is to squelch all scandal."

"By having me pretend to be your wife."

"Yes."

A hint of mischief touched her face. "Ah, but how will you fit even a pretend wife into your busy schedule?"

He shot her a quelling glance. "A pretend wife will not harangue me into dropping my activities to entertain her. A pretend wife will not divide my attentions from my work. A pretend wife will not turn my household upside-down in order to make it her own."

"In other words, a pretend wife will be entirely under your control," she said dryly. "What an appealing prospect for me."

He bristled. "Will you do it or not? It's a better prospect for you than any other."

She pondered that a moment, with her face turned east like a bloom seeking the sun. Why must she look so perfectly at home in his garden, among the chirping lapwings and blossoming lilacs? It made him want—

"This pretend marriage of convenience," she said. "What will it involve?"

"I won't expect you to share my bed, if that's what worries you," he retorted bluntly, half for her benefit, half for his.

Judging from her shocked glance, however, he needn't have worried about hers. Good God, did she really not know what she did to him?

That was probably just as well. Mustn't have her guessing that she tempted him. Women built cottages on less expectation than that. Bad enough that he'd have to be around her for weeks without being able to touch her.

"Actually," she said, blushing, "I was talking about more mundane wifely duties."

"I have a housekeeper, a butler, and other servants for those. I will expect you, however, to accompany me to the occasional social engagement to maintain the illusion. I'd want to start tonight by taking you to the theater. Nat and I were supposed to attend with his fiancée and her mother, but now—"

"Yes—what about your brother? How will you explain his disappearance?"

"I've already taken care of that."

"You can explain away an absence of days, weeks, even months?"

"It won't be months." *Please, God, don't let it be months.* How could he endure months of her teasing, her flirting, her alluring forbidden lips . . . "I've charged my best investigators with finding him. We suspect Nat has fled to the Continent. That's where he usually goes to avoid me after one of his . . . mishaps. Undoubtedly he figures it's easier to hide from me there."

"Is it?"

"It depends on how good a trail he left behind. But he won't evade the runners forever. I'm hoping for a few weeks at the most."

"You wouldn't want me to get too used to being Lady Ravenswood," she bit out.

"I wouldn't want you inconvenienced any more than necessary."

"How very considerate of you." She lifted a shaky hand to pluck the lilac from her hair, then held it to her nose as if sniffing it gave her solace. "And what happens if I refuse your proposition?"

He wished he could just give her the money. But that would prove disastrous for everyone, probably even her. In her typical naiveté, she thought she could simply step into her father's shoes in America. It wouldn't be that easy.

Better to let her think him an officious bastard for forcing her to agree to his terms than a "nice man" she could twist around her finger. "If you refuse, then I hope you have another source of funds, because you won't have a penny from me."

Her eyes began to flash and her shoulders to shake. "You would actually refuse to give me money after your brother—"

"Yes. And you can't return to America without it. You certainly can't start up a business."

"But I could tell everybody in England about my awful mistreatment at the hands of the Law brothers."

"I wouldn't advise that," he said in the coldest voice he could muster. "I am not a wise man to cross, Miss Mercer. Besides, who do you think people here will believe—you or me?"

She paled. "I thought you were worried about scandal."

"I am. But if you don't do things my way, there will be a scandal regardless. So I have nothing to lose by offering this. While you have much to lose by refusing."

An angry flush crawled up her neck. "This is blackmail!"

"Indeed it is."

She gazed at him a long moment, as if trying to assess his intent. Then taking him by surprise, she reached over to clasp his hand. "You wouldn't force me into this—I don't believe it. You're too much of a gentleman, too good—"

"I am *not* good." He shook off her hand as if it were poison. She mustn't think she could get around him by engaging his sympathies. Quickly, he rose to put some distance between them. "What I am is determined. When it comes to my family, my country, or my king, I will do whatever it takes to protect them."

"Even if it means forcing me to continue a farce I'm uncomfortable with?" she whispered in an aching voice.

He stared down at her, struggling to maintain his cool façade. "Uncomfortable or no, you'll end up richer and better situated with my scheme than if you cling to your pride and try fending for yourself."

Hurt etched deep lines in her golden brow as she gazed up at him.

Unable to witness her distress any longer, he turned away. "Come now, you know this is best. Even if I gave you every penny my brother stole—and I won't—you'd have to struggle to reestablish your father's business without its being legitimately yours. You'd have to return to Philadelphia under an embarrassing cloud of speculation."

"I don't care about that."

He whirled to face her. "No? You don't care if they claim that the viscount tossed you aside because you were common? Or worse yet, if they imply you were never married at all? Hasn't it occurred to you that your hasty return to America might rouse speculation that you'd been my mistress rather than my wife, and a rejected one at that?"

Judging from her horrified look, it hadn't. "You, sir, are an awful man!" she cried, apparently at a loss for how to refute his argument.

"That I am. But my shortcomings needn't stop us from playing this scheme out to the end."

She rose, her face a rigid mask. "You think not? All right, I'll agree to your outrageous request if you meet one condition."

"What?" he asked, instantly on his guard.

Her green eyes grew icily distant. "You must kiss me to seal the bargain."

Chapter 5

Never question your employer's choices regarding the dispersal of his funds. How he spends his money is a more private matter than how he spends his nights.

Suggestions for the Stoic Servant

Although Abby could almost smell Lord Ravenswood's alarm, she stood her ground.

"Isn't that a rather strange condition?" he asked in a strained voice.

"You want me to pretend to be your wife, yet you find me repulsive. That will make the farce even harder, don't you think?"

"I don't find you repulsive," he snapped.

"You recoiled when I touched your hand moments ago. What do you call that?"

He glanced away, and the tension in her belly tightened unbearably. She hated to force this, but she had to know this one thing. Her instincts regarding him had led her astray once. So this time she needed some sign that the gentleman she'd grown to care for in America wasn't a complete fiction. She'd trusted the gentleman; she didn't quite trust the viscount.

But if he could bring himself to kiss her, if he had any vestige of warm feeling toward her, then she might bring herself to trust him . . . at least with regard to this charade.

68

He finally returned his chilly gaze to her. "You'll agree to my terms if I kiss you?"

She hesitated. But what choice did she have? Without money, she couldn't go back to America. And there was Mrs. Graham to think of, too, both of them trapped in an unfamiliar city. "If you kiss me, I'll agree."

"You can't simply take my word for it that you don't repulse me in the least?"

"Not when your actions say otherwise." She steadied her nerves. "Believe it or not, my lord, I don't actually enjoy public humiliation. Last night's events provided me with enough of it to last a lifetime, so the prospect of enduring more every time you jerk away from my touch before God and everybody isn't exactly appealing."

"I see." A sudden flare of heat in his face was her only warning before he moved forward to capture her chin in a firm grip. His eyes shone down at her like steel through crystal. "Remember that you asked for this," he rasped. Then he lowered his mouth to hers.

She'd expected a brief brush of his lips, the absolute minimum he could get away with. What she got was beyond her experience . . . lips more fluent than language, stroking and caressing and molding, melting her bones into water and heating her blood to steam. Dear heaven, what had happened to the cold viscount, the aloof man of property and position who had no use for a wife?

This was the man she'd dreamed about, the man she'd come to England to marry.

The aroma of bergamot burst through her senses, overlaid by scents of lilacs and garden soil. Then she couldn't smell anything, for she couldn't breathe, couldn't think. The kiss went on and on, tender and urgent and thrilling. He bound her so thoroughly in its spell that she became a willing slave to his mouth, praying the bliss never ended.

But it did, of course. And much too soon.

He drew back, his eyes unreadable. Yet he still clasped her chin, still loomed close enough that his quick, coffee-scented breaths fanned her face. "Satisfied?" he clipped out, as if that were all he could manage.

"That's not exactly the word I was thinking of." Not when her heart pounded hard enough to shatter her breastbone and her muscles seemed to have been replaced by rubber.

A stark hunger glimmered in his face as he tightened his fingers on her chin. "I meant—have I sufficiently met your condition?"

"I-I . . . yes. It appears you can tolerate touching me after all."

"Despite what you think, it would be better if I couldn't, my dear." He regarded her mouth regretfully, his thumb tracing the line of her lip. "You might find that more difficult, but I would find it infinitely easier."

With that enigmatic comment, he released her chin and stepped away.

When his lordly mask dropped instantly back into place, she wanted to cry. Once more he wore that impersonal expression that so infuriated her. Yet the warmth of his fingers lingered on her jaw, his taste lingered on her lips, and pleasure mingled with agony in her breast.

Had she simply imagined the passion behind his kiss, the tenderness in his touch? Or worse yet, was he simply more adept at simulating deep feeling than she'd realized? Which man was the real Lord Ravenswood—the English friend who'd just kissed her or the haughty stranger who faced her now?

Either way, maintaining this charade of a marriage was going to be a lot harder than she'd thought. Because if that was the real man who'd just kissed her, then she was in deep, deep trouble.

Too late to back out, however. She'd made her demand,

he'd met it, and now she had to hold up her end of the bargain.

"Sit down, Abby," he commanded. "We have much to discuss."

Despite everything, a thrill shot through her. Even in America, he'd never used her Christian name. And though she knew he did it only because of their bargain, it sounded so sweetly intimate on his lips that it reminded her of the kiss they'd just shared. She sank onto the bench obediently, relieved to have something solid beneath her shaky frame.

"You'll need gowns, of course," he began, "in a variety of colors and fabrics as well as—"

"Excuse me, but shouldn't I keep wearing mourning?"

He scrutinized her current gown, making her squirm under his critical appraisal. "I don't consider unrelieved black bombazine suitable attire for even my sham wife."

"Oh." Though the Seneca in her had rebelled at the unnaturalness of wearing mourning for so long, she'd done so because Philadelphians expected it. Wouldn't the English do so, too? "Are you sure people won't think I'm a disrespectful daughter if I throw off mourning too quickly?"

"Not if they don't know. They'll only hear what I tell them about your father, and I needn't reveal how recently he died." He smiled. "But if you really want to—"

"No." Then realizing how callous that must sound, she added, "Mama's people only believed in mourning loved ones for ten days. Then they had a feast to send the deceased on. Even when Mama's own father died, she preferred to show her grief as the Seneca do. She always said the best way to honor the dead was to celebrate the living."

"She must have been a very wise woman."

She smiled. "She was. And speaking of my mother, my lord—"

"You needn't call me 'my lord,' Abby. You're my wife now, not my servant."

It surprised her that his lofty lordship didn't expect her to preserve the distinctions of rank at all times. "Then what do I call you?"

"Normally you would call me Ravenswood. But since we'll have a difficult enough time convincing people we're actually married, you'd best be more intimate and use my Christian name, Spencer."

"All right. Spencer."

A smoldering heat crossed his face, then vanished. "You were saying about your mother . . ."

"How will you explain her and my lineage?"

"However you wish."

"I wish you'd tell the truth, but since I know that isn't preferable—"

"The truth is always preferable, my dear. It's just not always wise. But in this case, it's both." His solemn expression showed he was serious. "If I remember correctly, your mother was a chief's daughter. I see nothing to hide in that."

Papa's family had seen much to hide. Hard to believe that a man of his lordship's station would feel any differently. "It's not my mother's class I'd expect you to hide, my lord."

"Spencer," he corrected.

"Spencer. It's my mother's race that I thought you might take exception to."

He sat down on the bench, and this time he was the one to clasp her hand. "Let us be straight on one thing. I've spent nearly half my life with people of all races and creeds. I've encountered 'savages' more wily than English spies, African women rivaling French courtesans for beauty, and Sikh lords as peace-loving as Quakers. I long ago learned not to make assumptions about people—including other Englishmen— based on their surface qualities. So your mother's race is of no concern to me."

"But it will be to other people."

"Other people will take their cue from me. It is all in how

it's presented. If I present your mother as an exotic Indian princess, then that's how they will regard her. I promise, Abby, I won't subject you to any humiliation."

In his typical arrogance, he actually believed that he could control what people thought of her mixed blood. She wasn't nearly as sanguine as he, having had too many slurs thrown her way as a girl. But he would learn such a thing for himself soon enough.

"All right," she murmured. "I'll let you handle that as you see fit."

"Good." Releasing her hand, he rose. "I'll have a dress-maker summoned to fit you for new gowns. You'll need at least five for day and six for night, not to mention—"

"Please don't spend a great deal of money on gowns I'll only wear for a while."

"I can easily afford to dress you while you're in London."

She rose, too, her pride pricked by his assumptions. "I'm not some pathetic waif who needs your charity, you know. If not for your brother, I could pay for these things myself. So I'd prefer a more modest wardrobe."

His eyes narrowed. "No viscountess of mine shall dress in anything less than the finest, madam. What I want I get, and right now what I want is to prevent my peers from speculating about my treatment of my wife. Is that clear?"

Embarrassment burned in her chest. No doubt the haughty wretch thought her so inappropriate a wife that he must spend pots of money to make her presentable. Very well, if that's how he wanted it . . . "Then I'll need more than gowns. I'll need bonnets to match all outfits, slippers for evening, half boots for day, extra reticules to suit different occasions, a couple of shawls, two pelisses at least—"

She broke off, annoyed by the smile growing on his face, then added, "Oh, and let's not forget chemises and petticoats and two nightdresses. Or are you only concerned with my public apparel? I suppose it would be all right with you if I went to bed naked since nobody who could 'speculate about' your wife would see."

His smile vanished. "The servants might see. Not to mention . . ." He hesitated, a dark awareness flickering in his gaze as it drifted down her body. Then, as if realizing where his gaze had traveled, he jerked it up. "I'll make sure you're given appropriate attire for every occasion, including sleep."

So, she thought with perverse satisfaction, the idea of her naked affected him. Apparently his reaction to their kiss hadn't been feigned in the least. He might not find her suitable as a wife, but he did seem to desire her. That should anger her, except that she could tell he didn't like it one bit. It must really annoy him to desire a vulgar American like her.

A mischievous impulse seized her. "What about drawers— are they generally worn among females of your set? And corsets. Will you require me to wear them, too? Or do you prefer the female form to be natural, so to speak? I did notice when I wore the corset that it pushed my chest up so—"

"There will be no corsets." His peremptory tone left no room for argument. "As for the rest of it, do as you please. I'll pay for whatever you order—just tell the dressmaker what you want. Now if you'll excuse me . . ." Whirling away, he strode off as if he couldn't escape her fast enough.

"The dressmaker won't have my gowns ready for a few days, Spencer," she called after him, not prepared to end the game just yet. This was too much fun. "What should I do in the meantime? Wear my black gowns?"

He halted to face her, irritation furrowing his brow. "I hadn't considered that." He stared off across the neat beds of blooming daisies swarmed by bees and butterflies. "I suppose you can have my stepmother's old gowns altered."

"You have a stepmother?" she asked, startled.

His expression grew shuttered. "I did. Dorothea lives in Italy now, I believe. I haven't seen her in years."

"Is that why neither you nor your brother mentioned her while you were finding out everything about *my* family and finances?"

He shot her a stony glance. "Dora and I didn't get along after she was estranged from my father, so I rarely talk about her."

"Oh." No wonder he'd said that estranged wives weren't that uncommon.

"She and Nat were close, so he sometimes mentions her, but I suppose he was too busy pulling the wool over your eyes to tell you the family secrets." Pain laced his flip words. His brother's betrayal had wounded him more deeply than he'd let on. "And that reminds me—I must go. I have to meet with the solicitor about all this mess. Not to mention arrange for the dressmaker and hire you a lady's maid—"

"Mrs. Graham is fine. There's no need to hire someone who'll just have to be dismissed after I leave."

"I'll make sure the maid isn't left destitute when this is over," he said, sounding faintly amused by her concern for a servant. "But although Mrs. Graham is suitable as your companion, you also need a real lady's maid to attend you. So if you'll excuse me, I'll see about having one engaged immediately."

Casting her a cordial bow, he walked off toward the house, his chestnut hair ruffled by the morning breeze and his long-limbed stride easy and sure.

Meanwhile she stood here reeling from what had just happened. Everything was moving so quickly. In one fell swoop she was acquiring a new wardrobe, a lady's maid, and a pretend husband who obviously believed that he must arrange every aspect of her role as his wife. No wonder he'd never married—what woman could live up to the high expectations he clearly held for any female in his sphere?

Though she supposed he had the right to have those expectations. He *was* a wealthy viscount, after all. Still, it grated on her that he seemed to think he must throw lots of money at her to make her even remotely presentable.

Very well, let him throw his money at her. It wasn't as if he'd given her any choice. So let him dress her and lead her about and present her to his friends if he must.

And when this was all over, she'd thank her lucky stars that the marriage had not been a real one after all. Because clearly Lord Ravenswood was much too lofty a sort for an everyday life with a plain American woman like her. Marriage to him would mean living in constant fear of doing or saying the wrong thing in public. What misery such a life would be.

Except when he kissed her.

No, she wouldn't think about that, wouldn't yearn for that. Because that way lay heartache and rejection, and she'd had enough of that on this trip, thank you very much.

Chapter 6

Gossip is a dangerous business. The prudent servant avoids it, except where it aids him in serving his employer.

Suggestions for the Stoic Servant

Spencer drummed his fingers impatiently on the curved arm of his drawing room sofa while he watched the annoying Lady Brumley scribble in her notebook with a bejeweled hand. Did the bloody woman have to write down every word he said?

When she glanced up, he stopped his drumming and forced a smile. The Galleon of Gossip was a shark among sharks. One whiff of blood, and she'd be all over him. She was already sniffing too closely to please him. Although she appeared to accept his tale about falling madly in love in America, she seemed to doubt the one about Nat.

Spencer glanced at the clock—he had only a few more minutes to convince her. He and Abby must leave for the theater at five if they were to escape the crowds and reach his box without having to field too many questions from nosy theater patrons.

Lady Brumley tapped her pencil on her notepad. "Let me see if I've got all this right. You say that during the assault upon that footpad last night, your brother was wounded. And now he's recovering at your estate in Essex."

"Exactly."

She lifted a cool glance to him. "You must be beside yourselves with worry."

"Indeed we are."

"Yet you're content to gallivant about London with your new wife while he is languishing away in the country."

"I have important duties here, as you surely know. If I thought Nat's injury was life-threatening, then I would certainly be at his side. But the doctor has assured me that it is not."

"Could I speak to this doctor?"

"Certainly. You know my family physician, Dr. Godfrey." Spencer barely suppressed a smirk. Lady Brumley would soon discover that he'd already anticipated any avenues she might explore to poke holes in his story. Not for nothing had he been a spymaster.

Evelina and Lady Tyndale had been told the same story as Lady Brumley. And everyone else involved had been told whatever he deemed appropriate. They were prepared to say whatever he commanded. Fortunately, they all liked Nat. And disliked Lady Brumley.

He didn't dislike the woman himself—her kind could be useful. But only when they suited *his* purposes.

"I suppose Lady Evelina is with him in Essex?" she probed.

"No. I discouraged it. Her presence would only tempt him to get around before he is ready, and we couldn't have that, could we? Besides, she has much to do to plan for the wedding. She can't be rusticating in the country with my brother."

"Well then, if it's such a minor wound that even his fiancée has abandoned him," she said slyly, "I'm sure we'll see him in London within a day or two."

He flashed her a tight smile. "Oh, it might be longer than that." That was the ingenious aspect to this tale—a wound could take as long to heal as Spencer required. Relapses could occur, Nat could be near death . . . indeed, if the bloody idiot didn't show up soon, he'd be wishing for death by the time Spencer got through with him. "But he's in good hands with my staff at Essex."

"Is he indeed?" Lady Brumley's snide tone told him she didn't believe half of what he said. But short of traveling to Essex and sneaking about the estate, she'd never prove he was lying. His staff, both in London and at the estate, was completely loyal to him. Spencer's man of affairs had left for Essex this morning to personally inform his estate staff of what they were to say if anybody asked about Nat.

Now Spencer just had to hope that Nat didn't turn up at the gaming tables in Bath or Brighton or somewhere else public to make a liar out of him.

He glanced again at the clock, then rose with a thin smile. "I'm afraid we'll have to finish this conversation another time. My wife and I are joining Lady Evelina and her mother at the theater tonight. I figured it would give the three of them a chance to become better acquainted, given the . . . er . . . awkwardness of last night's meeting."

Surprise lit Lady Brumley's face. Clearly she hadn't expected him to be so friendly with his future in-laws when something questionable was afoot. "Well, then, my lord, I shan't keep you from your lovely wife. I think I have all I need." She stood and cast him an arch smile. "For the moment, that is."

When she walked out of the drawing room, he followed grimly. He'd have to keep an eye on the Galleon of Gossip. She could make his life hell if he didn't handle her properly, and he had all the hell he could handle just now.

But when he and Lady Brumley reached the stairs just as his sham wife was coming down from the floor above, he realized he hadn't known the meaning of hell until that moment. Because although the lady's maid he'd hired wasn't starting until tomorrow, his wild American rosebud had blossomed into a stunning showpiece of satiny amaranth petals. And like the English despoiler he was, he wanted to reach up and pluck her.

Good God, look at that hair, ropes of raven silk piled loosely on her head. He could send them cascading down with one twist of his randy hand. And that gown—had it ever belonged to his stepmother? Dora had never looked like *that* in it. But it must have been hers, for the bodice—made for a slighter woman—strained to contain Abby's more ample attractions. Abby certainly needed no corset. The gown already shoved her breasts up too high as it was. If not for his mother's rubies, which partly obscured the view—

"Good evening, Spencer," Abby said hesitantly. "I hope this will do for the theater."

Bloody hell, he'd been so busy gawking that he hadn't said a word.

Thankfully, Lady Brumley was never speechless. "Certainly it will do. Anytime the sight of his wife makes a husband swallow his tongue, Lady Ravenswood, you can be sure he is pleased with her attire."

"Pleased" wasn't quite the word. Who could be pleased at the prospect of an evening spent lusting futilely after a desirable woman?

Apparently bolstered by Lady Brumley's words and his reaction, Abby turned coy. "And you, my lord?" She held her hand out to him. "Have you found your tongue yet?"

"I'm working on it." He took her hand as he surveyed her. The gown had turned out well. The deep amaranth made Abby glow with healthy color, while the addition of petallike flounces about the hem transformed it into fashionable attire. He'd have to double the dressmaker's payment.

"You're the loveliest thing I've ever seen, my dear," he added. "The theatergoers will have a hard time keeping their eyes on the stage and away from my box tonight."

Abby laughed, a musical sound that made his gut twist and his loins tighten painfully. "You're teasing me now."

"I'd never dream of it." Attempting to reassure her, he lifted her gloved hand to his lips. But her fingers were delicate as china, and when they trembled beneath his kiss, a surge of need hit him despite all his determination to rein in his reactions.

She blushed, then touched her free hand to the ruby necklace that had belonged to his mother. "Oh, and I should also thank you for these jewels. I wasn't expecting—" With a glance at Lady Brumley, she added weakly, "That is, they must be quite valuable."

Never mind their value—he'd sent McFee up with the bloody things so they'd shield that tempting bosom of hers from his gaze. But now that they did, he wanted to snatch them off just so he could stare at her in her full glory.

Instead, he forced his gaze back to her face. "What would a gown be without jewels?"

"What indeed?" Lady Brumley remarked slyly.

Ignoring the other woman, Abby shot him a meaningful glance. "I'll be very careful with them."

It took him a second to realize she was trying to reassure him that she knew they were a loan. "I'm sure you will." Annoyed by her reminder of their charade, he added, "And if you're not, it's no great concern—I'll just buy you more."

When Abby's eyes widened, flickering green and mysterious in the dusky light, he fought a dark urge to drag her into his arms and kiss her senseless right there.

Lady Brumley cleared her throat. "I see that his lordship was right." For once, her voice lacked sarcasm. "It's a love match after all."

When Abby paled, Spencer drew her down the last two steps, tucking her hand firmly in the crook of his elbow. "Did you think otherwise, my lady?"

The Galleon of Gossip regarded them with cool amusement. "I didn't know what to think."

Spencer led Abby down the next flight of stairs to the ground floor, leaving Lady Brumley to hasten after them.

"It's not every day that an English viscount of your standing takes an American wife, you know," the annoying woman said behind them.

"It's not every day an English viscount meets an American as fascinating as my wife," Spencer countered smoothly. When they reached the entrance hall, he gestured to the footmen, who scurried to fetch his coat and Abby's pelisse.

He flashed Lady Brumley an even smile. "If you'll excuse us, we'll be late if we don't leave now."

"Which theater are you attending?"

"Covent Garden." He helped Abby with her pelisse and donned his coat.

Lady Brumley snorted. "I was there only last week, and the first thing is a stupid trifle of a farce, nothing to bother with. You could miss that. Fortunately, the play after is much better." Removing a vial from her reticule, Lady Brumley waved it in the air. "Besides, before you run off I want to hear more about Lady Ravenswood's interesting concoction— this Medicinal Mead of her father's."

Damn. The cursed woman had that bottle of Mead he'd taken from Abby's reticule the night before.

"So *that's* where my vial went," Abby said as she reached for it. "I've been looking for it everywhere."

Lady Brumley returned it quickly to her own reticule. "I'm not done trying it out. You can have it back when I'm finished." She flipped open her notepad. "But so far it doesn't look promising. I tried it on my indigestion last night and nothing happened."

When Abby's hand tensed on his arm, Spencer covered it with his own and gave it a warning squeeze. "I'm afraid discussion of Mercer's Mead will have to wait for another time,

Lady Brumley. I agreed to pick up Lady Tyndale and her daughter in my carriage, so we cannot be late."

Maneuvering Abby past the meddlesome gossip, he headed for the door, secure in McFee's ability to dispose of the woman on his own.

But Abby called back before they got through the front doors, "Do try it again with some milk, my lady. I think you'll find it works better that way. And if it doesn't, come see me and we'll add another posset to it."

Tightening his grip on Abby's arm, Spencer pulled her out the door and down the steps into the waiting carriage.

As soon as she was settled on the seat opposite him and the doors had closed, he erupted. "You're not to see that woman in private, do you hear? She isn't as harmless as she appears. One heedless word to a shark like Lady Brumley and—"

"Speaking of heedless, you told her we'd made a love match." Abby drew her pelisse tighter about her shoulders. "How much more heedless can one get?"

"It was the only plausible explanation left," he said defensively. "No one would believe I'd married you to enhance my wealth or further my political career."

He regretted his bald words when she set her mouth stubbornly. "Thank you for reminding me that I have no rank or family connections to commend me to a man as important as yourself."

"I didn't mean—"

"I know what you meant. Don't worry, I won't forget my place again."

Bloody hell. He hadn't meant to prick her pride. Why was he always too blunt with her? Usually he had no trouble flattering women, but Abby was so direct it flustered him, prompting him to meet her with equal directness.

But that was no excuse. Leaning forward to clasp her gloved hands, he refused to release them when she tried pulling away. "I'm sorry. I don't mean to be such a cur—"

"And yet you are. It must come naturally." At that moment, she looked as haughty as any affronted miss and more a woman of "rank" than she realized.

"I'll make it up to you. Think of the next few weeks as your pleasure trip to London. I have duties at Parliament, but when I can get away, I'll show you the sights."

"Oh? You can take that much time from your career for your pretend wife?"

Her sarcasm made him wince. "I'll do my best."

She refused to meet his gaze, staring woodenly out the window at the sinking sun. "Don't bother. I don't want to see the sights anyway."

Her hands were rigid in his, which alarmed him. "But London has many grand places. We could take a boat along the Thames—"

"Which hardly compares to sailing on Lake Erie."

Good point. "We could see the Tower of London."

"Where they executed all the traitors?" She gave an exaggerated shudder. "No thank you."

"Then how about the . . ." He wracked his brain. This was not going well. "The theater? We could see every play."

"We have theaters in America, too, you know." She shot him a cool look. "But if you have any hundred-foot waterfalls or wild buffalo, I'd love to see those."

"I don't think—" Then he caught the glint of mischief in her eyes.

Why, the little minx was teasing him. Releasing her hands, he threw himself back against the squabs. "You enjoy having me at your mercy, don't you?"

She flashed him a decidedly impish smile. "After being told by the great Viscount Ravenswood that he'd rather deceive all his friends than be truly married to me, I'm entitled to my fun, don't you think?"

"When you put it like that, I suppose so." If she only knew

how eagerly he would embrace being "truly married" to her under different circumstances.

As they rode in silence, he indulged fantasies of that imaginary state. Every morning he'd wake up to her in his bed. After breakfast she would send him off with a tender kiss like the one they'd shared in the garden. At night she would transform his social duties into excuses to dance with her and hold her. Not that he'd need excuses if she were his wife—they could have their own private parties in his bedchamber with their only music the sounds of hot, naked lovemaking.

Ah, how glorious Abby would look naked, spread out on his bed. Her breasts—those same cursed breasts peeking above the edge of her gown to torment him now—would be the color of warm honey and just as sweet. The nipples would be a rosy brown, puckering up at the touch of his tongue—

"Spencer?"

"Yes?" He silently thanked her for dragging him from *that* idiotic fancy.

"What have you told Nat's fiancée and her mother about me?"

"That you're my wife. That I vowed Nat to secrecy about it, but had been waiting until you were free of family obligations before I brought you from America."

She lifted one delicate eyebrow. "And they believed that nonsense?"

"Whether they did or not, they'll say what I tell them to say to whomever asks."

"I swear, why does everyone put up with your ordering them about? You make them do what you want with the most high-handed disregard for what *they* want."

He'd been accused of worse. "Don't you do the same when necessary? For instance, with Mrs. Graham—"

"You must be joking. Mrs. Graham do what I tell her? Only if I trick her into it."

"So what did you tell her about this?"

"The truth, of course. No point in lying about it—she'd sniff out the truth no matter what I tell her."

"And she had no problem with the scheme?"

The late afternoon sun pierced the unshaded windows to gild her pensive expression. "Actually, she's delighted to have me play at being your wife."

"But I got the distinct impression she didn't approve of me."

"Oh, her approval waxes and wanes according to your intentions," she said archly. "As my husband, you can do no wrong; as my betrayer, you're the devil. Since at present you're my husband, she's kindly disposed toward you."

"Even though it's only a role."

She sighed. "She's hoping that the role will become a reality."

Alarm seized him. "But *you* understand—"

"Yes, Spencer, I understand," she said tightly. "Never fear—I'm not as naive as my servant. I realize this will never be anything more. Though you didn't help her notions any by having your butler move my things to the bedchamber adjoining yours."

"I have my own servants to consider—keeping a secret among so many will be virtually impossible, so it's better to let them think you're my wife in every respect. If you'd asked, I would have cautioned you not to confide in Mrs. Graham."

She shook her head. "It wouldn't have worked. I lack your talent for lying. The minute she asked me for details—"

"You would tell her it's none of her concern. She's your servant—it's her duty to follow your orders without question."

"I see." With a swish of satin skirts, she shifted in her seat.

"Just as it's the duty of your family—and those soon to be your family—to do what you tell them without question?"

He stiffened. "I have their best interests at heart. Because they know that, they allow me to guide their actions."

"Do they? Nathaniel seems to have missed that point."

He curled his fingers into the seat, struggling not to show that she'd struck a nerve. "Not for want of my trying to explain it to him." He cast her a false smile. "Let me worry about my family, all right? You just concentrate on playing your role convincingly."

"I think I've got the harder job," she said with a sniff.

"Come now, how can you complain? Serving as wife to a grouchy old statesman is every young woman's dream." When his sarcasm gained him a small smile, he added, "And anyway, think how hard it would have been if you'd married me in truth. You'd have years of my high-handedness to look forward to."

"Perish the thought." She tipped up her chin, eyes alight. "And thank you for reminding me that this is fortunately temporary."

"You're welcome." The coach joined a long line of other coaches and slowed to a crawl. "We're nearly to the theater, my dear. Prepare to act your part."

She shot him a quizzical glance. "But you told Lady Brumley we had to pick up Lady Tyndale and her daughter."

"I had to get rid of the woman somehow, didn't I?"

With a roll of her eyes, she sat forward on the seat. "You certainly have a penchant for lying."

"It's common in my business, I'm afraid."

Her pretty eyebrows arched high on her forehead. "I thought statesmen were supposed to be honest."

"Not that business, my dear. The spying business." The coach shuddered to a halt. "Don't bandy this about, but I was once a spy and later a spymaster."

"Really?" She shook her head as the footman opened the

door and pulled down the step. "I should have known. It explains why you're so good at the lying. You've had plenty of practice."

He climbed out, then helped her down, bending low to murmur, "Some gentlemen fence, some play cards . . . I lie."

She shot him a chastening look. "And so very well, too," she said sweetly.

After that, speech was impossible. Thanks to Lady Brumley, they'd arrived too late to avoid the crowds. Half the *ton* seemed to be entering Covent Garden, and even more of them were jammed into the theater's vestibule once they got inside.

He guided Abby through a throng of highly ornamented, heavily perfumed, and ostentatiously dressed patrons toward the grand staircase that rose to the lobby of the lower tier of boxes. Staving off any questions with a dire look at anyone who neared them, he planted his hand in the small of Abby's satin-sheathed back to lead her along. But he could scarcely keep from smoothing his fingers lower, following her gown's descent to the perfectly rounded bottom. Good God, this was going to be a bloody long night.

Then they reached the stairs, and the crowd forced him to let her ascend ahead of him. Wonderful. Now her sweet behind was at eye level where he could imagine it unveiled, the soft globes wiggling as he kissed each in turn, then reached between her thighs to find the dewy flesh—

This was insane. What idiocy had possessed him to concoct this scheme of a pretend marriage? No French torture could torment him more than Abby prancing before him with all her charms. Her utterly forbidden charms.

Thankfully, he was able to thrash his randy imagination into submission while they navigated the corridor running behind the boxes. By the time they entered his own box to find Lady Tyndale and Evelina already there, he'd achieved the closest approximation of normalcy any man could manage with a fetching female hanging on his arm.

"Allow me to present my wife, Lady Ravenswood," he told his companions. "Last night you weren't properly introduced."

Fortunately, Lady Tyndale and Evelina were too well-bred to comment on their first bizarre meeting. They murmured polite greetings and left it to him to carry the conversation. But apparently Evelina still regarded the American woman as a rival, for she studied Abby with wary eyes.

At last the music started and the curtains were lifted, signaling that they should take their seats. The farce proved as trifling as Lady Brumley had claimed, but Spencer wasn't paying attention anyway. He was too busy watching for Abby's reaction.

Despite her impudent claim about theaters in America, her eager concentration on the stage demonstrated that she'd rarely attended. Every witty thrust prompted her to smile; every ridiculous contrivance elicited her murmur of surprise. Unlike the faintly bored countenances of the other ladies, Abby's face was as malleable as the actors, showing all her delight.

He felt vaguely envious. How long had it been since *he* had relished each moment or taken such heedless pleasure in even the most absurd theatrics? Probably not since he was a boy, when he'd thought the world his oyster. That seemed so long ago.

At last the farce ended, prompting her enthusiastic applause. Thank God that was over. He'd have to find another way to entertain his wife, one that didn't sink him into maudlin remembrances. Odd how only Abby made him do that. Then again, only Abby made him want the impossible.

No doubt about it, Abigail Mercer was a dangerous woman.

As the interlude began, some friends of Lady Tyndale's entered the box to talk to Evelina and her mother, leaving Spencer and Abby to themselves. At first Abby didn't seem to mind. She asked Spencer about the theater, the other patrons . . . whatever took her fancy.

After a few moments, however, she turned to whisper, "Why does Lady Evelina keep staring at me?"

"I suppose she's still clinging to her silly notion that you are Nat's mistress come from America to prevent his marriage. She thinks I'm only pretending to be married to you to protect him. I told her it was absurd."

"Are you absolutely sure she believed you?"

"If she didn't, there's nothing I can do about it."

"Well, I can." She picked up her beaded reticule. "Look there, her mother and her friends are leaving the box. I'll simply go explain to Lady Evelina about Nathaniel."

"You most certainly will not." He stayed her with one hand.

"Why?"

"I don't want her to know the truth about us."

"I'm merely going to explain that I'm not Nathaniel's mistress."

"You can't talk about mistresses to a well-bred Englishwoman. It violates every propriety."

"To speak in a forthright manner violates propriety?" She rose to stare at him with thinly veiled amusement. "No wonder you English lost the colonies. What with all the lying and the 'propriety' and the evasions, how do you ever get anything done?"

As she crossed the box to sit down beside Evelina, he stared after her in fascinated amazement. Americans were mad—that's all there was to it.

Evelina stiffened, refusing to look at Abby, but that didn't deter his brazen wife. "Lady Evelina," she said cheerily, "I'm so glad to finally get this chance to talk to you. I need your help, you see."

"Yes?" Evelina said, venturing a glance at her perceived rival.

"Being new to London society, I don't know all the niceties of polite behavior. I was hoping you'd teach me, since your fiancée told me you were the perfect English gentlewoman. He said I could do no better than to emulate you."

Evelina looked intrigued. "Nathaniel said that?"

"Oh, yes. Hardly a day passed that he didn't sing your praises. 'Lady Evelina is the most beautiful creature in England' and 'Lady Evelina is the soul of kindness and generosity.'" She shot Evelina a shy smile. "I confess he made me envy you. I want to make my Spencer as proud of me as Nathaniel is of you, but I don't know how to go about it. Being American, I'm a complete dunce when it comes to such matters."

Spencer saw an odd confusion pass over Evelina's face, before she eyed him speculatively, as if to gauge his reaction to Abby's subterfuge. Could the girl possibly suspect the truth about his situation with Abby?

No, that was ridiculous. Why should she?

Then the fleeting impression faded as Evelina turned back to Abby. "What would you like to know?"

Spencer relaxed when the two women began conversing about fan use and servants and a lot of nonsense everyone knew, even Americans from Philadelphia. How clever of Abby to pretend otherwise to put Evelina at ease.

By the time the music played, signaling the beginning of the first act of Oliver Goldsmith's *She Stoops to Conquer*, Evelina and Abby were already calling each other by their Christian names and chatting amiably, as young women were wont to do. Then Lady Tyndale returned to take her seat, and Abby left Evelina's side to join Spencer.

When she sat down, he murmured, "Nicely done, my dear."

"You see, my lord?" Her eyes sparkled up at him. "Sometimes you can achieve better results by telling the truth."

He arched a brow. "So my brother actually did say all those things about Evelina?"

With a smug smile, she faced the stage. "Not in so many words, of course. But a little shading of the truth can be permitted in this instance, don't you think?"

His laughter was still echoing as the first act began.

Spencer had never seen Goldsmith's popular play. Normally he considered theater-going in the same vein as any other duty—he went there to placate his relations. Just as he attended the opera to observe what civil servant was involved with what singer in case such a tidbit might be useful in the future. Or showed up at a ball for appearance's sake.

But tonight, thanks to Abby, he watched the play merely for enjoyment, a decidedly unique experience. He noticed the clever repartee and double meanings. He paid attention to the characters and who was deceiving whom, who was in love with whom. By the time the fourth act neared to a close, he even found himself wanting to see what came next. When was the last time *that* had happened?

Then Abby turned to him, looking embarrassed. "I'm sorry, Spencer, I thought I could wait until the break, but I can't. I have to find the ladies' retiring room."

"Of course," he murmured, all thought of the play forgotten. "I'll take you. Better to go now anyway, while there's no crowd."

They slipped into the passageway with her apologizing the whole time until he lied and said he needed some air himself. He waited for her near the entrance to the retiring room, feeling rather pleased with himself. The night was going better than expected. She was enjoying herself and had befriended Evelina. That was a good start.

When she came out, they headed back upstairs, chatting

about the play until they reached the corridor behind the boxes. Trying not to disturb the other patrons, they fell silent as they hurried down the passage.

Then someone approached and they moved aside to let the person pass. That's when they heard the conversation wafting out of a nearby box.

"She's not his wife," said a female voice. "How can she be? An American of dubious heritage? Ravenswood would never marry so low. And has anyone actually heard him claim her as his wife?"

Cursing the fates that had allowed them to overhear such nastiness, Spencer tried to hustle Abby past the open box door, but she shrugged off his hand to stand frozen, her eyes wide and hurt.

"Someone at the betrothal dinner told me he wouldn't explain her at all," said another female. "So she must be his mistress."

"Don't be absurd," a languid male voice put in. "Ravenswood would never introduce his mistress to Lady Tyndale and Lady Evelina. No, it's probably his brother's mistress and Ravenswood is acting as a cover for the rascal."

Now Spencer stood frozen, mostly because he couldn't believe their idiocy. Bad enough that Evelina had thought it, but the rest of them? It was ridiculous.

"Ravenswood has certainly been keen on the marriage between Lady Evelina and his brother," the addlepated female said. "He'd do anything to make sure it takes place."

"Even marry some chit from America?" another addlepate asked.

"Of course he didn't marry her," the addlepated male retorted. "Ravenswood probably claimed that the American girl is his fiancée to explain her abrupt appearance at the betrothal dinner. I daresay that's how all the confusion about her being his wife arose. Still, it's beyond the pale for him to flaunt her before his future relations *here*."

Spencer wanted to smash his fist right through the thin walls to grab one of the unfeeling gossips by the throat, but he knew better than to give them such satisfaction. Then he caught sight of Abby's face. Bloody hell. He had to get her back to his box where she couldn't hear such poison.

Suddenly, one of the women said, "Oh, dear, the act is ending. Come on, Lucille, let's go and find an orange girl before the crowd comes out. I'm dying for citrus."

He and Abby were trapped. They couldn't make it past the box before the women came out. Then again . . . perhaps he should put all this silly gossip to rest for good.

Pushing Abby against the corridor wall, he stared down into her surprised face. "Play along," he whispered.

Then he kissed her.

At first he was too intent on listening for "Lucille" and her friend to be much aware of what he was doing. But soon other sensations crowded in to distract him. Abby's mouth, soft as roses and sweet as nectar. Abby's scent, a tantalizing blend of rosemary and wine. Abby's breasts, full and warm and crushed against his chest.

He scarcely heard the gasp of shock behind him as he pulled back to stare at her. He was already lost in the widening wonder of Abby's eyes and the breaths stuttering from between her parted lips. Her seductive, parted lips . . .

And before he could stop himself, he was lowering his mouth to hers again.

Chapter 7

A beautiful woman can tempt even the most discreet employer into indiscretion.

Suggestions for the Stoic Servant

In an instant, Abby forgot about the cruel gossip and poor Evelina and all the other things plaguing her since her arrival. Because Spencer was kissing her, really kissing her. And it was fascinating . . . amazing . . . and completely unexpected.

It was so unexpected that when his tongue pressed between her lips, she opened her mouth just to see what would happen. Then his tongue swept into her mouth in an intimate and very unexpected caress, and a thrill blossomed low in her belly. Hardly conscious of it, she flattened herself against him, breast to thigh, and a growl of satisfaction rumbled low in his throat, like the thunder god signaling the coming storm.

And heavens, what a storm. His mouth seduced hers in a possession as wickedly satisfying as thunderclouds conquering the sky on a hot summer day. Every nerve in her body sparked like lightning, every pulse pounded like a hard, beating rain. He drowned her in his scent, his touch, his strength, until she knew only the thrusts of his tongue and the tightening of his powerful arms about her waist.

Then things got really interesting. Through the thin layers of skirt and petticoat and chemise, she felt his male arousal rise against her softness, an unyielding proof of his need. She couldn't help it—this evidence of the incautious Spencer she'd known in America delighted her.

Half drunk with excitement, she lifted one hand to clutch his neck, crushing his starched collar. With a heartfelt groan, he kissed her deeply, savagely, his scent fogging her brain until she sagged against the wall to keep from dropping to the floor.

Never had she known such a kiss—mouths caressing, tongues entwined, hot breaths mingling with hot breaths until neither knew where one began and the other ended. His storm fed hers, raining pleasure over her parched earth so sweetly that she didn't even react when his hand swept up to cover her breast. With the expert ease of an accomplished seducer, he kneaded it through the satin.

Then someone cleared his throat. Abby started, tearing her mouth from Spencer's and pushing his hand from her bodice.

The storm had passed, but Spencer seemed to have trouble registering that fact. His other hand still gripped her waist possessively, and his eyes glittered a promise of more storms to come.

"Bloody hell, Abby," he whispered as shock and wonder filled his features. "Bloody, bloody hell."

"My lord, we are not alone," she whispered.

He stiffened. She could practically see his sanity return, see him absorb where they were and who was watching. Releasing her abruptly, he faced the onlookers, whose expressions ranged from horrified to amused. Then with a low curse, he snagged Abby's hand and towed her down the corridor toward his box.

Now that the music had risen, people were pouring out into the passageway. They shot Spencer curious looks as he hurried Abby past, but he ignored them, his face set in grim lines, his expression warning off any who approached. Abby had never seen him so out of control. She didn't know whether to be pleased or alarmed by this intense reaction.

They met Lady Tyndale coming out of Spencer's box, but Spencer didn't even pause for her explanation of where she was going. He just dragged Abby inside and shut the box's door in Lady Tyndale's face.

Evelina glanced up as they entered. "There you are. We were wondering—"

"You and everyone else." Spencer dropped Abby's hand to pace the limited confines of the box. "If people would only mind their own business, the world would be a better place."

When Evelina flinched at Spencer's harsh tone, Abby hastened to reassure her. "Don't mind Spencer—he's not angry at you. We just overheard some unsettling gossip, that's all."

"That's all?" He whirled on her with face alight. "Half the world thinks you're my brother's mistress, for God's sake!"

Noting how Evelina paled, Abby said quickly, "I think you disabused them of that notion by kissing me in the corridor."

"You kissed her?" Evelina sounded surprised.

"Yes, I kissed her. What of it? She's my wife, isn't she?" Spencer sucked in a shuddering breath, then stared at Abby, a frown carving his brow. "But I didn't intend— Forgive me, Abby. I never meant to embarrass you."

"You didn't embarrass me." He'd shocked her, thrilled her, and turned her world upside down, yes. But he hadn't embarrassed her. She hadn't had time to be embarrassed before he'd hustled her back to the box like a madman.

"You'd think people would have better things to do than speculate about matters beyond their concern," Spencer grumbled, though he seemed calmer.

Stepping up close, Abby lowered her voice. "I told you that this wouldn't work. They'd be fools to believe that a viscount—"

"They'll believe what I tell them to believe. And it's time I tell them what that is." He held out his hand. "Come, my dear, I will introduce you as my wife to everyone I see. That should put an end to this nasty gossip."

Lady Tyndale entered, her face pale. "I wouldn't go out there just now if I were you. I heard some ladies saying—"

"That Abby is Nat's mistress?" he snapped. "Don't believe a word of it."

"Uh . . . no. Actually, they're saying that she's *your* mistress." A dainty pink rose over the matron's cheeks. "It seems that you . . . well . . . really, my lord, most men do not kiss their wives so . . . and in public, too."

Apparently he understood the vague Lady Tyndale's babbling, for he squeezed Abby's hand in a crushing grip. "I am not 'most men,'" he retorted. "I will kiss my wife wherever and however I please, and I do not appreciate having idiots speculate about her simply because I . . . got carried away."

Lady Tyndale stiffened. "From what I understand, you did more than kiss your wife. And that would rouse comment no matter who you are."

Remembering the heat of Spencer's hand on her breast, Abby blushed furiously. No wonder they thought she was his mistress. Though that gave her an idea.

"Would you excuse us a moment?" she told Lady Tyndale and Evelina, then pulled Spencer aside and dropped her voice to a whisper. "Maybe you should just let everyone go on thinking I'm your mistress. Then when I leave, you won't have to maintain the farce of an estranged wife, and everything would be easier."

"For whom?" His eyes gleamed like polished steel. "My brother has taken enough from you—I will not have him take your reputation as well."

"My reputation in England won't matter once I return to America."

"It matters to me now." His eyes darkened. "I refuse to

compound my brother's crimes by letting society heap calumny on your head while you're in London."

His staunch determination to protect her warmed her so thoroughly that all she could manage in response was a tremulous smile.

"Now come with me." Tucking her hand in the crook of his elbow, he walked toward their companions, who were also whispering together. "I'll make sure it's understood that you're my wife, even if I must introduce you to every person here."

Evelina looked up. "Please don't act so foolishly, Spence."

He scowled at the young woman. "How I act is not your concern, Evelina."

"No, but your wife is." Her soft smile included Abby. "We're soon to be sisters, and I shouldn't like to see a sister maligned. Given what those gossips saw, I can't believe you'd want to subject your wife to the vile comments they'll undoubtedly make."

A lump caught in Abby's throat. The woman who had every reason to distrust her was championing her. Abby hated to repay her trust with deception, but what choice had Spencer left her?

Spencer went rigid beneath her hand. "They would not malign her to her face, not with me at her side. They know better."

"Perhaps. But they might give her the cut direct before you can introduce her. Then you'll have forced the issue and lost, because after snubbing her before their friends, they won't easily turn around and support her."

"You have a point," Spencer admitted tersely.

"I'm not sure what the 'cut direct' is," Abby put in, "but I've probably endured worse countless times." Apparently even Spencer's high station couldn't save her from humiliation. She forced nonchalance into her voice. "Really, the two of you mustn't worry. I have a thick skin."

Spencer's hot gaze searched her face. "Do you? I seem to recall a certain discussion in my garden that implied otherwise." When she dropped her eyes from his, he added in a low voice, "I promised to spare you that. I'll hold to my promise."

He left her to head to the top of the box where he stood with his hands braced against the balcony rail. As he surveyed the bustling theater, his jaw tightened. The chandeliers were going up—any minute now the fifth act would begin.

Spencer let out a deep sigh. "Evelina, how do you suggest we solve this?"

Evelina started. "You're asking me?"

Spencer turned from the rail with a tight smile. "Why not? Tonight you've shown you have a good head on your shoulders and an astute knowledge of London society."

Evelina's astonishment gave way to a pleased smile. Clearly Spencer had never asked for the young woman's advice before. Given how he spoke of his family—and his family-to-be—that was no surprise.

"I think you should present her formally." The fifth act began, so Evelina lowered her voice. "Mama is already having that ball tomorrow night to celebrate my betrothal. Why not make it a celebration of your marriage instead?"

"But Evelina," Lady Tyndale protested with a scowl for Abby, "that ball is supposed to be for you and Nathaniel."

"I know, but if Nathaniel is recuperating in . . . Essex, we can't celebrate our engagement anyway. So we might as well use the ball to help Spence."

Evelina's hesitation before the word "Essex" gave Abby pause, but she didn't dwell on it. She was too busy panicking over appearing at a ball tomorrow night. "No," she whispered, "I can't. My gowns won't be finished and—"

"At least one of them will," Spencer put in. "I already paid the dressmaker an ungodly sum to make sure one was ready right away."

"But *I'm* not ready. I haven't been to a ball in years."

"You'll be fine. Evelina is right—you should be formally introduced to society, the sooner the better. They can hardly claim you're my mistress if Lady Tyndale holds a ball to celebrate our union."

For heaven's sake, this was getting out of hand. "Really, Spencer—" Abby began.

"Thank you, Evelina," he said, ignoring Abby. "I told you that you have a good head on your shoulders. I couldn't have devised a better way to handle this myself."

"As for tonight," Evelina said, "you should probably not stay until the play is over. After you're gone, Mama and I will spread the news of your wedding and talk about the ball tomorrow night, just to prepare people. We'll say you're so much in love that you couldn't restrain yourselves and went home rather than embarrass anyone." A smile lit her face. "It's the truth, anyway, isn't it?"

"Of course." Spencer spoke the lie with perfect ease, curse him. Then he offered Abby his arm. "Come, my dear. I'm sorry you'll have to miss the rest of the play, but we'll attend another time."

She hesitated, but arguing with him about the ball in front of Evelina and Lady Tyndale was pointless, since she'd have to watch every word she said.

So she took his arm, murmured her good-byes, and let him lead her out to the waiting carriage. She held her tongue only until they were situated inside and headed home. "Spencer, I can't possibly be presented at a ball. I still have too much to learn about London society."

"It's not that different from American society." Drawing the shade up, Spencer stared out into the London street. "You said your father had you tutored in social graces and such—

you won't need more than that. And if you do, just follow Evelina's lead. She always behaves correctly."

His praise of Evelina gave her pause. "She *is* very elegant, isn't she?"

"Yes."

"And pretty, too," she said with an edge in her voice.

"Quite pretty." His gaze swung back to her. "But so are you."

Just not pretty enough. "Yet you think I should emulate her."

He looked annoyed. "Only if you're confused on some matter of correct behavior. Otherwise, follow your own instincts."

"You don't understand. I don't have any instincts here. America and England aren't the same, no matter what you say. And I haven't even been to a ball since before Papa became ill. The dances have surely changed, not to mention—"

"Abby?" he interrupted.

"What?"

"You do realize why I kissed you tonight, don't you?"

All thoughts of balls and dances fled Abby's mind. Dear heaven, she didn't want to talk about their kiss. He'd ruin it. She'd rather hug to herself the knowledge that for a few fleeting moments he'd found her desirable enough to forget she wasn't the sort of wife he wanted. "You kissed me to squelch the rumors about me and Nat." *Please let that end the discussion*, she prayed.

No such luck. "So you understand that the kiss was all a sham."

Anger burned up through her. How dared he try to take from her the one sliver of satisfaction she'd had since her arrival? "It was *not* all a sham. I know enough about men to know when they're . . . feeling things for a woman."

She thought she saw bleakness in the steel-gray eyes, but it must have been a trick of the street lamps, for when she looked again, he merely appeared annoyed.

"All right," he said tersely, "I'll admit I felt desire. But surely you know that a man can feel that physical urge for many women. I would have reacted the same if you had been any other beautiful woman pressed up against me."

Curse him for that. Why couldn't he have just left it alone? Unshed tears burned the back of her throat, but she'd never let them fall. She'd never let him know how much he'd hurt her. "Yes, I know exactly what you mean." She steadied her voice. "That's true for women, too. I daresay I would have responded the same to any handsome man with a talent for kissing."

She gained some satisfaction from the anger rising in his face. But her satisfaction was hollow, since his anger only stemmed from his foolish male pride and nothing else.

"I see," he bit out. "Then we understand each other."

"Yes, what a relief." She tipped up her chin with a bold smile. "I may be naive, my lord, but I'm not entirely without experience of the opposite sex. I've been kissed a time or two." What a complete lie. "I'm well aware that men often kiss women without meaning anything by it."

"Good. So long as you understand."

He actually sounded irritated. No, she must have imagined it. Why should Spencer be irritated? As usual, he was getting everything he wanted.

Including her attendance at a ball, since clearly the arrogant scoundrel would drag her there no matter what she said. Fine, let him drag her. She'd hold her head high as she fumbled her way through it. And if it turned into a disaster and she embarrassed him before all his friends, so much the better. Let *him* suffer some humiliation for a change.

Chapter 8

The prudent servant heeds his employer's commands even when they are wrongheaded, shortsighted, or utterly foolish.

Suggestions for the Stoic Servant

Spencer had spent the entire morning in the office of Sir Robert Peel, the new home secretary. He'd spent the afternoon in his own, dealing with urgent matters of state. So shortly after sundown he was relieved to see his friend and subordinate, Morgan Blakely, enter. He could use a diversion right now, and Blakely always provided one.

Unfortunately, this evening's diversion was far from diverting.

Blakely dropped a folded newspaper onto Spencer's desk and stabbed his finger at a headline—*Viscount Marries Exotic American Beauty*. "I can't believe I have to hear about this from Lady Brumley's column," Blakely said, though his eyes twinkled. "You old slyboots, how dare you get legshackled without telling your friends?"

Spencer waved Blakely to a chair as he scanned Lady Brumley's account. Though the Galleon of Gossip had dedicated the entire column to news of his marriage, she wisely hadn't mentioned her suspicions about Nat.

But she'd vastly exaggerated his and Abby's romantic

connection. Spencer winced as he lifted his gaze to Blakely. How much of the truth should he reveal? All of it? Could he trust Blakely's discretion?

His friend sat back with an expectant smile. "Spill everything, *mon ami*. Clara sent me to ferret out the details, and she won't be satisfied with less than the entire story, from first meeting to wedding."

Spencer frowned. "You should tell your nosy wife to mind her own business."

"I already did. She ignored me as usual. She figures you owe us inside information after how you threw us together three years ago."

"I was under the impression you were both happy about the marriage that resulted from my machinations. Is the bloom finally off the rose?"

"Hardly." Blakely grinned smugly as he folded his hands over his belly. "Clara is enceinte again."

"Ah." Spencer managed a smile through his sudden stab of envy. "Then congratulations are in order. And do tell your wife how much I admire her willingness to bear children to a rascal like you."

Amazing how calm he sounded. That came of years saying whatever the situation warranted, regardless of his feelings. Not that his congratulations weren't genuine. But he couldn't help his resentment—this would be Blakely's second child, no doubt one of many. Some men led charmed lives.

Which reminded him . . . "Sir Robert said to tell you that testing is complete on your brother's pistol design. Let Templemore know that the Home Office intends to have pistols made to it for all the officers."

"That should please him," Blakely said. "He's inordinately proud of his designs." He shook his head. "Though I think these days he's even more proud of his burgeoning family. Juliet is enceinte again, too—can you believe it?"

Devil take the man, he seemed determined to stay on the

subject of children. "I'm sure it was bound to happen given the way those two go on. Now about those pistols—"

"And since you've finally gotten around to acquiring a wife," Blakely cut in with a conspiratorial wink. "I suppose we'll be hearing a similar announcement about impending children from you before long."

The blow came too suddenly for Spencer to prepare himself, and the subsequent pain that lanced his chest knocked the breath from him. He hadn't even considered that people would expect him and Abby to be thinking about children.

But of course people were expecting that. He was getting on in years. Most men of his rank and wealth took wives for precisely that reason—to bear their heirs.

Some of his distress must have shown in his face, for Blakely frowned. "Sorry, old boy, I forgot that you don't much like children."

"It's not that." His farce of a marriage was suddenly too painful to endure. Perhaps he *should* tell Blakely the truth. He trusted the man with his life. Besides, Blakely already knew about the subterfuge with Nat. Spencer had sent word to him about it the first night of Nat's defection so that Blakely could handle the magistrate. He might as well hear the rest. "Actually, ours is not that sort of marriage."

Blakely's smile faded. "What sort do you mean?"

"It's not a love match, despite what Lady Brumley wrote. It's not really a match at all."

Spencer told Blakely the entire sordid tale, leaving nothing out except why he dared not make the marriage a real one. And he certainly didn't mention his persistent physical attraction to Abby. That was merely the normal reaction of a man who'd been without a mistress for too long. Yes, surely that's all it was.

"Thankfully," he finished, "Miss Mercer has agreed to play my wife until I can find Nat. It's very good of her, considering that Nat stole her dowry. And that I'm blackmailing her into it."

"It's not blackmail when she'll come out of the scheme twice as rich as before." A frown touched Blakely's brow. "Take care, my friend—hasn't it occurred to you that you have only her word about the dowry?"

He bristled at Blakely's implication. "Apparently you were a spy longer than was good for you. Not everyone is sly and deceitful."

"Apparently *you* were not a spy long enough. How do you know she's not some fortune hunter seizing this opportunity to become a wealthy viscount's wife? Or even cheat you out of five thousand pounds?"

"She wouldn't. It's not in her character, trust me."

Blakely looked unconvinced.

Spencer planted his elbows on his desk. "You'll meet her tonight. After that, if you can still tell me she'd use deception to gain a man in marriage or steal what doesn't belong to her, I'll eat my hat."

"Very well. And once you've settled things with your brother? What will you do with her?"

"Travel to America, sever the marriage by pointing out that it's not legal, and leave her there. Society will then only know of her as my estranged wife."

"And when you decide to marry in truth?"

He wasn't about to reveal that he never planned to marry—Blakely would plague him with even more questions than Abby would. "I'll cross that bridge when I come to it. At the moment my main concern is avoiding a scandal." He narrowed his gaze on his friend. "By the way, will you be able to maintain my deception about Nat and a footpad? Will the magistrate and his officers cooperate?"

"Hornbuckle didn't like it, but he agreed to it. And his officers are very loyal to him . . . and to you."

Spencer relaxed. "At least that's taken care of."

"Have you no idea where your brother is now?"

He shook his head. "I've got Bow Street men scouring the countryside and others investigating Nat's old cronies in London in the hope that one might lead us to him."

"In the meantime, this American becomes more firmly entrenched in your household every day."

"Let me worry about Abby," Spencer snapped. Then he softened his sharp words with a smile he didn't feel. "After all, you've got a real wife to worry about, not to mention an unborn child. You've no time to fret over *my* troubles."

"True." Blakely rubbed his chin. "And speaking of Clara, how much can I tell her?"

Spencer hesitated. It might be good for Abby to have a woman on her side who knew the entire situation and could advise her. "If you trust Clara's discretion, tell her all of it. But make her understand that she must not speak of it to anyone else."

"You know Clara—she's not a gossip," Blakely said. "But if it makes you feel better, you can caution her again yourself tonight at the ball."

"All right." Spencer looked at his watch. "Speaking of that, I'd better go." He rose. He had to get home to dress. "I'll see you there."

Blakely rose, too. "I look forward to meeting this interesting American whom you claim is incapable of using deception to snag a viscount."

"Now see here," Spencer bit out, "suspect Abby's motives if you must, but don't inflict those suspicions on her tonight. She'll be anxious enough as it is without having to endure your contempt."

"I'll be perfectly amiable, don't you worry," Blakely promised. His eyes darkened. "Besides, amiability is far more effective than contempt in eliciting information from a subject."

Spencer gritted his teeth, but knew he'd never talk his friend out of at least questioning Abby to determine her character. Fortunately, Blakely knew how to do it without rousing suspicion.

They walked out together discussing other matters, but as soon as Spencer entered his carriage, his mind had time to wander. To his consternation, it wandered back to his unwise attraction to his sham wife.

Last night's maneuver at the theater had been a mistake—he saw that now. Why had he assumed he could kiss Abby and remain unaffected? Even before her arrival, she'd plagued his thoughts constantly. And their fleeting kiss in the garden should have shown him how susceptible he was to her.

Yet he'd stupidly indulged himself last night anyway. Now he couldn't go ten minutes without reliving the heady pleasure of having her in his arms. All he could think about was his need to kiss her, caress her . . . make love to her.

He'd nearly done it last night, before God and everyone. She had this annoying ability to turn him into a slobbering fool whenever she approached. How did she do it? He'd never lost his head over a woman before, not even his last mistress—an exotic Frenchwoman who knew every way to please a man. How did one little American with rosemary-scented breath and an impudent, teasing manner make him forget everything but his need to plunder her delicious mouth?

Knowing she shared the attraction only made it worse. He had no right to take advantage of her willingness. Abby had a life to go back to after this was over. That's why he must keep his roaming hands to himself.

And keep from kissing those lips too sweet for prudence. Yes, that was the secret—never kiss Abby. Kissing Abby always led to disaster.

He could manage not to kiss her, couldn't he? Tonight they'd be under intense scrutiny—that should make it easy.

They'd have to dance a waltz or two, which would be sheer hell, but he'd simply have to tamp down his lust. Thankfully, he and Abby need not dance more than that, since no husband danced every dance with his wife.

He settled back against the squabs. Yes, he must treat her the way most English lords treated their wives—with respectful indifference—if he was to survive the evening without a lapse. He must find a way to gird himself against her charms.

Think about your work, he told himself. *Surely that will do the trick.*

Once he arrived home and set about preparing for the evening, he forced himself to think of Parliament, of the bills being proposed, of the troublesome resistance Sir Robert Peel was receiving to his ideas about a citywide police force. By the time he knocked at the adjoining door to Abby's bedchamber, thinking to accompany her downstairs, he was proud of how he'd reestablished control over his vexing desires. She was just a pretty woman, after all. Nothing to lose his head over.

Then Mrs. Graham opened the door, and all his hard-won control crumbled to dust. His wife was a vision even lovelier than he'd remembered. Rich folds of jeweled green silk fell from the high waistband to the floor. Lines of embroidery ornamented the gown with spidery designs in a lighter green, and a number of silk scalloped flounces adorned the hem.

But the lower half of the gown didn't worry him—it was the upper that sent his pulse into a frenzied pounding. Sweet God in heaven. With her hair loosely piled atop her head and her breasts partly exposed by the low-cut bodice, she looked delectable enough to shatter any man's control. He would never survive the night without kissing her. He wouldn't even survive the carriage ride. He'd have her in his arms so fast, it would knock the breath out of her.

"This will not do," he choked out.

The French maid, who'd been waiting silently for his reaction, said, "Monsieur?"

He scrambled for some reason to explain his consternation without revealing his susceptibility, and could find only one. "She doesn't look respectable." Pleased to have hit on a logical explanation for his objections, he hurried on. "They will never believe she is my wife when she looks like . . ." He searched for the least offensive word. "A ladybird." When the maid looked perplexed, he added in French, "*Une fille de joie.*"

Both Abby and the maid regarded him with horror.

"*Pardonez moi*, monsieur," the maid protested, "but this is the height of fashion. A very beautiful gown for madame, *non*? She look like a queen, not a *fille de joie.*"

"Under other circumstances, I'd agree, but this is a delicate situation. She must show herself to be a proper matron tonight, and this gown reveals too much of her—" He forced himself to sound reasonable. "It simply will not do. The neckline is too low."

"Spencer," Abby pleaded, "there's no time for anything else. The other gowns aren't finished, and I can't wear a day dress to a ball—that would insult your hostesses."

"Then use a fichu to cover your bosom." He glared at the wide-eyed maid. "I don't care how you do it—just cover her up, understand?"

The maid bobbed her head furiously. "*Oui*, monsieur, *oui.*"

"And another thing," he went on, "her hair should be pulled up tighter atop her head." So he wasn't tempted to let it down and run his fingers through it. He strode up to Abby, ignoring the way her face shone as red as ripe cherries. "I want ringlets here and here," he said, indicating her temples. "That's what all the young respectable women wear."

"But monsieur," the maid protested, "Madame's hair is not . . . how do you say . . . not for the curling. It will not look so pretty the way you say."

He crossed his arms over his chest. "May I remind you, mademoiselle, that it is your job to make it look pretty. Because if you cannot provide me with what I require—"

"Marguerite," Abby interrupted in a cold voice, "do as his lordship demands. The ringlets, the fichu, everything. He's paying for this, so he should get what he wants."

He stared at Abby, wary of her easy capitulation and vaguely uneasy about the way she'd worded her command. "Thank you." He studied her flushed face, his unease sharpening. "You do understand, don't you, my dear? You must look as unspoiled as the dew tonight if we're to quell the gossip."

"I understand perfectly, my lord. You want to turn me into an elegant English miss like Evelina."

"Devil take it, Abby, this is for the best. Once you're established as my wife, you can dress as you please, but for now you must let me guide you."

"Certainly, my lord," she said smoothly. "Whatever you think is appropriate."

Was she mocking him with her "my lords" and her "whatever you think is appropriate"? Well, let her mock him if she liked—he could not go out with her looking like that, not if he was to keep his hands off her.

"Very good." He ignored the sudden drop of temperature in the room and Mrs. Graham's fierce scowl. "We can leave as late as an hour from now, Abby. I trust that you can be ready by then."

Without another word he left, heading downstairs for the haven of his study and his cognac. Living with this sham marriage was proving a lot harder than he'd expected. He could only pray that the runners found his brother soon.

Chapter 9

Parties, dinners, and balls are the crucibles within which all important persons are tried, but not all emerge purified.

Suggestions for the Stoic Servant

Torn between awe and fear, Abby surveyed Lady Tyndale's modest ballroom. How had they crammed this many people in here? At least a hundred gaily bedecked ladies and gentlemen wandered in and out, intent on either dancing or examining her with all the subtle interest of wolves scenting fresh meat.

Even with Spencer beside her, she felt conspicuous. But now that he'd gone off to fetch her punch, she felt like the prime entertainment. Matrons rolled their eyes at her behind their fans. A cluster of young misses burst into giggles after every furtive glance at her hair. And some dandy—she thought that's what those fancy men were called—lifted his glass to his eye and with a supercilious smile frankly surveyed her attire.

"Don't mind them," Evelina murmured from Abby's side. "You'd think they'd never seen a viscount's wife before."

"That's not why they're laughing." Abby's chin trembled, partly from anger, partly from embarrassment. "They're laughing at this silly fichu stuffed in a ball gown."

Evelina lifted one perfectly plucked brow. "Why did you wear it if you knew it wasn't fashionable?"

"Spencer said the gown wasn't respectable without it. It's nonsense, of course, but he gave me no choice."

Evelina's lips tightened into a line.

"I wouldn't mind it so much," Abby went on, "if it didn't keep attempting an escape. The gown's not designed for use with a fichu, so it has no fastenings for it, and the pins keep coming out."

"Then just take it out and stuff it in your reticule," Evelina retorted. "Never mind what Spence says."

Absolutely not. He'd wanted a fichu, and she was going to give him one. Maybe after some of the gossip got back to him, his high-and-mighty lordship would finally acknowledge he didn't know everything. "Don't worry. After two trips to the ladies' retiring room, I think I've got it secured." Although if she relaxed her vigilance for a moment, the annoying scrap of lace would probably leap right out and attack somebody.

Another of her supposed "ringlets" drooped into her eye. She blew it out.

Evelina eyed her closely. "Was the coiffure his idea, too?"

"What do you think? He wouldn't listen when we told him my hair doesn't take a curl like yours does. I wish it did."

"Bite your tongue," Evelina said. "Last night every woman at the theater, including me, was envying your lovely thick hair so fetchingly arranged on top of your head. It looked ever so much more comfortable—and prettier—than our tight knots."

Abby eyed her askance. "You're just saying that to make me feel better."

"No, I'm not. Even Mama liked your coiffure, and while she may seem rather . . . er . . . dim, she's quite the arbiter of fashion. You may just start the next rage."

Abby didn't want to start the next rage. She wanted to be

inconspicuous. But that seemed impossible, no matter what she did with her hair. "Spencer said my coiffure made me look like a ladybird."

"What? That's ridiculous!"

"Is it? He might have been right." She gazed at the women, all of whom wore ringlets exactly like Spencer had dictated. Only hers weren't crisp and tight like theirs. Marguerite had done her best with the iron in such a short time, but it was a hopeless case. "He thinks he can make me look more refined, but you can't turn a sow's ear into a silk purse."

"Especially when it's already a silk purse," Evelina said stoutly. "Now see here—don't you listen to Spence. He doesn't know what he's talking about. You're perfectly adorable just as you are, and if he can't see that, he's blind."

Abby flashed Evelina a grateful smile. "Nathaniel was right about you—you *are* the most generous woman in England. I see why Spencer says I should emulate you."

"Does he really?" Evelina frowned. "Sometimes Spence is an ass."

Abby's jaw dropped. "What did you say?"

Evelina colored instantly. "Forgive me for my vulgarity, but that's what Nathaniel always says. He's right, too. Someone should instruct Spence on how to treat a wife."

"Oh, he's not so bad." It wasn't Spencer's fault that his brother had thrust her into his lap. "He's been very good to me. You should have seen the gowns he bought—I know they cost him a fortune. And the reticules and the shoes . . ."

"He bought you gowns and all that?" Evelina now wore an expression that on any other woman Abby would have called calculating. "And did he complain about having to spend so much on them? Some husbands do, or so I'm told."

"Actually, he insisted upon sparing no expense, even when I wanted a more modest wardrobe."

Evelina looked out across the ballroom floor, a slow smile playing over her angelic face. "Well, well . . . isn't that interesting?"

"What?"

Evelina started. "Oh, nothing." She tapped her fan against her hand. "Tell me, what do you think of our ball? Are balls this grand in Philadelphia?"

"Not by half. For one thing, nobody in Philadelphia actually has his own ballroom. We just roll up the carpets and push the furniture against the wall in the drawing room. Then somebody plays the pianoforte so we can dance." She gestured at the ballroom. "Your mother outdid herself with all this."

"You can thank your husband for that. He absorbed much of the cost. He even sent over his cook to prepare the food and loaned us his staff for things like polishing the ballroom floor. We could never have managed such grandness alone."

That explained a great deal—Nathaniel had described his fiancée's family as "often short of funds," and Abby had wondered how they'd afforded such a fine affair. "Why did Spencer do that?"

Evelina shrugged. "Once it became *your* celebration, he thought it only fitting that it be a bit more extravagant an affair."

"I wish he'd stop spending money like this over our . . . marriage." Their *sham* marriage. It made her uneasy.

"Nonsense—Spence has pots of money. So why not let him spend it on a superb orchestra instead of the three musicians we'd hired? Or provide those bright new French globe lamps instead of candles? Except for his grand house, which he only built to further his political career, he never spends his funds on anything frivolous or even fun. Work is everything to him. It has always driven Nathaniel mad."

Mention of the reckless man provoked Abby to defend

Spencer's seriousness. "Yes, I gathered that 'work' is of little interest to Nathaniel."

Too late, she realized she was speaking of Evelina's fiancé, but Evelina didn't appear insulted. Instead, she cast Abby a searching glance. "Things aren't always as they seem."

Abby blinked. Could Evelina know more about Nathaniel's activities than she let on?

She had no time to ask, because Spencer's bright globe lamps allowed her to be picked out even by undesirable guests. Like Lady Brumley, who now sailed toward them, a tiny golden ship perched impossibly atop her swirling coiffure.

Abby sighed. Spencer didn't want her talking to the woman. But what was she supposed to do—be rude? Only rudeness would rebuff the likes of a Lady Brumley.

"My dear Lady Ravenswood," the woman said, "I simply must talk to you about this Mead of yours. I don't understand why your father sold it as a cure for indigestion. I've tried it several times and it never works."

Abby stuck out her chin. "It always works fine for me, my lady. Did you try it with milk?"

"I tried it with milk, with honey, with tea—I tried it with everything but the dirty wash water, and it still did nothing."

Abby winced. "I don't know what to tell you. Maybe it's not the right combination of herbs to suit your digestion, my lady."

"Would you stop with all the 'my lady's', if you please? Good Lord, you'd think you were a servant."

Heat rose in Abby's cheeks. Spencer had said something similar—about her not being his servant. But how was she supposed to know the proper way for addressing people with titles? Nobody had told her, and although she was trying to learn by observation, none of it made any sense.

"In any case," Lady Brumley went on, "I think you're going about this Mead business all wrong. This shouldn't be a tonic at all. It's wonderful as a—"

"Good evening, Lady Brumley," Spencer said coolly as he walked up with two glasses of punch. Handing one to Evelina, he held the other out to the marchioness. "Have some refreshment, madam. I believe I shall dance with my wife."

Though Lady Brumley accepted the glass, she scowled at him. "Now see here, Lady Ravenswood and I were in the midst of a conversation. You can't always be whisking her off whenever I have the chance to talk to her."

"Ah, but I can." Spencer's eyes gleamed. "It's a husband's prerogative. Now if you'll excuse us . . ."

Giving Abby his arm, Spencer guided her toward the dance floor. Abby could only shrug helplessly at Lady Brumley, but in truth she was relieved. Talking to Lady Brumley was like navigating a strange house in the dark— one never knew when one might send a vase crashing to the floor.

She glanced up to find Spencer smiling at her. "Thank you for the rescue," she said.

"You're welcome." He led them to the center of the floor. She watched curiously as the other dancers moved aside, forming a space around her and Spencer. "But it wasn't entirely a rescue, my dear," he went on. "I want to dance with you. They're waiting for us to lead off the first waltz."

As the music swelled up from the orchestra, she panicked. "No, we can't," she whispered. Dear heaven, everyone was watching them.

"Why can't we?" Placing one hand on her waist, he held the other up with an expectant smile. "They think we're married, remember?"

"I don't know how to waltz," she hissed.

His smile faded. "What do you mean?"

"I mean I have no clue what the steps are or how to move or . . . or anything."

Casting a furtive glance around, he lowered his voice. "Why didn't you tell me?"

"Because you never asked."

His jaw grew taut. "But surely you've seen it done enough to manage a reasonable approximation."

"I've never seen it done and I've never danced it. So if you persist in a waltz, you'll only make us both appear foolish. Unless you can carry me about the room without anybody noticing."

Dropping his hands to his sides, he cursed under his breath, then said curtly, "Wait here," and strode off toward the orchestra.

Oh, no, what now? Mortified to her toes, she stood there alone on the floor. The music abruptly stopped, and every eye in the ballroom fixed on her with malicious interest. She wanted to sink right through the floor.

She'd nearly decided to make a mad dash for the retiring room when the orchestra struck up a different piece of music, something she recognized from balls in her girlhood.

Acting as if changing dances at the last moment was perfectly natural, Spencer approached to offer her his arm. "You *can* dance a reel, can't you?"

She nodded. Thank God he hadn't chosen something else she didn't know.

As he led her to the lines that were forming, he asked, "How could you not know the waltz? You had a dance master, and you said you attended balls in your youth."

"Yes, *in my youth*. Before the waltz reached America. By the time Philadelphians were dancing the waltz, I was spending all my time in Papa's sickroom. I told you, it's been years since I attended a social event of any kind. And I've never learned to waltz."

"I see."

But his rigid face showed that he didn't see at all. Her temper flared. "It's not as if I didn't warn you. Last night in the carriage—"

"Yes, you're right." His tight jaw softened. "I suppose I should have listened. I'll be more careful in the future, all right?"

"All right." But as they approached the head of the lines, she felt a moment's panic. "I hope you dance the reel the same way here as we do in America."

"I can't imagine why we wouldn't." He lowered his voice to a whisper. "And if the music should confuse you, just stop and I'll have them play something else. It might take a few tries, but eventually we should hit on one that works."

Horrified by the very idea of enduring such humiliation twice, she started to protest. Then his smile gave her pause. With a wink, he left her to cross over to the other side to take his place, and the truth hit her.

Spencer—the sober-minded statesman—was actually teasing her. And after she'd shamed him before all his friends, too. Would wonders never cease. Just when she thought that the haughty viscount had completely buried the friendly gentleman she'd known in America, he did something to flummox her.

When the dancing commenced, he flummoxed her again. Spencer was quite an accomplished dancer. She never would have guessed it—the reserved Lord Ravenswood light on his feet? Engaging in frivolity? Astonishing!

Yet his smooth skill put other dancers to shame. He even effectively covered the few slips that *she* made, which was nothing short of amazing. After a while, she relaxed and let the music carry her through the steps.

Thank heaven they resembled those she'd danced in her youth. Besides, her partner made it easy, his sure steps clearly mirroring what she was to do. His hand guided her in the turns with a deft security that carried her through as if he held her aloft. As if they were truly married.

Dear heaven, not *that* again. She could manage not to yearn for him to be her real husband when he was his remote and lordly self, but when he let down his guard like this, her heart flipped over. Every touch seemed a prelude to an embrace, every smoldering glance a promise of kisses so fierce and demanding and frankly male that just anticipating them set her blood to pounding.

By the time the reel was over, she'd forgotten the embarrassing aborted waltz. She'd forgotten her own name, completely absorbed by the heat of his arm beneath her hand as he led her from the floor, the citrus scent of his shaved jaw as he bent to whisper, "There are some people I want you to meet."

That certainly dispelled her pleasantly sensual haze. "You shouldn't introduce me to so many. It'll make it that much harder to explain my disappearance when this is over."

"Ah, but the Blakelys are my good friends. Blakely and his wife will stand by me no matter what happens. Besides, they already know the truth about us."

"You actually told somebody the truth? After all your insistence that scandal would fall on your head if you didn't maintain this farce?"

"I had to tell Blakely. He's my subordinate, and I needed him to help me deal with Nat. And since his wife would have wrangled it out of him eventually, I saw no point in his not telling her."

Abby tensed, partly because a waltz was playing again, prompting people to shoot her smug looks as they took the floor. And partly because she hated having his friends know the truth. "They must think me a very wicked creature for agreeing to this."

"Don't worry, they won't blame you—they're used to my schemes," he said dryly. "As long as you are your usual cheery self, Lady Clara will adore you. You're exactly the sort of woman she likes."

What did he mean by that? "And her husband?"

A sudden inexplicable gleam shone in his eyes. "I expect he'll have much the same reaction. Once he eats a little humble pie, that is."

Chapter 10

Memorize *Debrett's*. Failing that, always keep a copy handy for reference.

Suggestions for the Stoic Servant

When Spencer brought Abby over to meet the Blakelys, his eager anticipation wasn't even dampened by Evelina's presence. So Blakely thought Abby a fortune hunter, did he? Spencer couldn't wait to see how rapidly she turned the fool's suspicions around.

After introducing the couple to Abby as Captain Blakely and Lady Clara, he added, "Blakely is one of my oldest friends. I met him when he was in the navy and I was charged with obtaining dispatches from certain captains."

"I see," Abby said. "I thought you might have grown up with his lordship, the way you did with Evelina and her family."

"I didn't grow up with Lady Evelina and her family," Blakely said, perplexed.

Just as Spencer caught Abby's slip, Evelina said gently, "I believe, sir, she was speaking to her husband."

"But that means she called me—" Blakely winced when Spencer glared at him. "Oh, I see."

"I did it wrong, didn't I?" Abby said, her fingers clawing into his arm.

"No, no," the men both responded in unison.

Lady Clara glared at them. "Being polite won't do her any good, you idiots. I'm sure she wants to know the correct rules." She smiled warmly at Abby. "My husband is not generally addressed as 'lord' or 'lordship.'"

Abby cast her a grateful look. "I-I assumed he had a title, since you're called 'Lady.' I figured his military status was just more important, so that's why he's called 'Captain.' Captains do something useful, after all, but what do lords do?"

Blakely smothered a laugh. "Hear that, Ravenswood? Your wife's a very astute woman. What do lords do indeed?"

Evelina and Spencer both scowled at him as Lady Clara said sternly, "Morgan, stop that. You're embarrassing his lordship's poor wife."

"Wait, I thought *I* was his lordship," Blakely teased, then when his wife jabbed him in the ribs, added to Abby, "Sorry. It's nothing to do with you, Lady Ravenswood. It's just that I can never resist the chance to poke fun at your husband."

Abby was no more immune to Blakely's roguish charms than any other woman. She relaxed her talonlike grip on Spencer's arm. "I understand completely. I can never resist that myself."

"All the same, please ignore my scamp of a mate," Clara said. "He understands perfectly well how easy it is to confuse our English titles and manners of address. He didn't grow up in England, either, you see."

"And I was none too happy to be learning it all at thirteen when I started my formal schooling in Ireland," Blakely put in. "I threw *Debrett's* at the schoolmaster's head and got caned soundly for it. It took me years to grasp all the fine points. When my brother, who did grow up in England, first brought me into society, I insulted a baroness. Nobody ever told me how to address women possessing titles of their own."

"Women can have titles? Is that why your wife is called 'Lady' but you're not called 'Lord'?"

"Not exactly," Lady Clara responded, then began to explain.

Meanwhile, Spencer cursed himself for not preparing Abby better. The waltz, her stumbling over titles . . . all of it could have been prevented. Instead of rushing to head off a scandal, he should have listened to her fears. What had happened to all his skills of strategy? Why hadn't he realized he couldn't simply toss her into an ocean of complicated rules and expect her to swim?

Because she'd thrown him off his game. Thank God he hadn't known her during his days as a spymaster, or England would have lost the war. He'd never met a woman with such a cursed ability to distract him.

Glancing over, he winced to see her shove her fallen curls out of her eyes. Again. Perhaps the maid had been right about her hair—perhaps there was such a thing as hair that didn't take a curl. This wife business got more complicated by the moment.

"I shall never keep all the titles straight," Abby was complaining.

"Yes, you will, as long as Spence takes the time to help you." Now even Evelina was leaping to Abby's defense. The girl flashed Spencer a chastening glance. "You can't expect Abby to learn in one day what it took you and Captain Blakely half a lifetime to learn."

"Of course he can," Abby retorted with a hint of bitterness. "Don't you know? Lord Ravenswood can command anybody to do anything he pleases. Or so he tells me."

"Now, Abby—" he began.

"Lord Ravenswood does have the most annoying tendency to push people around," Lady Clara said, joining the fray.

"Indeed he does," Evelina remarked. "You should see how he's always laying down the law to Nathaniel."

Lady Clara nodded. "And you should hear how he manipulated Morgan and me three years ago. You would never believe it."

"Oh, I think I could believe almost anything about my husband." Abby's eyes gleamed impishly. "But don't chastise him too severely. He only does it because he knows so well what's best for us all. God forbid we should rule our own lives or make our own decisions when we have the all-knowing Lord Ravenswood to guide us."

This rapidly grew annoying. "Are you ladies finished sharpening your tongues on my hide?" Spencer said irritably. "Perhaps you'd like to flay Blakely here for a while. He has flaws, too."

"Ah, but mine aren't nearly as entertaining as yours," Blakely said jovially. "I have boring flaws, like my tendency to snore and my inability to take anything seriously."

"Spencer certainly never suffers from that flaw," Abby quipped. "Even his jokes are serious affairs."

"Lord Ravenswood tells jokes?" Lady Clara exclaimed. "I should very much like to hear that."

"My wife has never heard me tell a joke," Spencer said dryly. "That was probably her point."

"I've heard Ravenswood tell a joke," Blakely said with suspect enthusiasm.

"You have?" Evelina cried. "Oh, do tell us what it was."

Blakely grinned like some maniacal clown. "All right, let me see . . . When James I came into England, an old priest blessed him thusly: 'May Heaven bless you, and make a man of you, though it has but bad stuff to make it of.' *That* was Ravenswood's joke."

"Just as I told you," Abby said triumphantly, "even his jokes are serious."

"And not terribly funny," Lady Clara added.

"To be fair," Blakely said, "he did tell some funny ones, but they were all too bawdy to repeat in polite company."

"Why, Spencer, you naughty man!" Abby cried in mock horror.

Spencer glared at his friend. "I've never told a bawdy joke in my life."

"Yes, you did. You've forgotten it because you were drunk at the time. Remember that night in Paris when we finished off a bottle of Madame Dupuis's best brandy?"

Spencer scowled.

Rubbing his chin, Blakely added, "Though come to think of it, that's the only time I've ever seen you foxed. Hmm. The only time I ever heard you tell a joke is also the only time I ever saw you foxed. What am I to make of that?"

"Clearly my husband only has fun when he's drunk," Abby teased, eyes sparkling. "He tells jokes and quotes poetry—"

"Ravenswood quotes poetry?" Lady Clara put in. "This gets better and better. Whatever does he quote?"

Abby's smile faded abruptly. "Oh. I-I didn't actually hear him quote it. I just . . . that is . . ."

"Byron," Evelina said. "I heard that he quoted Byron: 'She walks in beauty like the night of starry climes and cloudy skies.' He was referring to Abby."

"Was he indeed?" Blakely exchanged a glance with his wife. "Ravenswood, you old devil. I'll have to ply you with drink more often."

Abby blushed furiously, but Spencer shot Evelina a searching glance. "How did you know about that?"

Evelina shrugged. "Nathaniel told me."

"You've spoken to Nathaniel?"

A look of panic flashed over Evelina's face that was gone so quickly Spencer wasn't sure if he'd seen it at all. "Of course. When he first came back from America. He told me about the night you were intoxicated."

How strange. What else had Spencer told his brother that night to make it memorable enough for Nat to mention it to Evelina? A gentleman never talked about another gentleman's inebriation to a lady. It wasn't done.

Then again, since when had Nat followed any rules?

"Well, he shouldn't have told you," Spencer said. "Some things are private."

Abby's face grew solemn. "Everything seems to be private with you, Spencer. Maybe if it weren't, you wouldn't be so serious all the time."

Beleaguered on all fronts, Spencer stiffened, then turned to his friend and changed the subject. "By the way, have you told your brother the good news yet? What does Templemore think?"

"He's delighted, of course." Blakely slid his arm about his wife's waist and stared fondly down at her. "He likes acquiring nieces and nephews almost as much as he likes siring sons and daughters."

Devil take it, he'd meant the news about the pistol design. But before he could correct Blakely, Evelina said brightly, "Oh, Lady Clara, are you enceinte?"

Lady Clara blushed. "Yes."

Abby broke into a smile. "Is it your first?"

"Our second," Blakely put in with the beaming smile of an expectant father. "We've got a little girl, Lydia. She's nearly a year old."

Just what Spencer didn't need tonight—talk of children.

"That's wonderful," Abby breathed. "I adore babies. I'd love to see her." The rapt envy on her face was like a punch to Spencer's gut.

"I'll bring her to visit sometime," Lady Clara said, then caught sight of Spencer's pained expression. She gave a weak smile. "When your husband's not around. Lord Ravenswood isn't terribly fond of children."

"Hogwash." Abby cast him a questioning look. "How could anybody not like children?"

"Oh, bachelors and newly married men never do," Lady Clara said dismissively. "But that's because they don't have any. They don't know what to do with them. You should have seen his lordship the first time I tried to hand Lydia to him. He recoiled as if she were a snake."

"I was afraid I'd drop her or something," Spencer lied through his teeth.

Lady Clara laughed, unaware of the torture she inflicted on him with every word. "Or you were worried she'd get spittle on your fine coat. That's a man for you—Morgan was much the same until he had his own child."

"I was not!" Blakely protested. "I liked children well enough. More than Ravenswood, at any rate."

"Well, you're less conscious of spittle on your coat, I suppose," Lady Clara said soothingly. "But I seem to remember some comment you made about squalling brats. Before you had any."

"All right, perhaps once," Blakely muttered.

"So are you hoping for a boy this time?" Abby asked, her face full of a woman's usual eagerness about anything concerning babies.

Spencer could take no more. "Come along, Blakely, let's fetch our wives some punch. That'll give them something better to do with their mouths than talk about children."

"Good idea," Blakely said as he left his wife's side. "Although I can think of even better things they could do with their mouths than drinking punch."

"Morgan, for shame!" Lady Clara said.

But Blakely merely laughed. Then Abby asked a breathless question about Lydia, and as Spencer walked off with Blakely, the women were happily discussing babies again.

He cursed under his breath.

Blakely laughed. "She's driving you mad, isn't she?"

Spencer strode purposefully ahead. "I don't know what you mean."

"That fetching American wife of yours. The one with the brilliant smile and laughing eyes and interest in babies."

Unaccountably disturbed that his friend had noticed

Abby's "brilliant smile and laughing eyes," Spencer glowered at Blakely. "I take it you no longer believe her to be a fortune hunter?"

"Any woman who'd tease the dignified Lord Ravenswood in front of his friends is no fortune hunter. Because a fortune hunter would assume that flattering you would gain her more than poking fun at you."

"Poking fun at me is Abby's favorite pastime," Spencer grumbled. "It's her way of paying me back for forcing her into this."

"You offered her twice her dowry. I don't call that force."

"All she wanted was a little of the money Nat took from her. And I refused to give it to her because I wanted to prevent a scandal."

Blakely cut Spencer an assessing glance. "That's not the only reason you refused, I suspect. You're keeping her here because you want her, don't you?"

Like I want air and food and water. But that had nothing to do with it. "If you're asking if I desire her, the answer should be obvious. What man in his right mind wouldn't? She's quite attractive."

"But not attractive enough for you to make her your real wife. I suppose a viscount does require someone more . . . appropriate in birth and station."

Spencer glared at Blakely. "You, too? Does everyone think me the most pompous man in England?"

Blakely looked unusually somber as they stopped beside the punch tables. "If you don't care about that, why not make the marriage a real one? God knows she'd be amenable. Every time she looks at you, her face lights up."

Spencer turned to the punch table, needing to do something, anything, to banish the intriguing idea of Abby's face lighting up when she looked at him. But his hands shook as he poured two glasses of punch. "I have no desire to marry, Blakely—it's as simple as that. It has nothing to do with her in particular. It's just that I wouldn't make any woman a good husband."

"That's absurd. Besides, eventually you have to marry somebody—if not your pretty American, then some other woman. You have to bear an heir. Even I know that's expected of you."

"I don't have to do anything I don't want. And unlike you I lack the urge to sire a lot of 'squalling brats.' I'm the one who doesn't like children, remember?"

"Clara's right—that will change once you have your own. So you needn't—"

"I do not want to discuss this." Good God, he couldn't even escape talk of children with his bloody friends. Spencer picked up the glasses and faced Blakely, staring him down. "My personal affairs are none of your concern, so stay out of it."

Blakely flinched. Then his face hardened. "Very well. I'll be sure to remember that in the future."

"See that you do."

Spencer walked off without waiting for Blakely to follow, before he said something else he regretted. He was tired of evading everyone's questions and tired of listening to their expectations for him. Let them think him officious or arrogant or unfeeling. It was better than having them know the truth, which would only garner their pity. He hadn't endured pity from anyone since his mother's death, and he wasn't about to endure it now, especially from his friends.

Even if it did leave him all alone in his torment.

Sometime later, Abby was feeling more hopeful about her ability to navigate the treacherous waters of London society. Lady Clara and Evelina had kindly given her a quick course in English titles. While it would take more than that to make her comfortable, she thought she could master the title business eventually.

Even Spencer's surliness when he'd returned to ask her to stand up with him for a country dance hadn't dampened her hopes. Especially since the dance had seemed to relax him and wipe some of the anger from his eyes.

Fortunately, he'd been perfectly cordial by the time the dance ended. He even managed a smile when Captain Blakely asked her to dance the Scotch reel, so she promptly accepted.

Captain Blakely led her to join the promenading couples. "You seem to be holding up your end of the charade very well."

Abby felt a moment's panic before she remembered that he knew the truth. "I'm trying. Though I'm not sure it was a good idea."

"Then why did you do it?"

She gazed stiffly ahead as they circled the room. "He gave me no choice. It was either play his wife or be thrust into the street penniless."

"He was bluffing. Surely you realized that. He would never leave a woman destitute. Especially one he likes."

She cast Captain Blakely an arch glance. "Spencer doesn't like me—he tolerates me. And he also . . . well, never mind that. Whatever else he feels, he keeps hidden."

"I still say he wouldn't have thrown you into the street."

She sighed. "I suppose that's true. But he offered to double my dowry. And to be honest, I felt I owed him something for trusting his brother. None of it would have happened if I'd been more skeptical of Nathaniel's claims."

"Why weren't you? You seem like an intelligent woman."

"Thank you." She flashed him a smile. "Spencer thinks I'm naive and overly optimistic. He thinks that's why I believed Nathaniel."

"Why *did* you believe him?"

Captain Blakely's kind manner encouraged her to be truthful. "I suppose because I liked Spencer more than I should have. I wanted Nathaniel's tales to be true."

"I can't imagine why. Ravenswood is a good man, but he's very sober-minded. Whereas you seem too spirited a sort for him."

She shook her head. "In America, he was different."

By then, they'd reached their positions, and the Scotch reel was too lively a dance to continue their conversation.

It was certainly too lively for brooding about Spencer. Besides, Captain Blakely danced creditably and she adored Scotch reels with their skips and sheer exuberance. The heady scent of the primrose and lilacs used for decor in the ballroom only enhanced her pleasure until she forgot all her troubles in the dance. By the time it finished, they were both laughing.

But after he led her from the floor, Captain Blakely drew her aside instead of bringing her back to their companions. Then he picked up their conversation where they'd left off. "How was Ravenswood different in America?"

She wished she hadn't mentioned that. She wasn't even sure if Spencer's behavior there had been real or feigned. "It's hard to explain. I mean, he's always been more serious than most men I've met." Staring down at her hapless fichu, she thought back to that time. "You must understand—the gentlemen I knew in America were either friends of my father's and much too old for me or men whose activities I considered frivolous."

"Certainly no one could call Ravenswood's activities frivolous."

"Exactly. And I found that vastly appealing. He was so earnest when he spoke about England, so passionate about his opinions. And he showed sincere interest in my mother's people. He never judged their practices and never disapproved of their culture."

"Their culture?" he echoed.

Oh, dear. She probably shouldn't have mentioned that, but now that she had, he might as well know the whole of it. "Although I grew up among my father's people in Philadelphia, my mother was from the Seneca tribe, the daughter of their chief." She gazed proudly at him, daring him to show some sign of contempt. "She had as much to do with my upbringing as Papa."

He flashed her a smile. "Ah. Then you had an advantage over me. Despite being a baron's son, I had only my mother to raise me. And since she had difficulties of her own, I ended up a pickpocket in the streets of Geneva until my uncle brought me back to England."

His words surprised her so much she couldn't muster a response.

He didn't seem to require one. "But you were explaining how Ravenswood was different in America."

"Yes." She ducked her head. "You see, though he was serious-minded, he was also kind and amiable and—"

" 'Amiable' isn't quite the word I'd use for Ravenswood."

"Yet that's exactly how he was. And he made me think . . ." She trailed off, not wanting to reveal the full extent of her own idiocy.

"Are you saying that he led you to believe an offer from him was forthcoming?" Captain Blakely asked in a clearly disapproving tone.

"No, no, nothing like that. He was never anything but the perfect gentleman. But we were friends, don't you see? That's why I was so eager to marry him. In America, I could talk to him about anything. He encouraged it. Even when he didn't agree with my opinions, he listened earnestly."

"And here?"

She stiffened. "Here he is arrogant and controlling and determined to have his own way no matter what I say."

"Ah, now that sounds like the Ravenswood I know."

"It's maddening, especially when I'm the one having to obey all his dictates."

"Not quite what you expected marriage to him would be."

"No, I thought it would be . . ." She glanced away. "Whatever I thought, I was wrong." Setting her shoulders, she managed to meet his gaze. "Not that it matters anyway. This is all a sham. Spencer has no interest in marriage just now, and certainly not to me."

"I wouldn't be too sure of that if I were you."

Before she could question what he meant, a low murmur in the room made her look up to see Spencer walk in with a stunning woman in a scandalously revealing gown. When the woman laid her hand on his arm and leaned in close to whisper something that he bent low to hear, Abby's heart constricted. "Who's that woman Spencer is talking to?" she whispered.

Captain Blakely was already staring at the two, his jaw tight. "Nobody of consequence. Come, let's join my wife and Lady Evelina."

As Captain Blakely led her back toward their companions, her heart sank. His reticence told her worlds. "She's his mistress, isn't she?"

"Of course not." When Abby raised one eyebrow, he sighed. "All right, Genevieve used to be, but she hasn't been for two years at least. They're merely friends now."

Very good friends, judging from how familiarly the woman touched him and how intently Spencer listened. Genevieve—the woman even had a mistress's name.

Her throat tightened. "Why would Lady Tyndale invite her here for this?"

"Lady Tyndale probably doesn't know who she was to Ravenswood. Genevieve was always discreet in her affairs, as was Ravenswood—few people realized she was his mistress. Besides, she's now married to some baron and quite respectable."

"Yes, I can see how respectable she is."

He squeezed her hand. "Really, Abby, the woman means nothing to him."

It sure didn't look that way. "Even if she does, I have no

right to complain, do I? I mean, it's not as if I'm really his wife."

"You still have the right to his respect. But I think you have it. I wouldn't make too much of this."

How could she not? After she and the captain reached their companions, she couldn't even concentrate on their conversation. Too many unanswered questions plagued her. Did Spencer have a current mistress? Would he expect to continue his visits to her while Abby pretended to be his wife? Did she even have the right to ask him not to?

Of course she didn't. But oh how she wished she did.

Abby made desultory conversation with the Blakelys even after Spencer joined them. But she brightened when the orchestra struck up a familiar piece of music for a cotillion. "Oh, I do love this song. They played it at all the balls when I was a girl."

"Then shall we?" Spencer offered her his arm with a smile.

She hesitated. That Genevieve was still in the room. What if Abby made some dreadful error in front of her? But this was her favorite, and she did know how to dance the cotillion very well. "All right," she said, taking Spencer's arm.

Unfortunately, fate seemed determined to vex her tonight. They'd already taken the floor when she felt a pin fall down inside her gown. Her earlier exertions in the Scotch reel must have worked it loose from the fichu.

Too late to do anything about it—she refused to stop short on the dance floor again. Besides, surely one pin wouldn't make a difference in how well her fichu stayed put. Would it?

But as they took their places in a circle of eight and began to dance, she realized one pin could make a lot of difference. Every movement prompted her fichu to creep. It crawled up from inside her bodice with demonic persistence.

Dear heaven, not now. If she could only make it to the end of the dance, she could escape to the ladies' retiring room to repair it. That was her only option. She couldn't shove it back down—there was no way to do it surreptitiously in the middle of the dance floor. And doing it blatantly would be almost as vulgar as letting it fall out.

For a brief moment, it seemed to halt its upward move, and she relaxed, figuring the other pins had caught it.

Then Spencer twirled her in a turn, and sly thing that it was, it leaped to safety. She made a grab for it but missed. In horror, she watched as the demon fichu fluttered to the floor and landed beneath a man's dancing shoe.

On the highly polished floor it might as well have been a marble, for the man's foot found no purchase and shot right out from under him. His partner followed him down with a little cry. Then two people tumbled over them until the entire group of dancers collapsed in a tangle of limbs and bobbing heads.

Except her and Spencer, of course. He'd managed to grab Abby and jerk her out of the way before she could be dragged under with the rest.

Now he stood gaping at the others as if they'd lost their minds. "What the devil?" he growled as he held out his hand to help up the first man who'd fallen.

The man came up with the fichu clutched in his fist. Stony-faced, he held it out to Abby. "I believe this is yours, madam," he said with that hint of a sneer all the English gentlemen seemed to affect.

Her mortification was complete.

Snatching the fichu, she fled, pushing through curious onlookers, disapproving matrons, and a score of laughing dandies. She couldn't stay there one more minute or she'd die of shame.

She headed for the retiring room, praying it would be empty. For once her prayers were answered. Slipping inside the deserted room, she sank into a chair and began to cry.

Tears poured out of her, too many to hold back, and they

turned to deep, wracking sobs for all the indignities she'd suffered. Her misery was so complete that she didn't hear the door open until somebody stepped inside. Why hadn't she thought to lock it?

But it was Lady Clara. The woman took one look at her and locked the door herself, coming to her side with such sympathy in her face that Abby cried all the harder.

"There, there." Lady Clara knelt before her to clasp her hands. "It's not as bad as all that."

"I br-brought down an entire d-dance floor with a f-fichu!" Abby blubbered. "How m-much worse can it be?"

"Not an entire dance floor—just a few people."

"It might as well have been the whole country," she whispered.

Lady Clara handed her a handkerchief. "It's not your fault, dear. Evelina told me that Ravenswood *made* you wear the fichu. If anybody should be blamed, it's him."

"I-I felt it slipping out . . . I should have refused to dance or . . . or . . . something."

"That would have been worse. You did what any of us would—hoped it would hold and made the best of a difficult situation."

Abby lifted her face to Lady Clara's. "I made a fool of myself. I made a fool of *him*."

Lady Clara's mouth tightened into a grim line. "I wouldn't worry about your 'husband,' if I were you. He doesn't deserve your concern after how he's coerced you into this silly scheme."

"B-but he only did it to prevent a scandal. And now I've put him in the middle of one. I've been the most horrible wife he could have chosen, and he knows it, too, or he wouldn't be talking to that . . . that woman."

Lady Clara looked perplexed. "What woman do you mean?"

"His mistress. Well, your husband says she's Spencer's former mistress, but—"

"My husband has an imprudent tongue," Lady Clara retorted, eyes ablaze.

"Don't blame him. I could see that she meant something to Spencer just from how she touched him. I know I shouldn't care, but . . ." She trailed off with a sob.

Sympathy suffused Lady Clara's face. "Oh, Abby, you poor thing. You love him, don't you?"

"No! No, don't be silly. It's just that when I came here I really thought we were married, and when I found out that we weren't . . ." She blew her nose without a care for how unladylike it looked. "And I-I did like him, you see. It's silly, but I wanted him to like me, at least a little."

"I think he does—in his own way. God knows I've always found the man too haughty for words, but when he's with you, he . . . softens."

Abby shook her head morosely. "He won't after tonight. I'll be lucky if he doesn't put me on the first ship to America."

"Isn't that what you want?"

Abby stared down at her hands, remembering how Spencer had kissed her last night. "Sometimes I do. But sometimes . . . Well, it doesn't matter. After tonight, he'll hate me."

"If he does, he deserves nothing but censure." Lady Clara squeezed her hands tightly. "Don't let that arrogant scoundrel bully you, do you hear? You are doing *him* a favor, no matter what he claims."

"But if I hadn't listened to his brother—"

"Stuff and nonsense. His brother wronged you, not the other way around. If you want to return to America, then demand your money and threaten to expose everything to the press if his lordship doesn't give it to you. But don't let him push you around. He has no right to do that."

Drawing her hands from Lady Clara's, Abby stared at the woman's fierce expression. Abby had been so caught up in her mortification that she'd forgotten whose idea this was. It certainly wasn't hers. She hadn't wanted to play this charade; she hadn't asked to be deceived and manipulated. That was all his and his brother's doing.

She tipped up her chin. "That's true—he doesn't have the right, does he? And I'll tell him so, too."

"Good for you."

Abby frowned. "But not here. Not with all those people out there watching." She glanced beyond Lady Clara to the mirror, and her heart nearly failed her. Dear heaven, she looked awful. Her hair had completely fallen. Her ringlets were a straight curtain about her face, her eyes were bloodshot, and her nose shone as rosy as a tippler's.

"I can't talk to him looking like this." She shot Lady Clara a desperate look. "I can't go back out there. Not until I appear at least moderately dignified. I have to go home before I can face him or anybody else. Will you take me?"

Lady Clara hesitated, then nodded. "But remember what I said—don't let him bully you. Because the minute you give a man an inch, he'll take more than a mile. And frankly, Abby, you can't afford to have anything more taken from you."

Chapter 11

When your employers leave the house to attend a ball, be waiting with liquid sustenance upon their return. Anything can happen at a ball.

Suggestions for the Stoic Servant

Spencer paced the edge of the ballroom, too frustrated to do anything else. He couldn't forget Abby's expression when she'd gazed on that ridiculous scene on the dance floor. He'd had more of an impulse to laugh at the tumble than anything. Until he saw her misery-ravaged face. Then she was gone before he could even think to stop her.

And now she'd apparently closeted herself off somewhere with Lady Clara. No one could tell him where, and it was driving him mad.

Evelina approached, but before she even reached him, he growled, "Where is she? Where's Abby?"

"Lady Clara took her home. I am to say she's indisposed. Will you make the announcement or will I?"

"You make it," he snapped and turned for the door. "I'm going after her."

Evelina blocked his way. "Not if you're planning to lecture her."

He glared at the generally angelic Evelina. "What I do with my wife is my concern."

"You bullied her into wearing that fichu, so I shan't let you chastise her for it."

"I don't plan on chastising her, for God's sake. Not that it's any of your business."

"Just remember when you speak to her that we're not all as smooth and collected as you. She's tried very hard to be what you wish, and right now she feels like a failure."

Her words brought him up short. Had he really seemed so exacting, so demanding that something like this could send her fleeing his presence in shame?

The scene in her bedchamber earlier came back to him—his insistence on the fichu, his comments about her hair. He'd instructed her on things she hadn't needed instruction on and had neglected to tell her what she desperately wanted to know.

No wonder she refused even to tell him she was leaving.

He looked at Evelina's determined expression and softened his voice. "I promise not to lecture her, poppet. Now will you let me pass?"

"After I say one more thing." A faint blush rose on Evelina's cheeks. "In future, you might consider not flaunting your . . . former paramours in front of her."

"Former paramours?" he asked in bewilderment. Then memory slammed into him. "But Abby didn't know who Genevieve was."

"Your idiot friend Captain Blakely told her."

Bloody hell. He had even more to apologize for than he realized. He could kick himself for talking to Genevieve, though it had been innocent enough.

Evelina went on. "I'll admit it was wrong of Mother to invite the woman in the first place, but she was peeved that you'd turned my engagement ball into a ball for yourself, and she did it out of spite. If I'd known, I would have discouraged it."

More mistakes to lay at his door. Good God, would this

night never end? "I shall make amends to my wife for conversing with Genevieve in her presence," he said tightly. "Anything else?"

Evelina swallowed, as if suddenly remembering that she never did things of this sort. "That's all."

He lifted an eyebrow. "It's enough, isn't it?"

"She deserves your respect, you know, even if she's not your true—" She broke off suddenly.

His eyes narrowed. "My true what, Evelina?"

"Your true love." Evelina squared her shoulders, then soldiered on. "I know you probably married her because you took pity on her situation with her father, but that doesn't lessen your obligation to be a good husband."

Once again, he wondered if she might know the truth. Could Lady Clara have told her, or even Abby? But if that were the case, why would she pretend not to know?

Unless . . .

"Have you spoken to Nathaniel since the betrothal dinner, Evelina?"

She paled, though she didn't flinch from his steady gaze. "How could I? You had him whisked away to Essex before I could even see him."

He stared at her a moment longer. But it seemed impossible that she could be in league with his brother. The honest Evelina would never approve of Nat's stealing a dowry. No, she was probably just upset about all that had happened.

"Very well," he said. "I have to go. Tell your guests that my wife fell ill and I took her home, all right?"

She bobbed her head.

He left after learning from the butler that Lady Clara and Abby had departed only a short time before. Good. He didn't want her to suffer in unwarranted misery longer than necessary. Evelina was right—Abby *had* tried hard to please him, and all she'd gotten to show for it was humiliation, the very thing he'd promised to spare her.

Well, he'd make it up to her somehow. Tomorrow he'd go buy her something special—some jewels or a fancy gim-crack or some such. Women liked those fripperies. And then he would engage her a dance master and a tutor. That way she'd feel better prepared for future social events.

But first he had to talk to her. To apologize. To soothe her wounded feelings and promise he'd be more careful of them in the future.

Fortunately, Lady Clara had already left by the time he reached home. He was in no mood to deal with both of them tonight. Bad enough he had to deal with Abby. The woman was a sensitive little thing—she'd probably be crying.

But he knew how to handle storms of female emotion. He'd had plenty of experience dealing with his former mistresses' tearful complaints—this couldn't be much different.

As McFee took his things, Spencer asked, "Where's my wife?"

"In her bedchamber, my lord. Mrs. Graham said she was retiring for the night."

Bloody hell, she was really upset, wasn't she? Well, he wasn't about to put this off until tomorrow while she let her misery eat at her.

Swiftly mounting the two flights of stairs, he strode down the hall to her bedchamber. Then he stopped short. Mrs. Graham stood guard outside. She moved to block the door the moment she saw him.

This was becoming absurd—all these women trying to protect Abby from him. As if he would actually try to hurt her. "I need to speak to my wife," he told the flame-haired Scotswoman.

"She don't want to speak to you. I'm to tell you that she'll talk to you in the morning."

"This cannot wait until morning. Step aside."

"No indeed. In any case, she's already in her nightdress, so you can't go in there. Wouldn't be proper."

He started to retort that he could see his wife in anything he pleased, then remembered that Abby's termagant servant knew the truth about the situation. Devil take them all. "Fine. I'll use the connecting door." He turned toward his own bedchamber.

"It's locked," she called out. "Just like this door here."

Now they were locking his own doors against him? Fury roiled up in him, swift and sure. "McFee!" he bellowed down the hall to the stairs. "Get up here now!"

His butler rarely ran anywhere, but the man had worked for Spencer long enough to know when his master had urgent need of him. McFee reached Spencer scant moments later, gasping for breath. "Yes, my lord?"

"The keys to my wife's bedchamber, if you please," he said, holding out his hand.

With a bob of his head, McFee fished out his key ring, then fumbled through it. Mrs. Graham looked on smugly as McFee went through all the keys once, then again.

At last the butler looked up with a barely contained look of alarm. "I . . . I . . . my lord . . . they seem to have . . . um . . . disappeared."

"That's what happens when you doze at your post, Mr. McFee," Abby's servant said with fiendish delight. "I wasn't about to have my girl helpless in a room where his lordship could come and go as he pleased, so I took the liberty of relieving you of them keys yesterday morning."

McFee's face lost his usual reserve. "You harpy from hell," he said with more venom than Spencer had ever heard him use. "How dare you presume to take *my* keys out of *my* coat and—"

"That's enough, McFee," Spencer broke in. This was getting them nowhere. He forced himself to address Mrs. Graham calmly. "I commend your concern for your mistress, madam, but in this case you're going about protecting her all wrong."

"Am I?" She stuck out her chubby chin. "That girl came in with eyes red as my hair. Seems to me any man who'd send his wife home all ravaged by tears don't deserve nothing more than a curt word and a fare-thee-well. Which is what I'm giving you."

"I didn't send her home—she came home on her own, without giving me the chance to apologize. Do you really think your mistress is better off crying in her room than hearing an apology from the person who brought her to tears in the first place?"

Uncertainty filled the woman's face. "An apology, is it?"

"Yes. I know I did wrong. I want to make amends." His voice tightened in spite of his efforts to control his temper. "But I can hardly do that standing out in the hall, can I?"

"Listen to the man, lassie," McFee said beside him. "He may be a Sassenach, but he's an honorable one. He will treat your lady properly."

Mrs. Graham looked from Spencer to McFee and back. Then she sighed and reached inside her apron pocket to draw out two keys. "All right then," she said in a whisper. "Long as you tell her that you had to wrestle me down to get them."

As Spencer took the keys, McFee muttered, "Now there's a thought."

He left McFee and Mrs. Graham squabbling in the hall. Entering his own room, he unlocked the connecting door into Abby's bedchamber. When he walked in, she was sitting on the tester bed facing the fireplace, her back to both doors. She was brushing her hair in long, sensual strokes that sent the silky strands rippling over her shoulders. Her thinly clad shoulders.

Devil take it, he'd forgotten what Mrs. Graham had said she was wearing. That muslin nightdress might as well be glass for all it hid of Abby's sweet charms. Especially when she shifted to put her profile to the fire. When the outline of her breasts showed clearly through it, his pulse thundered in his ears. Bloody hell.

Tamping down on his inappropriate response, he stepped into the room and closed the door behind him. Then he locked it to make sure her meddling servant didn't come charging in to interrupt him in the midst of his apology.

"What did he say?" she asked, probably expecting Mrs. Graham.

"He said he was sorry," Spencer told her hoarsely. "He said he hadn't meant to ruin the ball for you. He said he wanted to make it up to you."

Leaping from the bed, she whirled to face him. "You!" Horror filled her features as she clutched the neck of her nightdress in her fist. "How did you get in here?"

"It's my house, remember?"

Anger flashed in her eyes. "Only too well. You never let me forget it."

That's when he noticed her reddened eyes and nose. Remorse flooded him. "Oh, God, Abby, I didn't mean to make you miserable."

"You didn't." Her mouth trembled as she drew into herself, wrapping one arm about her waist. "I did it to myself by letting you tell me what to do. Well, not anymore, do you hear?"

"No, not anymore." He'd do anything to wipe that haunted look from her face. "We'll call a halt to balls and other such events for a while. I'll engage whomever you need—tutors, dance masters, governesses . . . whatever you want. As for the clothes, dress as you please."

"Really? Even if I look like a *fille de joie*?" she said with fierce sarcasm. "Even if I don't dress my hair remotely like the refined Evelina?"

"I was wrong about the hair and the clothes and the rest of it." And if he had to take cold baths twice a day for the next few weeks, he'd smile and endure her gowns no matter how provocative they were.

Though none of them could be worse than what she wore now. That nightdress might go up to her chin, but on its way it skimmed every curve with loving care. And with her hand around her waist pressing the fabric against the front of her, he could even see a shadow of the nest of curls between her thighs.

Breaking into a sweat, he jerked his gaze up to her face. "There's nothing wrong with how you dress, Abby." *At least not in public,* he added silently.

"But there's a great deal wrong with how I act."

"If there is, it's only because I didn't prepare you. I'm sorry I broke my promise not to subject you to any humiliation. I swear I didn't realize that . . . I didn't know . . ."

"That I had absolutely no knowledge of the rules for your society? I seem to recall telling you that."

"And I didn't listen. But I will from now on."

She shook her head. "There will be no 'from now on.' I can't do this anymore."

Panic seized him. "Of course you can. All you need is a little polish and—"

"And what? Society will welcome your stupid American wife with open arms? No, I don't need this." She tipped up her chin, eyes glittering. "Tomorrow morning you will write me a draft for five hundred pounds. That's only a tenth of what your brother took from me—that's all I ask from you until you find him. It should be enough to pay my passage back to America and enable me to take lodgings somewhere while I look into continuing Papa's business."

Good God, she was serious. She really meant to leave. "Abby—"

"If you don't give it to me," she went on, "I'll visit that Lady Brumley woman and tell her the whole story. I know she'll believe me. And then you'll have your scandal."

He felt as if she'd walloped him in the chest. "You hate me that much?"

A stricken look crossed her face. "I don't hate you." Her eyes glimmered with unshed tears. "I just . . . need you to know that I mean what I say. I can't continue this charade. I don't belong here. I can't help you."

"Yes, you can. You're the only one who can." He came toward her in a daze of disbelief. He acted on instinct, having lost all his bearings. He only knew he had to keep her here in London. With him. "You mustn't leave, not yet. I won't let you."

"You can't stop me, Spencer. For a while I let you convince me that I had no choice, but now I know better."

Frantically he wracked his brain for some argument to persuade her why she must remain. "What about Evelina? You may not care about bringing scandal down on my family, but what about hers?"

She swallowed. "There won't be any scandal if you just give me five hundred pounds and let me go."

"You think not?" He laughed harshly. "You don't think people will talk when my wife leaves me after living with me less than a week? How am I to explain it?"

"Tell them I discovered that we didn't suit." Her voice grew bitter. "After tonight's fiasco, they'll have no trouble believing that."

Determined to call her bluff, he marched up to her, fists clenched at his sides. "I won't do it. I won't give you a penny. I won't let you leave without seeing this through. Go tell that gossip-mongering witch whatever you wish. Anything she writes can't be worse than what they'll say about me if you leave."

She glared up at him. "Fine. Don't give me any money then. Clara said I could live with her until your brother returns. Once he does, I'll file suit against him for my dowry and see how you like that."

Bloody hell, now she had Lady Clara on her side. His anger faded into frustration. Everything he said merely strengthened her resentment against him.

"What do you want from me?" he bit out, an unfamiliar desperation seizing him at the thought of her leaving. "Do you want me to beg, is that it? Do you want to bring the 'all-knowing Lord Ravenswood' to his knees so you can pay him back for tonight's humiliations? Because if so, you're certainly succeeding."

A perplexed frown furrowed her brow. "Am I?"

"You know very well that you are."

"How does it feel, Spencer, to have your life clutched in somebody else's hands? To know that they can ruin your future, and you can't do a thing about it?"

Her allusion to her own situation reignited his temper. "The same way it felt the day you showed up on my doorstep. You're not the only one my brother wronged, Abby. You're not the only one having to adjust."

"True. So why not let me put an end to both our miseries?" A thin smile touched her lips. "Come now, admit it—if you weren't so worried about a scandal, you'd be delighted to see me go. One less nuisance to deal with, one less annoyance underfoot. With me gone, you can look for your brother at your leisure without the urgency of trying to regain my money. You won't have to act like you're married. You can return to your bachelor life. It will be nothing but a relief."

"It will be nothing but a torment." When surprise suffused her face, he glanced away, not wanting her to see how badly he needed her to stay. "If you leave, I'll know it's my fault you're struggling in America all alone. The guilt of what my family has done to you will prey on me, and I'll blame myself for driving you to flee."

"But you mustn't." She laid a gentle hand on his arm. "Nobody asked you to fix your brother's mistakes—you took it on yourself. You could have told me I was mad and thrown me out of the house or decried me to the authorities, but you didn't. You've gone beyond any possible obligation, and I know that. I only wish I could have been more helpful by better playing the part you required."

"There was nothing wrong with how you played your part," he said, shifting his gaze back to her. "If I hadn't meddled, tonight would have gone perfectly well." He covered her hand with his. "And even tonight wasn't all bad, was it? You got on well with my friends. You even seemed to enjoy the dancing for a while."

"When I wasn't bumbling my way through it." Humiliation flared in her eyes. "The rest of the time I was miserable. And you were embarrassed. I'm sure you were."

"To be with the most beautiful woman at the ball? I wasn't the least embarrassed. Despite the few things that went wrong, I enjoyed being there with you. I wouldn't have wanted to be there with anyone else."

She tugged her hand free. "Not even Genevieve?"

Bloody hell, he'd forgotten about that. "Certainly not Genevieve. If I could tolerate her company for an entire evening, I wouldn't have left her two years ago."

"You didn't have any trouble tolerating her company tonight." She lowered her eyes, but not before he glimpsed the hurt in them.

"We merely talked for a few minutes. She asked why I'd decided to marry after all these years, and I gave her some answer. There was nothing more to it than that."

"What did you tell her? That you'd grown bored with all your achievements and figured that civilizing a stupid American wife would provide you a new challenge?"

Cursing himself for what he'd unwittingly done to make her feel so wretched about herself, he reached out to tip up her chin with one finger. "I told her that my wife was the most enchanting woman I'd ever met."

Her lower lip quivered as she stared at him. "You lied, in other words."

He shook his head. "I never lie about essentials."

"Really?" A welter of confused emotions passed over her face. "Then tell me this, Spencer. Do you have a mistress?"

"I told you, Genevieve and I—"

"Not her. A regular mistress. Some ladybird stashed away in a little house in a less savory part of town. Because from what I heard tonight, half the married men do and nearly all the unmarried men."

"Good God, who did you hear all this from? I know Evelina and Lady Clara weren't filling your head with such ideas."

She arched one brow. "I spent a lot of time in the ladies' retiring room repairing my fichu. One hears things in the retiring room."

"If you heard anything about me, it was lies. I have no mistress."

"No one said you did, but . . . I also heard you're discreet." She swallowed. "As long as you stay discreet, it's all right. But it's bad enough to have people talking behind my back about the vulgar American—I won't have them talking about how you prefer your ladybird to your wife."

"There's no ladybird. There hasn't been one since Genevieve." He dragged his finger down her throat, then in widening circles over the petal-soft skin. Touching her like this was a mistake, yet he couldn't stop himself. "You're the first woman to interest me in a very long time."

Her eyes flared with suspicion. "I don't interest you—you said so yourself." Pain sharpened her words. "You said you only felt desire for me, and even that was no more than you'd feel for any beautiful woman pressed up against you."

He winced to hear his foolish comments thrown back at him. "I thought perhaps saying it would make it true. But it's not. It never was." He slid his other arm about her waist, seized by a need to reassure her. "I want you more desperately than I've ever wanted any woman. I keep expecting the urge to pass, but it hasn't."

As she stared up at him with those impossibly green eyes, he splayed his fingers over her throat, her lovely fragile throat with its madly beating pulse. "Even with your ridiculous droopy curls and that absurd fichu I foisted on you, all I could think tonight whenever I saw you was how badly I wanted to kiss you again."

She met his gaze evenly. "Then why don't you?"

That was all the encouragement he needed—that and the driving ache for her that he'd felt since the day they'd met. Slipping his hand beneath her heavy hair to clasp her neck, he drew her near to cover her mouth with his.

Just this one indulgence, he told himself. One sweet kiss to hold him for a lifetime in case he couldn't stop her from leaving.

Then her lips parted beneath his, and he knew he was lying to himself. He could never stop with one kiss from Abby.

Chapter 12

What goes on in your employer's bedchamber is none
of your concern. Forgetting that rule is the surest way
to lose your employment.

Suggestions for the Stoic Servant

Abby probably shouldn't have encouraged Spencer to
kiss her. What was she thinking? The wily rascal already had her wavering about leaving, and this only further
tempted her to stay. Was that why he was doing it?

No, she'd swear it wasn't. His mouth was too ardent in
plundering hers, his hold on her waist too urgent for this to be
some callous ploy.

And after all his sweet words and pleas, how could she resist? Especially when he was being the nice gentleman she'd
come all this way to marry. She delighted in having that man
kiss her again, so fervently, so deeply he made her palms
sweat. Why not enjoy it? She might not get another chance.

Winding her arms about his neck, she threw herself into it,
opening her mouth wider, touching her tongue to his. A
growl rumbled through him as he tightened his embrace,
sending an avaricious thrill up her spine.

After ravishing her lips for a while, he turned to ravishing
her chin and her jaw, raking his open mouth down her neck to
tongue the hollow of her throat. "Ah, Abby," he breathed, "I

dream about this at night, about holding you like this."

More sweet words. And she lapped every one of them up like honey. "Do you?" She dreamed of him, too, of stroking the close-cropped hair at the nape of his neck as she was now, touching him as intimately as a real wife.

"It's all I can think about. I even smell you in my dreams. What's that scent you wear, the one that smells like flowers and rosemary?"

"Not a scent," she whispered against his ear, pressing a kiss to the lobe and glorying in his sharply indrawn breath. "It's the Mead. I use it to sweeten my breath."

"And drive me insane." He dropped his head to nuzzle her collarbone through the nightdress, and she drank in his own heady scent, thick with musk and candle smoke and bergamot. "Every time I smell it, I think of you, of kissing you, tasting you . . . Oh, God, I want to taste you so badly . . ."

His hand found the small buttons at the neck of her nightdress and deftly unfastened them until it gaped open at the throat. "I want to taste this," he murmured, pressing his mouth to her bared collarbone. He danced his tongue along it as his fingers marched down the placket, working loose every tiny button. "And this." His head dipped to sow kisses in the furrow between her breasts.

She caught her breath. He should definitely not be taking such shameful liberties.

On the other hand, why not just a little more? Something to remember when she was gone.

Then before she knew it the placket gaped open clear down to the last button above her waist. Spencer's breath beat hotly against her skin as he drew the edge aside to expose one breast. "Then there's this," he rasped. "I've wanted to taste this most of all."

Before she could even consider being embarrassed, his mouth closed over her breast, sucking it hard, shooting wild sensations along her every nerve. He tongued her nipple mercilessly, until she gasped and clutched his head to her chest. When he slipped his hand inside her nightdress to fondle her other breast, she moaned and swayed against him, deliberately closing her eyes to the image of his mouth and hands on her breasts.

Because maybe if she didn't see it, it was just a dream she could indulge forever, without guilt or regret. It certainly felt like a dream, his tongue swirling over her nipple and his hand kneading her breast to a taut eager peak.

He smoothed his other hand down her backside to urge her hard against his rigid arousal, then dragged his mouth from her breast. "I shouldn't do this. I have no right to take advantage of you."

"You certainly don't," she agreed, then promptly pulled his head to her other breast so he could suck that one, too. As long as he was taking advantage . . .

Next thing she knew, he'd backed her up against the bed and was pressing her down on it, following her until she lay beneath him on the needlework counterpane with her thighs parted. Dear heaven, she was really in trouble now.

Eyes feverishly bright, he settled himself between her thighs. "Just a little longer," he promised hoarsely. Then his mouth proceeded to "take advantage" of her bared breast, lavishing such naughty caresses on it that she whimpered and strained up for more.

"I'll stop soon, I swear," he said as he turned to suck the other breast while his hand plumped and teased the still damp flesh of the first.

"Take your time," she murmured. "I'm in no hurry."

Besides, she wanted to feel his bare skin, too. She tugged at the lapels of his superfine coat until he shrugged it off and tossed it aside. His waistcoat and cravat rapidly followed. But when she went to work on his shirt buttons, he lifted his head with a dazed look. "What are you doing?"

"I get to touch you, too. That's only fair."

Hunger flared in his face. "Yes, only fair." Since she'd finished with his buttons, he tore his shirt off, then grabbed her hand and laid it on his chest. "So touch me and we'll be even."

Hardly, she thought as she skimmed her hand over thick muscle and taut skin. Hair whorled around his flat male nipples, which hardened to points at her caress. Hmm. What if she did to them what he'd done to her?

She leaned up to lick one tight nub, and he jerked. "Christ, you go too far, Abby."

But she noticed he didn't stop her when she licked the other. "It's only a little playing."

"You call this *playing*?" he growled.

"That's what Mama called it. She said it's what two people do when they desire each other. Before they make love." Abby always thought it sounded better than the actual act of lovemaking anyway.

Spencer drew back, his eyes suddenly solemn. "We're not going to make love."

Oh, no, he was starting to come to his senses. Next thing he'd be telling himself all that nonsense about how he had no time for a wife and how she didn't fit his plans for the sort of wife he wanted. She wouldn't let him, not yet. "Then let's just play for a while," she whispered, wrapping her arms about his neck.

"You don't know what you're asking." He fixed her with a gaze of such raw need she shivered. "You don't even really know how to play."

True, but she knew it didn't ruin a woman, and that was all that mattered for now. Mama had said that her and Papa's playing before they'd married was what had convinced Papa to ask for her hand.

A forbidden hope sprouted in her heart. If it worked for Mama . . . "Then teach me, Spencer." She tightened her grip on his neck. "So I'll know what it's like. We'll stop when it gets to be too much."

Skepticism filled his face. "I don't know if I can."

"What? I thought the great Lord Ravenswood could do anything he put his mind to." She tried to draw his head down to her breast, but he resisted, though his heavy gasps heated her flesh.

"So now you think to provoke me into it, do you?"

"If I have to," she said primly.

He bent his head to kiss her neck, then sucked on it hard. "Very well, you little seductress, we'll play. Under one condition." His gaze burned into hers. "That you stay in London and keep pretending to be my wife. That you don't go back to America until we find my brother."

She stiffened. "You'd resort to blackmail again?"

"If I have to."

Curse him for using something intimate and beautiful for his own purposes. Just for that, she ought to push him off her and walk right out.

But she wouldn't, because his request held more than calculation. He wanted her to stay not only to prevent a scandal, but to keep her close. Surely that meant something.

Maybe she was foolish to hope for a future with him, but he had no mistress—he was free. And he desired her. That was a start, wasn't it?

Besides, she couldn't go back to America without at least *trying* to convince him that they belonged together. Otherwise, she would always wonder if her cowardice had deprived her of her only chance of happiness with him.

"All right, I'll stay in England," she murmured. "But *I* get to say when we stop our playing tonight."

A savage light blazed across his face as he loomed over her, his large frame starkly outlined against the white canopy overhead. "If you mean to torture me, be forewarned—I can bear any torture if it makes you stay."

Then he swooped down to seize her lips with a greed that

matched her own, bold and ravening and unrelenting. His hand was rough on her breast, squeezing and plucking the nipple until she wriggled beneath him in an urgent quest for more.

Following his lead, she splayed her fingers over his chest, exploring every inch of the hair-coarsened skin drawn tight over sculpted muscle and unyielding bone. Tonight he was hers, and she wanted him to remember it. Tearing her mouth from his, she flicked her tongue over one of his nipples, then nipped at the other.

"So you want to tease, do you?" He forced her head back up for a brief kiss. Then he dragged his open mouth down to her breast, where he mirrored her earlier tortures, licking her nipple and sending a shiver dancing along her skin.

She thrust her breasts up higher so he'd suck them, but he only tugged at her other nipple with his teeth, then released it, leaving her aching for more.

"Please . . ." she whispered. Grasping his head, she tried to force it back so he'd take her breast in his mouth as he had before.

He chuckled. "Teasing goes both ways, my dear." He blew on her damp nipple, watching her squirm. "This is playing, too, you know."

Her eyes narrowed. She slid her hand down between them to rub the bulge in his breeches. "So is this."

When she withdrew her hand, he caught it and flattened it against the hard length of him. "Play fair, Abby."

"Only if you do."

That's all it took to have him sucking her breasts again, devouring them, caressing them with hot rasps of his tongue. So she responded as best her limited knowledge of men would allow. Letting his groans and eager thrusts against her hand be her guide, she fondled his aroused member through his breeches.

Until her hand slipped suddenly to one side to press his loin, and he jerked his head up with a curse clearly more of pain than pleasure.

She yanked her hand away. "I hurt you."

"It's nothing. Old war injury, that's all."

"So close to your—"

"Yes," he said tersely. Reaching down, he worked loose the buttons securing the fall of his breeches, then the buttons of his drawers.

"I-I'm sorry. I'll be more careful."

"Here, this will make it easier." With a smoldering gaze, he caught her hand and shoved it inside his drawers, closing her fingers around his naked arousal. "Hold on to the handle and you won't go astray." He cast her a wry smile. "If you're going to play, you might as well play right."

A treacherous thrill shot through her. Surely this went beyond playing. His rigid flesh felt large and strong and impossibly male, perfectly capable of being a weapon if she weren't careful.

Then his hand moved over hers, showing her how to rub him. And when her first tentative caress made him whisper, "God, yes, Abby . . . keep doing that," she realized she had a powerful weapon of her own—his need for her.

Triumph surged through her. She could do as she pleased with him. He even wanted her to. As she stroked him, he uttered sounds from low in his throat that she'd never heard— urgent, keening moans that fed her own need.

He pulled his hand out of his drawers, but only to catch the hem of her nightdress and drag it up her legs. As if to distract her, he kissed her again, but she was still acutely aware of that hand raising her hem. When he'd tugged the nightdress high enough so he could thrust his hand beneath to find the damp juncture between her legs, she wrenched her mouth free and stopped stroking him.

"Spencer, maybe you shouldn't . . ."

A recklessness had transformed his features into molten fire. "We're playing, remember?" He rubbed her, and excitement flooded her with warmth. "You're playing with me. I want to play with you." Then he thumbed a sensitive nub nestled in her curls, and she nearly went insane.

"Oh heavenly day . . ." she whispered as he cleverly caressed the bit of flesh, teasing and fondling until she strained against his hand. "That's . . . oh . . . it's too . . . oh, Spencer . . ." This felt too good to be mere playing.

"You stopped," he said in a guttural voice. "Don't stop. Let's play together."

When her pleasure-drugged brain finally absorbed his command, she returned to stroking his thick "thing" that felt almost alive in her hand. Then he lost all restraint. His mouth branded her everywhere—ravaged her breast, sucked her throat, plundered the hollow of her ear. But all her attention was focused on the wicked finger that drove inside her over and over.

As she tugged his aroused flesh, too, she half-consciously matched the rhythm of that hot, searching finger. Then he was thrusting two fingers deeply inside her, and his thumb was pressing her throbbing flesh, making her whimper and twist in a search for more of that exquisite excitement building between her legs.

When he increased his rhythm, she increased hers until their hands moved in tandem, their bodies slick with sweat, their breaths mingling in urgent gasps. A strange roar sounded in her ears, growing with each of his strokes until it pounded louder and louder and . . .

"Yes, Abby, yes," he rasped against her ear, "like that . . . oh, God . . . you're such a wild little thing . . . my wild rose . . . my wild darling . . ."

The word "darling" pushed her over some edge where the roaring erupted into a scream. It was hers, a shameless cry pouring out of her as light burst behind her eyes and her body went taut. Wave after wave of pleasure vibrated through her, catching her off guard, making her cry out again less violently.

Then his flesh jerked in her hand, and he gave a cry of his own, hoarse and guttural. It turned into a repetition of her name as a pulse shivered along the length of him and his "thing" went limp. Unsure of what she'd done, she yanked her hand out, but not before feeling a sticky wetness inside his drawers.

He rolled quickly off her to lie gasping at her side. "Good God, woman," he said after a moment, "you'll be the death of me yet."

A pleasant lassitude was stealing over her, but she fought it back in her worry for him. "Did I hit your war wound again?" she whispered. "I know I felt blood—"

"Not blood." A strangled laugh spilled out of his mouth. "That was my seed. If you can call it that."

Confused, she rose up on her elbow to look at him. "But I thought we didn't—"

"We didn't." His breathing was slowing to normal, but his eyes still smoldered. "It means we pleasured each other separately, that's all. You're still chaste, at least in the strictest sense of the word."

She didn't feel chaste. Now that she knew she hadn't hurt him, she felt wonderful. Like a woman, his woman. Of course she wasn't, but what they'd done felt too intimate to be merely pleasuring. And he'd called her "darling." Did he realize that?

Dropping back onto the bed, she snuggled close to him. Tentatively, she laid her hand on his chest, and he sucked in a sharp breath as if the slight weight wounded him. Yet he didn't push her away.

"Spencer?"

"Yes, Abby."

The cool distance in his voice gave her pause. Please, no, not the lofty lord again. She wanted the Spencer back who said sweet things to her about needing her beside him.

But she soldiered on. "I didn't mean for our playing to go so far. But I'm glad it did."

He said nothing, merely stiffening beneath her fingers.

Fear banished her enjoyment, but she wouldn't relent, determined to find out how far he would withdraw now that he'd had his pleasure. Forcing a teasing note into her voice, she asked, "So when will we be playing again?"

He uttered a low curse. Setting her firmly aside, he sat up to throw his legs over the edge of the bed. His spine was rigid as iron, and when she touched his back, he flinched. She dropped her hand, her stomach churning with disappointment.

"We can't play again, Abby," he choked out. "It's too . . . difficult."

"Difficult? How?"

"Makes things complicated."

Her heart sank. "Not for me. So it must 'make things complicated' for you."

"Exactly." He rose, still refusing to look at her. "Because if we keep playing, I'll want—" He broke off with a curse. "We just can't, all right?"

Then he faced her, and his eyes widened at the sight of her spread out on the white counterpane. His gaze dropped to her open nightdress, which still left one breast exposed, then further to the rucked-up hem she hadn't bothered to pull down, the one that bared her legs to the tops of her thighs. Desire flared in his face as he raked his hot gaze over her.

At last a shuddering breath escaped him. He took a step forward and hope leaped in her heart, but all he did was pull down her hem and draw the gaping edges of her nightdress together. "In future, it would be best if we hold any discussions between us somewhere other than your bedchamber. Or mine, for that matter."

While she still stared at him, shocked that he could put what they'd done behind him so easily, he scooped up his clothes and headed for the door. "I'll see you at breakfast," he said.

Then he was gone.

She'd cried so much already tonight she'd thought she had no tears left. She was wrong. They boiled out of her unchecked as she turned her face to the pillow.

How could he do this—be one man one moment and another the next? He'd called her "darling," and he clearly desired her. Yet he could thrust her aside as if she were . . . were a mere nuisance.

She fisted her hands against her throbbing eyes. That was the problem—he saw her as an impediment to all his grand career plans. He wanted her physically, but he didn't think she could be what he wanted in a wife.

Maybe he was right. She wasn't sure if she *could* be a wife to the officious viscount.

But there was another man beneath that façade, a man who desired her and cared so much for her that he'd swallow his pride and apologize for his mistakes. She could be a wife to *him*, oh, yes. And she wanted to be a wife to him, to have him speak to her in his old comfortable way, to have him share with her his hopes for England as he'd done before.

She lay back on the bed to stare up at the canopy. She wanted to unearth the buried Spencer, the man she'd sworn to be a wife to. She wanted to resurrect the Spencer who was kind and passionate and . . . and . . .

And who might be happy married to her. Because she now knew for certain that she wanted that gentleman for her own. She wanted to be that Spencer Law's wife until death did them part.

But bringing such a thing to pass might be tricky. For some odd reason, he insisted on clinging to his old aristocratic ways while he was in England. And he had this strange idea about marriage interfering with his ambitions. After tonight's ball, he was probably even more convinced that she wouldn't make a good viscountess. He might tolerate her ineptness to avoid a scandal, but he'd never tolerate it in a real wife.

So if she wanted to remain married to him, she'd have to assuage those fears. She'd have to teach herself how to be the right kind of wife. She'd learn the waltz and all those stupid titles and every silly rule of deportment in creation, whatever it took to become the elegant viscountess he thought he required. She'd show him that a wife could be an asset to his career, not to mention a handy thing to have about the house.

Yes, she would put her "naive American optimism" toward making herself indispensable to him, and she'd win him. Because naive American optimism beat out English cynicism any day.

A short while later, Spencer lay in his bed cursing himself soundly. Had he completely lost his mind, to agree to her "playing"? Bloody hell, if they ever played like that again, he wouldn't stop until he'd buried his cock so deep inside her that their marriage would be one in truth. Then there'd be nothing he could do about it.

Except make love to her every night, dine with her every day, touch her whenever he wanted, dance with her . . .

And watch her adoration turn to resentment and then hatred when months passed with no children. No babes in arms, no chattering boys, no mischievous girls. A lifetime chained to him with no children to occupy her while he spent his days at Parliament or the Home Office.

Because thanks to the iron fragments that had peppered his groin all those years ago, there would be no children from

him. Although most of the iron had been removed and his
privates were only slightly scarred, every doctor who'd examined him had voiced the same concern. A fragment had
sliced through some crucial part of his anatomy, and although everything worked fine, they doubted he could sire
children.

At first it hadn't bothered him so much. What randy young
soldier wouldn't like to rut whenever he pleased without fear
of consequences? And after the war, when his busy career
had given him time for only the occasional mistress, he'd enjoyed himself without concern. But when year after year had
brought no by-blows, the reality sank in. His seed might as
well be water for all the good it did. And if he couldn't sire
children, he could never sire an heir.

Or give his wife something all women wanted, her own little babes. So he'd sworn to remain a bachelor. Until Nat had
engineered this insane marriage to Abby.

If only . . . No, it was out of the question. Abby of all people would want children, and she deserved to have them, too.
He refused to deprive her of that. With her dowry restored,
she could make a real marriage, especially if she went to
a well-populated American city like New York where her
Senecan blood wouldn't matter so much. She could find
some nice fellow and have all the babies she wanted.

The thought of Abby in another man's arms hit him like a
blow to the chest, and he pounded the bed in futile anger. By
God, it wasn't fair. *He* should be the one marrying her, caring
for her . . . being teased by her.

He grasped at straws, frantic to find some way to keep her.
Perhaps she wouldn't care about his sterility. She might not
even mind adopting a child. That would be the same as having her own, wouldn't it?

Like hell it would. Spencer groaned as his stepmother's
image swam into his head. Someone else's children were

never the same—who knew that better than he? Women always wanted their own. Abby would, too. He just couldn't give them to her.

Perhaps he'd have been better off if the iron fragments hadn't missed his cock. Being able to bed any woman he wanted but not sire children seemed a mockery of his manhood as surely as if it had been destroyed.

But then he wouldn't have had tonight with Abby.

For a moment he savored the bittersweet memory of her hand wringing him dry. Hot, wild Abby . . . dampening beneath his caresses, tightening around his fingers, crying out her release as she brought him innocently to his.

And asking why he refused to do it again.

Bloody hell, what a mess. Now that she knew how much he desired her, she would expect it to lead to more. He'd convinced her to stay, but at what cost? He might have been better off letting her go back to America and brazening out the scandal.

But he wouldn't be brazening it out alone. Evelina and her mother would have to suffer it, too, especially once society began speculating about Abby's departure. Someone would assume that Nat's disappearance and Abby's disappearance meant something, and before he knew it, they'd be linking Nat to Abby again.

So she had to stay until Nat came back. Which meant he'd have to cope with his obsessive physical attraction to her.

There was only one way to manage it—throw himself into his work, squiring her only to the most important functions. She'd made friends of Lady Clara and Evelina—let them entertain her. Because if he were the one to do it, he'd soon find himself "playing" again, and that mustn't happen.

He must follow the same time-honored rules parents used to keep randy suitors from debauching their daughters. But since Abby clearly wouldn't enforce the rules, he'd have to.

Very well. No more private encounters. No more being alone with her in a room or carriage or any secluded place where he could seduce her. No more touching her, except when absolutely necessary, and then only in public.

Most importantly, no kissing. No kisses of any kind. Not if he wanted to keep this marriage a sham one.

Chapter 13

If your employer is deficient as a host, it is your duty to guide him. Otherwise you will spend all your time covering up his errors.

Suggestions for the Stoic Servant

The afternoon after the ball, Abby surveyed Spencer's dining room with an assessing eye, praying for something, anything, to be wrong with it. No such luck. Like all the other rooms, it was in perfect order. The man's staff was just too competent. She hadn't found a room yet that wasn't artfully arranged and immaculately kept. The silver had nary a pit, the sideboards were polished to a high sheen, and even the crevices of the fluted columns bracketing the doors were devoid of dust.

Heavenly day. How was she supposed to make herself indispensable to a man who had everything, including an efficient army of servants?

Especially when he wasn't even around to notice her efforts. A frown creased her brow. Spencer had left the town house long before she was even awake. Oh, she knew he had an important job saving England or whatever he did at the Home Office, but he'd been here for breakfast yesterday and the day before—why was today any different?

Because the silly man was avoiding her.

She touched the high neck of her day gown as she had several times already, putting her finger on the spot where he'd left his mark last night. Warmth flooded her insides. Spencer did desire her even if he was trying to ignore it. And his desire was one thing to commend her as a wife. Now she needed others.

In Philadelphia she would have impressed a man by making his favorite dish when he came courting. Maybe she should find out what Spencer's favorite dish was.

She sniffed the air. Maybe she could also do something about the house's faintly antiseptic smell of cleaning agents and vinegar. Cut lilacs in the vases would help. Or dishes of potpourri. A smile crept over her face. Yes, she could find orange peels in the kitchen and jasmine in the garden. And even if it proved too early for jasmine, there was always the Mead—

"Excuse me, madam," Mr. McFee said as he poked his head through the open door.

"Mr. McFee, I'm glad you're here. Do you happen to know what his lordship's favorite dish is?"

"Shellfish in butter, madam. Which is why we serve it every Friday evening."

"Of course you do," she said with a sigh.

"I came to inform you that you have a caller. It's Lady Clara Blakely. Are you in to callers?"

"I'm here, aren't I?" she said, bewildered by the question.

His lips twitched. "Yes, of course you are, madam. How unobservant of me."

She shot him a quizzical look. "Put her in the front drawing room and tell her I'll be right up."

"Very good, madam." McFee vanished like some servant sprite off to do her bidding.

How odd that Mr. McFee never called her "my lady." But then he probably knew she really wasn't one.

As did Clara, thank heaven. At least there was *one* person she could be herself with. Whisking off her apron, she paused beside a pier glass to check her hair and attire.

The new gowns wouldn't be finished for two more days, but the dressmaker had skillfully altered those belonging to Spencer's stepmother. By attaching an embroidered silk stomacher to cover the original high waist, the dressmaker had turned the outdated gown into a right fashionable one. Marguerite had dressed her hair in her old style, too, so no more droopy ringlets. Now she didn't look like the pathetic creature Clara had met last night.

Content that her appearance would suffice, she went up to meet her guest. As soon as Abby entered the front drawing room, Clara smiled amiably and rose to hold out her hand. "I would ask how you are, but I can see that you're well."

Taking Clara's hand, Abby pressed it warmly. "I have you to thank for that. I'll always be grateful for your kindness last night."

"I'm only glad you didn't take it all too much to heart." She searched Abby's face. "Or am I right in assuming from the absence of trunks in the entrance hall that you've decided to remain here a while longer?"

"Yes. Spencer promised not to tell me how to dress or wear my hair, and he apologized very nicely for all his bullying. So I'm giving him another chance." She could hardly say she'd traded her right to leave for a few stolen moments of scandalously delicious "playing." Or that she didn't regret one moment of it. "Anyway, I'm glad you're here. Have a seat, and we'll chat."

As soon as they sat together on the sofa, Clara faced her with curiosity shining in her eyes. "So Lord Ravenswood actually apologized, did he?"

"Better than that—he admitted he'd been wrong."

"That's a first."

"I know—I was too angry to appreciate it at the time, but it really is amazing. Now I almost regret plaguing him about his mistress."

"You mean Genevieve."

"Her . . . and any other mistress he might have."

"You *discussed* his mistresses?" Clara asked in clear disbelief.

"Of course. I had to know if he had a current one. Just because I'm his pretend wife doesn't mean I have to put up with being humiliated behind my back. So I asked him if he had one, and he said no."

"I can't believe you actually asked him that." Clara laughed. "I wish I could have seen his face. Lord Ravenswood isn't used to forthright women who don't play society games. Did he get all haughty as he usually does when he thinks someone's impertinent?"

Abby couldn't prevent a blush from staining her cheeks. "Um . . . not exactly. He asked me to stay, and then he . . . kissed me."

"Oh, better and better!" Clara said, practically beside herself with excitement.

"I'm not sure he thought so. He didn't *want* to kiss me, and he was annoyed about it afterward."

"Of course he was. Men always are." She patted Abby's arm. "But it's about time somebody annoyed his lofty lordship. He's had everything his way for far too long."

Abby suspected that wasn't entirely true, but she had no basis for that opinion yet.

Suddenly McFee appeared in the doorway. "Lady Brumley is asking if you are in, madam. What would you have me tell her?"

Abby sighed. The last person she wanted to see was Lady Brumley. But she had to face the woman sooner or later. She might as well do it with a friend at her side. "Have her join us, Mr. McFee, thank you."

As soon as Mr. McFee was gone, Clara asked, "Quickly, tell me what Lady Brumley was talking about in her column. I'm sure that's why she's here."

"You mean the one she wrote after Spencer's dinner party?"

"No, no, this morning's column. She said that the new Lady Ravenswood was keeping a treasure under her hat that would impress all of society once it was unveiled. What the dickens did she mean?"

"I have no idea." Abby jerked up in her seat, alarm gripping her. "Oh, no, what else did she say? Did she talk about my pitiful showing last night?"

Clara had no time to answer, for Mr. McFee appeared in the doorway to announce Lady Brumley. Abby rose to greet the new arrival with a sense of impending dread.

Lady Brumley breezed in like a ship in full sail. "I'm delighted to see that you are sans husband. Perhaps we shall finally have a chance to talk."

"Good afternoon." Abby tried not to show her anxiety. "You know Lady Clara Blakely, don't you?"

"Of course." Without waiting for an invitation, Lady Brumley headed over to Clara's side. "I'm glad you're here, too. You can help me convince Lady Ravenswood."

"Convince me of what?" Abby asked.

McFee cleared his throat, and she glanced up.

"Will that be all, my lady?" the butler asked.

She blinked. He'd called her "my lady." How very odd. And something in his expression said that he expected more than a cursory reply. When she hesitated, he mouthed a word that looked like "tea," and she started, mortified that she hadn't thought of it herself. But then she and Papa had rarely had callers in recent years.

"Uh, Mr. McFee? Would you please have some tea brought in?"

"Certainly, my lady," he said with an approving nod.

As soon as he'd disappeared, Abby turned to find Lady Brumley scowling.

"Come sit down, dear girl," the older woman said as she perched herself atop the velvet-upholstered sofa, and Clara followed suit. "You and I must talk about the behavior expected of a viscountess."

Abby's heart sank. The last thing she needed was a lecture from Lady Brumley about her mistakes at the ball.

"I'm sure she'll learn it all in time," Clara put in, attempting to intervene.

"She'd better learn it quickly, if she intends to keep a man like Ravenswood toeing the line," Lady Brumley retorted.

"There's no need to point out all my errors last night." Abby sank into an armchair across from the woman. "I know my dancing was disastrous and—"

"Oh, pish, who cares about dancing? You can learn the steps in an afternoon. No, I'm speaking of more important things—like how you address your servants."

"My servants?" Had she somehow managed to insult the unflappable McFee?

"A viscountess does not ask her butler to have tea brought. She commands it."

The very idea appalled Abby. In America, even the finest families had few servants, and those they did have tended to be resentful of authoritarian commands. Here in England, the servants seemed to accept their lot without question, which she found very peculiar. "But that's so . . . so . . ."

"Overbearing?" Lady Brumley finished.

"Yes," she said weakly.

"I should hope so," Lady Brumley answered. "How else can you show your servants that you're in charge of your own household? If you don't, they'll run roughshod over you and then gossip to their fellow servants about how 'common' their mistress is. Before you know it, the whole city will be talking about it."

"After last night, the whole city is already talking about how common I am," Abby said dryly.

"What fustian. Granted, they may be discussing how clumsy you are or how unfashionably you dress or even how American you are. But they haven't got round to 'common' yet, and you must make sure that they don't."

When Abby paled, Clara rose to her defense. "Really, Lady Brumley, I don't think you're helping—"

"Of course I am. The girl was clever enough to snag Ravenswood, wasn't she? No matter how she managed it, she can't rest on her laurels now. She must learn all she can about how a woman in her position behaves." She leveled a piercing glance on Clara. "And you must teach her. Your father gained his title late in your life, so you know how difficult it can be to learn all the niceties. Take her in hand, and I'm sure she will be socially presentable in no time."

"Given how freely you've expressed your opinions about a woman you barely know," Clara said icily, "I assumed *you* wanted to take on the task."

"Lord, no. I'm here about another matter entirely." Lady Brumley opened her reticule and drew out the vial of Mead she'd stolen, then brandished it at Abby. "This concoction of yours is marvelous. You hold a treasure in your hand, young lady."

Abby brightened. "So it finally did work on your indigestion."

"Indigestion? Oh no, I'm speaking of perfumes." She shook the bottle. "This is the finest fragrance I've come across in years. Have you any idea how difficult it is to find a decent perfume these days? One that is delicate, yet lasts?" She thrust the vial at Clara. "Smell this, and tell me if that isn't the most delicious scent ever to tickle your nose."

Clara's face clouded with surprise as she took the bottle, opened it, and sniffed.

"Pay her no mind," Abby put in. "Yes, I suppose the Mead does smell nice, but it's meant to be a cure—"

"Never mind what it's meant to be," Clara broke in. "I seldom agree with Lady Brumley, but in this case she's right. This is marvelous. Quite the loveliest scent ever."

"You see?" Lady Brumley straightened her current headdress, a bizarre turban of twisted silk and ribbon that featured a circlet of gold anchors. "Follow the lead of those fellows who created Eau de Cologne. They meant their elixir to be a cure, too—I heard that Boney himself drank bottles of it. Tried it once myself—nasty stuff. But as a scent, it became all the crack." Her eyes gleamed. "Until this, that is. Yours is twice as fine."

Abby glanced from Lady Brumley to Clara, who nodded her agreement. Just then, the maid brought in the tea. Mechanically Abby went through her duty as hostess by pouring it, but her mind was on Lady Brumley's startling assertions.

She'd always known the Mead had a lovely aroma, but she'd figured it was only her keen nose that made her notice it. She did use it to sweeten her breath, which wasn't unusual since plenty of medicines also worked as breath sweeteners.

But perfume? She'd never considered it a perfume. Then again, she didn't use perfume—Mama had always said that soap and water were all the perfume any woman needed. It had also seemed somehow unnatural to add a scent to one's skin.

"Why are you telling me this about the Mead?" Abby asked Lady Brumley.

"Because you should take advantage of it. I understand that his lordship has invested in your father's company and his brother is a partner, so if you can persuade them to produce the Mead as a perfume, it might become a resounding success."

Lady Brumley flashed her a calculating smile over the brim of her teacup. "Of course, I'd be happy to lend my assistance. A few hints in my column will have my readers clamoring for information about this new find. And with you and me both wearing it in public—and you, too, Lady Clara, if you wish—people will begin to ask about it. Then voilà, I'll reveal that it's all the rage and your husband's family will reap the financial benefits."

Lady Brumley added with a sly wink, "Your husband will be most grateful, I'm sure. His brother's injury makes the man unable to pursue the matter at present. But if you take matters in hand, the company will already be on a sound footing by the time Mr. Law is up and about again. Customers will be lined up to buy the Mead. That would increase your husband's investment and raise your usefulness to him. Men always like women who bring something other than their pretty selves to the marriage."

Abby hadn't considered that. Spencer owned half the company at present, and he'd always been concerned about his brother's future. If she could make keeping her a financial and familial asset . . .

Clara eyed the older woman with suspicion. "Why on earth are you interested in promoting this enterprise? What is it to you?"

Good question, Abby thought.

"Ah, you know me so well. And I do have an ulterior motive. For one thing, I want an endless supply of this fabulous elixir." She held the bottle up to the light. "What Lady Ravenswood gave me is already half gone."

"I didn't give it—" Abby began.

"Secondly, I expect a certain percentage of the profits in exchange for my help." She patted her elaborate turban. "My tastes are expensive, you see, and my dear departed husband didn't leave me quite as well off as I would like."

"That certainly explains your interest," Clara remarked. "But you're taking a risk, you know. What if Mr. Law never recovers from his wounds?"

Clara exchanged a glance with Abby. Yes, Spencer's brother might indeed never be found. But they could hardly tell Lady Brumley that.

"Pish, who needs a man for this?" Lady Brumley said. "Lady Ravenswood is the one who concocts the stuff. As long as she can provide the bottles and her husband approves—"

"Are you sure that he will?" Abby asked.

"Why wouldn't he want everyone talking about his wife and her fabulous perfume?" Lady Brumley asked.

"But I'd always heard that the English consider it crass for those of rank to be involved in trade."

"It is, but you're the inventor, my dear, and that's quite another thing. It's rather exotic for a lady to invent something. As long as no one knows you are participating in the actual business of it, it will only enhance your reputation."

"Lady Brumley has a point," Clara put in. "And it never hurts a woman to have something of her own. So that rather than being known as his lordship's wife, you'd be known as the lady who created the scent." She stared hard at Abby. "You see what I mean?"

Abby did. Clara figured that if Nat was never found and things got sticky with Spencer, she might have to start up her own company, if only to pay for passage back to America. And she'd need customers if she struck out on her own. Abby hoped it never came to that, but she supposed having something to fall back on wasn't a bad idea. "And you're sure that my husband will be pleased to see the Mead succeed?"

"This will make you the toast of the town." Lady Brumley shook the bottle of Mead. "After one whiff, ladies will be congratulating you for your superior nose, and your previous faux pas will be forgiven and forgotten. Your husband will be delighted."

"In that case," Abby said, "what do you need from me to make this work?"

Setting her cup down, Lady Brumley got right to business. "First of all, the mixture needs another name. I'm sorry, dear, but Dr. Mercer's Medicinal Mead isn't going to have ladies fighting over it at the nearest shops."

"How about Abigail's Aromatic Elixir?" Clara suggested.

"That sounds like smelling salts for maids," Lady Brumley snapped. "No, I was thinking of something like Scent of the Sea."

"You mean like brine?" Clara said dryly. "I think not."

"What about Abby's Scented Water?" Abby put in.

"Oh, no, that's much too plain," Lady Brumley said.

"I've got it!" Clara exclaimed. "Heaven's Scent—you know, like 'heaven-sent.'"

Lady Brumley pursed her lips in thought, then repeated the name a few times. "Yes, that's lovely. I like it. Heaven's Scent. I shall start talking about the new Lady Ravenswood's mysterious beauty secret in tomorrow's column. We'll have a week of hints to whet their appetites. By the time I'm done, they'll be clamoring for the secret."

"Or tired of hearing about it," Abby said, still a little skeptical of this plan.

"No woman ever tires of hearing about the latest beauty secret, my dear." Lady Brumley set down her half-empty cup of tea. "And after the hints, we must unveil the scent publicly. I have just the thing for it. I shall give bottles as gifts to the ladies at my breakfast a week from Saturday—you and your husband were already invited, of course. Then Sunday's column will feature the revelation about Lady Ravenswood's new scent."

"That's a wonderful idea," Abby said. "How many bottles will you need?"

"Oh, a hundred should do it."

"A hundred!" Abby exclaimed. Today was Thursday. That gave her only nine days. "I don't know if I can manage that."

"Of course you can. I'm paying for the bottles." She withdrew a bank note and handed it to Abby. "This should be sufficient to cover your expenses."

As Abby gaped at the amount of fifty pounds, Clara said, "She'll have the bottles ready, don't you worry."

"I'm not in the least worried." Lady Brumley rose to fix Abby with a stern look. "I always get what I want."

As Abby and Clara rose, too, Lady Brumley started toward the door like a ship tacking to face the wind. Then she paused. "One more thing, my dear ladies. Do keep this a secret. You may tell your husbands, but don't tell any of your friends."

"Why not?" Clara asked.

Lady Brumley rolled her eyes. "For effect, of course. I don't want anyone hearing of my discovery until *I* present it." She waited until she had their joint agreement, then swept from the room in a cloud of Mead scent and superiority.

Abby collapsed onto her seat the second the woman was gone. "Dear heaven, is she always like that?"

"Oh, yes." Clara sat down, too, and lifted her cup of tea. "Lady Brumley thinks herself the epicenter of polite society. Most of the time she's right."

Abby shook her head. "How can I have a hundred bottles of the Mead—I mean, Heaven's Scent—ready for Saturday? I haven't even found all the ingredients yet, or the bottles. Then labels must be hand-lettered, and the bottles cleaned . . ."

"But surely that won't take more than a few days," Clara protested.

"I only have two. It must sit at least a week for all the ingredients to meld properly. So I have to prepare and seal all the bottles by *this* Saturday just to have it ready for *next* Saturday. How on earth will I get everything done?"

"What you need is lots of busy hands to help."

"I suppose I could hire people, but I don't know how much of this fifty pounds I'll need for ingredients. And I don't want to bother Spencer's servants when they have their own duties." Especially after Spencer's comment about a wife's disrupting his household.

Clara straightened. "I have the perfect solution. Lord Ravenswood may not have told you, but I run a charitable home for the reformation of pickpockets. My young charges need to learn useful skills, and this could be perfect. You could show them how you make the perfume, and they could help you put the bottles together. One of my girls has a fine hand with lettering. I can't guarantee they won't bungle a few bottles, but—"

"That's an excellent idea," Abby broke in. "I would dearly love to meet them. I so rarely get to be around children, and I do adore them."

Clara laughed. "You might not adore these after you spend a few hours with them, but I know they'll adore you. The minute you walk into the Home—"

"The Home? We can't make the perfume at your institution—I doubt you have a large enough work area for the sort of project we're discussing. Besides, I don't want to cart the bottles back and forth once they're filled." Abby thought a moment, then added, "And there's plenty of room here, anyway. There's a huge schoolroom upstairs that's merely gathering dust. I'm sure Spencer won't mind if I take it over for a while."

"I don't know, Abby. Given how he feels about children, are you sure he'd want a lot of them running around his house?"

That brought her up short. "I hadn't thought of that." She pursed her lips. "But do you really think he hates children?"

"Is it worth risking his anger to find out?"

Angering Spencer needlessly wouldn't help her situation. She wanted to entice him into keeping her, not tempt him to throw her out on her ear. "No, I suppose not."

"Ah, well, it was a nice idea. And at least *I* can still help.

I'll bring a couple of the older girls—we've got two or three who might do. But I'm afraid I can't stay away from the baby all day—our new nursemaid is one of my young charges, and she's still nervous that she'll do something wrong. So I promised I'd stay close to home for a while. Though truthfully, Lydia is such a contented thing, I can't imagine she'll give the girl much trouble."

Envy mingled with yearning in Abby's breast. She'd wanted children of her own for so long. How lovely it would be to have Spencer's children.

But if he really hated children, he might not want any babes at all. No, he couldn't really hate children, could he? That didn't even make sense. Anyway, a man of his station was supposed to sire an heir. He'd swallow his aversion if only for that.

Though she didn't want him fathering children only out of a sense of duty.

"Abby?" Clara said, breaking into her thoughts. "Shall I bring some people?"

"Yes, of course. Bring them tomorrow, as many as you can manage. I'll make sure I gather the herbs, clean out the room, and buy the bottles and such today."

They settled the details of the project, and then Clara left. But long after she was gone, Abby sat on the sofa musing over their plans. If Lady Brumley was right, the Mead might give her entrée into society. And Clara could help her learn the niceties of social behavior. They could start discussing it tomorrow while they worked on the perfume.

Everything else was falling into place, too. As soon as her gowns arrived, she'd be able to show Spencer she could dress appropriately. And he'd sent word earlier that he'd engaged a dance master, so soon she'd be able to dance appropriately. She was well on her way to demonstrating her ability to be his wife.

Except in one respect. He seemed determined not to

chance any repeat of last night's "playing." Considering how easily he could avoid her by hurrying off to his office, she might never get to be alone with him again. She had to find a way to keep herself in his thoughts even while he was gone. She needed something to remind him of her . . . like a picture or a scent or—

She sat up straight and nearly crowed aloud. The Mead. Of course. A slow smile crossed her face. *I even smell you in my dreams sometimes.*

She'd make sure he smelled her in more than his dreams. He'd smell her at work, in Parliament, and yes, while he slept. All she had to do was slip into his bedchamber and sprinkle a little Mead on his cravats and his pillow—not so much that it was noticeable, but enough that the faint scent would work itself into his memory.

Now she had to sneak into his room without being seen . . .

Chapter 14

What your employer does not know will not hurt him.

Suggestions for the Stoic Servant

Irritated that he had to return home in the late afternoon, Spencer descended from his carriage at his town house. But a summons from the king could not be ignored, and he must change into more formal clothes for the meeting.

What a bloody nuisance. The House of Lords was discussing the prime minister's latest idiotic plan in this afternoon's session, and Spencer should be there to hear it. Instead he was dashing about London.

He only hoped he didn't run into Abby. He'd already spent half the morning mooning over her like a besotted half-wit, remembering the texture of her skin, the fine surprise in her eyes when he'd brought her to her release, the luxurious pleasure of plundering her mouth and her breasts and her . . .

He cursed under his breath. He had to stop this. The last thing he needed was to meet the king with his mind in his breeches. Dealing with the petulant King George required keeping one's wits about one.

"McFee!" he bellowed as he hurried through the front door.

The butler appeared, looking uncharacteristically flustered as he thrust a notebook into his pocket. Now that Spencer thought about it, he often caught McFee with a notebook. How odd. Though perhaps that was how the stalwart Scot kept the house in such good order.

McFee halted in front of Spencer, his face smoothed into a respectful demeanor. "Yes, my lord?"

"Tell James I need him upstairs. I have to dress for an appointment with the king."

"Certainly, my lord."

As the butler walked away, a proud smile cracking his usual reserve, Spencer sighed. Like all his servants, McFee gloried in having a master worthy of meeting with the king. Well, at least someone enjoyed Spencer's least favorite duty. Normally the home secretary took care of these audiences, but Sir Robert was in Manchester, so the task fell to Spencer, who barely tolerated His Majesty's whims.

It had been different when the man's father was king. During the periods when George III wasn't plagued with madness, he'd possessed a great deal of good sense and a love for his people that his son had never managed to muster. In contrast, George IV was a vain fool more concerned with fashion, food, and females than with his country.

But though Spencer chafed at the necessity for coddling the debauched king, he knew his duty. He always knew his duty.

Reminding himself he had but an hour to make himself presentable for His Finicky Majesty, Spencer hastened up the stairs and along the hall. Idly he noted the new purple cast to the corridor. Ah, pots of lilacs decorated the console tables, reflected all along the way by the mirrors. When had his housekeeper starting filling the place with flowers?

But another surprise awaited him in his bedchamber when he opened the door. His sham wife was bent over his bed, her sweet bottom jutting up in a most tempting position.

After half a day of imagining her in that position, among others, it was all he could do to keep from closing the distance between them, throwing up her skirts, and taking advantage of the fetching picture she presented.

Devil take her. Why was she here? Hadn't he told her they should never be alone together in either bedchamber? Angry to find her ignoring the very commands meant to preserve his sanity, he slammed the door shut behind him.

She jumped and whirled around so quickly that whatever she held in her hand slipped from her fingers to shatter on the wood floor.

As a powerful scent of rosemary and citrus engulfed them both, she stared woefully at the shards lying at her feet. "Oh, dear . . . Spencer, I'm so sorry. I didn't expect you—I'll fetch a broom at once." She took a step forward, and glass crunched under her flimsy blue slippers.

"Don't move!" He cursed himself for the impulse that had made him cause her to drop whatever had been in her hand. Taking two swift steps through the glass, he lifted her in his arms, then carried her past the danger.

"What are you doing?" she asked as she flung her arms about his neck to hold on.

"That glass will tear your slippers to shreds, not to mention your feet."

Her tender gaze was too adoring by half. "This is becoming a habit—your hauling me about in your arms."

"Can I help it if you always need rescuing?" he said gruffly.

"I wouldn't need rescuing if you weren't always taking me by surprise." She tightened her hold on his neck in a blatant invitation. "Not that I'm complaining. I like being rescued by you."

He caught his breath, achingly aware of her soft, fragrant weight. Her full mouth held a teasing smile, and her eyes sparkled with gaiety. For a second he actually considered tossing her on his bed and taking advantage of the sweet surcease she offered.

Then the door opened and his valet walked in. "Oh, I b-beg your pardon, my lord," the man stammered, already backing out.

"It's all right, James." Hastily Spencer set Abby on her feet and forced himself to pull his hands away. "Lady Ravenswood had a little mishap. Fetch someone to clean up this glass, if you will."

"Yes, my lord," James said and left them.

Disappointment flickered in Abby's eyes. But when he did nothing but stand there clenching and unclenching his hands to keep from reaching for her again, she sighed and turned away to stare at the glass. "I should clean it up myself."

"That's what I have servants for." Then he added more harshly, "What were you doing in my bedchamber anyway?"

The question seemed to throw her into a quandary. She fiddled with her apron strings. "Well, you see . . . I . . . um . . . was bringing you a little present, that's all."

"A present?"

"A bottle of the Mead." She waved her hand over the strewn glass, then babbled nervously, almost guiltily, "I thought you could use it to sweeten your breath or soothe your stomach or whatever you wished. You could even use it as a scent if you—"

"I don't use scent."

She swung a perplexed gaze to him. "That's not true. I've smelled bergamot on you many times. You must use *some* sort of scent. That's why I . . . um . . . thought of giving you a bottle of the Mead."

He took insult at being lumped in with those idiot gentlemen who perfumed their clothes and hair and bodies. "I assure you, I'm not some dandy trying to smell like a flower garden. I don't use scent. You're mistaken in what you thought you smelled."

"If you say so," she said with a stubborn tilt of her chin. "In any case, I've destroyed the only bottle I had left. I'm making more tomorrow, but I won't bother to make you any, since you don't 'use scent.'"

Was that sarcasm in her voice? Probably. She never seemed to believe him. "I'm sorry I made you drop your only bottle, but I didn't expect to see you when I came in here to change clothes."

She blinked. "Why are you changing clothes?"

"I've been summoned by the king."

"The king of what?"

Good God, she was serious. "England, my dear. We have one, remember?"

A blush stained her cheeks. "Yes, but I didn't think he bothered with regular people . . . that is . . . I-I didn't realize . . . I mean, I *did*, but . . . well, you're quite an important man then, aren't you?"

"Only when the home secretary is away on business. One of my duties is taking his place, and that includes meeting with the king when His Majesty requests it."

He waited for her reaction, expecting the same one his servants always had—pride in the connections they vicariously shared by being part of his household. Even as his sham wife, she was bound to feel the same.

So her frown took him by surprise. "It's rude of him to expect you to drop everything and run about for his pleasure. You probably have more important things to do." Planting her hands on her hips, she looked him over with feminine indignation. "And what's wrong with what you're wearing anyway? Why should you dash off to change clothes just because he can't stand a plain and honest coat?"

He burst into laughter. He'd been thinking much the same thing, but dared not voice his complaints aloud to anyone. Leave it to Abby to do it for him. "He's the king. He can order people about as he pleases."

"Really? Well, that's very obnoxious of him." She shook her head. "I don't know how you English put up with royalty. You ought to boot them all out and run the country yourselves like we do in America. We believe all men are created equal. You're just as good as he is, you know."

"Careful, my dear, you might want to keep that opinion to yourself," he said dryly. "They still hang people for treason here."

She lifted her hand to her neck in abject horror. "They could hang me for speaking my mind?"

"If your mind is treasonous, yes." A wicked urge seized him, and he bent low to add, "But don't worry—I'll make sure they only lock you in the Tower with the rest of the hardened criminals."

She gaped at him. Then awareness dawned in her eyes. "Why, Lord Ravenswood, I do believe you're teasing me."

"Not at all." He struggled to keep a straight face. "We Englishmen take our treason quite seriously. Why do you think the king has summoned me? To discuss what to do with my troublesome American wife who's preaching sedition in the streets."

"Is that so?" With a coy smile, she sidled up close to him. "And you would suggest that they put me in the Tower, would you?"

"We have to protect our populace from dangerous sorts like you Americans."

"Fine. Put me there if you must." Her eyes danced. "But only if you agree to visit. I'm sure you'd find it amusing to see me in chains after all the trouble I've been."

A vivid image of her in chains flashed into his mind. Then it turned into a lewder image of her naked in chains, offering up her eager mouth while his hands took wanton liberties with her breasts and her splayed thighs and the sweet hot place—

Good God, she was driving him mad. He should know better than to tease her—teasing led to flirting, and flirting led to other things.

He turned away abruptly to mutter, "I doubt that the king allows visits to criminals in the Tower." With a shuddering breath, he brought his unruly urges under control. "James will be back any minute to help me change clothes, so you'd best go." *Before I chain you to my side for the rest of my life.*

He shook off that dangerous thought. "And the next time you wish to give me a 'present,' hand it to McFee and he'll see that I get it."

"Why?" she challenged. "Are you afraid that if you let me loose in your room I'll ruin something else, something that doesn't belong to me?"

"No. I'm afraid that *I* will." When he glanced over to find her staring at him in bewilderment, he added harshly, "Just go, will you? I have to dress."

"But I wanted to talk to you about the Mead—"

"Not now, Abby. I don't have time."

"Oh, all right." She sniffed. "I see that your king isn't the only one who thinks he can order people about as he pleases."

As she stalked toward the door, all wounded dignity and feminine outrage, he actually contemplated running after her to beg her forgiveness with kisses. Instead he watched woodenly as the door closed behind her, leaving him once again alone.

Not for long, however. As he stripped off his coat and waistcoat, his valet returned with a broom-bearing servant in tow. The servant set about cleaning up the glass immediately. James, who carried a pail of steaming water, approached Spencer with his face full of excitement.

"An audience with the king, is it?" James said. "We'll have you looking bright as a new-polished penny in a thrice, my lord."

Spencer sighed. Time to return to acting as if a royal audience was an honor rather than an onerous duty. "I hope so. I've only got an hour." He peeled off his limp shirt.

"Shall I shave you before you dress?" James asked.

"Considering that His Majesty thinks facial hair is rude, I suppose you'd better." Spencer ran a hand over his faintly whiskered cheek and jaw. "Just don't nick me. Bleeding in his presence is probably illegal."

His valet laughed. "Don't worry, my lord, I'll be gentle as a lamb." James poured hot water into a basin and set out the shaving implements. Normally, Spencer paid no attention to James's machinations, but today he couldn't help noticing that James poured some liquid from a bottle into the shaving water.

Spencer flicked a finger toward the bottle. "What's that?"

"Bergamot oil, my lord. Just enough to soften the skin."

He stared at his valet. "Do you always use it when you shave me?"

"Of course. Every gentlemen should have a bit of scented oil in his shaving water—so the soap don't dry him out. And it has a pleasing scent, too."

So Abby had been right. He'd berated her for making him sound like a dandy, when all the time she'd simply been following her nose. Feeling like a cad, he sank into the chair that his valet indicated.

Spencer had never been so out of his depth as he was with Abby. He couldn't open his mouth without either hurting her feelings or turning her flirtatious. It was bloody annoying. Like last night, the way she'd looked when he'd left her after their outrageous and unwise fondling. Most women would have chastised him for taking such liberties. But not Abby, oh, no. She wanted more. She always wanted more than he could offer.

How he wished he had it to give to her.

And how he wished she hadn't broken that bloody bottle in here. The room reeked of it, keeping her in his mind constantly. He glanced over to the servant who was sweeping up the glass. "Be sure to scrub that floor when you're done with the sweeping. And use something to get rid of the smell. It's potent enough to choke a man."

And sweet enough to turn him into a slavering slave at the feet of the woman who smelled of it. Chains—hah! If anybody wore chains these days, it was he. He couldn't spend one moment without thinking of all the ways he wanted to make love to her. Forget the Tower—he'd like to chain her naked to his bed while he taught her exactly what happened to women who teased men without a thought for the consequences . . .

"I'll fetch your clothes now," James murmured, having finished shaving him.

Jerked from his erotic fancies, Spencer groaned. He had an erection. Again. Devil take it, he had to stop thinking of her, before James returned and noticed his bulging trousers. Otherwise, changing clothes would be bloody embarrassing.

He must think of something else. The king. Yes. That would deflate any man's ardor. He reviewed what concerns the king might wish to discuss. He pondered tactics for dealing with His Majesty. He contemplated the latest bill in the House of Lords. That dampened his lust enough to get him through dressing.

Until James tied his cravat. Suddenly, his image of Abby rose powerfully in his mind once more. Her scent seemed more intense than ever, as if that damned bottle of hers were being waved right under his very nose.

Bloody hell, this was insane. His mind was playing tricks on him. But if she did this to him when she wasn't even around, how would he ever manage when he had to be near her? He had to get the woman out of his house and back to America before she eroded his resolve completely.

Making a mental note to consult with the runners yet again for any news of his brother, he stood there holding his thoughts of her barely at bay, praying that the scent of her would pass before he left the house.

But it didn't. It seemed to follow him everywhere. He couldn't purge her from his brain, not in his carriage, not at the palace, and not even when he stood before the king himself. Abby's essence had infected him.

"Lord Ravenswood?" said the regal voice, and he realized with a start that he hadn't been paying attention to what the king was saying.

"Yes, Your Majesty?"

"Do you think we are wise to take this trip to Edinburgh in August? We would be the first king since Charles II to set foot in Scotland, you realize."

"That's true." Spencer dragged his wayward thoughts back to the matter under discussion. "Your Majesty must determine what you wish to accomplish with such a trip. Do you want to ascertain the concerns of the Catholics regarding Emancipation? Or merely to assure the Scots of the Crown's good will? In the first case, the trip is pointless, because you can do that here. But in the second, it might be beneficial."

When he caught the king staring at him as if he'd grown two heads, he realized he'd grossly misunderstood the situation. His Majesty merely expected Spencer to approve what he'd already decided to do.

Although Spencer considered himself a competent undersecretary, he was not a very good courtier. He couldn't simply toady to the king. "But I'm sure Your Majesty has considered all of that," he added smoothly.

"You are decidedly opinionated, sir," His Majesty said in a bland tone.

"Forgive me, but you did ask my opinion."

"Yes. And you gave it very bluntly, too, did you not?" The king hefted his portly frame from the creaking chair in the audience room and trundled toward the window. "You know, Ravenswood, that is what we've always hated about you.

You're too somber by half, too arrogant in your opinions, and always sure of your own perfection."

Spencer only wished that the last were true. And he had not known until now that His Majesty had taken such a strong dislike to him. Spencer saw his political future sliding down into an abyss. Yet he felt strangely calm, perversely pleased to be disliked by such a frivolous king.

His Majesty went on. "But of late we have come to believe you might not be as somber as we thought."

Spencer's eyes narrowed. "I beg your pardon."

When the king faced him again, his expression was stern, but his eyes twinkled. "We hear you've taken a wife. And not just the usual boring miss, but an American woman of dubious heritage with a penchant for causing trouble at balls."

Spencer hardly knew how to respond. "Er . . . yes, Your Majesty, I have recently married an American."

"Good for you. Threw all those stuffy matrons into a tizzy, I expect. They thought you'd take one of their insipid daughters for a wife, but you showed them, didn't you?"

"It does appear that way." It dawned on Spencer that the king had often suffered at the hands of the gossiping matrons who despised his profligate ways. The man must have felt unfairly maligned. So Spencer's aberrant act probably seemed a kind of rebellion against the very women who'd always tormented him.

If the man only knew.

The king flashed him a smile. "Makes us wonder if you don't have a jolly bone or two beneath that cool exterior after all. Good show, Ravenswood, good show."

The conversation was so bizarre that Spencer could only murmur, "Thank you" and wonder how the hell he'd gotten so lucky. If you could call it luck to have the king consider him the same sort of heedless fool that he himself was.

"We hear your wife is quite beautiful," His Majesty continued.

Every muscle in Spencer's body stilled. Despite the king's rumored liaison with the Lady Steward of his household, the man's eye always roved.

"Some would call her beautiful, yes," Spencer said non-committally, though anger knotted in his gut at the very thought of George casting his lecherous gaze on Abby.

"We should like to meet this American beauty." His Majesty's smirk showed he was perfectly aware of Spencer's sudden jealousy. "For May Day we will be attending Throck-morton's exclusive fête-champêtre. We understand there will be dancing and a maypole and even fireworks. Surely you were invited, so do bring your pretty wife to present to us. We should like to see how an American manages our quaint dances."

Spencer couldn't hide his shock. The king had never so much as expressed a desire to drink tea with him, much less required his attendance at a social engagement. Obliging His Majesty would enhance Spencer's political career immeasurably.

Except that Abby would never agree to it. If she felt uncomfortable at a smallish private ball, he could only imagine how she'd react to meeting royalty at one of Throckmorton's lavish May Day feasts. "I'm afraid that isn't possible, Your Majesty."

"What?" His Majesty's eyes narrowed. "And why not? Pray explain how appeasing a whim of your lord and king is 'not possible'?"

Though Spencer felt the noose closing about his throat, he chafed at having to explain himself, even to the king. "My wife still feels uncomfortable in good society. She was raised very differently in America and needs time to learn our English habits. She's never been around royalty, for one thing, and—"

"Nonsense, she'll be fine." The king's outrage vanished, replaced by a typical nonchalance. "We aren't entirely unaware of how Americans behave. We shall overlook any errors of propriety. We merely wish to meet the bold American who managed to capture the heart of one of our most haughty subjects."

Abby had captured something more volatile than Spencer's heart—she now held his entire future in her hand. The woman whose favorite pastime was teasing him publicly could easily ruin his political career in one fell swoop.

But that wasn't what annoyed him about this. What annoyed him was the realization that the king himself had an interest in her. Absurd though it seemed, Spencer didn't want to share his sham wife with anyone. Not even the man who could destroy him politically.

"I'll have my man mention to Lady Throckmorton that you and your wife will be attending, Ravenswood," His Majesty said.

It was not a question. "Yes, Your Majesty," Spencer said through gritted teeth.

A smug smile curved the king's fleshy lips. "Oh, and tell your wife to bring that treasure Lady Brumley spoke of in her column this morning. We should like to determine for ourselves if it's as marvelous as that old battle-ax hints at."

"As you wish, Your Majesty." He must get a copy of Lady Brumley's column at once to find out what the hell the king was talking about.

Because one thing was certain—Abby had unwittingly made a splash in society. Spencer only hoped her splash didn't drown them both.

It was long after dinner before Abby finally got the chance to stand back and survey her handiwork. Everything in the schoolroom was nearly ready for tomorrow. She and Mrs. Graham still had to finish clearing it out and make room on the long table for stations where she and her friends could letter and glue on the labels, fill the bottles, and tie on the ribbons. But the table had plenty of chairs ranged around it, thanks to Spencer's obliging servants, and she'd managed to find every ingredient she needed to make the Mead . . . the Heaven's Scent.

Privately, she thought Lady Brumley's plans were crazy, but if her ladyship dictated that the Mead be perfume, why not indulge them? What did Abby have to lose?

"It's a pity you couldn't accept Lady Clara's offer to use her children for this." Mrs. Graham gathered up the books scattered on the table and arranged them on shelves around the room. "It would've made it all go faster, and they'd have liked doing it, I warrant. But after what his lordship's servants told me about his feelings toward children, I guess you were right not to take her up on it."

Abby tensed as she reached for a box. "What did his servants say?"

"That he complains about the boys across the street. I'll admit they're a rowdy bunch, always sticking their noses where they don't belong, but that's no cause to banish them from his garden like he done. They weren't hurting nobody."

"Spencer is a very private person. He works hard and has to listen to boring speeches all day, so when he comes home, he just wants to relax in his own quiet garden. Can you blame him?"

"That ain't the only time. Mr. McFee told me that Mr. Law once gave the boys permission to play in the garden whenever his lordship weren't here, and when his lordship got wind of it, he put his foot right down. Said he'd best not find any boys skulking about his garden without his say."

A chill ran down Abby's spine, but she ignored it. Spencer had a right not to share his garden with anybody. It meant nothing. He might have been worried that the children would hurt the plants or steal the fruit.

Although that seemed petty for a man as rich as Spencer.

Mrs. Graham went on. "But Mr. McFee said you're right

to keep them away. He said having children here would set his lordship's temper off something fierce. And you don't want that, do you?"

No indeed. Abby had already had one close call this afternoon when Spencer had come upon her just as she was dripping Mead onto his pillow. Thank heaven she'd already finished scenting his cravats or he would really have lost his temper, especially considering how he felt about scent. She certainly didn't want to risk his ire again.

At her continued silence, Mrs. Graham added, "Mr. McFee also says—"

"Enough about that snobbish butler," she said peevishly. "Since when do you listen to him? I thought you hated him."

To her surprise, Mrs. Graham actually blushed. "I do. Most of the time." She suddenly became inordinately busy with arranging books. "That don't mean he can't speak sense once in a while. Especially when it comes to his lordship." She shot Abby a concerned glance. "I was hoping that the viscount would keep you for his wife, but I'm not so sure anymore. He's a bit more toplofty here than he was in America, don't you think? Besides, men who don't like children don't make good fathers."

"He's a bachelor," Abby said, balking at hearing her own concerns voiced so blatantly. "Bachelors always consider children to be nuisances. That's all it is."

Or at least she hoped that was all it was. She wished she could find out for sure without provoking his anger. Because Mrs. Graham did have a point about men who didn't like children, and Abby fully intended to have children of her own one day. She hoped to have them with Spencer.

Mrs. Graham gave a dramatic sigh. "I just hate to see the man break your heart."

"He can't break it if I don't give it to him. And I'm much too practical to give it to a man who doesn't want it."

Not to mention too sensible to discuss the ownership of

her heart with her nosy servant. She picked up a box and began to unload its contents. "Take a look at these bottles, Mrs. Graham. Do you think they'll do? I tried to get pretty ones, but I had to take what I could find in the rag and bottle shops."

Suitably distracted, Mrs. Graham rounded the table to examine the bottles. "They're a bit grubby, but we can clean them up easy enough."

They were so engrossed in their evaluation that they didn't hear anybody approach until a deep voice said, "I'm back."

Abby's pulse leaped as she whirled toward the open door. Spencer leaned against the doorframe, watching them with an unreadable expression. His well-fitted knee breeches of royal-blue kerseymere left nothing to the imagination, and the matching swallowtail coat with its velvet collar and gilt buttons skimmed his broad shoulders, muscled chest, and lean waist in loving detail. He looked powerful, rich, and dangerously handsome.

And completely inaccessible to a woman like her. Or was that his point in dressing so extravagantly?

No, of course not. He'd been to visit the king. Lucky king.

She tamped down her stammering pulse. "You look well."

"You look busy." He smiled, and her pulse went positively mad with glee. With a flick of one long finger, he indicated the table. "What's all this?"

"Mr. McFee said I could use the schoolroom as a workshop for making the Mead. I would have asked you, but you weren't here."

Pushing away from the doorframe, he strolled toward her pots and funnels and brazier for heating water. "It's a rather large manufacturing operation for a few bottles, isn't it?" Restlessly, he prowled the room, examining all her materials. It made her nervous, especially when she felt Mrs. Graham's watchful eyes on her.

Abby ignored the woman. "Actually, I hope to produce

more than a few bottles. When Lady Brumley called on me this afternoon, she suggested that I present the Mead as perfume. She and Clara convinced me to go along. We're calling it Heaven's Scent."

He picked up a bottle and turned it over in his hand. "Appropriate."

"Do you think so?" she asked, warmed by his interest. "I thought they were both crazy, but they insist it smells pretty enough to sell. Lady Brumley has already put in a large order, so Clara's bringing a few friends here tomorrow to help me produce them."

A pained look crossed his face. "You may have to put that off, my dear. You're going to be much too busy to fool with the Mead right now."

"Oh?" she said, instantly put on her guard.

"I know I said we wouldn't attend any more balls and such for a while. But an engagement has come up that we can't avoid."

Her eyes narrowed. "What sort of engagement?"

He sighed. "His Majesty is attending Lady Throckmorton's fête-champêtre on the first of May. I've had my invitation for weeks, but I hadn't planned to go. Now he's insisting that I do so. And that I bring you, too, so he can meet you."

"Oh, my lady, the king himself wants to meet you!" Mrs. Graham cried, all her distrust of his lordship apparently vanishing. "Only think of it!"

Abby's fingers curled convulsively around the back of the chair in front of her. "No, I can't."

He leveled his gaze on her. "You can. Besides, we have no choice. Believe me, I like this no better than you. I tried to excuse you from it, but the king would brook no refusal."

"Why on earth does he want me there anyway?" Abby grumbled, stung by Spencer's reminder that the last thing he wanted to do was introduce his nobody of a wife to the king. "Has he run out of jugglers and jesters and players to amuse him? Does he figure that a clumsy American will give him hours of entertainment?"

A muscle ticked in Spencer's jaw. "Don't be absurd."

"Surely he heard what happened at the ball—"

"He doesn't care about that." Spencer shifted his gaze to the fireplace. "He says he . . . wants to meet the woman who captured my heart."

A bitter laugh erupted from her. "Then I'm not the one he wants, am I?"

Spencer slapped the bottle down on the table. "He *thinks* you are, and that's all that matters. I can hardly set him straight, can I?"

Dragging the chair out from the table, she slumped into it, her mind awhirl. She wanted to show Spencer she could be his wife in every respect and make him proud of her. But starting at the tiptop of society wasn't what she'd had in mind.

"It won't be so bad," he went on. "You'll have to spend more time with Clara and the dance master, that's all. And you have nearly two weeks to prepare."

Two weeks? To be ready for royalty? If she made a fool of herself before the king, Spencer would never stay married to her. "That's not long enough. I promised Lady Brumley a hundred bottles of Heaven's Scent by her breakfast a week from Saturday so she can give them to her friends. I have to meet that quota before I can do anything else. That leaves me only a little over a week, if you don't include Sundays—"

"You'll simply have to put Lady Brumley off."

"I can't put her off—I already promised! She's putting it in the newspaper and everything. She may not be the king, but she has the power of the pen behind her, and you don't want me getting on her bad side, do you?" His black scowl was her answer. "Besides, you know even two weeks won't make me ready for a meeting with the king."

"Ready or not, the king has asked to meet you, and you

must oblige him. If you don't, it could destroy my entire future in the government."

"But if I do oblige him, I will most certainly destroy your career."

"Nonsense. What happened to your American ideas about all men being created equal? He's only a man after all, Abby, and no one to be afraid of. A few hours ago you were telling me that I was just as good as he is."

"Exactly. *You*, Spencer. *You* are just as good as he is."

"So are you."

"Maybe, but you English don't see it that way. How someone behaves in society matters so much more here than in America. And if I were to ruin your future by some bumbling mistake—"

"You won't." He leaned forward to plant his hands on the table across from her. "Come on, Abby, I need you. I'll give you whatever you want if you'll do this for me."

"I don't want anything—"

"She wants that expensive wardrobe you bought her," Mrs. Graham interrupted from beside Abby. "She gets to keep every stitch of it and carry it back to America."

Spencer's gaze shifted instantly to Mrs. Graham. "Clearly I've been discussing this with the wrong person. All right, she can keep the wardrobe. It's not as if I'll have any use for it after she's gone." His eyes narrowed. "What else does she want?"

"Now see here—" Abby put in.

"She wants them rubies you put on her night before last." Mrs. Graham crossed her arms over her ample chest. "And not just the ear bobs neither—the whole parure."

"Done. What else?"

"Stop it this instant!" Abby leaped to her feet to cast Mrs. Graham a fulminating look. "I want none of that, and you know it."

"If he's willing to pay—"

"I'm not going to accept jewels or clothes for this like I'm some . . . some ladybird," she hissed at her servant. She faced Spencer with a proud stance. "I'm not *that* desperate."

His gaze softened. "All right. So what will you accept?" His voice was low, earnest. "I'm willing to give you anything, Abby. What do you want?"

She stared at him uncertainly, taking in his firm, determined jaw, the soft mouth that could kiss a woman into oblivion, the arms that had held her so tenderly.

You, she thought. *I want you.*

She doubted he'd take that for an answer. Besides, she didn't want to get him by forcing him into it. She wanted to convince him they could be happy married to each other, sharing a life, having children . . .

Children. Yes, she could ask for something that would answer her most nagging question about him. "You have to let me complete Lady Brumley's order."

"Fine," he snapped. "As long as you spend the rest of the time preparing to meet the king, do as you please with that."

"That's not all." She dragged in a deep breath. "If I'm to let it sit for a week, I have to produce those hundred bottles by this Saturday, so I need more hands to get it done. Clara offered me the use of her reformed pickpockets. If you'll let me, I want to bring the children here tomorrow to help me bottle the Heaven's Scent."

He scowled. "Why can't you have them help you at the Home?"

"I don't want to haul all my materials over there. Besides, Clara doesn't have the room for such a big project." Abby swept her hand around her. "But you have plenty of it here. With fifteen or so eager hands, I can have the bottles put together far more quickly than a few friends and I could do it."

"Use my servants."

"That would disrupt your household." Sarcasm edged her voice. "I thought you didn't want it disrupted by a wife's activities. Or was that just hogwash?" She knew perfectly well that it was, but he'd never admit it.

When he turned away to mutter a low oath, she added, "It's not as if the time would be wasted either. Clara can instruct me in etiquette and titles and such while we fill bottles and letter labels."

"She can do that without the children here."

Abby thrust out her chin. "That's what I want, Spencer. Take it or leave it."

He shot her a frustrated glance. "That's all you want? The children to help you?"

"Yes."

"I'd rather give you the jewels." When she opened her mouth to protest, he held up his hand with a sigh. "All right, bring them here. But only if I don't have to put up with them running about underfoot. On Fridays Parliament adjourns early, so I'll be home for dinner at seven. I want them gone by then, understand?"

"Yes." She understood perfectly. He wanted everything his way.

Well, he wasn't going to get it. This was her chance to test his reaction to children, and she would take full advantage of it. Even if she annoyed him a little in the process.

Chapter 15

A household with children requires a butler with certain skills. Do not go to work for an employer of child-bearing age unless you are prepared to learn them.

Suggestions for the Stoic Servant

Abby could hardly contain her pleasure. Surrounded by babbling children of varying ages, she sat at the long table in the schoolroom, cutting lengths of ribbon. It was hard to believe these sweet-faced angels had ever been thieves . . . except when they were working. Then their clever hands moved so quickly she could hardly follow them.

"What a delight they are," she told Clara. "You've taught them well."

Clara raised an eyebrow as she meticulously lettered a label. "You didn't see Jack trying to lift that porcelain figure of a shepherd on his way up the stairs or Mary gauging the silver with her eagle eye."

Abby's eyes went wide. "They wouldn't really steal from *us*, would they?"

"If they thought they could get away with it."

Clara reached over to steady the hand of a seven-year-old pouring finished perfume from a pitcher into a bottle. The girl, whose name was Lily, smiled shyly.

Abby melted. "Oh, I don't care. Let them steal if they want. God knows Spencer can afford it."

"Watch what you say," Clara warned, though her eyes sparkled. "I'm trying to teach them *not* to steal, you know."

"I wouldn't steal," Lily said stoutly. "I ain't stolen since I was a little 'un."

Clara laughed. "That's because you know you'd be in trouble with me if you did."

Lily screwed her face up as she poured more liquid into a new bottle. "I didn't like stealing anyhow. Too scary when you get caught."

Abby could hardly imagine a girl of seven having to steal, much less a "little 'un." But she'd heard it wasn't unusual in London. It wasn't even unusual in Philadelphia, but London seemed to have more pickpockets—and crueler punishments.

No wonder Clara was so dedicated to her Home.

"Will we be able to provide Lady Brumley with her bottles?" Clara asked, glancing toward the schoolroom windows and the darkening sky outside.

"I think so. How many are there now, Jack?" Abby asked the wiry-framed eleven-year old who was gluing labels on bottles.

"We're up to eighty-nine, milady." Jack scowled over at Lily. "It would be ninety-one if not for the two that Miss Fumble-fingers knocked over."

"But there was a spider!" Lily stuck her lower lip out petulantly. "I hate spiders."

"So do I." Abby reached across the table to pat Lily's hand. "Don't worry, two bottles won't break us. And we can work a while longer, can't we, Clara?"

"Yes, but I'll have to send word to the Home for them to keep dinner back for us."

"Nonsense, you're eating dinner here," Abby said. "I've already arranged it with Cook. It's the least I can do after you've helped me so much."

Clara chewed on her lower lip. "What about Spencer? Are you sure he'll approve of having all these little devils at his dinner table?"

"He told me they could come here, didn't he?" she answered evasively. "Besides, it's a special menu—soup and pork pies and sausages. I tried to choose things the children would like." And that Spencer might enjoy, too.

She jerked up straight. "Mrs. Graham, you did show Cook how to make the clam chowder, didn't you?"

"I did indeed." Mrs. Graham tied a bit of ribbon around a bottle neck. "You should have heard the silly man, complaining about putting bacon in with them clams. 'Next you'll be wanting mussels with your roast pork,' says he. I told him that her ladyship wanted it that way, so he'd best be doing it right. Mr. McFee will make sure he does. He's seeing to the lemon ices, too."

"Lemon ices!" Jack exclaimed. "Heigho, chaps, did you hear that? We're having lemon ices tonight!"

"You'd think I fed them only gruel and gravy," Clara said wryly as the news ran through the children.

Their delight thrilled Abby. "Oh, you know children. Half of their excitement probably comes from being able to have their treat away from home."

"I doubt it. The Home could never afford to serve them all lemon ices in April. It costs a fortune." Clara eyed Abby curiously. "I hope you know what you're doing."

"I do," she said, though she wasn't at all sure. But she had to find out if Spencer really did hate children. And if he resented the expenditure, that would tell her something, too.

The schoolroom door opened, and a young nursemaid came in carrying a large, gurgling infant on her hip. "The wee one's just up from her nap, my lady," the girl said, "and I thought you might not mind if I brought her up here with the rest of you."

"Of course we don't mind," Abby answered for Clara as

the children clamored to see the baby. Abby held out her
hands and shot Clara a glance. "May I hold her?"

"Certainly," Clara said with a smile.

Looking harried, the young nurse seemed only too happy
to hand the child over. Abby could see why. Lydia was quite
a large nine-month-old. Hauling her up two flights of stairs
must be no mean feat. Entranced by Lydia's liquid brown
eyes and sweet baby scent, Abby cradled the dear thing
close. Oh, if only this were *her* baby, hers and Spencer's.

As she stared fondly down at the infant, the door opened.
"What the devil is—"

Her head jerked up at the sound of Spencer's voice, but her
words of welcome died as she saw the pure shock in his face.
His eyes were riveted on her and the baby, and he stiffened
until he rivaled one of her glass bottles for unyielding rigidity.

"Forgive me for interrupting." Every word was clipped,
spoken through a taut jaw and tight lips. Dragging his eyes
from the baby, he lifted his head. "Abby, if I might have a
word with you in the study . . ."

She nearly gasped to see the icy anger in that wintry gaze.
"Yes, of course," she breathed. But inside she was dying.
Now she had her answer concerning his feelings toward chil-
dren. Unfortunately, it wasn't the one she'd hoped for.

Spencer paced his study, barely restraining his urge to
smash something. He had to get control of himself before she
came, but that seemed impossible. He was a grown man, for
God's sake—how could a lot of children turn him into this
seething bundle of rage?

Because they'd been surrounding Abby. Because she'd
been holding little Lydia—for he had no doubt of who the
baby was—and staring down at the infant with such yearning
it still sent pain knifing through his gut to remember it.

Devil take her! She'd deliberately kept those children here

for him to see—he was sure of it. And after he'd ordered her to have them gone before he got home.

The door opened and she slipped inside, but he gave her no time to speak.

"What are those brats still doing here?" he growled. The shock in her eyes drove the knife deeper in his gut, but he couldn't hold back his bitter words. "I told you I didn't want to see them. And it's nearly dark outside, so don't pretend you forgot the time."

Though she paled, she held her ground. "We weren't finished."

"I don't care." He kept seeing her with that babe in her arms. He could never give her a babe, never be the one to bring that tender look into her eyes. It tore at him more deeply than he'd expected.

He gritted his teeth. "I want them gone, do you hear? I want them gone now."

She thrust out her chin. "I can't do that. They deserved some reward after all their hard work, so I promised them a nice dinner. And I'm not going to renege just because you don't like having your careful little life upset."

Upset! Good God, if she only knew. "Very well, serve them dinner if you must. I'll go to my club. But if I ever see them here again—"

"You won't." She scowled. "If I'd had any idea how strongly you felt, I wouldn't have subjected them to your temper. I know you don't exactly approve of frivolity, Spencer, but I never expected you to take it out on mere children."

"Take it out—What the hell do you mean? I've done no such thing."

"Oh, your displeasure was very clear to them, I assure you. They endure enough from everybody else for being pick-pockets—they don't need your condescension, too."

"You think this is about their being pickpockets?" he said incredulously.

"What other reason could you have for being angry over the presence of children?" She eyed him coolly. "I wouldn't blame you for fearing that they might steal some of your gimcracks and silver. I mean, without the evidence of your lofty social standing that you must parade before—"

"For God's sake, it's not that." He faced her, feeling oddly like a child himself, being chastised by the schoolmistress. "If I was worried they'd steal from me, I would never have hired one of Lady Clara's charges as a groom."

She gaped at him. "You did?"

"Yes. Years ago. And two of my footmen were once her charges." But they'd been nearly grown—not children who could torture him with thoughts of what might have been. "Ask Lady Clara yourself if you don't believe me. This has nothing to do with their being pickpockets. I just don't like children." He cast her a pointed glance. "As you know very well."

"I heard your friends say such nonsense at the ball, but I didn't credit it. Why would a grown man take a real dislike to what are simply younger versions of himself?"

Her gaze was steady on him, and he had the uneasy feeling she was baiting him.

Well, he would not be baited, and he certainly wouldn't tell her his shame so he could watch her anger turn to pity. Especially not now that he'd seen the yearning in her eyes when she'd held little Lydia. She wanted children, and he could never give them to her. Nothing would change that. "Perhaps the grown man doesn't like having his peace disrupted, his home invaded, and his opinions challenged at every turn."

"Are you talking about the children now or me?" she asked quietly.

He sucked in a steadying breath. "I don't wish to argue

with you, Abby." Snatching up the satchel he'd left on his desk when he'd first come in, he brushed past her toward the door. "Give them dinner and get rid of them. I'll be at my club."

But when he opened the door, he was hit with a bustle of noise coming from the entrance hall. What were the bloody devils up to now? He strode down the hall, heedless of Abby hurrying to keep pace with him. As he burst into the foyer he saw Lady Clara helping her children sort out hats and gloves.

Abby rushed past him. "Wait a minute!" she protested to Lady Clara. "Where are you going?"

Lady Clara shot Spencer a furtive glance. "We thought it best if we return to the Home and leave you and your husband in peace."

A curly-headed imp pouted at Spencer. "And without sausages, too. It ain't fair."

"Hush, Lily," Lady Clara admonished the girl.

Abby turned to stare at Spencer expectantly, and something twisted in his gut. He knew what she wanted of him, the willful wench.

"There's no need to go," he bit out. "I'm heading off to my club anyway. Abby has an entire dinner prepared—it would be a shame to let it go to waste."

Joyful cries erupted in the entrance hall even as Lady Clara tried to quell them. "Really, Lord Ravenswood, if you'd rather we go—"

"No," he said firmly. "Please stay." He glanced over to McFee, whose hands were already filling up with the gloves and hats that the children had thrust back at him when Spencer made his announcement. "McFee, fetch me my coat and hat."

"Certainly, my lord," the unflappable butler said as he handed his burden over to one of the footmen.

Abby herded the imps together, casting Spencer a grateful smile over her shoulder. "Come this way, children—it's nearly time for dinner anyway, so we might as well go on to the dining room."

"But do it quietly," Lady Clara added with a glance in Spencer's direction. "All this noise is surely giving his lordship a headache."

He wanted to tell her that the noise was the least of his complaints, but he held his tongue. He just wanted them gone. Yet before they'd moved an inch, a crash sounded from the drawing room upstairs, followed by a loud rattling noise.

What the— Spencer strode up the stairs toward the sound, while the rest of his unwanted guests surged behind him. He reached the drawing room just in time to find a boy of middling age trying frantically to right a table as a silver bowl wobbled about on the floor. Beside the boy was a box. Beyond him stood the satinwood cabinet that Spencer generally kept locked. It wasn't locked now.

"Jack!" Lady Clara hissed as she came up beside Spencer. "What in the dickens are you doing?"

Jack thrust his chest out with a hardened pickpocket's belligerence, but the fear behind the false bravado was unmistakable, even to Spencer. "I only wanted to see what was in there." The boy gestured to the cabinet. "I was being careful when I opened it."

After picking the lock, Spencer thought with irritation.

"While I was trying to figure out how to get this here box open, I-I stumbled and . . . I didn't mean to knock over the table." The boy's gaze flew unerringly to Spencer, whom the older boys knew and feared, since he was in charge of all the magistrates in London proper. "I wasn't trying to steal nothing, my lord. Honest, I wasn't."

"Lord Ravenswood, I am so sorry—" Lady Clara began.

But he cut her off. "It's all right. Boys will be boys." He found it easier to deal with annoying children than cute ones. Besides, he grew tired of being regarded by Lady Clara and the children with either fear or horror.

Stepping up to Jack, he righted the table and picked up the box the boy had set down. He hesitated, staring at its fanciful painted exterior. Then he sighed and with a flick of his finger, released the catch. The box opened like an accordion, fanning out to three times its length.

Jack's eyes went wide. "Odsfish, what is it?"

"A children's peep-show box," Spencer explained curtly. "Here, hold it toward the candle and look through this hole. Then you'll see the fox hunt."

As Jack warily took the box and lifted it to his eye, Spencer could almost envision the three-dimensional scene he'd gazed on a thousand times as a boy. Created by layers of cut-out paper spaced evenly apart like the sets on a stage, it showed scarlet-clad huntsmen riding to hound. They galloped through trees toward the bloodred sun, actually a bit of thin red paper covering a hole through which the candle shone in the back.

"Hang it all, that's fine, it is," Jack exclaimed.

Spencer glanced back to find Lady Clara and Abby watching him, their mouths agape as the children crowded around to get a better look at what was going on.

Snapping out of her surprise, Abby walked toward the cabinet, glanced at the ten boxes inside, then stared at Spencer. "You have a collection of peep-show boxes," she said matter-of-factly.

A flush rose over Spencer's face. "I do not have a 'collection' of anything," he grumbled. "You make me sound like some silly schoolboy. Next you'll ask to see my bag of 'treasures' containing chips of pink quartz and bits of kite string."

A curious Lady Clara advanced nearer, with the children pushing in behind her, but Abby merely stood there regarding him with a steady gaze. She swept her hand to indicate the interior of the cabinet. "If this isn't a collection, what do you call it?"

He jerked his gaze away from her. "A random assortment of peep-show boxes that I just happened to acquire when I was young."

"And that you keep in a special cabinet," Abby said, laughter in her voice.

"A locked cabinet," Jack interjected helpfully.

Spencer glowered at the boy. "Yes, locked. So how did you get into it, pray tell?"

Jack swallowed hard, his eyes growing huge.

"Oh, stop trying to change the subject," Abby put in. "Face it, Spencer, you've been found out. The great undersecretary of the Home Office has a collection of peep-show boxes. It's nothing to be ashamed of."

"I'm not ashamed of it." He couldn't believe he was standing here defending his boxes to a lot of children and his sham wife. He added sullenly, "And it's not a collection. It's a random assortment—"

"You might as well give up, Lord Ravenswood," Lady Clara put in, her eyes gleaming with amusement. "Abby's right—you've been found out."

"And maybe if the children ask nicely," Abby added, "his lordship will let them look inside his special boxes. He might even show them how they work."

As a children's chorus of pleas filled the air, at first tentative, then more querulous, Spencer swung his gaze to her in alarm. Abby watched him steadily, those pretty green eyes demanding something from him. Bloody hell, did she actually expect him to *invite* swarms of children to torment him?

Clearly she did. And the plaintive cries of Clara's charges only made it worse—they had so little, and denying them something so small when it would give them such great pleasure would be churlish indeed. Even he could not be that cruel.

But he'd make Abby pay for putting him in this situation in the first place. Oh, yes, he wouldn't be the only one to suffer.

Somehow he managed to keep his voice calm. "I'd be happy to demonstrate the boxes to the children."

His reward was a shout of hurrah from the little imps—and a hopeful smile from Abby. Both nearly made him retract his promise. Instead, he gritted his teeth and threw himself into hell.

The next hour passed in a daze. Children bombarded him everywhere, at first wary and aloof, but soon creeping under his guard. They began by looking over his shoulder as he crouched to show a small doe-eyed boy how the peep-show box with the lake scene worked. Soon they were tugging at his arm to pull him over to this box or that and then slipping tiny, fragile hands in his, ignoring how he stiffened.

But the final insult came when Spencer retreated to his favorite bergère chair to escape the onslaught. The gap-toothed urchin named Lily who'd earlier bemoaned the loss of the sausages had the audacity to follow him and clamber onto his knee.

Eyes solemn, she held out one of Spencer's boxes. "I can't make it work, sir. I look through it, but I don't see nuthin'." Her lower lip trembled as if she were on the verge of tears, and Spencer felt his gut twist.

Just what he needed to make this night a complete disaster—a sobbing child. A sobbing *cute* child, all riotous black curls and soulful blue eyes. Devil take it.

"You see, Lily—" Reluctantly, he took the box from the girl, who'd been aiming it toward his chest, and turned it so the other end faced the fireplace to his left. "You have to tilt the box toward the light. It has to have light behind it— from the candle or the fire."

He shifted her so the girl could look through the peephole, and in an instant the child's expression changed from despair to surprised pleasure.

"It's a horse race." Lily glanced up at Spencer. "Do them horses move?"

He couldn't suppress a smile. "Watch," he said, and reached beneath the box with both hands to clasp the strings this particular box contained.

When he pulled in alternate rhythms, making the horses bob up and down inside, Lily crowed with delight. "They're off! Look at 'em go!"

A strangled laugh eked past the lump in Spencer's throat. "It's not as good as a real race, but at least you can control who wins."

Watching Lily center all her energy on a silly trifle of an image proved a sublime torture. If not for his war injury, this might have been his own daughter sitting on his lap, holding the peep-show box with the irreverent casualness of the young and foolish.

Pain scoured his soul, and his eyes sought out the woman bent on upsetting his life. Abby beamed at him. She probably thought she was doing him a favor, forcing him to face what he professed to dislike so he could see it wasn't so bad after all. Like a wild rose, she was overgrowing his house and his life.

First there was her "playing" and then her appearance in his bedchamber and now the children. It was almost as if—

An uneasy suspicion suddenly hit him. Could she possibly think to . . . No, surely she knew better. He'd made his wishes on that score perfectly clear.

Lily glanced up at him. "Do you got any boxes that show stuff for girls?" she asked hopefully. "You know, like . . . like fancy dances and ladies in coaches?"

"I'm afraid not." But there were such things. "You like ladies in coaches, do you?"

"Ever so much." She smiled timidly. "'Specially when they're as nice as Lady Clara and Lady Ravenswood. Lady Ravenswood smells like Mama used to, all sweet-like."

"Used to?"

Tears welled in her eyes, and he cursed himself for even

raising the subject. "Mama went to live in heaven. I don't got a daddy. He went to sea afore I was born."

The lump in Spencer's throat thickened. "Who took care of you before you went to live at the Home?"

She wiped her tears away with one small fist. "My uncle. But he kept sending me out to steal." A troubled frown creased her smooth brow. "I don't like stealing."

"Good for you," he said fiercely. "You just keep obeying Lady Clara, and you won't have to steal ever again." He made a mental note to double his donation to the Home this year.

The unbelievably cute thing snuggled closer to him. "I like you. You're not so mean as all the boys say." She thrust her nose into his cravat and inhaled. "And you smell sweet-like, too. Just like Lady Ravenswood."

He chuckled in spite of himself. "Do I?"

"Sure you do." She shoved his cravat up in his face. "See?"

To humor her, he sniffed. Then sniffed again. That was Abby's scent on his cravat, all right. But he hadn't put it there. His eyes narrowed.

McFee entered the drawing room to announce, "Dinner is served." But the butler's reserve slipped when he caught sight of Spencer with Lily perched on his lap. "Er . . . my lord . . . do you wish . . . that is . . . I have your coat and hat ready if your lordship still intends to go to your club."

Lily gazed up at Spencer. "You don't want to be going to no club, sir. There's lemon ices for dessert here. I bet that club don't have lemon ices."

"Lemon ices?" Spencer shot Abby a telling look. Did she plan to spend him into debtor's prison as well as plague him with children? "How did you find lemon ices at this time of year?"

She looked nervous. "Um . . . Mr. McFee helped me."

When Spencer arched one brow at his butler, the man went rigid. "Her ladyship asked what dessert would be most calculated to appeal to children, and I suggested lemon ices. I did not worry about the difficulty of obtaining it."

"Or the expense," Spencer said dryly.

As both his sham wife and his butler colored, Spencer shook his head, feeling despair grip him. They had him trapped, all of them. If not for the hopeful expression on Lily's face, he would have wished them to the devil and gone off to the club anyway.

But he hadn't sunk so low that he would hurt the feelings of a little girl who couldn't know how her every winsome smile inflicted fresh pain.

Spencer gazed solemnly down at Lily. "Well then, poppet, I think you're right. I wouldn't want to miss lemon ices for dessert. Especially when my wife and my servants went to such great lengths to get it."

Abby was all smiles again. Oh, yes, the woman was certainly up to something. He'd play along for now, but later he would get the truth out of her. And if it was what he thought it was, she wouldn't get away with thwarting him. Not anymore.

Chapter 16

Never question what happens behind locked doors.

Suggestions for the Stoic Servant

Abby had relaxed while Spencer was with the children, but now that they were sitting down to dinner, she tensed up again. Spencer's brooding glances unnerved her, making it hard for her to breathe. And when the footmen brought the soup around, she forgot to breathe entirely.

Especially when Spencer stared down at his bowl and asked, "What's this?"

She licked her dry lips. "It's . . . um . . . clam chowder. An American dish. I thought you might like it. I-I mean, since you like shellfish and all."

His gaze shot to hers as he dipped his spoon. "How did you know that?"

"The servants," she said noncommittally, watching as he tasted the soup.

The children were skeptical enough of the unfamiliar dish to wait until he pronounced judgment. When he realized every eye was on him, Spencer slowed his movements. He took another spoonful, but this time he swished it around in his mouth and looked deep in thought as he swallowed.

When he merely dipped his spoon again, she'd had enough. "Well?" she snapped. "What do you think?"

He ate calmly. "About what?"

"The soup, of course!"

"Oh, the soup." When Abby glared at him, he relented. "It's quite good, Abby. Best soup I've ever tasted." He arched an eyebrow at the children. "Don't you all think so?"

That was enough to have them digging in. Soon they were exclaiming over it, eager to please both their hosts. And Spencer's smug smile made her want to throw something at him.

Still, the rest of dinner went very well. Spencer even surprised her with his deft ability to entertain. He regaled the children with stories about visiting Italy and floating in a Venetian gondola alongside the swans.

When Jack sullenly proclaimed he didn't like swans, Spencer said, "I know what you mean. God only gave swans beauty to hide their rank stupidity."

The children squealed with laughter.

They'd just finished the lemon ices when Spencer blotted his mouth with a napkin and stood. "I regret that I must leave you, but I've work to do." He slanted an enigmatic glance at Abby. "After our guests have gone, my dear, I'd appreciate it if you'd stop in at my study."

"Certainly," she said, though something in his manner struck her as odd.

Clara had noticed, too, for later when she was leaving with the children, she said, "You don't think Lord Ravenswood is still angry about the children being here, do you?"

"Of course not. He was perfectly nice to them. I'm sure he just wants to go over tomorrow's plans with me."

But once everybody was gone and she headed off toward his study, her unease returned. She didn't know why, but it wouldn't abate.

When she reached Spencer's study to find the door ajar,

she halted. Her mouth went dry as she peeked in to find him standing between the fire and his massive mahogany desk in his shirtsleeves.

Spencer in shirtsleeves—how strange. She scanned the room until she found his coat and waistcoat slung over an armchair. But he'd draped his cravat over his shoulder like a soldier's colors, and that gave her pause, too. He rarely dressed casually outside his bedchamber.

A tendril of foreboding crept around her heart, but she willed herself to ignore it. She was being silly. She had nothing to fear from him. What if he did dress casually in his own home? He had a right to walk around in his shirtsleeves if he pleased.

Even if he'd never done so before.

Studying him through the cracked-open door, she sought some sign of his mood. But though his profile was to her, she could tell little from the carved line of his jaw, the unsmiling mouth. He merely looked pensive as he swirled some dark liquor in a tumbler with one hand and balanced a peep-show box with the other.

"Come in, Abby," he said without turning around.

She started. Her blood inexplicably clamoring in her ears, she pushed the door all the way open and walked in.

Yet he still didn't face her. "Close the door behind you and lock it."

The clipped command stirred up butterflies in her belly. Maybe she had something to fear after all. "Why?"

"I don't want the servants barging in on our private discussion."

"Oh." That made sense, yet her hands trembled as she shoved the door closed and turned the key.

When she faced him, he'd set his empty glass on the desk next to him and was turning the peep-show box over in his hands. Firelight sketched unholy shadows over his profile, rousing her sense of unease to new heights.

As always, she met her fears boldly. "You said you wanted to see me."

"Yes." He kept staring down at the painted box. "You like children, don't you?"

"Of course. Who doesn't?"

He glanced to her, one eyebrow raised.

"And don't try to tell me again that you don't," she went on quickly. "I won't believe it. I saw you with those children. You were compassionate and entertaining—"

"I can put a good face on things when I need to," he bit out.

"Hogwash. You could have gone to your club any time you wanted. But you didn't. And no man who hates children would have told them jokes and tolerated them climbing all over him." She crossed her arms over her chest. "You enjoyed yourself with those little darlings, admit it."

Slowly he turned toward her, still holding the box as his steely eyes searched her face. "Is that why you brought them here? To find out if I could tolerate children?"

The butterflies fluttered madly in her belly. "No! I-I needed them to help me."

"And that's why you planned an entire dinner for them. One that included dishes meant only for them as well as dishes meant only for me."

That was harder to explain away. "I . . . um . . . merely didn't take seriously your words about having them gone by dinner."

It sounded lame, even to her ears. He fixed her with a disturbingly level gaze. "You had no ulterior motive for your actions, no reason beyond your aims with the perfume."

The very fact that he asked the question gave her pause. But she wasn't about to admit her reasons for her behavior. "Of course not," she managed to say.

"I see." His smile might have put her at ease if it hadn't been so very . . . mysterious. It wasn't like Spencer to be mysterious. Evasive, perhaps, or cool, but not mysterious. What in heaven's name was he thinking?

Eyes gleaming, he held up the box. "I've got something to show you."

Her pulse leaped in apprehension. Did this mean the inquisition was over? And why show her yet another peep-show box? "I don't remember seeing that one earlier."

"I don't keep it with the rest. My father gave me the others when I was a boy. This one is from Nat. He found it in Paris a few years ago."

"Oh." She sounded like an idiot, but she couldn't help it. His strange behavior made her very jittery.

"Come take a look," he said, a peculiar tension in his voice.

"All right." Crossing the Turkish carpet on shaky limbs, she held out her hand.

Instead of putting the box in it, he tugged her toward him. Turning her in his arms, he leaned against the desk and settled her between his parted thighs so her backside rested against his groin. He anchored her there with one powerful arm clamped about her waist.

Heavenly day. Was he simply trying to torture her? Or had he finally accepted the attraction he'd been fighting at every turn? And if that was the case, why now?

A thrill coursed through her to feel him thickening beneath her backside. Then he pressed a kiss into her hair, and her thrill twisted into anticipation. She didn't care why he'd changed his mind. He was holding her and kissing her—that was enough.

He pushed the peep-show box into her hands, then bent his head to whisper. "Look in it, Abby."

Wondering what a peep-show box had to do with anything between them, she muttered, "Oh, all right," and lifted it to her eye.

It took a moment for her to register the image, even though he held her facing the fire so that light shone through the back aperture. But as her gaze adjusted and the image formed in her vision, she gasped.

The scene was a bordello. Scantily clad women lay sprawled in various scandalous positions, touching themselves, being touched by men . . .

She jerked back from it, hot blood flooding her cheeks. "I . . . It's—"

"—an erotic peep-show box. Not all of them are for children, you know."

"Oh."

His deft hand stroked back and forth over her belly, raising wanton shivers even beneath the layers of gown and chemise. But when his other hand began working loose the buttons of her gown at the back, she didn't know whether to be delighted or alarmed.

"Wh-what are you doing, Spencer?" she whispered.

"I think you call it 'playing.'" His breath warmed her neck, heated her blood.

"I thought you didn't want us to play again," she said warily.

"Sometimes a man can't help himself." He went on unfastening buttons until he had her gown completely open in the back. Taking the box from her, he set it on the table. Then he tugged her gown completely down, letting it drop with a rustle at her feet. "But then you were counting on that, weren't you?"

Fear warred with excitement in her chest. "I don't know what you mean."

He dropped something about her neck, and only when the scent hit her did she realize it was his cravat. "You put the Mead on my cravats, didn't you? That's why you were in my room the other day. It took me until this evening to figure it out. When one of the girls commented on my sweet smell, I realized the scent was too strong to be simply the figment of my imagination."

Panic clutched her chest. "Sh-she smelled your own scent on your cravats, that's all. I know you said you don't wear any, but—"

"James set me straight—apparently he puts scent in my shaving water. But I went up to my room after dinner and checked the freshly washed cravats. They all smell like this." He drew the silky fabric over her nose, then let it slither to the floor. "Like you, your scent. You may as well admit it."

When she said nothing, he murmured, "Ah, such a stubborn little wench." Then he reached around in front of her to untie her chemise. She tried to face him, but he held her forcibly in place.

"Another thing," he went on, "and this time I want the truth. Why did you want to have the children here, Abby?"

Dear heaven, he was back to that. Had he figured that out, too? "I told you—"

"No. The real reason. You knew how I felt. So you had a purpose for convincing me to let you bring them here, and then for keeping them past the hour I'd dictated. I think I know what your purpose was. I just want to hear you say it."

She gave up. "All right, curse you. I wanted to see if you really hated children. And I think I proved that you don't."

"I see." He sounded oddly calm as he dragged her chemise down to her waist, leaving her breasts completely exposed. The chill air made her nipples pucker into hard buttons, and his breath on her neck quickened. "So it was a test, was it?" he whispered in her ear, then tugged her earlobe with his teeth.

All her nether muscles tightened into an aching knot centered between her legs. "Wh-what do you mean? What sort of test?"

His arm snaked around her waist again, but this time right

over her bare flesh. "To determine if I'd make a suitable husband."

Heavenly day, he'd figured *everything* out. "Don't be silly. If we're going to separate in the end anyway, why would I care?"

"Good question." His finger circled her navel, then darted in it. "I wondered the same thing. And I could only come up with one explanation—you want to make this marriage permanent if you can."

She wasn't fool enough to admit *that*. "Certainly not."

"No?" His fingers danced along her ribs.

"No."

"Still stubborn, I see." His voice now held an edge. "Tell me, Abby, have you any idea what it's like to live with heaven dangling always beyond your reach?"

She frowned. "That's an odd question."

"I know. Answer it anyway."

"All right." She thought of how this past few days had been, living as his wife but not his wife. "I think I do. Yes."

With a growl, he flattened his large hand over her belly and tugged her hard against him, forcing her to feel every inch of the bulge beneath his trousers. "I think not. I think you have no idea what that's like."

She didn't know how to answer and barely even had time to wonder what he was getting at before he ordered, "Pick up the peep-show box and look inside again."

The ever-curious and wicked wanton in her found his demand vastly interesting. The well-bred lady in her recoiled. "Why?"

"Because I told you to. You're my wife. And wives in England obey their husbands without question if they know what's good for them."

The implied threat sent a shiver along her spine. "I'm only your pretend wife."

"Funny how you only notice that when it suits you." When she stiffened, he softened his tone. "Just do it, all right? Think of it as a game, an erotic game. You like playing erotic games, don't you?"

Not when you're acting so strangely, she nearly said. Then he pressed a hot, openmouthed kiss to her neck, and all her objections melted into nothing.

"Look in the box, Abby," he coaxed again.

Through her haze she saw him thrust it into her hand as if he didn't trust her to pick it up herself. With a sigh, she grabbed it, then lifted it so she could look inside.

"Good girl." He flexed his fingers on her bare belly. "Now tell me what you see. Start at the left and describe everything."

Feeling the blood rush into her cheeks once more, she said in a whisper, "There's a woman st-standing by a curtain."

"And how is she dressed?"

"She isn't," she said in a small voice.

He feathered kisses over her jaw as if to reward her for her honesty. "Go on. What's she doing?"

"You already know what she's doing," she accused him.

"Yes. But tell me anyway." He sucked her earlobe. "It's a game, remember? And you do like games."

Why did he keep saying that? "She's . . . well . . . got a man standing behind her holding her—"

"Like I'm holding you."

She blinked. "Yes. Exactly."

"And what is she doing with the man?"

Now that she was catching on to the "game," a perverse excitement blew through her. "She's pressing the man's hand to her breast."

"Show me."

Abby hesitated, but his gruff command hung like a tantalizing promise in the air. If she just played the thunder god's game, she could ride the wind, tame the storm. She caught his hand and pulled it to her own breast, then pressed it there. "Like this."

With a growl of approval, he began to fondle her, palming her breast, teasing the nipple, and in general making her crazy. His caresses dragged the breath from her lungs, leaving her gasping and craving his mouth on hers.

She turned away from the box to seek his lips, but he merely moved his head to the other side of her neck and began to rain kisses on her sensitized skin.

"Go on," he rasped against her ear. "Keep talking. What about the woman in the middle? What is she doing?"

"Clearly you've looked in this box more than once," she said, faintly annoyed. "You seem to have the entire picture memorized."

He laughed harshly. "Pretty much. Even a serious-minded man has to have some pleasures." His fingers tweaked her nipple just enough to get her attention. "Tell me what's in the middle, Abby."

With a gasp, she returned her gaze to the image inside. "The woman is sprawled in an armchair with her gown open. The chair has gilded legs and—"

He nipped at her ear. "I don't care what the chair looks like. Describe the woman."

"She's sitting in it with her legs parted, that's all. And there's a . . . black pillow or something between them."

A strangled laugh escaped him. "It's not a pillow. Look closer."

Perplexed, she shifted the box to catch the light better. "All right, so the pillow is hairy, but . . . oh . . ." A blush spread over her cheeks. "You're right—it's not a pillow."

"No. It's a man's head."

Curiosity got the better of her. "What's he doing?"

His fingers had stilled on her breast. "You tell me," he said in that rumbling tone that always sent the butterflies to knocking around inside her.

"I . . . I suppose he's . . . kissing her."

"Where?"

"You know where," she whispered.

This time he took pity on her and put his own hand where he wanted it—down beneath her chemise, which still covered her below the waist, to rest right on top of the curls clustered between her thighs. "Here?" he asked huskily.

Her mouth was too dry for speech. All she could manage was a nod.

His palm cupped her there, rubbing her and making her collapse against him, weak-kneed. His other hand returned to fondling her breast, and she thought she'd died and ascended right into the clouds. It felt so delicious, so very delicious to have his hands on her, all over her. Then he dragged one finger up to part her curls and toy with a certain sensitive spot so adroitly that she moaned and swiveled her hips forward against his teasing hand, wanting more, needing more.

"Would you like me to kiss you there?" he said hoarsely. "Like in the picture?"

That seemed wicked in the extreme, yet the thought of having his mouth on her heated flesh . . . "I-I don't know," she admitted.

Apparently that was answer enough, because he slipped from between her and the desk to move in front of her. Setting the box aside, he stripped her chemise completely off. Then he nudged her legs apart and knelt between them atop her rumpled clothing.

A wave of expectation swept through her when he parted her curls with an impatience that seemed to rival her own.

As he stared at the tender flesh he'd exposed, a hint of uncertainty crossed his face. "I was right, wasn't I? Your reason for finding out if I really hated children was to see if there was any hope of making this marriage permanent?"

She wanted to deny it, but it was hard to lie to a man who was eyeing one's private parts as possessively as the thunder god surveying his domain. When she didn't answer, he glanced up and read her answer in her face.

Thunderclouds rolled over his face. "I thought so."

She opened her mouth to explain, to make him see that a marriage between them could work. But then he kissed her right there between her legs, and her mind went blank.

Oh, dear heaven. This wasn't a kiss at all. It was . . . it was . . .

Erotic. Amazing. And thoroughly maddening. His tongue did things she'd never dreamed a tongue could do. Her eyes slid closed as she reached for his head, threading her fingers through silky hair to hold him closer.

"Do you like that, Abby?" he drew back enough to growl. "Does it please you?"

"Yes . . . oh . . . yes."

With a grunt of satisfaction, he returned to laving her with his tongue, mouthing her so expertly she writhed and bucked and sighed. With his talented teeth and tongue and lips, he dragged her forward toward her pleasure, like the wind kicking up, blowing all before it, pushing everything into flight. Each caress of his clever mouth swept her farther and faster and higher until she started to leave the ground, started to soar . . .

He jerked back abruptly. Shaking off her convulsive grip on his head, he rose to his feet. She cried a protest as she crashed to earth without ever taking flight.

"Spencer, please . . ." she whimpered, but though his eyes blazed with his own desire and his trousers bulged, he ignored her plea. As she reached mindlessly for him, he backed toward the door, his tortured expression sounding the death knell to all her hopes.

Anger thundered in his voice. "Now you really do know what it's like to have heaven dangled just beyond your reach."

Pain sliced through her. He'd purposely brought her to the brink of fulfillment. Then left her here with no intention of finishing it. "Why are you . . . doing this?" she whispered, every inch of her body still throbbing with unmet need. "Because . . . because I went against your wishes today?"

With a ragged curse, he reached behind him to close one fist around the doorknob. "I told you nothing would come of our sham marriage. I told you I didn't want to make it real, but you persisted with all your games." The snick of his unlocking the door echoed in the intimate room. "Well, I can play games, too. So the next time you decide to scent my cravats or bring hordes of children here or tease me into 'playing,' remember that. If you do any of it again, I swear I'll give you what you're asking for and take you to bed."

A long, shuddering breath rocked his rigid frame. "But it will change nothing, do you hear? Once I find Nat, you're returning to America, ruined or not." He raked her with a blatantly needy glance. "Or if you really want to stay in London, I'll happily set you up in a nice house in Chelsea as my mistress." His voice was storm wrapped in ice, as cold and unyielding as a winter tempest. "But I will never make you Lady Ravenswood in truth. Do you understand me?"

Shocked by the fury emanating from him, she could only nod.

"Good." Jerking open the door, he stalked out and slammed it closed behind him.

For a moment, all she could do was stare after him, feeling battered and tossed by a whirlwind of emotions—thwarted desire . . . shock . . . despair.

And finally anger as it dawned on her what he'd done. He'd brought her in here purposely to tempt and tease her before dashing all her hopes with his curt withdrawal and bitter words.

Her gaze fell on the peep-show box, and her anger surged higher. Him and his temptations—why had she ever thought she might want to stay married to the heartless beast? With a curse, she snatched up the box and hurled it against the door.

Tears burned her eyes, but she fought them back as she stormed about the room, snatching up clothes. He could only stomach having her in his life when it suited his purposes, when he controlled everything and could rid himself of her whenever he pleased. He'd actually offered to make her his mistress. His *mistress,* mind you!

She jerked her chemise on over her head, then yanked her gown up and shoved her hands through the sleeves. Oh, yes, he would stoop to make her his mistress and have her share his bed, but God forbid she should encroach upon his career or his plans for the future by wanting . . . by wanting . . .

By wanting to be his.

She lost the battle with her tears. Collapsing on the floor, she let the sobs pour from her without restraint. She could never be his—the wretch had made that perfectly clear. All this time she'd misunderstood everything. She'd thought that his willingness to oblige her, his thoughtful attentions, and yes, his sweet kisses and caresses had meant he really was the wonderful gentleman she'd known in America.

But there was no wonderful gentleman—there was just the officious viscount. Yes, he desired her, but that was all. He wanted only her body, not herself. Nothing had changed from when she'd first come here—she was still the naive American fool with no connections to speak of, too unsuitable to be the wife of the wealthy and important undersecretary of England's blessed Home Office.

She scrubbed at her tears angrily with her fists, furious at herself for mourning the loss of him when he'd never been hers in the first place. If he'd only given her time, a chance to prove herself . . .

No, he was too sure of what he wanted for that. But that

didn't mean she couldn't still prove herself. She could do it just to show him that she could. And rub his nose in it.

Drying her eyes on her sleeve, she stared blindly at the fire. Why not? Why not get a bit of revenge on him for his coldness? She would become the quintessential English lady. She'd go to that May Day fête and meet the king, as coolly elegant as any lady there. She'd make him regret that he hadn't snatched her up when he had the chance. And when he finally came begging, she'd refuse him flatly.

Just see how he liked that.

Spencer sank against the wall outside his study. Her sobs had subsided, thank God, long after they'd deflated his rampant erection. Nothing quelled a man's lust like the sound of a woman's tears, especially when they belonged to a woman he desired with uncommon desperation.

He shouldn't have stayed here to listen. He should have headed straight to the privacy of his bedchamber to deal with the problem of his arousal. But it had seemed patently unfair to find his own satisfaction after leaving her with none, since she didn't have the sophistication to know how to pleasure herself.

Instead he'd stood motionless in the dimly lit hall while she'd vented her temper by throwing things. And then he'd stayed to punish himself, to listen to her heart-wrenching sobs and endure every stab of pain they inflicted.

Because he deserved to share her misery after what he'd done.

Devil take it, he should never have let his temper get the better of him. He'd gone too far. But after that dinner from hell where he'd seen just how sweet life with her could be if not for his inability to sire children, he'd snapped. If he hadn't done something, she would have kept on with her tactics designed to bring him to heel.

At least one good thing would come of this. She would hate him now. And that was just as well. He could handle her hatred better than he could handle her hopeful looks and her none-too-subtle attempts to tempt him. Just knowing she was in his house was more temptation than he could stand—he didn't need her actively seeking to seduce him. Or worse yet, to coax him into keeping her.

You should tell her the truth. Have it out. That would squelch her hopes at once.

Perhaps. Or she might protest that his inability to sire children didn't matter. She might even really believe it didn't. Until later, after he'd been lulled into giving her his heart and soul. Then it would be just like with Father and Dora—years of not having her own children would wear on her until she destroyed the marriage in her discontent. Leaving him alone again.

No, better not to risk that.

McFee appeared at the other end of the hall. When he spotted Spencer, he headed toward him with purposeful steps. Spencer pushed away from the wall and strode to meet his butler, relieved to have some household nonsense to take his mind off Abby.

"One of the runners is here with news of your brother, my lord," McFee said without preamble. "Shall I bring him to your study?"

"No!" Spencer dragged one hand through his hair. "No, Abby is in there and doesn't wish to be disturbed. I'll meet with him in the front drawing room."

"Very good, my lord." McFee glanced toward the study door. "Should I fetch Mrs. Graham to attend her ladyship?"

His stomach roiled at the thought of that harridan finding her darling mistress cursing Spencer's name, but it occurred to him that Abby might have trouble dressing herself. "That would probably be a good idea," he said wearily.

"As you wish." But McFee remained standing there, looking distinctly uncomfortable. He tugged at his cravat and cleared his throat. "I'm not sure if I should presume to tell you—"

"You shouldn't," Spencer broke in.

McFee colored, but went on. "Forgive me for my impertinence, but I thought you might wish to know . . . that is . . . well, sir, you are missing some items of clothing."

That brought Spencer up short. Glancing down at his shirt and trousers, he stifled a curse. Good God, she had him so scattered he hadn't even noticed his state of undress.

"Thank you, McFee. Put the man in the drawing room, and I'll . . ." He paused. He could hardly go back in his study to fetch his clothes. "I'll be there as soon as I've stopped in my room for fresh attire."

"Of course, my lord."

True to his profession, McFee walked off without daring to speculate on why his master was gadding about so improperly clothed or why Spencer couldn't simply put his cravat, waistcoat, and coat back on.

Thank God for discreet servants. At least there was one place where his commands were never questioned. God knew his wife questioned them often enough.

He groaned as he climbed the stairs. His *wife*. Thinking of her like that was what had landed him in trouble in the first place. She would never have taken the notion to make their marriage a real one if he hadn't succumbed to her sweet offer that they "play" in his bedchamber.

So unless he wanted her to become his wife in truth, he mustn't think of her as one. He must think of her as a guest, nothing more, who just happened to be using his name at the moment. Never mind that he wanted to seduce her every chance he got. Never mind that her presiding over his table felt natural and right.

She was not his wife and never could be—why couldn't he get that through his thick skull?

Because she dogged him everywhere. Even now in his room, as he washed her scent off his face and hands, he could taste her, musky and female, on his tongue. He could even still feel her flesh quiver beneath his mouth. She'd trembled as she'd obeyed his stern demands, yet her excitement had been evident in her rapid breaths and hot sighs. And that had fired his own excitement.

He'd wanted so badly just to thrust himself deep inside her, join her to him irrevocably. He'd only resisted the urge by remembering the yearning in her face when she'd held that damned baby in her arms. The yearning he could never satisfy.

With a curse, he donned fresh clothing. Then he went to meet the runner, praying that there was news this time. The sooner he brought Nat home and banished that alluring female from his life, the better.

As Spencer entered the drawing room, a gangly young man with penetrating eyes and a cowlick rose to give Spencer a deep bow. "Good evening, my lord. I'm sorry to call so late, but I thought you'd wish to have this news as soon as possible."

"Of course." Spencer gestured toward the man's chair, and the runner resumed his seat. Spencer was too restless to sit, but instead went to pace before the fire, clasping his hands together behind his back. "So have you found him?"

"Er . . . no, not yet. But we've made a rather surprising discovery. He didn't flee to the Continent, as we expected."

Spencer shot the man a surprised glance. "That was always his refuge before."

"We have three witnesses who saw him on the coaching road headed north. Unfortunately, the trail grows cold in Derbyshire. Our last news of him is from when he bought a horse in Derby. He must have left the main road there, which will make him harder to track, but not impossible. Somebody is sure to have seen him or given him shelter. Unless he has friends in that vicinity whose direction you could give us."

"He has no northern friends that I know of. And if it's gaming he's looking for, the best places for that outside of London are in the south of England."

"Precisely, my lord. That's why it took us so long to find his direction. None of us expected him to go that way, so it was the last route we explored." The runner leaned forward. "But I have a theory about why he's there."

"Oh?"

"As you'd requested, we traced his steps in the days before his disappearance. We discovered that he had meetings with three captains of industry. He met each one at a private room in a hotel. Unfortunately, none of the three is in the city at the moment for us to question. We're trying to locate them. But one of them is a resident of York."

"To the north."

"Exactly. And Derby is on the way to York."

Spencer rubbed his chin as he stared into the fire. Captains of industry. Could Nat have taken the dowry to use in building up Dr. Mercer's company? But why? If that had been the purpose, he'd have been better off asking Spencer just to invest the money. Spencer had already agreed to that, and without being entangled in marriage.

Which meant Nat probably wasn't using the funds for any legitimate enterprise, damn his hide. The idiot might as well bet the money on a hand of cards.

Spencer was going to kill him. *When* he found him.

"I would suggest," the runner went on, "that men be sent to the estates of all three gentlemen. Someone might have seen him thereabouts, and we might pick up the trail."

"Excellent idea. Follow it out. And keep me informed. I want to hear the second he is located, understood?"

"Certainly, my lord." The runner rose, obviously aware he

was being dismissed. "It won't be much longer, I warrant."

It better not be, Spencer thought as he ushered the man out. Because if Abby remained in his house much longer, he would go stark raving mad.

Chapter 17

Loyal English servants can only pray that the present fascination with French culture will eventually wane.

Suggestions for the Stoic Servant

A week and a day after her disastrous encounter with Spencer in his study, Abby paced Lady Tyndale's drawing room with a very unladylike impatience. But she couldn't help it. Mr. McFee had said to pick up Lady Tyndale and Evelina at ten A.M., and it was already half past. Abby refused to be late to Lady Brumley's breakfast, not with her ladyship presenting Heaven's Scent to all her friends.

When Abby's stomach growled, she ignored it. Though she'd been awake since eight, she'd had so much to do to prepare that she hadn't even munched some toast. But there'd be food at the breakfast.

Lady Tyndale breezed in, followed closely by Evelina. "Ah, there you are, my dear. It's so good of you to include us in your party while our carriage is being repaired."

Abby stifled a smile. Apparently the mythical Tyndale carriage had been in repair so long it could have been remade thrice over. Which was probably why Spencer offered the use of his whenever possible. "We'd best go. We don't have much time."

239

Though Lady Tyndale and Evelina looked perplexed, they dutifully followed Abby out to the carriage. Before climbing in, Lady Tyndale spoke privately to the coachman, no doubt giving him her usual cautions about not driving too fast.

Once they were all inside, Lady Tyndale asked, "Where's his lordship?"

"We have to pick him up at the Home Office." Abby ordered the driver to go on. "Can you believe he's working on a Saturday?"

Evelina laughed. "I suspect he merely wanted to avoid accompanying Mama and me on our errands before the breakfast this morning."

"Errands?" Abby asked.

"Since we had two urgent errands to run regarding the wedding, his lordship said we could use the carriage. He did tell you, didn't he?"

"Yes, of course." Abby wasn't about to reveal that Spencer avoided talking to her whenever possible these days. "As long as we're not late to the breakfast—"

"There's plenty of time," Lady Tyndale put in. "It doesn't even start until two."

Abby blinked. "What? Are you sure?"

Evelina pulled something from her reticule and handed it to Abby. "It says so here on the invitation."

Abby stared at the gilded card. She hadn't actually seen the invitation. Spencer had received it long before she'd even arrived in London, but when she'd been told to pick up the ladies at ten, she'd assumed . . .

"You did know, didn't you?" With an obnoxious titter, Lady Tyndale nudged her daughter. "The poor child probably thought we were going right there. As if anybody would have a breakfast at eleven. Who would come?"

Abby hated that titter of Lady Tyndale's. She hated being called "the poor child." Most of all, she hated that despite her efforts, Lady Tyndale still regarded her as a vulgar foreigner. Abby refused to suffer any more of the woman's condescending remarks.

"Don't be silly." Abby adopted the cool viscountess tone she'd been using on Spencer. "I knew it was this afternoon. I just wasn't certain of the time."

Evelina, always more perceptive than her mother, looked unconvinced. "You did eat something before you left, didn't you?"

"Of course. Who would wait to eat until so late?" *A vulgar foreigner, that's who.*

Somehow in the midst of Clara's instructions on the habits of polite society, she'd neglected to mention that breakfast affairs took place mid-afternoon. Pray heaven these wedding errands included visiting bakeries about a cake.

No such luck. First they called on the vicar to discuss the ceremony. He offered them tea and nothing else. After all, who would need to eat so early? Then they went to the dressmaker—conveniently located nowhere near a pastry shop— for the fitting of Evelina's gown.

After the first hour, her hunger grew unpleasant. After the second, it became annoying. By the end of the third, it was downright overwhelming. Only Lady Tyndale's patronizing smiles kept her from begging them to accost a strawberry vendor.

By the time the three of them climbed into the carriage outside the dressmaker's, Abby wondered just how long a person could go without food, anyway.

"Thank heavens that's done," Evelina said as they settled into their seats. "We can head for Lady Brumley's now."

"It's too early," her mother protested. "It's just half-past one. We might have time to visit the milliner about your veil. Not a soul will be at the breakfast before three."

Three! "But we still have to pick up Spencer," Abby said hastily, "so we might as well go on." Which would take them another half an hour. Heavenly day.

Thankfully Lady Tyndale gave in. Unfortunately, it was now Spencer's turn to delay them. They waited on him half an hour before he finally hurried down the steps to the carriage.

"Good afternoon, ladies," he said as he got in. Ordering the coachman on, he took his seat beside Abby. "Sorry to keep you waiting, but I didn't expect you so early."

"Your wife was concerned we might be late to the breakfast," Lady Tyndale complained before Abby could answer. "I told her no one shows up at these things on time, but she insisted that we come on."

Abby forced a smile for Spencer's benefit. "I merely didn't want to insult Lady Brumley." Or starve. But she'd crawl on her knees over hot coals before she'd admit her error to *him*. It had taken her a week to achieve her air of serene sophistication—she wasn't about to ruin it now.

Lady Tyndale snorted. "The marchioness would not be insulted, I assure you, my dear. Really, you Americans have such strange ideas."

As Abby flashed Lady Tyndale a cool smile and searched for the perfect "elegant" phrase to change the subject, Evelina said quickly, "Lord Ravenswood, were you able to get much work done?"

He seized on the topic with apparent relief. "Yes. Quite a bit actually. When no one is there, I get more done than usual."

"Poor man, you work far too hard." Lady Tyndale smiled thinly at Abby. "I swear your husband is always hastening off to the office or the House of Lords or something."

Her unspoken criticism was readily apparent. Newly married gentlemen weren't supposed to work so hard. Wives were supposed to make their homes so cozy that they felt no need to rush off on weekends.

"I enjoy working," Spencer said tightly. "There's much to do before Parliament is out of session."

That effectively ended Lady Tyndale's attempts to condescend to Abby in front of her husband. An uncomfortable silence fell over the carriage.

Restlessly, Spencer shifted his position on the seat beside her. When he settled again, one of his knees was thrust up against hers. She shot him a veiled glance.

He wore the same brooding scowl he'd worn increasingly in the past week, but otherwise, he looked good enough to eat. Literally. That ruby cravat pin could be a cherry floating in a sea of whipped cream . . . sweetened whipped cream that frothed above an expanse of white marzipan studded with peeled almonds . . .

Not almonds. Buttons, for heaven's sake, they were inedible *buttons* on his white marcella waistcoat. She jerked her gaze away. If she didn't eat soon, she might devour them anyway, just to feel something go down her throat other than saliva.

Of course, then he'd have no buttons and his waistcoat would pop open to reveal the thin shirt beneath, a coating of white icing that she could lick off his broad chest . . .

Dear heaven, hunger was making her delirious. And now Evelina was staring at her undoubtedly flushed cheeks.

The young woman smiled. "Doesn't your wife look lovely today?" she asked Spencer.

He cast Abby a cursory glance. "Yes. She does indeed."

Annoyance flickered in Evelina's eyes. "I think that turban looks so elegant on you," she told Abby. "Is that a new purchase?"

Abby nodded, grateful for the distraction from her gnawing starvation. "Lady Brumley helped me pick it out, actually." She patted the white satin. "Since my hair doesn't take a curl well, I thought this would be a good compromise."

"It's exquisite. Indeed, your whole ensemble is very fashionable."

"Thank you." When out of the corner of her eye, she saw Spencer's scowl deepen, she added, "Mr. McFee said I look quite the Englishwoman. What do you think, my lord?"

Shifting to stare out the window, he growled, "He's right. You look, act, and sound 'quite the Englishwoman.'"

His sharp-edged tone exasperated her. What did the wretched man want from her anyway? She'd done exactly as he'd asked this past week. She'd relinquished her hopes for any future with him and kept their association on a cordial plane. Yet that hadn't seemed to please him—he'd been as surly as a goat these past two days.

Could her new refinement already be affecting him? Perhaps he began to regret his eagerness to rid himself of her. The idea appealed to her enormously.

Well, he'd seen nothing yet. Clara had fully prepared Abby for the rules, habits, and peculiar customs of fashionable society. Although Spencer had accompanied Abby to a few private dinners, he'd had no chance to see her behavior at a large social affair. She was determined to surprise him with her social prowess.

When they arrived at Lady Brumley's, Abby steadied her nerves. This was it—the real test of what she'd learned. If she navigated this successfully, she could surely handle meeting the king at the May Day fête.

Now if only she could ignore her acute hunger a few moments longer. There was probably some horrible social protocol that prevented one from mowing down people on the way to filling one's belly. But dear heaven, the smells of food wafting to her from Lady Brumley's gardens where they were headed were positively delicious.

Thankfully, the moment they strode onto the lawns, Abby spotted Clara standing alone by a hawthorn bush. Good—she could be herself with Clara and confess to her starvation. She could finally *eat*. "Excuse me," she told her companions. "I see my friend over there. I'll just go say hello."

Lady Tyndale and Evelina gave polite nods as she hurried off, but to her annoyance Spencer fell into step beside her. Why must he choose *now* to breach their cordial wall of distance?

"I truly am sorry I kept you waiting," he said in a low rumble. "I didn't think about the fact that you might want to be here on time."

"Don't be silly—it was no problem at all." She had to get rid of him. She refused to let him see her attack the eatables like a ravenous dog. "You don't have to squire me around, you know. I'll be fine."

Her less-than-subtle hint was completely lost on him. He scowled. "You must be really annoyed at me if you're trying to run me off."

"I'm not annoyed, Spencer." "Annoyed" didn't begin to describe how she felt at the moment. "Desperate" was closer. She fought to modulate her voice as Clara had taught her. "A lady is never annoyed. It's not fashionable."

Oh, how she hated that word. *Fashionable.* The very sound of it was vacuous. Especially since only a fear of being *un*-fashionable was keeping her hungry just now.

Fortunately, Clara spotted them and came to meet them. But they'd barely exchanged greetings before Spencer grumbled, "Would you please tell Abby that Lady Brumley probably didn't even notice that we're late?"

Clara laughed. "Lateness is fashionable, Abby."

There was that nasty word again. "I realize that." Abby cast a longing look at the food tables. "It's my husband who continues to harp on the subject."

"You won't even look at me, for God's sake," Spencer retorted. "I know you're angry."

"Why would I be angry?" Abby said sweetly.

"You know why, damn it." A muscle twitched in his jaw. "Because I kept you waiting while I finished up at the Home Office. Well, I do have duties and responsibilities, Abby."

"No one said you didn't."

"You went into the office on Saturday, Lord Ravenswood?" Clara put in. "Parliament doesn't even have sessions on Saturday."

Abby's hold on her temper was slipping, especially since Spencer would not *go away.* "He wasn't interested in working, I assure you. He simply wanted to avoid trundling about town with Lady Tyndale. He left that to me to do. Of course, he didn't bother to warn me about it."

His scowl deepened. "I know I must have said something—"

"You didn't, believe me. I would have remembered."

When Clara burst into laughter, they turned twin glares on her.

Her eyes were twinkling. "What a convincing performance. No one will doubt for a second that you're married. You both play the role to perfection."

That effectively ended the discussion and brought Abby to her senses. Viscountesses did not publicly argue with their husbands. She couldn't believe she'd allowed him to provoke her that far. She wouldn't succumb again, no matter how hungry she got.

Since Lord Surly Britches now had to find something else to vent his general grumpiness on, he turned to survey the grounds. "What in God's name is all this mess anyway? Did a linen draper spill his goods atop Lady Brumley's trees?"

Irritated by the man's steady refusal to leave, Abby obliged him with a cursory look at their surroundings. Then she took another. What in the world—

Lengths of white gauze had been bunched and draped over branches of trees to resemble great puffs of cotton. Or maybe clouds?

Eyes narrowing, she surveyed the overburdened tables, each of which sported angels crafted of pastry, napkins folded

to resemble wings, and huge marzipan centerpieces that
looked suspiciously like pearly gates. Awareness dawned.

"It's paradise, Spencer," Abby said.

He looked skeptical. "If this is paradise, I prefer purgatory."

"No, no, I mean the decor. The gauze in the trees is meant
to be clouds and the angels and things . . . It all represents
paradise. Heaven."

"Ah. That would explain the harpists."

There were harpists? Abby glanced about in surprise to
find nine of them in groups of three, playing in different parts
of the garden. She didn't think she'd ever seen more than two
harpists in one place in her life.

"It's because of Abby's perfume, you know," Clara explained. "Because of Heaven's Scent."

"That's precisely why I didn't want to be late," Abby said
coolly. "Lady Brumley is presenting my scent to all her
friends today."

"I realize that," Spencer said. "I'm not entirely oblivious. I
just thought you were cranky because I delayed us. I'm sure
you haven't eaten since breakfast, and it's nearly three now."

Abby finally admitted defeat. It was either that or lunge
wildly for the food tables. "I haven't eaten at all today,
Spencer."

"What?" Spencer exclaimed. "Whyever not?"

"Speaking of oblivious . . ." Clara muttered under her
breath.

All the irritation building in Abby since she'd discovered
her error now exploded. "This is a breakfast, remember? Nobody bothered to tell me that breakfast comes in the afternoon for the 'fashionable.' I thought it started at eleven. And
by the time I figured out that it didn't, I was already trapped
into running errands with Lady Tyndale."

"Good Lord, you must be starving," Clara said.

Abby gave her friend a wan smile. "I've passed beyond starving into a state of delirium—those tables over there look more like paradise by the moment."

"What are you waiting for, Lord Ravenswood?" Clara said as Spencer stood there agape. "Go fetch your poor wife some food, for pity's sake."

"I'm sorry, Abby, I didn't realize . . ."

Clara gave Spencer a little shove. "*Now*. Before she expires on the spot."

"Thank you," Abby murmured as Spencer hurried off.

"You should have said something sooner. I would never have guessed from the way you were acting that you were starving."

Good. At least she'd managed to maintain her viscountess manner to some extent. "I considered making a mad dash for the food myself," she confided in her friend. "But I didn't want Spencer to see."

"Why not?"

"I was hoping to come out of this with my dignity."

Clara laughed. "Who needs dignity when one can have a guilt-ridden husband catering to one's every need?" She gestured to where Spencer prowled the tables, deflecting anybody who tried to engage him in conversation. "Look at him scurrying about. He knows you can hold this over his head forever."

"Or at least until Parliament is out of session," Abby said tightly.

Clara searched her face. "He might surprise you. Anyone can see that you two belong together. Even Morgan says so."

Spencer was returning, so Abby stifled her retort, but she couldn't stifle her irritation at Clara's misguided matchmaking. Even if Spencer decided she was worthy of him after all, she would never accept such condescension. She wasn't that desperate.

But it was hard to maintain her convictions when he was

being this sweet. He handed her a fork and a plate so over-loaded with assorted dishes that she wondered how he'd managed to pile so much on there so quickly.

He hadn't even filled a plate for himself. Then again, Lord Perfect had probably thought to eat before he left the house.

"Go on," he said with a faint smile. "Don't wait for me, for God's sake."

She took him at his word. Seizing on the one recognizable item—a meat pie—she ate a bite and sighed. Pure bliss. But then anything edible would taste like bliss just now.

"I brought you the *homards a gratin*, the *gelinotte*, *les épinards à l'essence*, and that *la veau en croute* you're eating. I hope that's all right."

"It's fine," she mumbled between bites.

"You do know what all of that means, don't you?" he persisted.

She had no clue, but she nodded as she swallowed the last bite of *la veau*. The Viscountess Ravenswood must be completely at home with the French language, after all. She devoured the green blob, then went to work on the bony, sauce-colored blob she was fairly certain was some kind of small fowl.

Spencer's eyes narrowed on her. "I suppose the English penchant for all things French must seem strange to you."

"Not at all," she said between bites of the creamy, fishy-tasting stuff.

All right, so she did think Englishmen crazy for calling roast ham *le jambon à la broche* and pouring a lot of sauces over perfectly good joints of beef and mutton just to make them "French." Abby Mercer would have voiced her opinion. The Viscountess Ravenswood, however, must take such fashionable idiocy in stride.

As if reading her mind, Spencer went on, watching her closely as he spoke. "Some might consider it odd that we English persist in glorifying French culture, when we just finished fighting a war with France. Some might even say it appears that the French won the war after all."

Simply because people in polite society used French phrases instead of good English ones? Or insisted upon patronizing French dressmakers and hiring French chefs instead of using the perfectly acceptable talents of their countrymen? No, indeed. Why would anyone say that?

With her intent gaze on Abby, Clara chimed in. "Then there's the way fashionable ladies always insist on hiring French lady's maids. And if strained finances force the ladies to hire English ones instead, the poor maids must agree to pretend to be French."

"Don't you find that a little silly, Abby?" Spencer prodded.

She dabbed at her mouth with a napkin. Yes. She thought it was ridiculous. But she'd managed to go all week by keeping her real, undoubtedly vulgar, opinions to herself—she wasn't about to ruin all her hard efforts now by voicing them. "French lady's maids are more adept at dressing hair and such, that's all," she countered, trying to guess what a proper Englishwoman might say. "And why would one want to appear to hire the incompetent?"

"Why indeed?" Spencer looked fit to be tied as he glowered at nothing.

With a furtive glance at him, Clara said, "Lord Ravenswood, isn't that the home secretary standing over there under that horse chestnut tree with Lord Liverpool?"

"Yes. And I'd best go speak to him." Taking Abby's empty plate, Spencer strode off, stopping only long enough to drop the plate on a nearby table and take a cup of punch offered by a passing footman.

The second he was out of earshot, Clara murmured, "You know, Abby, you can speak your mind and still be an elegant lady."

"Not around Spencer, I can't. I won't have him looking down on me anymore."

The footman with the punch had reached them, so Clara snagged two cups, handing one to Abby. "But I don't think he does. Despite your husband's seeming seriousness, he's rather progressive for his class. He knows how to accept people for who they are and not what society says they should be."

A lump stuck in her throat. "Except in the case of his pretend wife."

"What do you mean?"

Lifting her cup to her lips, Abby took a quick swallow. "Come on, Clara. Why do you think he resorted to this farce in the first place? Because he didn't want to stay permanently married to a woman like me, and this was the only way he could think of to extricate himself from the situation without a scandal."

As if aware they were talking about him, Spencer glanced their way. When his gaze met hers, he lifted his cup in a silent toast, a faint smile touching his lips.

Deliberately, Abby turned her back on him. "Spencer has made it very clear that the socially inept Abigail Mercer is not the sort of wife he wants. She doesn't have connections and polish and all those things a statesman needs in his mate."

Clara looked startled. "He told you that?"

"He didn't have to. He gave me some nonsense about how his career takes too much time for him to manage a wife at this point in his life. But I knew it was only words. He doesn't want *me*, that's all."

Slanting a curious look at Abby, Clara sipped her punch. "Are you sure?"

"Oh, believe me, I'm as sure as a woman can be." She hadn't forgotten the painful lesson he'd taught her in the study. Whenever she found herself falling under his spell again, she reminded herself of it.

"I don't know, Abby," Clara mused aloud. "A man doesn't

watch a woman as obsessively as Spencer is watching you now unless he desires her."

Abby followed Clara's gaze to where Spencer still stared after her, paying little attention to his companions. His smile had vanished, but his silvery gaze ate her alive, roaming down her body, touching on her lips, her breasts, her belly . . .

The arrogant wretch—he had no right to look at her as if he wanted her when he knew he would never act on it. She tipped up her chin. Fine, let him look. Because he'd never have the chance to touch her again, not after what he'd done to her in his study.

"Half the women here would kill to have their husbands look at them like that, you know," Clara said. "It's plain to see that he wants you."

"Yes, he does. He wants my body—it's the rest of me he's not interested in."

"I don't think that's true. I've known him a long time, and I've never seen him look at anyone like that. It's more than desire, it's . . . it's yearning."

Abby snorted. "Spencer hasn't yearned for anything in his life. He has everything he could possibly want."

"Men can't always say what they yearn for. Oh, they know what they desire, but not what they need. And Lord Ravenswood needs you. I'd wager my life on it."

"Then you'd lose it." Abby wanted to hope, but she didn't dare. Her hopes had been too cruelly dashed before.

"You can't give up on him now." Clara shot her a smile. "And if it truly is just your lack of polish worrying his lordship, you'll overcome that deficiency. You've come so far already."

Abby forced a smile. "Oh, of course. Now that I've learned the language of the fan and how to curtsy to a duke, I can be the perfect viscountess."

"You know what I mean. You're more confident than you were even a week ago. And you fit in. You really do."

"That's kind of you to say, Clara, but we both know I can never really fit in. I don't have connections or wealth—"

"Lord Ravenswood has had ample opportunity to marry a woman with those things, and he hasn't. In fact, you're the first woman he's shown any serious interest in."

Abby opened her mouth to protest, but Clara quickly added, "And don't tell me he had no choice. He could have claimed that you were his mistress or paid to have you packed off on a boat . . . he's got a whole army of police at his command, you know. He could have done with you as he pleased. But he hasn't."

"Because for all his faults, he's an honorable man." Most of the time.

"And because he respects you. If he thought as little of you as you say, why would he have even suggested this pretend marriage?"

She wanted to ignore Clara's remarks, but they gnawed at her as fiercely as her hunger earlier. Although Spencer had offered to make her his mistress in his study, she suspected it had been more of a threat than a real possibility. Why else had he refused to pursue that avenue earlier on?

Clara leaned close. "I know how you can determine if your background matters to him. Go over and join him while he's talking to Sir Robert Peel and Lord Liverpool, men of supreme importance to his career. If Spencer really is ashamed of you, he'll try to head you off when he sees you coming. Or he'll allow you only a few words before he hustles you away. Then you can be certain how he feels about you."

"Yes, and I could also leap in front of a galloping Thoroughbred to see if Spencer deigns to save me, but I'm not going to."

"Coward."

"Refraining from embarrassing myself in front of the prime minister and home secretary of England isn't cowardice. It's sensible."

"Is it any worse than agreeing to meet the king?"

"That's different. I'm being forced into that."

"By your husband, who supposedly is ashamed of you."

"He was forced into it, too. But he made it clear he wasn't happy about the idea."

"Then show him he's wrong about you. Show him you can charm his lofty friends simply by being yourself, not some approximation of an elegant Englishwoman." She eyed Abby speculatively over her cup. "Unless, of course, you don't think you can."

Abby scowled at her friend. Curse Clara for knowing her so well. Abby never could resist a challenge. "If I make a fool of myself, you'll have to answer for it. When Spencer berates me, I'll blame *you*."

Clara smiled smugly. "Fine. I'm not afraid of his lordship. The question is, are you?"

No. But she was afraid of appearing the fool before him again. She was afraid of raising her hopes only to have them dashed once more. And she was terrified of finding out for certain that she was right, that he really held her in complete contempt.

Which meant there was only one thing to do. Meet her fears dead on.

Chapter 18

The more lofty the personage, the more circumspect you must be. You must wait until they initiate any familiarity before you respond in kind.

Suggestions for the Stoic Servant

Spencer's eyes narrowed when he saw Abby head toward him looking so determined. No telling what she was planning. Thanks to his idiotic actions a week ago, her artless expression no longer showed when she was up to mischief.

He sighed. She wouldn't be up to mischief anyway, would she? Not the refined faux Englishwoman she'd become. He hated this new Abby. He hated her distant air and her quiet sophistication, her refusal to say what she thought. Most of all, he hated that she no longer hung on his every word or regarded him with transparent adoration.

Never mind that he had only himself to blame for driving her to treat him so distantly. Like a querulous child wanting what he couldn't have, Spencer wanted the old Abby back. He missed her pert opinions. He missed her teasing, her flirting, her smiles.

She smiled now, too, but without warmth. It was killing him. He'd always thought himself in hell to have her so sweet and tempting beneath his very nose and be unable to act on his need. But that had merely been purgatory. Hell was being

255

deprived of the real Abby, being doomed never again to bask in the light of her attention.

"There you are," Abby said as she approached, wearing her remote smile, the one he loathed. She tucked her gloved hand beneath his arm. "I was just wondering where you'd gone off to, my dear."

The meaningless endearment sliced through him. Ignoring the savage pain, he turned to his companions. "Gentlemen," he said, "I don't believe you've met my wife."

She inclined her head toward them with perfect self-assurance. "It's so good to meet you. My husband has told me much about you both."

"I only hope he didn't make us sound too stuffy," Sir Robert retorted with a wink.

Spencer gritted his teeth. Sir Robert's gallantry toward the fairer sex had never bothered him before, but it bloody well bothered him now.

But Abby warmed to it like a cat stretching in the sun. "Don't worry—Spencer speaks highly of all his fellow statesmen."

"And how are you enjoying our fair city, madam?" Lord Liverpool asked, all supercilious condescension. "I'll wager it's quite different from your colonial towns."

Her smile grew a bit forced, but she didn't rise to the bait. "Having seen so little of London, I honestly don't know. My husband promised to show me the sights, you see, but he hasn't yet had the chance."

"I would imagine not." Sir Robert flashed her a faintly lascivious glance that made Spencer want to throttle him. "Newlyweds generally prefer to engage in more interesting activities at home."

"Oh, yes, we read quite a lot," she said as blithely as an innocent, though her faint blush showed that she knew exactly what the bastard meant. "But I was referring to how hard

Spencer works. He spends so many hours at the Home Office that he hardly has any time for leisure."

"The business of government must go on, Lady Ravenswood," Liverpool said in stern reproof. "Even new husbands cannot thrust their duties aside to engage in frivolity."

Spencer half hoped to see Abby chide the pompous toad the way she'd always chided Spencer for his seriousness.

But she'd grown much too elegant for that. "You're quite right, Lord Liverpool. The weight of the country is on the shoulders of you all, so England must come first."

Liverpool nodded, a little mollified. "Exactly what I'm saying."

"And are you married?" she asked in a conversational tone.

"I was indeed, until my wife died. And I intend to marry again. It's important for a man in my position to project an air of stability to the country."

"Ah. So English statesmen do consider having wives and families important to their careers. I'd been led to believe otherwise."

Her pointed words weren't lost on Spencer, who scowled.

"Of course they're important," Liverpool went on, oblivious to the tension between husband and wife. "As long as a statesman's wife understands her place, that is."

That arrested Abby's attention. "Her 'place,' my lord?"

"As a support and helpmeet to him, of course," Liverpool intoned. "The statesman's wife should put no demands on her husband. His activities in the public sphere place enough on him as it is. She must accept that she will only receive those few attentions he can spare. She must concentrate on easing his way whenever possible."

Sir Robert shot Spencer a glance meant to prod him into stopping Liverpool's idiotic opinions. But Spencer was waiting with bated breath for Abby's response.

She didn't disappoint him. "And if she does make demands on her husband?" Her smile was deceptively sweet. "What then? Should he deny her what she wants?"

Liverpool didn't even see the trap closing in. "Certainly, if her demands interfere with his aims. He must use a firm hand, cut her off before she grows too willful."

"I see," she said noncommittally. But there was no mistaking the mischief creeping over her face.

Hope leaped in Spencer's heart.

"Then you needn't fear for me," she went on. "My husband never hesitates to use a firm hand. Why, only the other day he threatened to have me chained up if I didn't behave."

Spencer nearly crowed aloud. Ah, there it was—the old Abby. Thank God for Liverpool and his crackbrained ideas. Rampant pomposity always brought out the devil in her. "What could I do?" Spencer said, inciting her to further deviltry. "You were being so troublesome."

"Well, it was certainly an effective way to remind me of my 'place.'"

Liverpool blinked, first at her, then at Spencer, clearly unsure whether to believe them or not.

But Sir Robert threw himself eagerly into the spirit of things. "And where were you planning to chain your recalcitrant wife, Ravenswood? Have you a dungeon beneath your town house that none of us know about?"

"I figured I'd put her in the Tower. I'm sure His Majesty wouldn't mind lending me a cell, given the trouble he had with his own wife. What do you think, Liverpool?"

The reference to the late Queen Caroline stymied Liverpool even further, since he'd been one of the men to advocate strict measures regarding her behavior. "Er . . . I . . . I would not advocate chaining, of course, but—"

"Why, the whole lot of you could chain your wives in the Tower when they misbehave." Abby's eyes gleamed with amusement. "I understand it's large enough for it. And that could prove advantageous to me, if I manage to stay out of it myself. Because if enough statesmen chain their wives in the Tower, leaving you gentlemen free to come and go as you please, you might not have to work so hard." She grinned. "And Spencer could finally take me on a tour of the city."

"Lady Ravenswood, I would not condone—" Liverpool began.

Sir Robert erupted into laughter. "She's pulling your leg, old chap. Chaining wives in the Tower indeed. Can't you tell when a woman's joking?"

Thoroughly delighted with his wife, Spencer joined Sir Robert in his laughter.

But Liverpool didn't find the conversation nearly so entertaining. Since he apparently couldn't decide whom to glower at the most fiercely, he settled for glowering at them all.

Belatedly, Spencer attempted to soothe the man's ruffled feathers. "Please excuse my wife, Liverpool. She has a tendency to tease. I did threaten to chain her in the Tower if she didn't behave, but she knows perfectly well I didn't mean it."

"What?" Abby exclaimed in mock disbelief. "I thought sure you were serious. You are always serious. Everybody knows that."

When she graced Spencer with one of her old teasing smiles, he exulted in it. Impulsively, he caught her hand beneath his and squeezed, thrilled by the pretty blush that stained her cheeks. He hadn't made her blush in a week.

"A serious nature is much to be preferred over an impertinent one," Lord Liverpool pronounced, his face as dour as an executioner's.

"Don't be so stodgy," Sir Robert said gamely. "The woman's an American, and everyone knows American women speak their minds."

"Only when Englishmen threaten to put them in their places, sir," Abby quipped.

"You married an English husband," Lord Liverpool cut in. "It might behoove you to remember it the next time you speak so idly, madam."

"Oh, for God's sake, man—" Sir Robert began.

"And you, sir," Liverpool went on, fixing a disapproving gaze on Spencer. "A pity you didn't heed your father's mistake when you chose your own wife."

The insult to Abby cast an instant chill over the conversation. As Spencer watched mortification banish Abby's mischievous smile, an ungovernable anger possessed him.

"My father's mistake was in marrying a woman half his age," he growled, staring Liverpool down. "And as I am not yet in my dotage and my wife is not fresh out of the schoolroom, I fail to see any similarity between his marriage and mine."

Liverpool's frigid smile held his usual contempt. "Ah, yes, I forgot. You went off to school after your father married Lady Dorothea—no doubt you missed hearing about your stepmother's wild escapades, impudent manner, and utterly frivolous character."

"I heard. I also heard that you offered for her before my father did, and she turned you down. Apparently, you only found her character to be frivolous after she proved to be uninterested in *you*."

When Liverpool's lips tightened and he looked as if he might speak again, Spencer went on, "Now if you'll excuse us, gentlemen, my wife and I have friends to seek out."

Settling his hand in the small of Abby's back, he led her off toward the punch table, inwardly seething.

As soon as they were out of earshot, Abby whispered, "Spencer, I'm sorry. I should not have been so frank."

"Nonsense. The man's a pompous ass, always has been."

"But I shouldn't have teased him. It won't happen again, I assure you."

Liverpool's comments were making her retreat into her

new cool manner, and the very thought drove Spencer mad. "You mustn't let that humorless old fool's words affect you. You couldn't have known that he has no sense of humor. Or that the doddering idiot actually believes all that rot about a woman's place."

"I gather you don't much like his lordship."

He gazed down at her still ashen features. "I don't like any man who insults you. If he'd been anyone else, I would have called him out for it."

Her eyes went wide. "Don't be silly—you would have done no such thing."

"No man insults my wife with impunity."

Shifting her gaze across the lawn, she said in a small voice, "So I suppose what he said was true. All that stuff about your stepmother being impudent and frivolous."

Spencer stiffened. Devil take Liverpool for raising such questions in her head.

They'd reached the punch table. As Spencer took a cup and filled it, he glanced at the guests nearby, but they were all engrossed in conversations. Handing Abby the cup, he filled one for himself and lowered his voice. "For the most part it's true. Then again, Lady Dorothea was only twenty when she married my father, and plenty of women are frivolous at that age."

"Twenty?" she exclaimed. "How old was your father?"

"Forty-eight. He married her about two years after Mother died bearing Nat."

"That's why Lord Liverpool called the marriage a mistake?"

Spencer drew her away from the others. "Dora was . . . lively and youthful, probably too much so for Father. She wanted constant attention, and Father couldn't give it to her."

"That must have been very hard for her."

"I suppose. She hid it well, at least at first. She tried to mother all of us and outrageously spoiled Nat, who was only a baby. Even my older brother, Theo, who was still alive at that point and at school, got her lavish attention when he was home."

"So you liked her?"

"Not at the beginning, but that wasn't her fault." He stared down into his punch glass. "I was at a difficult age. Ten-year-old boys aren't very amenable to new mothers. I resented her, but she didn't seem to mind. She used to laugh and call me 'His Little Highness.'" He shot Abby a rueful smile. "I suppose I was overly serious even then."

Abby didn't smile. "You'd just lost your mother two years before, Spencer. Any child would be serious under such circumstances."

Her sympathy crept inside to warm that aching spot in his heart reserved for memories of his stepmother. Leaning back against the tree, Spencer sipped his punch. "Anyway, I grew to love her almost as much as I had my own mother. The trouble was, she wanted her own babies, and Father refused to give them to her. He said he already had three sons. Apparently when he'd offered for her, it was under the condition that she relinquish any hope of having her own children with him. She must have married him with the intention of changing his mind later, for she pressed him about it through the years. He always steadfastly refused."

"But they shared a bed?" Abby asked, clearly perplexed.

"Of course. I suppose he merely took precautions." He stared off across the lawn, his face rigid. "Anyway, matters began to deteriorate. Toward the end, all they did was argue about her desire to have children. Fortunately, I wasn't home much. I went off to school at twelve. When I returned home and England was heading off to fight Napoleon again, I begged Father to buy me a commission in the army so I could escape watching Dora and Father destroy each other. I wasn't the heir at that point, so he readily agreed."

"How old were you?"

"Eighteen. Two years later, once Nat started school and Theo was sowing his wild oats in London, Dora was left alone with Father." He gave a ragged sigh. "I suppose she couldn't take it anymore. She started running wild, behaving outrageously, flirting with other men. When none of that swayed Father, she ran off to Italy with some count."

"Your father must have been devastated," Abby said, her face rapt with pity.

"I don't know. I was at war. But according to Nat, Father didn't care. He cared more when Theo died in some idiotic brawl in a gaming hell a few years later. Nat finished school and followed in Theo's reckless footsteps. And Father—" He sucked in a heavy breath. "Father took pneumonia and died a few months after Theo."

"Did your stepmother return after his death?"

He shook his head. "Nat receives the occasional letter from her. I . . . um . . . wouldn't answer the ones she sent me, so she stopped writing me. But Nat says she married the count after Father's death, and they have several children. Which is all she ever wanted." Her own children, not those of some other woman. That's what Abby would want, too. The thought punched pain through his chest. "So there you have it. The sordid tale of my stepmother and why she was completely unsuitable for my father."

"As I am for you," she said softly.

His head shot up. "I didn't say that."

"Lord Liverpool did."

"He's an idiot."

"Is he?" she asked, her eyes searching his.

Suddenly a mad chiming sounded a few yards from them, making them both swing around to see what was going on.

Lady Brumley stood in the midst of the lawn, surrounded by a coterie of footmen ringing bells. In keeping with the party's theme, she wore white, and she'd actually abandoned her ship headdresses for a golden halo, of all things. Spencer rolled his eyes.

When she had everyone's attention, she gestured to the footmen to stop ringing. More footmen lined up behind her, carrying either trays that held glasses of champagne or baskets full of ribbon-accented bottles.

The marchioness scanned the crowd until she caught sight of Abby. "Ah, there you are, my dear." She gestured for Abby to join her. "I want you by my side for the announcement."

With a blush, Abby handed Spencer her punch glass and hurried over to stand next to Lady Brumley. Spencer drained his punch and set both glasses down on the nearby table. This should be interesting.

"Now then, my friends," Lady Brumley began. "I have a special treat for my female guests today."

She nodded to the footmen, who threaded through the crowd, stopping to offer champagne to the gentlemen and beribboned bottles to the ladies. Spencer kept a watchful eye on his wife as he took a glass of champagne, wondering if all this public attention might embarrass her. But she seemed perfectly at ease.

Lady Brumley went on. "My good friend Lady Ravenswood has invented the most astonishing fragrance I have ever had the pleasure to experience. From the first time her ladyship wore it, I was so taken by its delicious scent that I had to have it. She was kind enough to give me her very own bottle."

Lady Brumley smiled down at Abby, who smiled back serenely. Spencer stiffened. He thought he'd banished that cordial façade, but apparently he'd only peeled it back for a moment. Just as that cursed turban hid her lush hair, her new refined manners hid the old Abby from him.

"You all know what I'm like," Lady Brumley continued. "When I find something I enjoy, I don't rest until everyone hears of it. So I persuaded Lady Ravenswood to provide me with bottles of Heaven's Scent for *all* of my closest friends to try. I think you'll be as impressed with it as I was."

Curious, Spencer glanced around. Women were already removing the stoppers and cautiously sniffing the contents of the bottles. Here and there some touched the scent to their wrists, then turned to have their neighbors smell it.

"In any case," Lady Brumley finished, "the bottles are yours to keep—a gift from myself and Lady Ravenswood. So enjoy the rest of my breakfast, and do tell us what you think of it. For myself, I intend to wear nothing else."

Those guests whose hands weren't full clapped politely, and the rest broke up into small groups. Except for the women surging toward Lady Brumley and Abby, and now Clara, too. Guests soon surrounded all three ladies.

"Your wife's concoction seems to be meeting with great success," a low voice said from beside him.

Spencer glanced over to find Blakely sipping champagne. "When did you arrive?"

"Not long before Lady Brumley's little speech." Blakely grinned. "I stayed away 'working' as long as I could without making Clara suspicious. I knew this was going to be a very dull party." He held up his glass. "Typical women's fare. And the damned woman has harpists. Harpists! Leave it to Lady Brumley."

Indeed. "I don't like Lady Brumley," he told Blakely. "She's a bad influence on Abby."

"How so?"

"Surely you've noticed the difference in my wife. She's turned into a damned English lady, all cool and collected. She only voices her opinion if you hold her feet to the fire. The rest of the time, she's as false as a wooden shilling."

"And you don't like that?" Blakely probed.

"No, I don't like it. It's unnatural." Especially for a woman who'd always spoken freely.

Now she was far too sophisticated for that. Spencer

glanced over to where the crowd around Abby and the marchioness grew larger by the moment. His eyes narrowed as he saw Lady Brumley hand out little cards to the ladies. Even Evelina, who looked a bit peaked, braved the crowd for one.

Then she turned and spotted Spencer. She came right over. "I've been looking for you, my lord," the young woman said as she started to tuck the card into her reticule.

"Let me see it," he murmured. When she handed the card to him, he read the single line in gilt: *Jackson's Apothecary in the Strand.* "What's this?"

"It's the address where interested parties can purchase Heaven's Scent. Abby told me just now that Lady Brumley had them made up so that if ladies asked where to get more perfume after the breakfast, she had somewhere to send them." Evelina smiled. "Abby couldn't very well sell it out of your house, you know. That would be vulgar."

"I didn't know she was selling it at all."

Blakely cast him a sly glance. "I thought Abby told you. Clara said you knew."

"I knew Lady Brumley wanted bottles of the stuff, and Abby was supplying them, but—" But what? What else had he thought she planned to do with them? "Yes, I suppose she did tell me."

Evelina removed the card from his hand. "Anyway, I came over to inform you that Mama and I are leaving. Mama's head is plaguing her."

"You don't look so well yourself."

A wan smile touched her lips. "I'm fine. And don't worry about the carriage—we found friends to take us home. So you and Abby can stay here and enjoy yourselves. Good afternoon."

As Evelina walked off, Spencer drank deeply of his champagne, trying to quell the sudden alarm in his chest.

"Abby's success must be quite a relief to you," Blakely said. "Now you needn't worry about her when you part ways.

She's got her business going without your brother, so her need for the money he stole is probably no longer as urgent. I understand Lady Brumley paid her a fifty-pound note for those bottles she gave away. And depending on what arrangement they made with the apothecary for subsequent purchases—"

"Devil take Lady Brumley," Spencer muttered.

"Why? What's wrong now?"

"Don't you see? With fifty pounds, Abby could leave me."

Blakely chuckled. "She wouldn't get very far, especially since she already used some of it to produce the perfume."

"You don't know how much more Lady Brumley might have given her. Or how much she'll get from this apothecary person."

"Why do you care? If she leaves, that means she no longer expects anything from you. You should encourage that. Then you could look for Nat at your leisure."

Christ, Abby had said much the same words to him the night of the ball. "It's not the money I'm worried about. It's the scandal."

Spencer drained his glass, then took another from a passing footman. With enough money, Abby could just slip away. Last week, she'd agreed to stay as long as he needed her, but that was when she'd still hoped to make their marriage permanent. That night in the study, he'd killed those feelings.

Now she couldn't possibly care what happened to him. This new Abby, the one with the poised smile and the elegant damned turban, had no heart. "I could easily wake up tomorrow morning to find her gone. That would certainly start tongues to wagging."

Blakely arched an eyebrow. "It's not the possibility of scandal that bothers you, I suspect."

"Of course it is." But it wasn't, and that realization rocked him to his boots. He wanted Abby to stay. He wanted her here because he needed her here. Even if she remained aloof, even if she never teased him again, he had to have her with him, and not just as his sham wife, either. Despite all his efforts, he'd lost the battle to resist her. Bloody, bloody hell.

"You're worrying over nothing," Blakely said. "Abby wouldn't leave you hanging just because she got a few pounds in her pocket. Besides, didn't you offer her a great deal of money to stay until the end? She'd be a fool to throw that away."

True. But she'd threatened to do it once already, and he'd only kept her here by unwittingly raising her hopes for the future. Now that he'd dashed them, she had no use for money except to escape *him*.

And now the marchioness was handing Abby some other piece of paper, which his bloody wife was tucking into her reticule, cool as you please. Probably another bank note she could use to run away.

"Damn Lady Brumley to hell," he muttered under his breath.

Blakely clapped his hand on Spencer's shoulder. "Come on, stop taking this all so seriously. What you need—what we both need—is a good bottle of stiff brandy, *mon ami*." Blakely called a footman over and made his request. The servant scurried off to do his bidding. "Our wives will probably be otherwise engaged for some time. So we might as well make the best of it."

Chapter 19

Never argue with an intoxicated lord.

Suggestions for the Stoic Servant

Night had already fallen by the time the crowd of women around Abby and Lady Brumley thinned. Two or three were quizzing Clara, but Abby was finally getting a chance to relax. "Phew!" she murmured under her breath to Lady Brumley. "I can't believe how enthusiastic these ladies are about a perfume."

"Didn't I tell you they would love it?"

"They love it because you told them it was fashionable to do so," Abby said dryly.

"Nonsense. The scent stands on its own. Though I like to think I did what I could."

"I can't tell you how grateful I am for all your help," Abby said. "If Heaven's Scent succeeds, it will mean more to me than you can imagine." She would no longer have to worry about what might happen if Nat was never found.

Lady Brumley waved her hand dismissively. "You need not worry, my dear. I shall be much amazed if it isn't an instant success. The ladies are probably already speculating that your fabulous scent was what snagged you a rich husband like Ravenswood." She glanced beyond the ladies talking to Clara. "Speaking of your husband, I believe that's him headed this way."

Abby swung her gaze around to find a grimly determined Spencer stalking toward them. Captain Blakely followed close behind, shoulders slumped.

"Ravenswood looks angry," Lady Brumley added. "You did tell him about this, didn't you?"

"Of course." Abby set her lips. "Pay him no mind. He's been such a grump lately I hardly know what to do with him."

"Men are simple creatures, my dear. Keep them well fed and well pleasured, and they are content. Since I doubt you have to worry about the former, you must concentrate on the latter. Take him to bed. That always brings a man right out of the doldrums."

Shocked by her ladyship's forthrightness, Abby could think of no answer but the truth, and she could hardly tell the woman that.

Besides, by then Spencer had reached them. "It's late, Abby. Time to go."

"Late?" Lady Brumley smirked at him. "Why, my dear Lord Ravenswood, it's only seven o'clock. Why the rush to get home?"

He fixed the marchioness with a glittering gaze. "I don't believe I was speaking to *you*, Lady Brumley."

His voice carried to the other women, who fell into an uncomfortable silence.

"Don't talk to her like that," Abby said in an undertone. "Her ladyship has been most kind to me."

"If you can call it that." Spencer stepped close to grab Abby's arm. Though he seemed steady enough, he reeked of brandy. Which might explain why he went on speaking loudly enough to be heard by those standing nearby. "I call it meddling in other people's affairs."

Lady Brumley's smirk vanished, replaced by a steely anger that brought high color to her heavily powdered cheeks. "Perhaps, Lady Ravenswood, you should go home with your husband after all. He seems to forget the courtesy he owes a hostess."

"I owe you nothing," Spencer grumbled, and now Abby could hear the faint slur to his words. "My wife owes you nothing."

"Ravenswood, old fellow, you're going about this all wrong," Captain Blakely muttered.

"He's clearly foxed," Abby retorted. "I suppose I have you to thank for that, Captain Blakely."

"Probably." Clara took her husband's arm. "Come now, my dear, let's go home. You've done quite enough for one night."

As Clara drew the protesting captain away, Spencer said, "I am *not* foxed. I meant every word, Abby. She's taken advantage of you quite enough. Come on, we're going, too."

"Taken advantage—" Abby wrenched her arm free. "That's an unfair assertion, and I'm not going anywhere with you until you apologize."

He glowered at her. "I refuse to apologize to that rumor-mongering—"

"Go on, my dear," Lady Brumley put in, her smirk returning. "There's no point to arguing with a man in his cups."

Spencer whirled on her. "I am not in my cups, I'll have you know. And furthermore, madam—"

"You're right—we should go," Abby muttered. All too aware of the curious ladies who remained nearby listening to every scandalous word, she dropped her voice. "I can't imagine what's possessed you. But we're leaving before you can make us a laughingstock."

"You're bloody right we're leaving." Wrapping his arm about her waist, Spencer towed her toward the house and thankfully lowered his voice. "And you're never to come here again, do you hear? That gossiping witch is not to be trusted."

Abby rolled her eyes. What on earth had brought all this on? What had happened to the calculating spymaster, the cautious statesman? Glancing back to the marchioness, who waved her off as gaily as if mad husbands routinely dragged their wives from her breakfasts, Abby called out, "I'll pay you a visit tomorrow!"

"You are not paying that woman any more visits," Spencer ordered as he hurried her through the house. He nearly stumbled in a corridor, the only indication that he wasn't quite in command of his faculties. But he caught himself quickly enough to continue their ridiculous march. "Not tomorrow, not ever."

"You're insane." As they halted in the foyer, Abby wrenched her hand from his grasp. "I may be your pretend wife, but that gives you no right to choose my friends."

"Watch your tongue, for God's sake," Spencer hissed, jerking his head toward the footmen standing nearby.

"Why? You certainly aren't bothering to do so. At least I'm speaking sense."

With a sullen scowl, Spencer ordered a footman to call for his carriage, then turned back to Abby. "I'm merely looking out for my wife."

"By embarrassing her before the world? Tell me something, Spencer. If Lady Brumley is such an untrustworthy gossip, why on earth would you give her something to gossip about by behaving like a complete madman in front of her?"

He opened his mouth to retort, then shut it. Good. At least the idiot had enough sense left in his brandy-soaked head to realize she was right.

A footman helped her on with her pelisse, while another edged close enough to offer Spencer his coat and hat. Spencer grabbed both and clapped his hat on his head, but he dropped his coat. When Abby reached for it, he glared at her as he bent to snatch it up himself. Surprisingly, he didn't overset himself, but he fared less well with getting it on.

He finally threw the thing over his arm with a mumbled "It's not cold enough for a coat." When she merely raised an eyebrow, he added, "I'm not foxed, I tell you."

"No, of course not," she said primly. "Eau de brandy is all the fashion these days."

A profound change came over him. He looked wild, almost desperate. "What have those women done to you?"

She blinked at him. "What women?"

"Lady Brumley. And Clara. You used to be so—"

"Your carriage is here, my lord," the footman said.

Spencer nodded, then offered his arm to Abby. "Come on then."

Abby hesitated. "What about Evelina and Lady Tyndale?"

"They got tired of waiting for you and found another way home."

The implied criticism sparked her temper again. Only with difficulty did Abby hold her tongue until they were inside the carriage.

But the minute they were in their seats and headed home, she tore into Spencer. "Isn't it enough that I've spent half my time learning the waltz and how to curtsy and a thousand other ridiculous rules that I'll never use after this? Must I also put up with your bad moods and your controlling ways and—"

"I don't give a damn if you learn to waltz. But you promised to see our sham marriage out to the end, and I won't have you breaking your promise."

"What are you talking about?"

"Lady Brumley and the money she gave you." He leaned forward, his fierce gaze lit by the carriage lamps. "I know about the fifty pounds. And whatever other funds she handed you tonight."

Abby gaped at him. "She didn't hand me any other funds. She did give me a fifty-pound note last week, but that's all."

"She gave you something tonight, too," he persisted. "You put it in your reticule."

As it dawned on her what he meant, she opened her reticule. "It wasn't money." Finding the papers Lady Brumley had given her earlier, she thrust them at him. "It's a contract with that apothecary who's selling Heaven's Scent. She wanted me to look it over before I signed it."

When he unfolded the sheet to find that she was telling the truth, he seemed only slightly mollified.

She snatched it back from him. "And anyway, it's none of your concern what she gives me."

With a steely glint to his eyes, he grabbed her hand before she could put the contract away. "I thought you said half of the business belongs to me as your husband."

"You said you didn't want it, remember?"

"And you said you'd see this out to the end. But now you think to get enough of your own money to buy passage to America and sneak off before I can even stop you."

So *that* was what had set him off, making him behave like a complete idiot. He still worried about his stupid scandal. "Oh, for heaven's sake, I'm not sneaking off anywhere. What would make you think that?"

She tried to tug her hand free, but he refused to let go. "You didn't tell me about the fifty pounds."

"Why should I? It had nothing to do with you."

Setting his shoulders mutinously, he extricated the contract from her hand and shoved the folded paper into his coat pocket. "Then you won't mind if I show this to my solicitor. To make sure Lady Brumley and this Jackson fellow don't cheat you."

Of all the low, controlling— "I can handle my own business affairs, thank you very much. And since I'll have to do so eventually, I might as well start now." She held out her hand. "Give it back to me, Spencer."

"After he's looked at it. After you've fulfilled the terms of our agreement."

"You're being completely unreasonable, you know." Preparing herself for a fight, she stripped off her gloves and stuffed them into her reticule.

"I am not." He crossed his arms over his chest. "You don't know Lady Brumley like I do."

"And you don't know me like you think you do either. I'm not the naive little incompetent you persist in seeing me as. Lady Brumley isn't taking advantage of me, I assure you. And furthermore—"

She broke off when the carriage shuddered to a halt. The footman swung the door open and Spencer leaped out, then turned to help her down. In the moment when his hands gripped her waist, she reached inside his coat to grab the contract. Then she hurried up the stairs, confident that she could outstrip him in his current state.

But he surprised her by overtaking her at the top. "Damn it, Abby, give me that," he said, grabbing for her arm.

Thrusting her elbow into his ribs, she spared only a glance to see him stumble back a few steps before she hastened inside. Ignoring his low oath behind her and the footmen's astonished expressions, she breezed past them, tucking the folded paper down inside her bodice. Spencer would certainly not go there for it, not when he was so determined to stay free of her temptations.

She headed straight for the stairs, hoping to escape to the safety of her room, but Spencer caught up to her on the second step. Swearing under his breath, he seized her by the waist and hauled her back toward his study.

"Stop it!" she protested, digging in her heels. She hadn't entered his study since that horrible night last week. "I'm not giving it to you, no matter how you browbeat me."

Spencer halted. "Unless you want me to grope inside your bodice right here in front of the servants," he warned in a low voice, "you'd best come along like a good girl."

Abby glanced back to see three footmen and McFee gaping at them. She blushed. "You wouldn't dare act so scandalously."

"After what I just did at the breakfast, do you really think I'd hesitate to act scandalously in front of my servants?"

She swallowed. Good point. This time when he tugged, she went willingly. But as soon as they were inside the study and he'd shut the door, she broke free.

Spencer watched in fury as his wife backed away from him. All right, so he was behaving like a besotted ass, but between the brandy fogging his brain and the nagging fear in his gut that she'd flee to America the second his back was turned, he couldn't seem to stop himself.

As he stalked toward her, she crossed her arms over her chest, her dark eyes alight with anger. "Don't you dare try to get this by force."

"Then give it to me." Holding out his hand, he approached her. "I won't have you taking the proceeds of your scent and scurrying off to America when I'm not looking."

She darted behind his desk. "I promised you I wouldn't."

"That was before," he said as he edged around the desk, "when you thought I would stay married to you. Now you have no reason to stay."

To his surprise, anger exploded in her face. "Except my promise. Which you apparently think means nothing. I'm only a frivolous American chit, right? I don't believe in honor or principle or—"

"That's not what I meant. Where the hell do you get these maggoty ideas?" He rubbed the back of his neck in acute frustration. "I only meant that . . . well, I know you hate me now. After what I did to you here in this very room—"

"I don't hate you for that." Warily, she slid around the opposite end of the desk. "You did me a favor by showing me the futility of my hopes."

"Ballocks." Good God, he really was foxed to use such crude language with her. But her dishonesty infuriated him. Abby had never lied to him before. "You're formal and distant with me . . . you put on airs as if to mock me—"

"Mock you!" Shock warred with anger in her face. "You warned me off, and I took you at your word. I'm only doing what you wanted."

"I didn't want you to turn into this . . . this . . ." He scoured her with a contemptuous glance. "This coldhearted creature who never gives a genuine smile and sneaks around behind my back."

"How dare you!" Color stained her cheeks as she balled her hands into fists at her sides. "Yes, I acted without consulting you, because you wanted that. You wanted me to stay out of your way and not to bother you."

She had him there. "Yes, but—"

"And as for my airs, you complained when I was the naive foreigner with the thoughtless tongue, trailing after you like a . . . a lovesick puppy. So I worked hard to make myself the perfect pretend viscountess you thought was necessary to your plans." To his horror, tears filled her eyes, and she brushed them away fiercely. "But that didn't please you either. It seems nothing is good enough to please you, Lord Ravenswood."

Two things hit him at once. One, she'd actually thought that he wanted a perfect viscountess. Two, she still cared enough to want to please him. "I never complained about what you were, only what you wanted from me."

"It's the same thing. I wanted to be your wife in truth, and that didn't suit you. Today I even figured out why. You thought I was just like the stepmother who left you—foolish and reckless and all those things you didn't want in a viscountess."

She'd taken everything all wrong. And Liverpool's stupid words had only made it worse. "You were nothing like Dora, do you hear?" he said firmly. "There was *nothing* wrong with how you were. You were perfect from the beginning."

She glared at him. "Certainly. I was so perfect that you went to extraordinary lengths to shatter my hopes for our marriage. I was so suitable to be your wife that you . . . you humiliated me and threatened me."

Bloody, bloody hell. All this time, he'd been so focused on keeping himself from seducing her that he hadn't stopped to think how she might see his adamant refusals. "I swear that your suitability had naught to do with it. I told you from the first—"

"Oh, yes, your career prevents you from marrying." Her bitter sarcasm cut him to the heart. "I'm not an idiot—we both know it has nothing to do with it. In August, Parliament will no longer be in session and you'll have time to settle in with a wife. If you want to, which you don't." Tears glittered in her eyes. "At least not with me."

Her every word sank him deeper into hell. All this time she'd thought it was she he objected to, while he'd blithely gone on assuming that she'd believed his facile explanations. He should have realized she was too clever for that.

But how could she think he didn't want her for his wife when he spent every hour aching to keep her? "You're right, I lied about my career having anything to do with it. But I swear my desire to remain a bachelor had nothing to do with your suitability—"

"Stop it! You're only saying that because you're worried about me running off and causing a stupid scandal. Well, I'm not running off, but neither will I stand here and listen to your lies. Whether you like it or not, I've got my business going, and I won't let you interfere just because you don't trust me to keep my promises."

Taking him off guard, she lunged for the door. With a

curse, he bounded toward her, somehow managing to intercept her at the end of the desk. Grabbing her by the waist, he lifted her and set her atop the desk, then sandwiched her legs between his thighs to trap her.

She beat at his chest. "Let me go, you . . . you bully, you!"

"I can't," he said hoarsely. He caught her flailing hands and pulled them behind her back. "I know I should. I know it would be better for both of us, but I can't." Pure instinct drove him now, instinct and need and a hunger for her that wouldn't be assuaged. It was pointless to fight it anymore. "I won't let you go."

Her struggling lessened as she stared at him, disbelief painfully evident in her face.

Drawing her hands together behind her back, he manacled both with one of his own. "It has nothing to do with a fear of scandal, not anymore. I want you to stay, and I'll do whatever I must to make sure that you do."

Lifting his free hand to his mouth, he used his teeth to remove his glove. He kept his eyes on her as he reached inside her bodice to search for the contract. When a purely female gasp erupted from her and her fearful gaze softened, his own need flared into white-hot desire. It took all his control to focus only on searching for the contract between her breasts and not think about tearing her bodice in two so he could feast on the tender flesh that brushed his fingers.

No, he could never let her go. "I don't want you to leave, not now, not ever."

A hint of despair crossed her face. "You don't know what you want."

"Wrong again." He found the contract and removed it, tossing it across the room well beyond her reach. Then he leaned close to brush his mouth against her ear, drinking in the lilting fragrance of her hair. "I know exactly what I want. I want you."

When he kissed her ear and she shivered, he exulted in her

response. He might have wounded her deeply, but at least she still felt this for him. And it had been so long, too long . . .

"I won't be your mistress, Spencer," she whispered. "Not even for a few weeks—"

"I don't want you to be my mistress." He should never have made that idle threat. He should have realized from the beginning that he would always want her to stay. That would have saved them both some pain.

But he would make it up to her, now, tonight. "I certainly don't want you to be the perfect viscountess. I want you to be yourself, my wife. That's all."

"You said you would never—"

"I know what I said," he rasped. "I was wrong."

He saw the question in her eyes seconds before he seized her lips with his. His heart roared in triumph when after a moment's hesitation, she opened her mouth to him. He kissed her deeply, thoroughly, seeking to blot all doubt from her mind.

He should do it by telling her the truth. And he would. But not until after he'd proved to her how sweet it could be between them, how much he needed her. He refused to risk losing her by telling her everything now.

As she melted inch by inch against him, he released her wrists to remove his other glove. Then he went to work on the buttons of her gown.

She tore her lips from his, her eyes huge in her face. "If this is another cruel trick—"

"No," he said hoarsely, nuzzling her pretty earlobe and then the scented patch of skin beneath it. "It's no trick, I swear. I simply can't stand to be without you anymore."

When she looked as if she'd protest further, he kissed her again, throwing his everything into it to distract her from what he was doing with her buttons. And it worked . . . until he tried to slide her gown off her shoulders. Then she jerked back from him with an expression of panic. She attempted to wriggle off the desk, but he wouldn't let her.

"Let me make love to you, my darling," he whispered. "I need you. My God, I need you so much."

Twisting her head to the side, she murmured, "You say that now when we're playing, but later—"

"No more playing." He caught her by the chin to turn her face up to his. "I want you in my bed. Tonight. And every night after." Shrugging off his coat and waistcoat, he reached for her gown again.

But she caught his hands in hers. "You're too foxed to think clearly."

"Or perhaps I'm just foxed enough." He didn't feel all that foxed, however. Yes, he'd had one too many brandies, thanks to Blakely, and his brain was a little fuzzy, but he knew quite well what he was doing. He was taking Abby— his wife—to bed.

He forced a smile. "You once told me I only have fun when I'm foxed."

That was the wrong thing to say. Her face clouded over, and her grip on his hands tightened. "Yes, but then you come to your senses the next day and regret it. You'll regret this, too." She cast a furtive glance about the study, and her uncertainty seemed to deepen. "If you even finish it."

Bloody hell, he would never live down that last act of idiocy. And he was certainly paying for it now. To think he'd actually believed a week ago that it might be *good* if she hated him.

Well, he'd discovered to his chagrin that having her hate him was sheer hell. Even having her distrust him was a torment, though he couldn't blame her for her distrust. Twice he'd started something and not followed it through, and the second time . . .

Guilt dealt a blow to his gut. What an idiot he was. He

shouldn't have started this *here*, in the very place where he'd destroyed her dignity.

Tugging one of his hands free, he lifted it to cup her cheek. When he ran his thumb over her soft skin and felt the dampness there, his guilt deepened to a gnawing ache, and he swore to make it up to her.

"You have every reason to think ill of me, darling. I've been unfair to you, I know. But never again. I'll finish it this time, and I won't regret it." Well, perhaps that last wasn't true, but he wouldn't dwell on that right now. "I want to consummate our marriage. We'll go upstairs to my bedchamber, away from this cursed room—"

"No. It has to be here, where you shamed me."

He stared at her. "Why?"

"Because I want it to be here, that's all."

Her insistence gave him pause, but he wasn't about to argue with her. "All right."

She warily searched his face, then thrust her chin up stubbornly. "And you have to do something else, too."

"What?" He suspected he wasn't going to like this.

"You have to be first to take off all your clothes."

Chapter 20

Your employer's secrets are a sacred trust. It is your honor to keep them, and your shame if you do not.

Suggestions for the Stoic Servant

Curious to see his response, Abby held her breath.

Spencer's eyes narrowed. "Is that why you want to stay here in the study?" he asked hoarsely. "Turnabout is fair play? You plan to do what I did to you and leave me here naked and aroused?"

She tilted up her chin. "Do you think that's what you deserve?"

"Yes."

His unhesitating answer tipped scales already teetering in his favor. She *had* briefly considered doing to him what he'd done to her. After all, she'd sworn not to fall under his spell again. She'd promised herself that once she had him regretting his actions and wanting to keep her, she would spurn him as cruelly as he'd spurned her.

But now that the moment was here, everything was different. Perhaps he really had always liked her just as she was. Why he'd fought staying married to her at first was still a mystery, but he wasn't fighting it now. Or at least she thought he wasn't.

Still, she wasn't taking any chances. He could change his

mind between here and his bedchamber. Or get halfway through the seduction and pull back in regret.

No, if he wanted her, he'd have to prove he meant it. He'd have to risk the same thing she'd risked for him time and again—his pride.

Careful to keep her expression unreadable, she reached up to smooth back a lock of his disheveled hair. "There's no way you can know what I'll do, is there? I mean, since I've turned myself into this coldhearted creature who sneaks around and all."

He winced. "I suppose I deserve that, too." He searched her face, his eyes hot, intense. "So this is a test of my sincerity?"

"A test. Or my revenge." She refused to lower his risk. "Take your pick."

A muscle worked in his jaw as he glanced away. She wondered if she'd gone too far, expected too much.

Then his gaze swung back to her, hard and determined. "Well then, we should do it right." Leaving her seated on the desk, he strode over to an oak chest, removed something she couldn't see, then turned back to her.

When she saw the box in his hand, she froze. "No."

"It's a different one, Abby." He ambled toward her with the easy strides of a hunter keeping pace with his prey. "But if you want to do to me what I did to you—" He handed the peep-show box to her.

Despite her apprehension, curiosity got the better of her. What could it hurt to take one look? Preparing herself for something shocking, she gazed inside, then swallowed.

Dear heaven. This was definitely naughty. The caption said "Circe and Ulysses." In keeping with the myth of the beautiful witch who'd enticed the great Greek traveler on her island, not only was the woman in the image naked, but the man was, too. Naked, and yes, fully aroused. He lay on a bower of leaves, his well-knit chest, sturdy thighs, and jutting member exposed to Circe's mouth and hands, which caressed him with the most astonishing intimacy.

She jerked her gaze from the box and strove to look nonchalant, not all that easy considering she blushed furiously enough to light a room. "How many of these wicked boxes do you possess, anyway?"

A half smile ghosted over his lips as he dropped onto the chaise longue to remove his boots. "Only those two."

"A likely tale," she said with a snort.

"The only way you'll find out for sure is to stick around for a while. As my wife, you can search the whole damned house from top to bottom and unearth every one of my dastardly secrets." He rose, his smile vanishing. "Or if you prefer to make me suffer as you did and walk away, you now have the means to do that, too. I won't stop you."

After striding over to the door in his stocking feet, he locked it. The snick of the key echoing in her memory decided her. Maybe she ought to give him some of his own back before she forgave him. If he would endure what she'd endured, he had to be sincere.

"Very well," she said. When he turned back to her, eyes alight with curiosity to know which choice she'd made, she added, "We'll try the box."

His eyes darkened to wet slate, and he looked so lost she almost relented. But it was about time his lordship learned what it was like to never know where one stood.

She slipped off the desk with the peep-show box in hand, feeling her gown gap open at the back. Ignoring the cool air on her skin, she strolled up to him and held out the box. "Look in it and describe what you see."

"I don't need to look in it. I know the image well enough."

She planted one hand on her hip. "For heaven's sake, are your friends and fellow statesmen aware of your private vice of looking at naughty peep-show boxes?"

He arched an eyebrow. "I doubt it. Why? Do you plan to tell them?"

Feeling a surge of power, she tapped the box with one finger. "I might."

"Then I might have to tell them I'm not alone in my vice." His gaze scoured her from turban to slipper, coming to rest on her bosom. "That my pretty wife has a penchant for the things as well."

When his husky words tightened a knot of need in her belly, she cursed herself for her easy response. He wouldn't manipulate her this time. She wouldn't let him.

Setting the box aside on the desk since he didn't need it, she took hold of his cravat. "Describe what's in the middle of the image," she commanded as she unknotted the scrap of silk.

His quickening breath wafted over her, the faint scent of brandy mingling with his ever-present citrus tang. "A man and a woman are lying on the ground."

She yanked his cravat off, then went to work on his shirt buttons. "And how are they dressed?"

"They're not."

At the hint of amusement in his tone, she snapped her gaze up to find him smiling. "Just you wait," she warned. "I liked this part of the game, too, remember?"

That wiped the smile from his arrogant lips. Feeling pleased with herself, she removed his shirt and tried not to stare. But it was impossible.

He and Ulysses could have been twins, with their sinewy chests and waists firm as carved marble. The thin trail of hair from his throat to his belly beckoned her gaze further down to where it disappeared beneath trousers that clearly bulged. The very sight profoundly affected her pulse, making it throb in the most surprising places.

Heavenly day. If he'd been this aroused when he was tempting her that night, how had he ever walked away?

By being his usual controlled self, of course. And she could be just as controlled. "So tell me," she whispered through a throat gone suddenly dry, "what is the woman doing to the man?"

"She's kissing his chest," he said quickly.

She pressed her mouth to his nipple, running the tip of her tongue over the already hard point. "Like this?" she asked as she feathered kisses over his muscular chest to his other flat male nipple.

"Yes," he choked out.

Tugging on the other nipple with her teeth, she reveled in the rough groan that erupted from his lips, a groan that only deepened when she reached down and flicked open the buttons of his trousers. "What else is she doing?" She circled around to stand behind him as he'd done to her before.

"She's caressing his stomach with one hand and . . ." He sucked in a hoarse breath when she slid her hand over his abdomen from behind, stroking the taut flesh, slipping her fingers beneath the gaping waistband of his trousers to unbutton his drawers.

"And what?" she prodded. "What is she doing with the other hand?"

"Fondling his . . . er . . . staff."

"Show me," she demanded. This part of their game she remembered only too well, the way he'd coaxed her to put his hand on her flesh.

"Good God, Abby, when did you become such a provoking wench?"

"I wasn't the one to start things and not finish them," she said coolly. "That was *your* tactic."

"Don't remind me," he rasped. "I must have been insane."

"So let's see if you've come to your senses. Show me how the woman is touching the man, my dear Lord Ravenswood."

Grabbing her hand, he drew it inside his drawers to close it around his hard flesh. "Like this, my little torturer. Happy now?"

"Not yet," she whispered against his solid shoulder. "But I'm getting there."

She couldn't believe he'd endured her teasing to this point. Her heart lightened more and more by the moment. Taking pity on him, she began to stroke, up and down, relishing the fierce rigidity of his thick "staff," the way the blood pulsed beneath her fingers, the way he sighed and moaned with every daring caress.

Using her free hand, she shoved his trousers down past his hips. Then she continued to fondle him, but she couldn't resist kissing his back, too, and rubbing her nose over the smooth skin, rich with the musky scent of pure male. Soon he was moving his hips and thrusting his flesh into her hand, his own hands curling into fists at his sides.

Suddenly he jerked back against her and caught her hand to stay it. "If you want to leave me naked and aroused, darling, you'll have to release me."

"Why?"

"Remember our 'playing' in the bedchamber?"

That was all he had to say to make her stop. She'd done this to him then, but he'd found satisfaction as a result of her fondling.

Her eyes widened. He could have found satisfaction now, too—she wouldn't have known enough to prevent it. So he'd really meant what he'd said about not stopping her if she wanted revenge. By warning her, he'd even aided his own downfall. Nothing could show his sincerity more.

Her heart breaking free of all doubt and fear, she laughed and drew her hand from his drawers. When she circled around in front of him, he was staring at her as if she'd lost her wits. Bending down, she removed his trousers completely and tossed them aside, then reached for his drawers.

He caught her hand. "No."

"Naked and aroused, remember?" she teased.

He didn't smile. "I have . . . scars, Abby. Ugly ones."

Ah, yes, his war wounds. She'd forgotten.

He gave a grim laugh. "Though I suppose that would enhance your revenge—to leave a scarred and naked man standing pathetically unfulfilled in his own study."

Her heart twisted in her chest. Time to end this. "Or . . ." she said as she walked over to the door, "we could move the game to a more comfortable place, like your bedchamber, where I could kiss your scars at my leisure to make them better."

She turned the key.

When Spencer heard the click of the lock, he assumed she meant to leave him here. Then her words registered. He whirled toward her, hardly able to believe his ears.

But there was no mistaking her open smile. She'd forgiven him. She wanted him. She was giving him a chance.

Without a word, he stalked up to haul her into his arms and kiss her with all the feverish need he'd suppressed for a week. Her eager response sealed her fate. He would make her his wife in truth tonight, and to hell with tomorrow.

By the time he drew back, the violence of his need had him reeling and her swaying on her feet. "Let's go upstairs," he whispered. He reached past her to open the door, then stuck his head out, relieved to see that nobody was around now except a sleeping footman at the end of the hall nearest the entrance.

"Since I have no intention of dressing and giving you a chance to change your mind, my darling," he went on, "we'll have to take the back stairs to my bedchamber. Just in case any of the servants are still up. It would be embarrassing to be caught like this."

"Embarrassing for you, maybe," she said in a husky murmur. "I'm fully dressed."

"Not for long," he promised, reaching for her gown.

With a giggle, she darted through the door and raced pell-mell for the back stairs. He swore as he raced after her, but she didn't slow her steps until she'd passed through the door into the stairwell. When she hesitated to catch her bearings, he caught up with her. Before she could escape, he dragged her gown off and tossed it over his shoulder.

But when he reached for her petticoat, too, she broke free and ran laughing up the stairs ahead of him. He followed more slowly, though he couldn't resist calling out, "I don't mind if you run, my dear, as long as you're naked by the time I catch up to you."

Peals of laughter drifted down to him, then were cut off as she disappeared through the door that opened into the upstairs hall. When it occurred to him that she could lock him out of his bedchamber if she decided to really torment him, he quickened his pace. By the time he'd reached his room and burst through the unlocked door, she'd dispensed with her petticoat and was stripping off her second stocking.

Dropping the stocking, she rose with a welcoming smile. He halted, his mouth going dry at the sight of her clad only in her chemise. She still wore that damned turban, but the rest of her . . .

Good God in heaven, she was choice. Her sheer chemise, a fragile wisp of muslin, clung to her breasts. Mysterious shadows on the fabric hinted at her nipples and the triangle of hair between her legs. Framed by the golden hangings and oak posts of his bed, she looked as erotic as any wanton in his private peep-show boxes. Except for one thing.

"Take it off," he rasped.

Her gaze grew sultry as she reached for the chemise ties.

"No, not that. I mean . . . yes, that, but first that nasty turban."

"Nasty?" She reached up to unpin it. "You don't like my turban?"

"I loathe it," he said earnestly.

Looking perplexed, she removed it. "Why? I figured you'd

find it more acceptable than my other style, the one you claimed made me look like a ladybird."

When she went a step further and unpinned her hair, letting the mass of it drop like a curtain of ebony silk about her shoulders, his pulse beat feverishly. "Is that why you wore it?" He strode up to yank the turban from her hands and throw it aside. "One more way to rub my nose in my crimes?"

"No, I really thought you'd prefer it."

As some of what she'd said earlier came back to him, his eyes narrowed. "Like you thought I would prefer your refined manners and your coldness?"

"Yes. Or at least admire and respect me for them. That's all I wanted."

Lifting his hand to her hair, he wound a hank of the petal-soft strands about his hand and kissed them. "So that wasn't a punishment, either."

She shook her head, the skin between her eyebrows puckering in a tiny frown. "The punishment was supposed to come when you realized I'd become the viscountess you wanted. Then I was going to 'rub your nose' in the fact that you'd thrown me away because you thought I wasn't good enough."

A low chuckle escaped his lips. "Well, you certainly showed me. Just not the way you'd planned." He cradled her head in his free hand. "I missed you, Abby."

She stared at him, bemused. "I never went anywhere."

"Yes, but you were different. I missed your teasing and your shy smiles. I missed the—how did you put it?—naive American with the thoughtless tongue, who trailed after me like a lovesick puppy." He ran his fingers through the shimmering silk of her hair. "I'm going to say this once and for all—there was never anything wrong with you."

"Spencer—" she began, a skeptical look on her face.

"I mean it. I only complained about your hair and your gown

before the ball because they made me desire you too much. I thought that if you dressed more like an Englishwoman, I wouldn't spend every waking moment aching to bed you."

She cocked an eyebrow. "Did it work?"

Chuckling, he cupped her breast through her chemise. "Does it look like it worked? No, it just made me want my wild American rose back. And the more you cultivated the English variety, the more you drove me insane."

"But if you thought I was fine the way I was before, then why—"

He halted her question with a kiss. He knew what she would ask and knew what he should answer, but he was self-ish enough not to want to ruin this. Better to make love to her so thoroughly that perhaps the truth wouldn't matter when he told her afterward.

Ignoring his conscience, which screamed that he was be-ing unfair not to tell her now, he lost himself in the warm vel-vet of her mouth, the sheer pleasure of her embrace.

When he drew back, her eyes were alight with mischief. "You're still wearing your drawers, Lord Ravenswood. And as I recall . . ."

Swiftly, he stepped back and stripped down to nothing. Thank God the fire was behind him—he doubted she had enough light to see the scars on his left flank. And when she stared at his cock, then jerked her gaze up with a blush, he re-alized her maidenly modesty would work in his favor as well.

"Your turn." He reached up to unfasten her chemise and push it off her shoulders. In two tugs, he had it pooled at her feet, baring her completely to his hungry gaze.

As he skimmed his hand up the lush fullness of her hips to her sweetly slender waist and then higher to beneath the full breasts that he ached so badly to touch, she stammered, "I-I guess I'm darker than most English women."

Only the need to reassure her kept his hot lust in check.

"No darker than an Italian." Smoothing his thumbs over her rose-brown nipples, he exulted when they tightened into buds. He shot her a wicked smile. "And you know what they say about Italian women."

"No, what?" She sucked in a breath as he swept his other hand back down past her golden belly to stroke the riotous black curls between her thighs.

"That they're passionate. That they revel in a man's caress." When he delved deep to find her petals already well nectared, he smiled. Drawing his hand up, he showed her his glistening finger. "The way you do. I know half a dozen Englishmen who'd give their eyeeth for a passionate wife, no matter what color her skin."

Though she blushed, her eyelids drooped in a sultry look. "Then come make me your wife, my lord."

No maidenly reluctance for his Abby. Like the wild rose he'd craved for so long, she reached up to twine her arms about his neck and pull his head down for her kiss.

He met it feverishly, stabbing his tongue inside the open bud of her mouth. Without breaking the kiss, he backed her toward the bed and tumbled her down upon it. Covering her with his body, he nudged her thighs apart with his knee so he could settle his legs between them. Then he returned to caressing the dewy flesh hidden in her sweet curls.

She gasped when he slipped two fingers inside her slick passage. She was so deliciously wet he just wanted to bury his raring cock inside her. But she was a virgin, and he must take it slow. So he settled for plundering her with his fingers as he dropped his mouth to ravish her breasts. He sucked one, then the other, drunk with the fragrance so uniquely hers.

At first she cradled his head against her, but as he drove his fingers over and over inside her hot satin, she repaid the caress by dancing her hand along his flank to grasp his erection.

He groaned aloud. The first stroke of her eloquent hand

was already more than he could bear. "I want to be inside you, darling." He lifted his head from her breast. "Guide me inside you."

Her hand stilled. "I-I don't know how."

Slowly he withdrew his fingers from between her legs. "Let my staff take the place of my fingers. Lift your knees and guide me in. I don't want to hurt you more than necessary." He gazed down at her through heavy-lidded eyes. "You do know that—"

"Yes. It's all right." Her teasing smile reassured him. "Mama told me everything. She said the man must break through a woman's innocence to harvest the pleasure the way a bear breaks through a hive to harvest the honey."

"That explains why beehive and honey pot came to refer to a woman's privates," he said wryly. "But please tell me bees don't fly out whenever a man deflowers a virgin."

"Don't you know?"

He shook his head. "I've never taken a woman's innocence, darling."

She laughed. "Well then, there's only one way to find out what happens, isn't there?" She pulled on his cock, and he clamped down the urge to thrust into her hand. Instead he let her draw him in until his tip brushed the slick folds he craved.

When she looked uncertain of what to do next, he brushed her hand aside. Trying to go slowly, he entered her. But as her silky sweet heat engulfed him, it was damned difficult not to plunge in to the very root. "My God, Abby, that's good," he said in a guttural voice. "You can't imagine what it feels like to be inside you."

"You can't imagine what it feels like to have you there," she said dryly.

Noting the game smile that grew stiffer the farther he inched inside her, he paused to let her adjust to him. But it took every ounce of his control. When she wriggled beneath him, probably seeking a more comfortable position, he thought he'd ex-

plode right then. Especially when it made him slip even further
into her snug honey pot.

Then he came up squarely against her virginal obstruc-
tion. His gaze locked with hers, but before she could tighten
her muscles in fearful anticipation, he muttered, "Hold back
the bees," and broke through in one plunge, planting himself
so deeply inside her, he thought he could feel her beating
heart.

Though she gasped, she didn't wail or cry or any of the
things he feared a virgin might do. If anything, she looked intrigued. "No bees, my lord."

"Thank God," he muttered as he fought for mastery over
his raging need.

Then she drew his head down for a kiss, and he lost all
sense of place and time and control. He didn't even realize
he'd begun moving until her hands tightened in his hair.

Slow down, he told himself. *Keep it easy.*

As if that were possible. It was his beautiful Abby beneath
him, his wonderful Abby dragging her open mouth along his
shoulder, his teasing Abby kissing the chest muscles rigid
from the effort of holding himself off her. Her petal-soft lips
only increased his need.

"Stop . . . kissing . . . me," he commanded, now barely
able to leash his control. "Or I'll . . . never hold out."

"Until what?" Her eyes gleamed as she leaned up to run
her tongue over one of his taut nipples.

"Until you can . . . find pleasure . . . in this, too."

She laughed, wildly, happily. "No reason to hold out."
Digging her fingernails into his upper arms, she clung to him
like a vine. "Having you make me yours is pleasure enough."

"No, it's not nearly enough." Reaching back, he tugged
her leg up. "Wrap your legs . . . about my waist. It will feel
better for you."

Her eyes shone with curiosity, but she entwined him in
those delicious legs of hers. The shift in position planted him

even farther inside her, if that were possible, and his need grew so intense, he could scarcely hold back his release.

He pounded hard, grinding against the tender center of all her pleasure, determined to make her share his excitement.

She gasped. "Heavens . . . that's . . . oh, my . . ."

A laugh tore from him. "Better?"

"Lord, yes . . . Spencer . . . dear heaven . . . Spencer . . ."

Her head twisted from side to side as her legs gripped his waist, sucking him in until he could feel her muscles start to tighten and her breath quicken to a ragged cadence.

"You're my wife now," he rasped. "You won't leave me."

"Never," she vowed. Then she convulsed around him and cried, "Spencer . . . oh, Lord . . . I love you!"

That drove him over the edge. With a strangled cry of his own, he thrust deeply to spill his seed inside her. Her "I love you" thundered in his head as he poured himself into her. Her "I love you" echoed through his taut muscles as he collapsed atop her.

Oh, God, now he had to deal with the "I love you" he did not deserve.

Chapter 21

It is not always wise to know the secrets of one's employer. Some secrets are better left private.

Suggestions for the Stoic Servant

As Abby lay with Spencer draped across her in a heap of warm, fragrant male, she wondered if it might be possible to die of happiness. Certainly her heart felt near to bursting with her joy.

She smiled against the bergamot-scented cheek that lay so close to hers. No, she wouldn't allow herself to die. Not now that she finally had Spencer for her own.

Tightening her arms about his muscled back, she cradled him close. Hers. He was hers forever, irrevocably hers. Spencer would never make love to her if he didn't mean to keep her. He was too much a gentleman for that.

His breath warmed her cheek as it slowed to normalcy. "Are you all right, my darling?" he murmured, then kissed her ear. "Not too much pain, I hope?"

"Pain?" She laughed. "There was pain?"

His rumbling chuckle made his chest vibrate against her breasts. "Apparently not." He rolled off to lie on his side facing her, his eyes gleaming. "A less trusting husband might worry that you'd lied about your innocence."

She flashed him an arch look. "And you, my lord? What do you think?"

"That I'm damned lucky to have a wife who's a natural wanton." He propped his head on one hand while his other idly stroked her belly.

With a saucy smile, she skimmed her own hand down his ribs and waist to his hips. He faced the fire now, and for the first time the scars riddling his left side were fully illuminated.

She couldn't help staring. The hair that had brushed her fingers earlier when she'd stroked him grew thickly on the right, but on the left was only a smattering interspersed with puckered scars.

She lightly traced one. "I never did get to kiss these and make them better."

"If that works, you'd best not tell anyone," he said, his voice suddenly strained. "Or droves of wounded soldiers will soon be beating down our doors."

"How did it happen?"

"At the Battle of Bussaco, a man next to me was kneeling to aim his flintlock when it misfired and the barrel exploded. I was luckier than he was—a fragment of metal entered his brain and killed him instantly. The fragments that showered me merely wounded me."

"Why does it still hurt? I mean, that time when I touched you—"

"You merely happened to hit a fragment still imbedded in the flesh."

"The doctors left all that metal in you?" she said incredulously, wondering if English doctors were completely mad.

"No, of course not. But a couple lay too near my vital organs to risk removing them."

"Oh." She explored his scars very carefully. "Does it pain you much to have them in there?"

"Only if I should happen to bump hard against something."

"Or if your overenthusiastic wife presses them," she quipped.

He didn't respond. She glanced up to find him watching her with a brooding look so shadowed it struck alarm in her chest. "Spencer?"

"When you said you loved me, did you mean it?"

"Of course I meant it." So he'd heard what she hadn't intended to speak aloud. And her declaration must not have been completely welcome, judging from his expression and the fact that he made no similar declaration.

All her pleasure faltered. *Please, God, don't let this be like the night we were in my bedchamber. I don't think I could bear it.*

"There's something I should have told you long ago, my darling, and most certainly before we made love." Guilt flashed over his taut features. "But I didn't want to risk losing you."

Thank heaven. "You won't lose me."

He flinched. "I might. Especially after you hear this." He hesitated, his hand stilling on her belly as he stared beyond her with that bleakness she'd sometimes seen in his face. "You were right—my career had nothing to do with my unwillingness to stay married to you. It certainly had nothing to do with your suitability as a wife. To be honest, until you came along, I'd never planned to marry at all."

"Never?"

"No. I didn't tell you, because it would raise questions I didn't want to answer. Now I have no choice." He dragged in a breath, then went on unsteadily, "You see, I can't . . . I can't have children."

Relief coursed through her. Was that all, him and his silly ideas about children? "If you're going to tell me again that you don't like them—"

His tortured gaze shot to her. "I didn't say I *won't* have children, Abby. I said I can't."

She stared at him, uncomprehending. "But we just—"

"Yes, all my parts work. I'm not impotent. But I am sterile." He shifted to lie on his back and stare up at the damask canopy. "One of the metal fragments that entered my flesh apparently injured me in a way that prevented my seed from reaching my . . . er . . . staff. So although I can make love and find release, my spirit has no seed." He lowered his voice to an aching whisper. "I can't sire children."

As the full ramifications of that struck her, her blood slowed to sludge in her veins. Dear heaven, if that was true . . . With a sinking dread, she dropped her gaze inexorably to the scars on his loins. Now she noticed those that crisscrossed his privates.

"Are you sure?" she asked, still not wanting to believe it.

With a sigh, he tucked his hands under his head, exposing his tufted underarms. "Countless doctors informed me when I was first wounded that I might never sire children." Firelight streaked across his rigid jaw. "And countless years of my sowing my wild oats without ever producing a by-blow have proved them right."

The torment shadowing his features deepened. "Why do you think I fought this marriage so hard? Because all women—and you in particular—deserve husbands who can give them children. I can't." He paused, and in the stillness the crackling of the fire sounded as loud as pistol shots. "If you stay married to me, it will always be just the two of us."

The words echoed in her brain, a solid blow to all her recent joy. No children. Ever.

Suddenly so many things made sense. His irrational behavior that day she'd brought the children here. His violent reaction to her attempts to seduce him. The way he seemed to desire her one minute and resent her the next.

She ought to be glad it wasn't her he objected to, yet all she could think was *No children, ever*. No babies like Lydia or scamps like Jack. In a daze, she slid off the bed and wandered the room until she found her chemise. But even the motion of putting it on couldn't silence the endless clamoring of her fevered brain.

No children, ever.

When she faced him again, he was sitting up with his back propped against the headboard and his lower body now covered by the golden counterpane. He watched her with a furtive gaze that turned remorseful when he caught sight of her probably dumbfounded expression. "I know I should have told you before I took your innocence."

She thought of all she'd suffered by believing that he considered her unsuitable to be his wife, and anger flared to life inside her. "You should have told me long before then." Sarcasm lent her words an edge. "The day I arrived to announce that I was your wife might have been an appropriate time."

He stiffened. "It's not something a man likes to admit to just anyone. I've never told a soul before you. Well, except for Genevieve. But she considered my sterility an advantage. For everyone else—"

When he glanced away, a muscle tightening in his jaw, she felt an unwanted stab of sympathy. How hard it must be for an English lord expected to sire an heir and carry on a dynasty to learn that he couldn't do it. He would certainly never admit such an unmanly lack to his friends.

But what about to his family? "Does Nat know?"

"No." He frowned, as if some thought had occurred to him, then shook it off. "He wouldn't understand."

"How do you know if you don't tell him? He's your brother, for heaven's sake." When his surprised gaze shot to her, she stalked up to the bed. "But that's the trouble with you, Spencer. You won't tell any of us a thing. You engineer these elaborate schemes to protect your family from scandal, but you don't bother to inform *them* of why you're doing it. You simply march on with your usual arrogance, telling us it's none of our concern while you shut us out of your life."

His eyes glittered in the firelight. As she turned to walk away, he snagged her arm and tugged her down to sit beside him. "When you first arrived, you took me by surprise. It's not as if I owed you any explanation then. *I* hadn't been the one to manipulate you or deceive you. And since I had no intention—or so I thought—of continuing our marriage, I saw no point to revealing a secret I considered very private."

"Yes, but what about later? When you realized I cared for you?"

He swallowed. "I was afraid you'd say it didn't matter. And that I'd want so badly to believe you that I'd be lulled into thinking it was true. I was afraid that when you came to your senses and realized it did matter, you'd want to be free of me. I was afraid that the pain of losing you after having you would be too much to endure. I thought it better not to risk it."

She stared down at her hands. "Far better to let me think that you considered me a silly fool with no social graces and nothing but my body to commend me."

"Devil take it." He clasped her by the chin, forcing her to meet his gaze. "I thought you believed my tale about my career. If I'd had any idea you thought such nonsense—"

"You would have told me the truth?"

He released her chin abruptly. "Perhaps. I don't know. I only realized tonight how you were interpreting my resistance to marriage."

"Yes, what about tonight? What made you change your mind about our future? Why are you now willing to risk the pain of losing me, as you put it?"

A feverish need shone in the silvery depths of his eyes. "I realized I already couldn't bear to lose you. And I hoped that if we shared a bed, you might stay. At least for a while. It was utterly selfish and wrong, I know, but I can't regret it. I—" His voice dropped to a choked whisper. "I've never wanted anything as much as I want you, Abby."

Her pulse quickened. He looked so earnest. How much

had that admission cost a man as proud and seemingly self-sufficient as him? Still, he'd said nothing of love. And what did he mean, "at least for a while"?

"Let me see if I understand you," she said. "You want me to remain your wife."

"I have no right to ask it under the circumstances, but yes. I'll take however long you're willing to give me and consider myself fortunate."

Temper flared in her chest. "You value yourself too little, Spencer."

"I value you too much. You have a right to expect children. I can't provide them. Eventually that will bother you. When it does, I don't want you to feel as if you're . . . trapped in this marriage. There's no reason we can't put my initial plan into place five months, two years, ten years down the road. You're still young, after all."

She gaped at him. "Whatever do you mean?"

"When you tire of our childless marriage, we'll go to America, dissolve it legally, and separate."

"After living together and being together for years—"

"The courts don't have to know that. We can invent a reason we didn't find out until—"

"It's not the logistics I'm questioning. How could you think I'd leave you after living with you for more than a day?"

His lips tightened into a grim line. "I'm giving you an out, that's all."

"Maybe I don't want an out. Maybe I believe that marriage should be 'until death do us part.'"

"I'm sure you do. For now. But I can't give you children, Abby."

"Still, there are other options. You don't have to have children of your own blood. There are foundlings and—"

"No." His face shone starkly angry in the flickering firelight. "I won't take in foundlings."

Alarm seized her chest. "Why not? Surely you don't really

believe that nonsense about a child's lineage dictating his character. Even if you do, we could find some gentlewoman who has made a mistake—"

"It has nothing to do with bloodlines," he snapped.

"If you don't care whether the child is of your own blood, then I don't see what difference it makes who gave birth to it."

"It makes a difference, believe me. It always makes a difference." The bitterness in his tone gave her pause. "There are bonds of blood between a mother and her own child that don't exist between a woman who merely takes in another woman's child."

"A mother," she echoed. So *that's* why he was being an idiot, suggesting a marriage with no permanency and forbidding even the possibility of adoption. "I notice that you say nothing about the bonds between a father and his child."

"That's different. The father doesn't carry the child, but the mother—"

"You're saying that if a woman doesn't carry a child in her own womb, she will not love or care for it properly."

He looked flustered. "I'm only saying it's not the same, that's all."

"She really hurt you, didn't she?"

"Who?"

"Your stepmother."

Releasing an oath, he slid out from under the counterpane and went to jerk on his drawers. "It has naught to do with her."

"It has everything to do with her. She married your father under certain conditions and then wanted to change them. She mothered you, then abandoned you."

"It wasn't her fault. She expected what any woman has a right to expect, and when she realized what she'd given up she regretted it."

"As you think I'll do." Anger mingled with pity to clog her throat. "So you're taking no chances. You won't commit to a wife whom you're sure will leave you eventually, and you certainly won't bring any children into a marriage where the mother might abandon them because they lack some essential 'blood bond.' "

"Abby—"

"Better to prepare yourself for heartbreak from the beginning, right? That way you won't be surprised when the woman turns out to be just what you expected—a soulless creature with no honor, no sense of responsibility, and no loyalty."

He whirled on her, eyes alight. "You always twist what I say to make it seem as if I think ill of you."

"Don't you?" She approached him with an aching heart. "A woman of character stands by her choices. She doesn't leave a man she loves and children who need her simply because she changed her mind. But apparently you think I'm not a woman of character."

"I think you're too young and inexperienced to know what you want from life. It's no reflection on your character if in time you discover you want more than I can give."

"Every person, young or old, risks the possibility of their life not turning out as planned. Especially when it comes to marriage. They might find they aren't suited for marriage after all. Or their spouses might die of an early illness. Taking a risk on another person is what marriage is all about."

"Don't talk to me of risk," Spencer said fiercely. "I'm risking more than you can imagine by continuing this marriage, knowing what could happen."

"Knowing what could happen and planning for it are two different things, Spencer. There's no risk in holding your heart in check and refusing to consider adoption. Because if anything goes wrong, you've lost nothing. You already knew it would go that way. But there's no gain in that, either. It's like a man who must leap a chasm to reach his heart's desire on the other side. If he tells himself he can't make it and never even tries, how can he gain his dream?"

"What do you want from me?" he asked hoarsely. "You want me to build a life and a family with you, knowing what could happen? I don't think I can do that. But I don't want you to go, either."

She swallowed. "Then I'll need a few days to think about this. Because if I stay, it will be forever. Maybe you can be married by halves, but I can't." She steadied her gaze on him. "So I have to decide if I can give up any possibility of having children, my own or someone else's, simply because you won't risk it."

"And if you can't?" he bit out.

"Then we'll finish out your plan as before—maintain our pretend marriage until you find Nathaniel and then go to America to dissolve it."

"I don't want that, damn it," he exploded. "Why can't you just let things go on as they are?"

"Until I grow so in love with you that I can't break away? All the while watching the years pass as I realize I never made a conscious decision to give up everything for you? The outcome will be exactly as you predict—my bitter regrets might poison any sweetness between us. I won't take that chance."

She started toward the door to her bedchamber, but he reached out to stay her. When he drew her back into his arms, she stiffened.

"There's no reason you can't share my bed in the meantime," he murmured into her hair.

"No." She wriggled free of his too tempting embrace. "You aren't the only one with a heart to protect. I love you, Spencer, but I won't let you use my love—or my enjoyment of your lovemaking—to bend me to your will. I'll come to your bed if I decide to stay, and not before."

He jerked her around to face him, his eyes steely bright. "We'll see how long you resist me when I'm actively seeking to seduce you."

"If you so much as attempt to steal a kiss," she threatened,

"I'll move out of this house and into Clara's until I've made my decision. Is that understood?"

A muscle worked in his jaw. "All right, no kisses. For now." He approached to tower over her, every inch of his taut, muscular frame screaming his confidence in his ability to sway her. "But only because I allow it and not for very long. Rest assured that if you dawdle about making up your mind, no one—not Blakely, not Lady Brumley, and for damned sure not Clara—will stop me from claiming you as my wife."

"At least for a while, right?"

He glowered down at her. "I wouldn't be the one leaving in the end."

"How do you know? If there's no solid promise between us, you could just as easily tire of me as I could of you. After all, you could dissolve the marriage with one little trip to America."

"But I wouldn't," he protested.

"No, of course not," she said bitterly. "You're a man of character. I'm the one whose character is in question."

"Devil take it, Abby—"

"You'll have my decision in a few days." Sick at heart, she turned toward the connecting door to her bedchamber.

"Wait!" he said when she laid her hand on the knob.

"Yes?"

"I'm sorry I didn't tell you about my sterility before. You had the right to hear of it while it could still do you some good. I should never have been so selfish as to ruin you for marriage to any other man when I knew I could only offer you half a marriage."

She flashed him a wan smile. "After you, there could never be any other man. I was ruined for marriage long before you took my innocence. But I don't regret it. So neither should you."

Neither should you. The words echoed painfully in Spencer's ears as he watched her walk out of his bedchamber for what might be the last time.

That awful thought stole the breath from his lungs and the joy from his soul. If she didn't decide to stay, he honestly didn't know what he would do. Life would mean nothing to him without her here. But how could he meet her terms?

Devil take her bloody stubbornness and talk of risk. *He* was the one who had to live every day with the knowledge of his inability to produce children. What did she know of risk?

She came halfway around the world to be with you on the word of your lying brother and a few paltry letters. She tried to make herself into what she thought you wanted. And even though you made her no promises, she came to your bed, knowing it would ruin her for any other man.

All right, so perhaps she did know something about risk. But she was too young to realize how time could wear on a person, remind her of things she'd missed, make her regret her choices . . .

The way Dora had regretted hers.

Bloody hell, this wasn't only about Dora. All women wanted children, or at least all the ones he knew.

A woman of character stands by her choices.

Yes, but would Abby stand by hers? The urge to have babes of one's own was powerful. Why else were all his friends procreating like rabbits?

Returning to his bed, he swore at the sight of her virgin blood staining the golden counterpane. To hell with her lofty ideas about risk and marriage. No matter what her decision, he had to keep her here long enough to show her the wonderful life they could have together.

At least she'd said she wouldn't leave until he found Nat. That would buy him time to convince her. In fact, the more time that passed without Nat's being found . . .

A slow smile crossed his lips. Abby wouldn't be leaving him anytime soon, not if he could help it.

Chapter 22

In certain situations, servants should be seen and not heard.

Suggestions for the Stoic Servant

Early in the evening on Monday, only two days after the night Abby and Spencer had made love, a knock came at the door of Abby's bedchamber while she was in her dressing room, drying off from her bath.

"Mrs. Graham, would you answer that?" she called out. "It's probably Marguerite with my gown."

"About time, too," Mrs. Graham said from the other room. "Dinner's in an hour."

Abby heard the door open and the murmur of conversation, but she never heard the door close. Curious, she donned her wrapper and strolled out into her bedchamber. No one was there. Had Mrs. Graham gone to check on the gown? If so, she was being terribly lax—she'd left the door ajar.

Rubbing the towel through her hair, Abby strode up to close it, then stood transfixed by the amazing sight that appeared through the crack.

Heavenly day. Mr. McFee and Mrs. Graham, locked in an intimate embrace.

She really shouldn't spy. But didn't she have a right to know what went on with her own servant? Someone had to look out for the woman's interests, after all. Although, judging from the passionate kiss he was bestowing on Mrs. Graham, the butler himself aspired to that position. Or was it their first such encounter?

Holding her breath, Abby peered through the crack. When after a moment Mr. McFee actually slid his hand down to squeeze Mrs. Graham's ample bottom, Abby nearly bit her tongue through while trying to hold back her laugh.

Definitely not the couple's first kiss. Or else the butler was awfully forward for a man of his reserve.

"That's enough of your tomfoolery, Arthur," Abby heard Mrs. Graham murmur. "Now go on and scribble in that notebook of yours. Plenty of time for the other business tonight when we can be private."

Abby jerked back from the door, but not before she heard him say, "I'm counting the moments, lass."

Vaulting across the room, Abby settled herself before the fire to dry her hair just in time. Mrs. Graham walked in and blinked to see her mistress sitting there with her brush and comb. "Oh, done bathing already, are you?"

Abby had to fight back her smile. "Yes. Where's Marguerite?"

"It wasn't her." A faint flush spread over the woman's cheeks as she turned away. "It was only one of the other servants, bringing something from his lordship for you." Mrs. Graham came over to hand Abby a small velvet case.

All thought of Mrs. Graham and Mr. McFee vanished as Abby opened it. Her heart caught in her throat. "Heavenly day," she whispered as she drew out a jewel-encrusted vinaigrette pendant.

"Look at that engraving," Mrs. Graham said in awe. "And the chain, my lady, the chain! Why, it's got to be gold."

"It could be bronze chased in gold." Nonetheless, the gems on the little container looked suspiciously costly. She tamped down her ready delight. Trust Spencer to find the perfect gift to tempt her.

Taking the vinaigrette, Mrs. Graham examined it with a shrewd eye. "Aye, it's gold, all right. And I'm near to certain these is emeralds. His lordship asked me this afternoon what gown you'd be wearing for dinner, and I told him the green one. No doubt that's why he sent Mr. McFee . . . er . . . that is, the servant up with this."

Abby frowned. That wasn't the only reason. "Spencer is the most infuriating, manipulative, and arrogant male to ever drive his wife purposely insane." She thrust the case at Mrs. Graham. "I know why he sent it."

"Because he's courting you."

"Trying to seduce me is more like it." She worked her comb through her tangled hair. "That's why he 'accidentally' brushed my fingers every time he handed me a hymnal at church yesterday. And why he's always touching my arm in the carriage when he reaches to open or close the window." He hadn't violated their agreement once by trying to kiss her. No, his seductions were more subtle. But every bit as effective.

She'd actually caressed her own breasts in bed last night and imagined it was Spencer's hand on them. For shame!

"This isn't mere seduction, love—these are emeralds. They must cost a fortune." She removed something from the case and held it out to Abby. "At least read the note."

With a sigh, Abby took it and read aloud, "To my lovely wife, for the next time you faint in my arms. This belonged to my mother." Tears stung her eyes. "Oh, the man is wickedly clever. He knew if he bought me jewels I'd accuse him of trying to buy my affections. So instead he finds an appropriate gift that's not only costly but belonged to his own mother—"

She swiped away her tears. "He means to persuade me I'm part of the family now. Even if I'm not."

"You could be." Mrs. Graham reverently returned the pendant to its case. "If you weren't so stubborn."

Abby bit back the impulse to tell Mrs. Graham the whole sordid tale. She'd already told the woman that his lordship had asked her to stay as his wife, but she hadn't explained why she balked at accepting his offer, other than to complain about his faults of character. Going into detail would mean revealing Spencer's secret, which she had no right to do. Especially when her servant was about as discreet as a signpost.

When Mrs. Graham set the case in Abby's lap, Abby wanted to scream. "You only support his lordship's suit because you want to stay in England yourself," Abby said bitterly, "so you can be with your Mr. McFee."

Mrs. Graham gaped at her. Then her eyes narrowed. "Spying on us, were you?"

"It's not like the two of you tried very hard to hide what you were doing."

Crossing her arms over her chest, Mrs. Graham pouted. "A little harmless kissing is all. I think I got a right to that after all my years of service."

Feeling instantly contrite, Abby reached over to pat her arm. "Of course you do. Don't mind my grumbling. I'm pleased you've found somebody after all these years, really I am. But don't let your own happiness blind you to the truth about Spencer. If I stay married to his overbearing lordship, he'll order me around from dawn to dusk."

"Most men do. A sensible woman just ignores their jabbering. She nods and says, 'Of course, my love, whatever you want,' then does as she pleases."

Unfortunately, doing as she pleased wasn't an option for Abby. She couldn't make Spencer adopt children or take a risk. He had to decide for himself to do those things. Which he would never do.

Because that would mean his trusting something—
someone—beyond his control. "I don't fancy a union where
my husband is always trying to control me." Abby tossed
down the comb to pick up her brush. "And that's what marriage to Spencer would be like."

Mrs. Graham took the brush from Abby's hands and
dragged it soothingly through her hair. "Can you blame the
man for trying to control things after the life he's had?"

Abby caught her breath. Could Mrs. Graham know of
Spencer's sterility? Surely not. Spencer said he'd never told
anyone. "What do you mean?"

"He's had nothing but tragedy, poor man, and all of it beyond his power to stop. His mother died when he was still a
lad. Then his father took a wife—too young a wife, if you ask
me—and they commenced to be miserable. His lordship
finds his own place in the army and is making something of
himself when his oldest brother dies. Now he's the heir,
whether he wants to be or not. So even though he's got a career he likes—if Mr. McFee is to be believed—he's expected
to put it aside."

"But he didn't."

"No, by then he'd started fighting the fates. First thing he
did after his brother died was become a spymaster."

"You knew about that?"

"I did." Moving around to the front of the chair, Mrs. Graham urged Abby's head forward so she could brush the hair
out from underneath. "Arthur . . . I mean, Mr. McFee . . .
knows all about his lordship. Been with the Law family since
the boy was in leading strings. Saw it all—the stepmother running off and the father dying of shame over it." She brushed
harder. "One more thing his lordship couldn't prevent."

Not to mention the accident that happened about that time
and ended all of Spencer's hopes for children. The woman
did have a point—what a lot of tragedy for one man to suffer.

"Suddenly," Mrs. Graham went on, "he's the viscount

himself, with an estate and a rascal of a younger brother to manage, not to mention his duty to his country that he don't want to give up. It's hard to handle all that if you don't order people about. After a while, you get used to it. You feel safer making everybody follow your rules."

"Yes." Abby couldn't keep the hurt from her voice. "Because he doesn't believe they're capable of thinking for themselves. They can't be trusted to run their own lives."

"Oh, lass, don't you see? The man is afraid to trust what he can't control. All the things he couldn't control gave him grief. So when he comes upon a sweet lady like yourself, who he don't know what to make of, he's plumb flummoxed. But that don't mean he won't come round in the end. Once he gets to know you better."

The door opened and Marguerite hurried in with Abby's gown, effectively ending the discussion.

Still, Mrs. Graham's words lingered in Abby's head the whole time the two women were helping her dress for dinner with Spencer. If she could be sure that Spencer would come to his senses eventually, she might stay around just to be with him.

The problem was, what if he didn't? What if she committed to him only to find he could never commit to her? She would give up any possibility of children.

But did it really matter if she never had a child to cradle in her arms, to teach and spoil and love? She sighed. Of course it mattered. Still, a foundling child would be enough for her. She could love any babe she took into her caring, whether she'd borne it herself or not. Maybe in time she could convince Spencer of that . . .

The way his stepmother had convinced his father to do as *she* wanted? Abby swallowed. Spencer was his father's son—once he plotted a course, he didn't change it easily. And did she want a marriage where she was forever waiting for him to trust her?

That was the question. And an hour later, as she and Spencer sat down to dinner, she was still no closer to answering it.

Nor was he making it easy, with all his sly seductions. "I see you're wearing the pendant I sent up," he said.

"Yes." She'd let Mrs. Graham and Marguerite talk her into it. But judging from his hungry gaze trailing down to where her breasts cradled the heavy vinaigrette, that was a mistake.

"It looks perfect on you," he said in that husky tone that roused her blood fever every time . . .

She swallowed. "Thank you."

Though the man was all the way at the end of the dinner table, nearer the door, she could feel his gaze as hot on her as if it were a caress. She tried to ignore it as the footmen brought the oysters, tried to concentrate on her food.

But she found herself casting him furtive glances every so often. And when during one of those glances he forked an oyster, then swirled it in melted butter the way he'd swirled his tongue over her breasts the other night—

"You're not eating your oysters," he said, a knowing smile touching his lips. "Worried about the effect they might have on you?"

"What do you mean?" Mesmerized, she watched as he ate the oyster and licked butter from his lips. The way he'd licked at her lips, then parted them to—

"Some say oysters are an aphrodisiac."

"What's an aphrodisiac?"

"Something that arouses a person's passions." He ate another, and a drop of butter landed on his chin. After wiping it with his finger, he sucked it off his fingertip. The way he'd sucked her tongue, the skin of her neck, her aching nipples—

Curse him. "Really?" Defiantly, she stabbed an oyster with her fork, then thrust it into her mouth and chewed, hardly tasting it. "That's ridiculous. I never noticed any such effect. Oysters usually give me dyspepsia."

That didn't deter him for a second. His mouth crooked upward. "Well, if you have dyspepsia later, just let me know. I'll be happy to rub your belly for you."

And your breasts. And your thighs. And the delicate, needy flesh between them.

She jerked her gaze away. Heavenly day, now she was doing the seducing for him.

The rest of the meal went no better. If she watched him eat, she imagined all the naughty things his mouth could do to her. But if she didn't watch, she imagined that her bread glistening with butter was his bared chest glistening with sweat, that the beef roast was his thick thigh, that the erect sausage . . .

She snorted. Erect sausage, indeed. But when dessert arrived, a quivering mound of custard with a cherry in the center that looked exactly like a nipple, she'd had enough.

"Excuse me," she murmured as she rose from the table. "I . . . um . . . don't want dessert. The oysters, you know."

She hurried for the door, but before she could pass Spencer, he reached out to grab her arm and tug her onto his lap.

"What on earth are you doing?" she hissed with a furtive glance at the servants.

"Rubbing your belly." His expression teemed with wickedness. "To help ease your dyspepsia." He cast the gaping footmen a warning look. "Leave us. And tell the rest of the staff that anyone venturing near the dining room before I call for them will be dismissed forthwith."

After the servants vanished, she tried to wriggle free, but he wouldn't let her. She glared up at him. "How dare you imply to them that you and I are in here—"

"What? I don't know about you, but I'm merely soothing my wife's indigestion. And since that requires my holding you in a scandalous manner, I thought you might prefer to have them gone."

"A likely story. I warned you that if you so much as attempted to steal a kiss—"

"I'm not attempting anything." His large hand covered her belly, then began to knead it in slow, sensuous motions. "I'm merely banishing your dyspepsia."

She sucked in a breath when he splayed his fingers wide over her lower abdomen, the warmth of his flesh feeding the warm ache between her legs. "You . . . you know that's not all you're doing."

"What a suspicious mind you have. Here I am, trying to be courteous, and you suspect me of having an ulterior motive." His hand swept up and down now, once, twice.

But when it brushed the underside of her breast on its third circuit, she caught his hand. "That's because you do. And I won't allow you to break our agreement—"

"You said nothing about my not being able to touch you."

"I implied it."

"You said, 'If you so much as attempt to steal a kiss.' That leaves enormous room for interpretation, my dear." He shifted her on his lap until she sat forward with her back pressed to his firm chest. Then he started rubbing her belly with his other hand.

A sudden surge of memory hit her . . . of that night in the study when he'd held her like this and caressed her and turned her to putty . . .

She groaned, hardly noticing when the hand she'd been clasping slipped from her grasp. Now he stroked her belly with both hands, side to side, up and down. "Surely it . . . violates the . . . spirit of the rules for you to touch me like this."

"Like what? In a manner meant to ease your discomfort?"

"Well, no, but—Wait a minute, stop that!" Exactly when had the sneaky wretch begun unfastening the buttons of her front-opening gown? "That is definitely not—"

"I'm only making you comfortable." He went on unbuttoning. "This gown is much too tight on your stomach. It's no wonder you have dyspepsia." He swept his hand inside to boldly caress her belly through her chemise. "Besides, I can rub it better if I don't have to contend with layers of fabric."

"If you think I'm going to let you . . ." She trailed off with a moan when his hand suddenly dropped down to stroke her right between the legs. "That's not . . . my belly . . ." she protested weakly.

"Sorry, my hand slipped." He danced his fingers sensuously up her abdomen.

Put them back, she thought, then cursed herself for her weakness. But the man was both clever *and* persistent, a combination she found incredibly seductive. Besides, if he wanted her so badly that he'd risk these dangerous touches when he knew she might run off to Clara's any minute . . .

"The problem is your chemise, you know," he went on smoothly. "We really should open it."

She rolled her eyes. "I can't wait to hear your reason for that bit of cheating."

"I'm merely saying it prevents me from seeing where I'm putting my hand." Now that her gown gaped open from neckline to thigh, he easily tugged the ties of her chemise loose. "Let's just move it out of the way, shall we?"

An uncontrollable urge to laugh bubbled up inside her. "You are incorrigible," she said, fighting to maintain her resistance and losing rapidly.

"I'm only trying to be helpful." He swiftly opened the short placket of her chemise. "That's what a good husband is supposed to do, isn't it?"

"A good husband is supposed to honor his wife's wishes," she said dryly.

"Precisely. Surely you don't *wish* to suffer from your dyspepsia."

When his hand slipped inside to fondle her breast, she shoved his hand down, then shifted back around to sit across his lap and eye him sternly. "I thought moving the chemise out of the way was meant to prevent your hand from slipping."

"My hand didn't slip." A smile ghosted over his lips as he again cupped her breast. "From what I understand, indigestion often causes pains in the chest as well as the belly. I thought I'd take care of those, too." With a roguish smile, he thumbed her nipple, blatantly, erotically.

The beginnings of a laugh escaped her lips before she squelched it. "Next you'll be telling me that indigestion sometimes causes pain in one's privates."

"Now that you mention it—" he began, sliding his hand downward.

"Spencer Law," she said, trying to sound severe as she caught his hand and drew it out of her chemise, "you know very well I wasn't suggesting—"

"Of course you were." He stuck his other hand inside her chemise. "And I'm more than willing to help."

Stifling a chuckle, she grabbed that one, too. "What if I tell you I lied about the dyspepsia? Will you stop this?"

"Certainly." Eyes twinkling, he tugged his hands free of her grip, but only to start unbuttoning his waistcoat. "However, it seems that *I* suddenly have dyspepsia. And since I was kind enough to help you in *your* hour of need . . ."

She couldn't help it. A laugh boiled out of her. "You have got to be the most persistent, exasperating—"

"And helpful." He leaned forward enough to shrug off his coat, then his waistcoat. "Let's not forget helpful."

She gave up. What woman could stand firm in the face of such blatant and egregious manipulation? Especially when he was manipulating her in the very direction her heart wanted to go.

Not to mention her body. Now that he had her thoroughly aroused, she wasn't about to let him leave her unfulfilled. "By all means, let me be helpful, too." She reached for the buttons of his trousers. "Just tell me where it hurts, my lord."

Clearly realizing that he'd won, he gazed on her with a look that mingled triumph with rampant need. "Everywhere." He dragged his shirttails free of the trousers she was unbuttoning, then grabbed her hand and slid it up underneath to cover his chest. "Here." He slid it lower over his abdomen. "And here." His eyes slid closed as he pressed her hand beneath his gaping waistband. "And definitely here."

He shuddered deliciously when her fingers found the arousal still cradled by his stockinette drawers. Anticipation surged through her to feel him so hard, so ready. She stroked him through the fabric, delighting in the guttural groan it wrung from his throat.

"Better?" she asked with a teasing smile.

"Not yet."

She shifted toward him so she could touch him more easily. Caressing his chest with one hand, she fondled his staff with the other until his breathing increased to rapid-fire gasps.

But when she leaned up to kiss his mouth, he jerked his head back, his eyes flying open. "No kisses, remember? I won't have you claiming later that I broke the rules."

As if he hadn't already. But one look at his fierce expression told her he was serious. She smiled coyly, then drew her hand from beneath his shirt to stroke his mouth. Rubbing her thumb over his lower lip, she said in a throaty whisper, "Do you really think you can make love to me without kissing me?"

Desire streaked across his face like lightning scoring the sky. "If I have to."

"You don't," she said, then drew his head down to hers.

After two days of pent-up desire, their kiss exploded instantly into a violence of turbulent need. He stabbed his tongue deep; she sucked it deeper. Soon they were battling for mastery, his mouth ardent and determined while hers gave as much as it got.

He shifted her to straddle his lap so he could thrust both hands inside her chemise, one to fondle her breast, the other to "slip" down between her legs. As he drove two fingers inside her, he tore his mouth from hers.

"I want you now, my darling," he rasped against her cheek. "I don't think I can make it upstairs."

"Then don't."

Apparently that was enough answer for him. Grabbing her about the waist, he set her off him so he could wriggle his trousers and drawers down. She leaned against the table and watched wide-eyed as his impudent "staff" sprang free.

"You see how bad my dyspepsia is?" he ground out. "What will you do to ease me, wife of mine?"

With a playful smile, she licked her finger, then stroked a circle over the insolent crown of his aroused flesh.

Spencer groaned. "Teasing wench."

She laughed and shrugged off her gown and chemise. Her drawers rapidly followed. "I've still got dyspepsia, too. And what will you do to ease mine?"

Desire flared in his gaze as he raked it down her naked body. "What do you think?" Reaching for her, he settled her astride his thighs until his staff rested like a hot, heavy promise against her belly.

"That seems a very naughty remedy, my lord. Whatever will the proper Mr. McFee say to his master performing such wicked acts in the dining room?"

"He won't say anything if he knows what's good for him," Spencer growled. "Besides, even McFee should know that a man needs a little dessert after dinner."

A sudden gleam shone in his face as he reached behind her. When he brought his hand back, it was full of custard. "Time for dessert, darling," he said as he smeared it over her breast.

"Spencer!" she exclaimed as the cool wet stuff dripped off and began to slide down her belly. "What—"

He seized her breast in his mouth, and her protest turned to a groan. His lips and tongue were everywhere, sucking and licking and generally driving her insane.

Dragging his mouth free, he gazed up at her with eyes alight, then licked his lips. "Mmm. I can see we'll be having custard often for dinner."

He reached behind her for more, but she scooped it from his hand when he brought it back. "Don't be greedy. You have to share with your wife."

She smoothed it over his chest, then bent her head to lick it off. Moaning, he leaned back to give her better access.

Heavenly day, but he tasted good, and not just because of the custard. Had it been only two days since she'd tasted his warmth, smelled his tangy scent, felt the smooth flesh jerk in response to the caress of her mouth? His male nipple met her tongue like a currant floating unexpectedly in one's custard, and she nipped it, wishing she could devour all of him.

Maybe then he'd really be hers. Maybe then she could feel sure she had him forever.

That sobering thought made her sigh against his chest, but he didn't allow her any regrets. Sticky with custard, one of his hands sought her breast to tweak and tempt the nipple while his other plundered her between the legs, plucking deftly at her own currant before driving his fingers deeply into her. She groaned and pressed herself against both his hands.

"I want to be inside you," he murmured.

"You're already inside me," she quipped.

His gaze glittered a warning. "You know what I mean."

"Then you know what to do."

Frustration filled his face. "You're on top. You have to help."

"Help what?" She mustered an innocent smile as she

stared down at the male flesh growing impossibly larger against her cleft.

"Devil take it, woman, do you want me to beg?"

"Absolutely. You deserve to beg after how you've acted the past two days, you and your not so subtle attentions and your furtive touches and your sly insinuations—"

He swallowed the rest with a sensual kiss that he probably meant to distract her.

She jerked back with a laugh. "But of course you won't beg, will you? You always ask if I want you to, yet never once have you begged me for anything. The great Lord Ravenswood never begs."

His eyebrow crooked upward with the arrogance of a thunder god. "Certainly not. Why should I beg for what we both want?"

This time when his insolent mouth came down on hers and brazenly took what it wanted, he didn't stop with that, oh, no. Like a wicked divining rod, his fingers returned unerringly to the very source of her spring, then worked it until her fluid flowed hot and thick for him and the hollow ache between her legs grew to a gnawing hunger only he could satisfy. But when she ground herself against his hand, he withdrew it abruptly.

"No more of that until I'm inside you," he vowed as he grabbed her hips. "So if you know what's good for you, my wild rose, you'll rise up on your knees and take me."

She would have balked at his tone of command—and his scurrilous tactics—but she wanted him too much. Trying not to look overly eager, she did exactly as he bade.

He moaned when she slid down on him completely. "My God, Abby, you weren't the only one suffering, you know. I've spent two days craving your hands on me, wanting your kiss, needing this."

What woman could resist such a thrilling admission? With a coy smile, she rose and came down again . . . and again, relishing the rough breaths she forced out of him, the rough moans he couldn't repress . . . and the sweet delight of having control over him for a change.

"That's it," he choked out. "Ah, darling, yes . . . like that . . . you do that so well."

The praise further swelled her enjoyment. All right, so maybe he wouldn't ever release his control enough to beg, but at least he could release it enough to let her take charge of their lovemaking. How many other men would?

And this felt so good, so . . . so erotic. When his mouth sought her breast and she angled forward to help, it got even better. The spot between her legs that always ached for him now pounded squarely against his pelvis. Feverishly, she increased her pace, seeking more of that incredibly delicious sensation. Like a swollen stream massing behind a dam, excitement gathered just there, beating against the dam over and over until the dam strained to hold it back . . .

"Yes . . . Yes . . ." he rasped. "You're mine now . . . Never forget it . . ."

How could she? No matter what happened, he'd always be part of her. He was the tide of her ocean, the thunder of her storm. And when he suddenly surged deeply to release a hot flood of his essence inside her, he burst her own dam, drowning her in the most exquisite pleasure, sweeping away everything before it . . . all her fears, her uncertainties, her insecurities.

Until the waters subsided, slowly but inevitably. Until their pulses receded to normal and their breathing fell into a steadier current. Clasping him tightly to her breast, she tried not to think of what she'd just done and how it complicated everything.

Then he whispered against her ear, "I love you."

And just like that her joy returned. With a little murmur of surprise, she settled back on his knees to stare at him, half in fear, half in hope.

"I love you," he repeated, his gaze perfectly sincere. "I think I always did."

"You didn't." Though her heart soared, she hadn't yet become completely irrational. "But it's all right. If you love me now, that's enough."

"No, really, I did." He kissed the tip of her nose. "Almost from the first time I saw you. You were wearing braids and standing in your kitchen in a cloud of purple while you stripped stalks of dried lavender."

She blushed. "I wish you didn't remember that. You and Nat arrived a day before your letter said to expect you, and I wasn't prepared. I'm sure I looked awful when Mrs. Graham brought you into the kitchen."

He fingered the pendant she still wore around her neck. "You looked sweet and pretty and innocent. Your cheeks were flushed, and crushed lavender petals were sticking to your apron. I wanted to dust them off just so I could put my hands on you." He grinned. "Then I wanted you to dust me off so I could have *your* hands on *me*."

"Really?" she said archly. "The way I remember it, you assumed I was a servant and said, in a very uppish tone, 'Please inform your master and mistress that Lord Ravenswood and Mr. Law have arrived.' "

He chuckled. "And you said, with a saucy smile, 'Please inform Lord Ravenswood and Mr. Law that the mistress is aware of their arrival and will take them to the master once she's changed her clothes and washed up.' Nat laughed his fool head off."

"You didn't. My impertinence probably appalled you."

"Not so much appalled as surprised me. You gave me no chance to respond before you flounced off toward the door. And once I got a good look at your impertinent and exceedingly fine derriere, I thought of only one thing—what it would be like to strip off your gown and ravish you right there in your father's kitchen." He released the pendant to run his finger over her breast and then her nipple. "I should have followed my impulse. It would have saved us months of frustration."

She laughed. "And sent Papa into a miraculous recovery as he chased you to the altar with a flintlock."

"Exactly."

As he kissed her in a sweet confirmation of all his love, her hope swelled even higher. If he truly loved her, then surely he meant to commit to the marriage. And that was all she wanted.

Spencer was stiffening again inside her when a knock sounded at the door to the dining room. He wrenched his mouth from hers with a curse. Glancing back at the door, he called out, "I told you not to disturb us!"

There was a short silence. "Yes, my lord, I know." It was McFee's hesitant voice. "I most humbly beg your pardon, but Lady Evelina has come to speak to you about an urgent matter concerning your brother. She awaits you in the front drawing room."

At the mention of Nathaniel, Spencer's returning erection died inside her. "Very well. Tell her I'll be there shortly."

"Tell her *we'll* be there shortly," Abby called out, then slid off Spencer's lap.

As the sound of McFee's footsteps receded, Spencer stood. "There's no need for you to go, Abby." Dipping a napkin in water, he rapidly washed the remaining custard from his chest. "Why don't you head upstairs to my bedchamber and wait for me?" He grinned. "And take the extra custard with you."

"No, indeed, my randy husband." She cleansed herself, too, then pulled up her chemise and tied it. "Anything that concerns your brother concerns me. So we're both going. The custard will have to come later."

With a heavy sigh, he muttered. "Oh, all right. I suppose

the sooner we get it over with, the sooner we can have more dessert."

They dressed and made themselves as presentable as possible under the circumstances, then headed for the drawing room. In the hall they saw McFee, who stiffly refused to meet their eyes when they started by.

Her embarrassment was acute . . . until she remembered what she'd seen earlier outside her bedchamber. Mr. McFee had the audacity to look down his nose at *them*, for heaven's sake?

A perverse impulse seizing her, she paused. "Oh, Mr. McFee, I wanted to thank you for coming by my room earlier to bring Spencer's gift. I'm only surprised you didn't wait around to hand it to me yourself. When I first came out of the dressing room, you and Mrs. Graham were nowhere to be found."

Mr. McFee's ruddy complexion deepened to scarlet. "I . . . er . . . thought it best to leave the box with Mrs. Graham."

"Yes, I gather that. She was most appreciative." She waited until McFee's eyes swung to hers in alarm, then added, "Of your trust in her, I mean."

As she moved on, Spencer bent to whisper, "What was all that about?"

"It seems my servant and your butler have formed an attachment to each other." She leaned up close to his ear. "I saw them kissing in the hall when they didn't know I was watching."

Spencer stared at her. "My McFee? And your Mrs. Graham? Are you sure?"

"Oh, yes. They made an assignation for later." She grinned as they neared the stairs. "And he even squeezed her bottom."

Spencer burst into laughter.

"Shh," she hissed, "he'll know we're talking about him."

"I hope he does. He's probably discussed my shortcomings with the other servants for years."

She thought of what Mrs. Graham had said. "Probably."

"So tell me," Spencer added as he dropped behind her on the stairs. "How did he squeeze her bottom? Like this?" He grabbed her left buttock with one hand, then cupped the right in his other. "Or was it more like this?"

Giggling, she hurried up the stairs to escape him. "I swear, Spencer, sometimes you are very wicked."

"You're just now finding that out?" he teased as he caught up with her.

"You hide it well beneath your seriousness."

"Either that, or you simply bring out the devil in me," he whispered.

She was still laughing when they entered the drawing room together.

Chapter 23

The wise servant avoids involvement in his employer's family relations.

Suggestions for the Stoic Servant

Abby's pleasure vanished when she caught sight of Evelina pacing the drawing room, her hands worrying a handkerchief much too violently for her generally mild manner. "Thank God you're here, my lord," Evelina exclaimed. "You have to help me."

"Of course," Spencer said in soothing tones as he left Abby's side to take Evelina's hand in his. "What do you need?"

"I have to speak to Nathaniel right away."

Only Spencer's rigid stance betrayed his sudden agitation. "Why?"

Evelina hesitated, her anxious gaze shifting beyond Spencer to where Abby stood. Finally she steadied her shoulders and whispered, "I'm carrying Nathaniel's child. And if he doesn't come back to marry me soon, everyone will guess what we've done. Mama will never forgive me, and my sisters will have no future." She burst into tears.

A desperate look crossed Spencer's face as he folded the weeping woman in his arms. "There, there, don't fret. It'll be all right."

Poor Evelina. How could it be all right when they didn't know where Nat was?

"How far along are you?" Spencer asked.

"Well . . . since we only . . . were together the one time after he first returned from America . . . I figure it's . . . not quite two months," the girl gasped between hiccuping sobs. Gazing up at Spencer, she wailed, "So you have to get him back here right away!"

Spencer shot Abby a questioning glance, but she had no idea what to tell him to do or say. Evelina still thought Nat was in Essex.

"My . . . my last letter to him," Evelina went on, managing to stifle her sobs, "the one telling him about the baby, was returned from Wales in the post this afternoon. Now I have no way to locate him and—"

"Wales?" Spencer's eyes narrowed. Releasing Evelina, he stepped back to stare at her. "Why did you write to him in Wales if he's recuperating in Essex?"

Coloring, Evelina dropped her gaze. "I . . . er . . . you see . . . I knew he wasn't in Essex. Because he came to visit me before he left town the night of your dinner."

"What?" Spencer roared. "And you never told me?"

"Please don't be angry," Evelina pleaded. "He made me promise not to say anything; he told me it would ruin all his plans."

"For what?" Spencer growled. "To abandon and humiliate you publicly while he waltzed off to spend Abby's dowry?"

"Of course not!" Sniffing, Evelina walked over to sit on the sofa. "His plans for you. And Abby."

Now intensely curious, Abby took a seat beside Evelina. "What are you talking about?"

Evelina wouldn't meet Spencer's angry gaze. Instead, she fixed Abby with a pleading look. "He wanted Spencer to marry you, so he made it happen. And then he ran away to make sure that Spencer didn't undo everything he'd done."

"He ran away because he'd stolen Abby's dowry," Spencer put in.

Evelina shook her head violently. "He said he only took the dowry to make sure she came here for the money. And her father's business concern."

"You believed that idiocy?" Spencer strode before the sofa, agitation threading his voice. "Come on, Evelina, you know Nat. How could he resist such a large sum?"

A stubborn fierceness filled her face. "He didn't take it for that reason, I swear. Nathaniel did it for you, because he loves you. He knew you'd never marry when you believed you couldn't sire—" She broke off with a blush.

Spencer halted, his face draining of color. "He knew about that?"

She bobbed her head. "He said you told him in America when you were foxed."

Looking as if he'd taken a blow to the chest, Spencer wheeled back to drop into a chair opposite them. "My God . . . I'd had so much to drink that night . . . I don't even remember . . ." He glanced up at Evelina. "That's why he manufactured the marriage and brought Abby here?"

"Nathaniel didn't think you should be without a wife simply because of some doctor's ill-considered opinion."

The enormity of Nathaniel's assumption roused Abby's anger. "So what did he do, just pick the first woman he thought might fit the bill? The first one he could manipulate? Without even caring that Spencer didn't want her?"

"No!" Evelina shot Abby an apologetic glance. "It wasn't like that. He knew Spence wanted you. He said that Spence talked about you, even talked about marrying you." She glanced to Spencer. "That's true, isn't it?"

Spencer's gaze fell warm and tender on Abby. "Yes. Before I got too drunk to remember anything, I do remember talking about Abby. Nat suggested I make her my mistress. I told him she deserved marriage."

Abby flashed him a shy smile. He'd thought of her in terms of marriage even then? When he'd said he'd desired her from the moment they met, she'd thought sure he was putting a rosy face on the past. But maybe not.

Evelina was watching Spencer eagerly. "You see? Nathaniel was sure you wanted her, so he got her for you."

Shifting his gaze back to Evelina, Spencer gave a harsh laugh. "*Got* her for me? Like . . . like someone purchases a horse? Good God, Evelina, that's insane. What about Abby? How did he know *she* wanted *me*?"

"She married you, didn't she?"

"Because she thought I wanted her."

"And because her other choices were awful. He did it for her, too, you know."

Spencer snorted. "Right. He deceived her and her father, forged papers, deceived me, and then left you here alone out of the goodness of his heart. To help his poor brother to a wife." He shook his head. "I don't believe it. He wanted Mercer's company and he needed the wherewithal to revive it, so he hit upon this mad plan of a proxy marriage."

"Nathaniel would never—"

"Perhaps you're both right," Abby put in, though she understood his feelings of betrayal. "The dowry and the company may indeed have tempted Nathaniel, but if he'd wanted only that, he would have taken the money and left me in America. He wouldn't have paid my passage here so I could uncover his deception. And he had to know I couldn't manage such a trip financially without his help."

That seemed to give Spencer pause. He leaned forward to fix Evelina with an intent gaze. "What reason did he give for caring whether I married or not?"

"You started talking about his being the heir, and he panicked. You know Nathaniel. He doesn't want the responsibility of an estate and a title. He only wants a comfortable portion for us and our children, nothing more. I'm sure he'll give every penny of the dowry back when he returns. He doesn't want the money."

"Then why was he in Wales?" Spencer persisted.

Abby wondered what Wales had to do with anything.

"I-I don't know," Evelina stammered. "I guess he had nowhere else to go, so he visited friends there. He usually writes to tell me where he'll be . . . except for this time. The week before he was in Wales he was in—"

"York?"

Evelina looked perplexed. "Well, yes. How did you know?"

"My runners discovered that he'd met with three men of business in the weeks before the dinner. No doubt he was already making use of Abby's dowry. One man was from York, one from Wales, and a third from Bristol. Unfortunately, by the time my runners reached York, Nat was gone. And he evaded them in Wales, too."

Evelina looked appalled by this obvious proof of her fiancé's perfidy. Then a fierceness passed over her features. "Well, whatever he was doing doesn't matter now. If you're right, then your men are waiting for him in Bristol. They'll bring him back, and then you can question him yourself about his actions."

Paling, Spencer jerked to his feet to pace before them. "Unfortunately, no one is waiting for him in Bristol. Not anymore."

"What do you mean?" Evelina asked as a sudden chill swept through Abby.

"Night before last I sent a message to my men, ordering them back to London."

The very night they'd made love. Abby felt the bottom drop out of her stomach. "Why?"

His defiant gaze swung to her. "Why do you think?"

It dawned on her then. Because if she decided against staying, she still couldn't leave until Nat showed up. And how could Nat show up if Spencer's men weren't looking for him?

Why, that sneaky, conniving—He wasn't satisfied with influencing her decision by seducing her. No, Spencer left nothing to chance, and certainly nothing to *her*.

Tears sprang to her eyes, but she ruthlessly restrained them. After all his sweet words of love in the dining room, after everything Mrs. Graham had said, she'd lulled herself into thinking they might have a future after all.

Yet he'd said nothing to indicate he'd changed his mind about their future. His dismissing of the runners wasn't a good sign either, even if he'd done it two days ago. And what if his admission of love was only one more tactic for coaxing her to stay?

Was she doomed to always be his Dora-in-waiting? If she stayed, would he spend every day anticipating her leaving until his fears and suspicions poisoned even their love?

Her uncertainties settled like a stone in her heart. She had to know if he still saw their marriage as temporary.

"Lord Ravenswood?" Evelina said, drawing them back to the girl's present predicament. "Can you send more men to Bristol? One way or the other, you must bring Nathaniel home."

"Yes, of course I must." Spencer looked relieved to have something other than Abby to focus on. "But since my men haven't been successful until now, I don't want to chance their missing him again. Once he leaves Bristol, we've no way of knowing where he'll go next. So I'll bring him back myself."

"You can't do that," Abby said coolly. "The May Day fête is in two days, remember? You said that the king demanded your presence."

"It doesn't matter. The king cares more about your presence than mine anyway. I'll attempt to be back by then, but if

I'm not, go on without me. Blakely and Clara can accompany you."

Approaching the sofa, Spencer squatted before the still-distraught Evelina. "Don't worry, poppet, I'll find him. Go home and stop fretting. Get plenty of sleep." He chucked her under the chin. "This baby may end up my only heir, so we can't chance his being born on the wrong side of the blanket, can we?"

"All right," the poor girl murmured.

My only heir. Abby's heart sank. He'd only need an heir if he refused to adopt children.

Or was there some rule against adopting an heir in English law? She clung desperately to that possible meaning behind his words.

Spencer stood, then drew Evelina to a stand. "How did you get here?"

"I . . . I took a hackney."

"Then I'll bring you home on my way out of the city." He cast Abby a glance, his jaw going taut as his gaze met hers. "Evelina, why don't you go tell McFee to call for my carriage? I'll be along shortly."

With a nod, Evelina left the room.

Abby rose to face him. "Why would Evelina's babe end up being your only heir?"

"You know why. I can't have children."

"And won't adopt them?"

He tensed. "We've been through this before, Abby—"

"Yes. And I see that nothing has changed." How foolish of her to think that it might. "Once more you're manipulating everything according to your wishes and ignoring mine. A pity that Evelina had to throw all your plans out of kilter. But I'm sure you're already working on some other way to keep me here against my will."

"Against your will?" he echoed. "Surely you're not letting my one mistake—"

"Of course. That's the sort of woman I am, aren't I? A frivolous idiot who will flee on a whim if you don't take measures to force me to stay. At least for a while, that is. Until my complete lack of character makes me run off with some Italian count—"

"You know very well I don't see you like that. I love you."

His heartfelt words made her hesitate. She'd waited so long to hear him say them, and today he finally had. So why wasn't she throwing herself into his arms? A few weeks ago, she had been happy to be married to him even without love, happy to have some small chance at being his. And now that she knew he loved her, she ought to be jumping to accept things on his terms. Why wasn't she?

Because things were different now. A few weeks ago, he'd been almost a god to her. Despite all her professed ideas about democracy and equality, in her heart she'd still thought Spencer worthy of any sacrifice. But she hadn't thought herself worthy of the same. Now she realized that he was just a man, no better and no worse than she. Yes, he deserved love and a full life . . . but she did, too. And if in his stubbornness and cursed arrogance, he couldn't see that she deserved better from him than a temporary arrangement, then their marriage was doomed from the start.

So she stood her ground. "You love only the Abby who adores you and sacrifices for you and would do anything to be with you. You don't love the Abby who expects the same thing of you."

He scowled. "And you don't love the man who can't give you children."

"Oh, but I do. I don't care if you give me children. But you won't even consider other options. My wishes don't count. You decide we should have a temporary marriage and not adopt, and that's how it must be."

"It's the best thing—"

"For you, yes. Then you needn't risk anything by putting

your faith in me, a fickle woman. Well, I've got a surprise for you, Spencer. I won't remain in a marriage where you refuse to trust me, to take some chances for my sake." She sucked in a breath, then spoke the only words she could. "I'll wait until Parliament is no longer in session, but after that, I want to go home."

A stricken look passed over his face. "You're going to leave me?" He searched her face, his eyes going cold. "Of course you are." His grim laugh cut her to the heart. "Odd, isn't it? You're doing exactly what I predicted after all. But I suppose it's just as well that it comes sooner rather than later."

With that cruel sally, he left.

As her heart shriveled up into a dried weight in her aching chest, she crumpled onto the sofa. She'd been a fool to think he'd ever trust her. He'd been waiting for her to abandon him from the moment they met, and no amount of love could have changed that.

He was right—it probably was better that the break came sooner rather than later. So why must it hurt so much?

Chapter 24

The servant should avoid gossiping about his employer's affairs unless it seems necessary to ensure his employer's happiness.

Suggestions for the Stoic Servant

Spencer's next few hours passed in a blur. After taking Evelina home, he tracked down his runners, who'd just returned. They told him all they knew and handed him written reports. Then he went to Blakely's, told him as much as he dared, and asked him and Clara to accompany Abby to the fête. By the time Spencer left London, it was past ten o'clock.

Now he sat in his coach rubbing his bleary eyes as he tried to read the runners' reports by the poor light of the carriage lamps. There wasn't much of use in them—when his men had left Bristol, Nat hadn't yet arrived there. But that was to be expected, considering the dates of Evelina's correspondence and Nat's departure from Wales.

One reassuring bit of information was that Sir Horace Peabody, the man Nat was supposed to be meeting, was in residence at his estate outside Bristol. With any luck, Spencer would reach the place no more than a day or two after his brother.

Thank God. Evelina was right about one thing—Nat must be brought back to London at once and forced to face his responsibilities. Besides, Spencer couldn't wait to get his hands on his brother. Throttling would be too good after the way Nat had ruined Spencer's life with his heedless machinations.

Tossing the reports aside, he turned down the lamp, then sank against the squabs. He ought to sleep while he could. Posting through the night, they'd probably reach Bristol by tomorrow evening, and he'd need all his strength for dealing with Nat.

He closed his eyes, but that was a mistake. Without the reports to distract him, he was free to think about Abby, to imagine her in all her aspects.

Abby settled across his lap all flushed and sated. Abby sharing an understanding look with him over Evelina's head. Abby looking betrayed.

With a curse, he straightened to stare out the window into the moonlit night. Damn that bloody woman to hell. Why must she plague him so?

Because he wanted her. Even after everything, he wanted her. He'd been so close to convincing her to stay. A few more days, a few more encounters like the one in the dining room, and Abby would have been his. But no, he'd had to ruin it by telling her about calling off the runners.

Why hadn't he lied? Why hadn't he claimed he wanted to go to Bristol to join his men? That's what Spencer the spymaster would have done.

But Spencer the husband was too besotted to think straight. Spencer the husband had recently developed this annoying habit of telling his wife the truth. Even when he knew what would happen if he did.

All the same, he'd meant what he told her—it was just as well that it ended now. At least this way he didn't get used to having her in his bed, to waking up with her in his arms, to sharing a laugh over the peccadilloes of society.

To loving her.

You love only the Abby who adores you and sacrifices for

you and would do anything to be with you. You don't love the Abby who expects the same thing of you.

What rot. Simply because he'd taken a few devious steps to keep her? The very fact that he'd go to such extremes ought to show her that he loved her.

Nathaniel did it for you, because he loves you.

Evelina's claim made Spencer scowl into the darkness. His actions and Nat's weren't the same. Nat had ignored Spencer's wishes—

Once more you're manipulating everything according to your wishes and ignoring mine.

He groaned. Devil take it. Yes, perhaps Abby was right—he had ignored her wishes. But what did she expect when her wishes were so unreasonable and ill-considered—

Nathaniel didn't think you should be without a wife simply because of some doctor's ill-considered opinion.

This was insane. He was not like his presumptuous and reckless brother, damn it. Every proud bone in his body balked at the thought.

All right, so perhaps he *had* been presumptuous in his measures for keeping Abby with him. But his determination to stick to his decision about the rest of it had been right—she'd proven it herself. Look how eager she'd been to leave him. If that's how little it took to drive her away, it was better he suffer for it now than later, after he'd fallen more deeply in love with her.

Why should he live a guarded life, worried that one of his heedless actions might send her fleeing any minute? What sort of lasting joy could he find in a marriage where he always had to tread lightly, where he couldn't simply relax in the knowledge that she would never—

A stillness came over him. That she would never leave him.

Bloody, bloody hell. That's exactly what she'd been trying to tell him. That if they drifted into marriage without committing to it, they would always be too careful with each other to be honest, too fearful to be secure . . . too untrusting to risk all for happiness.

He threw his head back against the squabs. She was right. She'd been right all along. A marriage where neither party could trust its permanence could bring no lasting joy.

So if he wanted to keep her, he'd have to do as she demanded—sacrifice his need to control the outcome and simply trust her. Trust her not to leave and to be satisfied with their childless marriage.

He shook his head. No, he'd have to trust her with more than that. He'd have to trust her with children who were not her own. Because she'd made it clear that she wanted children.

A sudden memory assailed him, of Abby cradling Lydia in her arms. That one brief glimpse had been enough to show him how fondly she regarded the child. How much more fondly would she regard a babe she'd cradled from early on, a babe they brought into their home together, a babe she would teach and nurture herself? That he could teach and nurture, too.

The longing that gripped him swelled so powerfully he could no longer resist it. The chasm was before him. He could leap it with her. Or like a coward, stand there and watch her leap it alone and ride away on the other side.

He refused to be a coward.

As he made his decision, a peace fell over him so sweet, he wondered why he'd ever fought so hard. What a fool he'd been. His wife had offered him more from life than he'd ever expected to have, and he'd very nearly thrown it away.

Thank God for Abby's stubbornness.

His first impulse was to turn the carriage around and race back to London to tell her before she could harden her heart further against him. Unfortunately, that was unwise. Evelina needed Nat now, and Spencer dared not risk the fool's getting away.

But once Spencer returned to London and had his wife in his arms again . . .

That thought alone enabled him to finally sleep.

The rest of the trip passed in a haze. Night turned to morning and then to afternoon as he ate and drank and relieved himself when necessary, but mostly he slept. And dreamed of Abby. Of their future. Of impish boys tugging on her skirts as they demanded ices, and cute chubby-cheeked girls who adored their papa . . .

When he came awake from his last doze to find that the sun had already set again and Bristol was close at hand, relief coursed through him. He wanted to fetch Nat and be done with this, so he could go home to Abby.

His wife.

With that thought ever-present, he sought out his brother. Thankfully, Sir Horace's estate was well known in town. More importantly, the innkeeper who gave Spencer its direction confirmed that a gentleman from London had already visited the Peabody estate twice. In fact, the innkeeper said, the man was there that very evening.

Elation gripped Spencer. It was almost over now.

Then a strange thing happened upon his arrival at the Peabody estate. The butler seemed unsurprised to see him, even going so far as to say that "the gentlemen" had been expecting him for dinner, which was sadly now long past. Though curious about how anyone could be expecting him for anything, Spencer held his tongue as he followed the servant to Sir Horace's study, where the gentlemen were "having their port and cigars."

But after Spencer was announced and had entered the room, two things rapidly became apparent. One, Nat was definitely the "gentleman from London." And two, Sir Horace had indeed been expecting the Viscount Ravenswood.

"Capital! You made it after all," said the genial Sir Horace, whom Spencer had never laid eyes on in his life.

Nat, however, looked as if he'd seen a ghost. "Spence? Why on earth are you—" The man caught himself. "Yes, it's wonderful that you arrived in time."

Something odd was going on, and Spencer had a funny feeling he wasn't going to like it. "In time for what?"

"The signing of the papers, of course," Sir Horace put in as he poured another glass of port, apparently for Spencer. "We waited until after dinner in hopes that you might arrive, even though your brother had shown me the documents giving him the authority to complete the purchase. He said he feared you wouldn't make it here yourself to sign everything and receive the bill of sale, but I'm so pleased that you did."

So, his devious sneak of a brother was at it again, was he? "I assure you, my pleasure far surpasses yours," Spencer said dryly as his gaze bored into Nat. At least his brother had the good grace to look guilty. "Remind me again of exactly what it is I'm buying."

When Sir Horace frowned, Nat gave a nervous laugh. "Don't mind my brother. He enjoys a good jest from time to time." He shot Spencer a pleading look. "The bottle works, Spence, don't you remember?"

"Bottle works," Spencer repeated. Nat had stolen Abby's dowry for that? What the bloody hell did Nat want with a bottle works? And why buy it in Spencer's name?

"Yes," Nat went on hastily, "to produce Bristol blue bottles for the Mead. As a gift to your wife."

Spencer's eyes narrowed. "Of course. I forgot." He flashed Sir Horace a smooth smile. "Unfortunately, I've changed my mind about the purchase. If you'd be so good as to return any funds my brother handed over—"

Sir Horace rose, his bulbous nose reddening. "He hasn't handed anything over yet—we haven't completed the transaction. But this is highly irregular, my lord. I demand to know why you would send your brother to purchase my bottle works and then withdraw for no apparent reason. Why, I spent half the day yesterday showing him around the factory. Then you snap your fingers and expect to undo everything?"

"It's my money, isn't it?" Spencer drawled. "And until I sign anything, it remains my prerogative to change my mind. Which I have."

"Sir Horace, if you could just give me and my brother a moment to speak alone—" Nat began.

"No need for that." Spencer reached over to grab Nat by the arm. "Come on, Nathaniel. You have an appointment in London for which you're already two months late."

"What?" Nat asked as Spencer dragged him toward the door.

"I say, old chap," Sir Horace called out, "are you sure you don't want to take a look at the property yourself before you change your mind? We could go round in the morning—"

"I'm sure." Those were Spencer's last words before he hauled his brother through the door and off down the hall toward the entrance.

"Let go of me, you bloody fool," Nat hissed. "I can walk unassisted."

"That's precisely what worries me," Spencer said, not even pausing in his march for the door. "I fear you'll head unassisted in the wrong direction."

The butler blinked as they swept through the entrance hall, but hastily leaped to open the door. Moments later, Spencer and Nat were in the carriage.

As soon as it set off, Nat exploded. "Do you have any idea how long it took me to set that up? How many bottle works I looked at before I settled on that one? And Peabody was giving it to me for a song, too, only forty-seven hundred pounds."

"Of Abby's money," Spencer snapped.

"Not her money. Yours. The dowry belongs to the husband."

He snorted. "Funny how the husband hasn't seen a penny of it."

Nat stiffened. Reaching inside his pocket, he pulled out a wad of bank notes and tossed it at Spencer. "Here. That's what I was going to give Sir Horace."

He counted them, surprised to find that they did indeed come to forty-seven hundred pounds, only three hundred pounds shy of the five thousand pounds in Abby's dowry. Three hundred was scarcely enough to cover Nat's expenses and Abby's passage to England.

Nonetheless . . . "I thought her dowry was in gold coins."

"I changed them in America before I left. I'm not idiot enough to travel to England with five thousand pounds worth of gold coins in my pockets. There are pirates who roam the seas, for God's sake."

Spencer could only gape at him. "So you really were buying that factory for me? Or rather Abby?"

Nat shrugged. "Actually, when I left America, I'd hoped her father would live a while longer. Then when she came here I'd have the factory bought and the beginnings of the business established here, all neatly tied up in property you or she might be reluctant to sell out of hand. So she'd stay to help me run the thing, and you'd be around her all the time, and there'd be the problem of the marriage . . ."

"And perhaps Abby and I would think it better just to let things lie."

"Or you'd do something noble like insist on maintaining the marriage for her sake, and she would agree." Nat gazed steadily at his brother. "That woman was half in love with you before she even left America. She spent nearly every day after your departure mooning over you. That's why I knew my plan would work. She wanted you, and you wanted her. I knew you wouldn't let her leave once she got here."

Spencer shook his head in sheer amazement at his brother's audacity. "The only reason I didn't let her leave initially was because you were missing and I couldn't risk a scandal. So your original plan would have failed miserably.

If she'd arrived according to *your* plan, and you'd told me you'd spent her dowry on a bottle works, I would have sold the factory at a loss, paid her off, and cut your allowance to compensate."

"And let her go back to America alone?" Nat snorted. "You would have had to take her back there, if only to dissolve the marriage. And you know how those long ship passages are . . ." Nat thrust his chin out defiantly. "You both liked each other, and I knew it. You just needed an excuse to be together long enough to realize it for yourselves."

"An excuse which you provided by marrying me off without informing me."

"If I'd informed you, you wouldn't have married her. And you know you wanted to." Nat scowled. "I certainly wanted you to. I wasn't about to let you make me heir to all the blasted Ravenswood properties and the blasted Ravenswood title. A position for which I'm ill-suited, as you ought to realize by now."

Spencer opened his mouth, then closed it. Yesterday he would have exploded into fury at his brother's characteristic habit of seeing his actions only through his own distorted glass. Today was a different matter. "So you took the bull by the horns, so to speak."

His calm tone seemed to give Nat pause. The young man eyed him warily. "Somebody had to. You certainly weren't going to."

"And you knew exactly what was right for me, what I was capable of handling, and what I ought to do."

Nat looked downright fearful now. "Well . . . I wouldn't put it quite like that—"

"Why not? That's how I always put it when I made choices for you." He settled back against the seat, pinning Nat with a dark glance. "I'm proud to see you following so closely in my footsteps, really I am. But since I have more experience in trying to run people's lives without consulting them, let me give you a little helpful advice. First of all, never try to run more than one person's life at a time. It's too complicated, and you risk their taking actions on their own that might destroy your carefully laid plans."

Nat sank against the squabs, crossing his arms sullenly over his chest. "If you're trying to tell me my scheme didn't work, I won't believe it. Evelina kept me very well informed about how the two of you are getting on."

"Ah, Evelina, the first person who didn't act according to your plan. Let's talk about your fiancée and her letters. The last one was returned from Wales, since she didn't have a new address to send it to."

He flushed. "My letter's on its way to her. I didn't have time to post it in Wales. I was in too much of a hurry trying to outstrip some rogues shadowing me—I assume they were yours." His eyes narrowed. "I thought I'd given them the slip. How did you know where to find me?"

"Oh, my runners found out all about your business contacts. And when Evelina came yesterday evening, desperate to reach you—"

"Desperate?" he asked with a frown. "Why? Has something happened?"

Spencer glowered at his brother. "Ask yourself what you were doing two months ago when you should have been keeping your prick in your trousers, and you'll have the answer to that question."

Nat blinked, then stared at him, stunned. "Evelina? She's . . . she's—"

"With child. Congratulations."

"My God," Nat said hoarsely, "I'm having a baby."

For the first time in his life, those words didn't strike envy into Spencer's heart. "I believe *she* is the one having the baby." He leveled a stern glance on his brother. "And she is the one who will suffer society's disapprobation if you don't marry her at once."

Nat's pleasure turned to alarm just that quick. "Is she all right?"

"She will be, once you're there. But the only way to preserve her reputation is if the two of you elope immediately, making people think you simply couldn't wait for a wedding. That way her mother—who's not the brightest candle in the sconce and is liable to cause trouble if you tell her the truth—won't be involved."

"Yes, whatever you say," Nat murmured, still looking dazed.

"Then you'll have to take her to Essex once she's close to her time and keep her there for a while so people won't speculate about her exceedingly early baby."

"Right." Nat glanced up. "Essex. You mean the estate?"

Spencer eyed him askance. "Unless you own a house in Essex that I don't know about."

"You would . . . let me go back there even after—"

"It's your home and you're my brother," he said evenly. "Of course I would let you go back there."

"My God, Spence, I don't know what to say." Then his face hardened. "Oh, of course you would let us go there. Can't risk a scandal." He gave a bitter laugh. "That's why my plan to keep you married to Abby worked. I can always count on you to fix my mistakes, not because you give a damn about me, but because you have to maintain a certain image. That's why the lofty Ravenswood can't tell his brother he's sterile, except when he's too drunk to know what he's saying. Can't have people thinking he's weak, you know."

A deep sadness settled into Spencer's chest. He'd known that his relationship to Nat had deteriorated through the years, but he'd always blamed Nat for that. Or Dora and his father. Perhaps it was time he acknowledge his own part in it and try to make amends.

"I want you at the estate because Abby and I will be there once Parliament is no longer in session." If Abby forgave him, that is. If she didn't— No, he wouldn't think about that. "If you truly wish to make a go of this business, you and Abby will have to develop a plan for it. She's already selling the Mead in London as a perfume, so you might want to consider pursuing that avenue."

Nat gaped at him as if he'd gone mad. "You would let me . . . and Abby—"

"Let you? Good God, man, you're twenty-nine and an expectant father. If you're not ready to choose your own path in life by now, you never will be."

With a surge of excitement, Nat leaned forward to grab Spencer's hands, squeezing them fiercely. "You won't regret this, Spence, I swear. I'll make the best of this chance. I'll make you proud of me."

"There will be conditions, of course," Spencer said gruffly, unused to such effusive emotion from his brother.

Releasing Spencer's hands, Nat settled back into his seat. "Whatever you want."

Spencer stifled a smile at his brother's enthusiasm. "Your firstborn child?"

Shock filled Nat's face.

"I'm joking," Spencer said hastily. "For God's sake, I'm joking."

Nat eyed him suspiciously. "You never joke."

"Then it's about time I start, don't you think?"

A slow smile lit Nat's face. "Yes." He started nodding. "Yes, I suppose it is."

They'd reached Bristol proper now, and a thought occurred to Spencer. "Do you need to stop at the inn to gather your belongings?"

"I can always send for them from London." Nat flicked his gaze over Spencer. "But you look pretty haggard. Why don't you take my room in the inn tonight, and let me go on in a mail coach?"

"I can't. I promised Abby I'd be back in time for the Throckmortons' May Day fête tomorrow night. I'm supposed to introduce her to the king, and I know she's nervous. That's why I posted through the night to get here, and why I intend to post through the night to get back."

Nat stared at him. "Despite having such an important political engagement tomorrow, you came all the way to Bristol after me just because Evelina asked?"

Spencer sighed. "I know I've been something of an ass from time to time, Nat. But I have always wanted only the best for you."

Nat ventured a smile. "You probably find this hard to believe, but I did the same for you." He glanced down at his hands. "You are . . . I mean . . . Abby does make you happy, doesn't she?"

A laugh swelled in Spencer's throat that he barely managed to check. "You have just presented me with quite a dilemma. On the one hand, I don't want to encourage this deplorable habit you've developed of behaving like your older brother."

Nat's head shot up, his eyes narrowing. "And on the other hand?"

"She makes me insanely happy." As Nat broke into a grin, he added severely, "However, I have not made *her* terribly happy. And I'm not sure if she'll be able to forgive me for that." He added, his throat tight, "Before I left London, she said that she was leaving me as soon as I could take her back to America."

"Why, for God's sake? You must have done something, said something . . . Wait, please say you didn't tell Abby you're sterile."

"Of course I told her. She had the right to know."

"But you're not even certain that you are."

Spencer frowned. "I'm a bit hazy about what I said to you

in America—but surely I mentioned that I've never used any methods to prevent children with my mistresses. And none of them have ever borne me a by-blow."

"How do you know *they* didn't use something? Light-skirts sometimes use methods a man can't detect, like sponges or pessaries."

"I suppose that's possible. But there was Genevieve, who knew the truth, so she had no need to use anything. I told her that my mettle lacked mettle."

Nat laughed. "And of course she took you at your word. Never mind that you were a spymaster and a lying dog. When you said she needn't prevent children, she listened."

Spencer could only stare at him.

"Didn't think of that, did you?" Nat asked, eyes twinkling. "Of course not. The great Ravenswood expects it to be so, and it is. Well, not everybody heeds your pronouncements, dear brother. They simply don't tell you they're ignoring you."

Spencer hardly knew what to think. Nat was right—it had never occurred to him that Genevieve might not believe him. Was it possible he might actually be able to—

He squelched the thought before he could hope. "No," he said firmly. "Genevieve would never have hidden such a thing from me. And we were together for three years."

"Suit yourself, you know the chit better than I do. But even if you're right and you can't sire children, you can always take in foundlings."

"That's what Abby said. That's partly why she's . . . leaving me. I told her I would never do it."

"Why not?"

"It seems silly now, but at the time I was thinking of how Dora left us."

"Dora? You let our stepmother and her disastrous marriage to Father stop you?"

Nat sounded so incredulous that Spencer got defensive. "Well, yes. She wanted children, and Father wouldn't give them to her. And clearly we weren't enough for her, so she ran off."

"For a man who used to be a spymaster," Nat said, shaking his head, "you can sometimes be damned oblivious."

"What the hell does that mean?"

"Our not being 'enough for her' wasn't why she left. Granted, I know she wanted children, but that wasn't the main trouble. What made her grow to hate Father was his refusal to share her bed. For years, apparently."

"What? How do you know?"

Nat crossed his arms smugly over his chest. "If you'll recall, dear brother, I was at home for most of their marriage while you were at school. And I wasn't averse to spying on the servants. I was rather sneaky about it—that way I heard the juiciest gossip. And they gossiped. A lot."

"About Father's marriage bed?" Spencer said, outraged.

"Among other things. I heard from Father's valet that he'd only married her to give us a mother. Then I heard from Dora's maid all about how disillusioned Dora became when she realized he didn't love her. That same maid also said that Father had banished Dora from his bed when she started plaguing him about children. I guess he was afraid she would trick him one night into . . . well . . . you know, completing the dirty deed, so he stopped taking her to his bed. That was years before she left."

For the second time in an hour, Spencer stared at his brother in dumb disbelief.

"I didn't blame her a bit for running off," Nat went on. "I'd run off, too, if my choice was between an old grouch who wouldn't touch me and a young and virile Italian."

Spencer shook his head. "Why didn't you ever tell me?"

"I figured you knew. The rest of us did, even Theo. Besides, you were never home, remember? You went straight from school to the war, and when you returned, you'd become this serious and scary patriarch who was always ordering everyone about. I wasn't going to tell you anything that might spark your temper."

A mad laugh escaped Spencer's lips, then another and another. When his brother eyed him warily, Spencer said, "I've been even more of an idiot than I dreamed."

"Have you?"

"It was Dora I kept thinking about whenever I refused to marry. It was my memories of Dora that made me say the most awful things to Abby and tell her a lot of nonsense about women and children not their own . . . That's why she got angry at me. Because I wouldn't trust her. Because I wanted everything my own way."

Nat searched his face. "And now?"

He sighed. "Now I just want Abby. If she'll take me."

"Of course she will. Tell her you love her, that's all. You do, don't you?"

"Yes. And I already told her." With a frown Spencer glanced out the window. "But I fear I'll need something stronger than words to restore her faith in me after all I've put her through."

They rode a while in silence, listening to the carriage creak as it strained up the hills, then rumbled furiously down. The three-quarter moon rose, casting a soft eerie light over the same hedge-divided fields of meadowsweet and betony Spencer had passed on his way from London. Thank God for fine weather and a dry road. If their luck held, they might make it in time for the Throckmortons' fête. The first step in persuading Abby of his sincerity this time must be keeping his promises.

Suddenly a thought occurred to him. "What time is it, Nat?"

Nat turned up the carriage lamp, to look at his pocket watch. "After midnight."

"The fête starts at seven P.M. tomorrow. Even with stopping to change horses and eat, we should make it, don't you think?"

"Or be no more than an hour late. Why?"

"Because once we're in London, I want to make a quick stop."

"Where?"

"At the foundling hospital. To find out what they require. If I can tell Abby I set up an appointment for us to talk to them later, she'll have to believe I mean what I say."

"Before you go taking in a bunch of foundlings, perhaps you should first make sure you can't have children of your own. Talk to one of your mistresses and see if they used any preventive methods."

Spencer nodded. "Genevieve. If she didn't use anything, it's obvious I can't sire children. She's pregnant by her new husband scarcely a year after they married. But if she did use something . . ." If there was any possibility he could sire children of his own, he could at least offer Abby that hope.

"Two stops then," Spencer went on. "Just drop me at Genevieve's. I won't be long. I'll take a hack from there to the foundling hospital and then home to dress. I know you want to get to the fête and find Evelina as soon as possible."

"Thank you, Spence." Nat leaned forward and patted his brother's knee. "It'll be all right, you'll see. Abby would be a fool to leave you."

Spencer shook his head. "After what I've put her through, she'd be a fool to stay. But she came all the way to England to be with me because of the promises made by a scoundrel like you. So maybe she'll stay because of promises made by a scoundrel like me."

Chapter 25

If you should be so privileged as to work for an employer who consorts with royalty, take great care to learn the proper way to attend such lofty personages.

Suggestions for the Stoic Servant

"Heaven's Scent is a decided success," Clara told Abby as they stood on the periphery of the crowd at the Throckmortons' May Day fête. "Half the ladies here seem to be wearing it, and Mr. Jackson told me yesterday when I was at his shop that he's placed orders for a hundred bottles since Saturday."

"That's nice," Abby said absently.

"Nice? It's wonderful. Only think of how well the business will do as word gets around."

"I'm sure you're right." She ought to be thrilled by this chance to be financially secure without having to rely on her dowry. Given Nat's unscrupulous behavior, there was no telling how much might be left of it. Even if a large portion remained, Spencer might withhold the money indefinitely in an attempt to keep her here longer. So she had to have the funds she would gain through Lady Brumley's scheme.

Yet all she could think was the more money she got, the sooner she'd be able to leave Spencer. And leaving Spencer was going to kill her.

"Are you sure your husband is keeping an eye out for him?" Abby asked Clara.

Though Captain Blakely had been stationed near the ballroom entrance, Abby had glanced there, too, from time to time. Still no sign of Spencer.

Clara chuckled. "You really are worried about him, aren't you? But you needn't fret yourself—he'll be here. He wouldn't miss anything so important to you."

"It's not me I'm worried about. I don't want Spencer to suffer if the king takes his absence as an insult." Bad enough that her "estrangement" from Spencer would soon subject him to comment, no matter how carefully they handled it. She refused to also be responsible for damage to his career.

"What a considerate wife you are," Clara said smoothly. "I take it you survived Spencer's temper last Saturday night?"

The night when he'd made love to her so sweetly, then told her he didn't believe her capable of fidelity, loyalty, or honor? "Yes," she said noncommittally. She'd survived—if you could call this state of numb despair survival.

"Are you all right, Abby? You've scarcely spoken two words since Morgan and I picked you up."

"I'm fine, really I am," Abby said. The blatant lie was all she could manage tonight. Eventually she'd have to tell Clara what had happened, but not until she had decided how much to reveal.

"Well, well," Clara said, fixing her eyes suddenly on the entrance. "The prodigal comes home."

Abby's cursed heart leaped as she turned to look. But it was only Nathaniel, who spoke to Captain Blakely just inside the doors to the ballroom. And without Spencer.

"Excuse me," Abby muttered as she hurried off toward them.

Captain Blakely looked up just as she approached and with a frown leaned toward Nathaniel as if to say something.

But before he got a word out, Abby heard Nathaniel say, "He won't be long at Genevieve's, I'm sure, and then—"

"Shut up, you fool," Captain Blakely growled as Abby halted, her heart sinking.

When Nathaniel turned to see her there, his face turned the color of chalk.

"He . . . he went to his mistress?" she whispered. Good heavens, he couldn't even wait until she was out of London before he took up with the woman again?

"No!" Nathaniel exclaimed. "It wasn't like that, Abby. He wanted to find out if she—" He glanced at Captain Blakely, then came up to Abby and pulled her out of earshot. "He went to find out if she ever used any sort of measures to prevent children. You know, in case he isn't as . . . damaged as he at first believed."

She stared at him, not sure what to think. Spencer was trying to find out if he could have children? Was this one more way to keep her here? Did he intend to promise he could sire a child whether he could or not?

When she scowled, Nathaniel went on hastily, "He went at my insistence. I told him he should be sure he was sterile before he visited the foundling hospital to discuss—"

"The foundling hospital?" A tiny hope sprouted in her chest. "He's planning to go to the foundling hospital?"

"Not planning to go." Relief filled Nathaniel's face. "He's there now. That's where he was going after he left Genevieve's."

Her hope burst into flower. If Spencer was willing to take in foundlings, that meant—

"He does love you, you know," Nathaniel said. "Don't let my blundering ruin everything."

Ruin everything? She was beside herself with joy. Spencer must really love her if he was considering possibilities, looking into the future, *their* future.

Ready to explode with happiness, she was about to reassure Nathaniel that his *blundering* hadn't ruined anything when she checked herself.

This wasn't the first time Nathaniel Law had blundered in his brother's life. Though his slip of the tongue had proved harmless enough, his earlier actions had nearly wrecked several lives. And all because he blithely thought to do his brother a "favor."

It was time the younger Mr. Law learned to stay out of his brother's affairs. And hers. Smoothing her features into a cold mask, she said, "He went to his mistress, Nathaniel. Surely you can't expect me to forgive that."

Panic spread over the young man's features. "But not for . . . It wasn't like that. And he was going to the foundling hospital straightaway after—"

"A likely story."

"It's the truth!"

"Oh, I'm sure that's what he told you, but thanks to you I've learned the hard way that men like Spencer meet their needs wherever they must. I was handy enough, but now that I'm leaving, he's gone off to his old mistress."

"No!" Nathaniel looked positively sick. "You must believe me—he wants you to stay! He loves you, he—"

"I'm not stupid enough to believe your lies twice. I'm leaving tomorrow, and there's naught you can say to stop me."

"Oh, God, you can't do that," Nathaniel began.

"Enough." Time to send him off, before he caught on that she was tormenting him on purpose. She wasn't about to relieve him of his agitation too easily. Let him stew over his mistakes for a while. "Isn't that your fiancée I see over there with a young gentleman? I suggest you take care of your own affairs and stop worrying about mine."

Nathaniel glanced over to where Evelina was fortuitously skirting the circle of dancers that surrounded the massive maypole erected in the middle of the spacious ballroom. A handsome fellow had given her his arm, and they seemed to be conversing quite pleasantly. Nathaniel scowled.

"Don't go anywhere," he grumbled. "I'm coming back in a moment to continue this discussion." Then he headed for his fiancée.

Abby smothered a laugh. Not if she could help it. She fully intended to rub young Nathaniel's nose in his perfidy for as long as Spencer went along with it. But that might be difficult—right now she was so happy she couldn't pretend to be mad at him for long.

Spencer had gone to the foundling hospital! Even though his political future was at stake if he didn't show up here, he'd gone to the foundling hospital for her. The realization of what that meant made her giddy.

"Lady Ravenswood," a tart voice said behind her.

She whirled to find Lady Brumley standing near her with a portly gentleman and three finely dressed ladies. One look at the man's elegant and costly attire was enough to bring Abby to instant panic. Good heaven, he could only be—

"His Majesty has expressed a desire to be introduced to you, my dear," Lady Brumley said, eyes twinkling. She performed the introductions swiftly. Abby dropped into a curtsy that she hoped was the right one.

When she straightened, His Majesty took her hand and kissed it with regal chivalry. "We would have left it to your husband to perform the office, but he doesn't seem to be here."

"N-no, Your Majesty." Frantically Abby tried to remember everything Clara had taught her about addressing the king. "He . . . er . . . was delayed by a very urgent personal matter. But he'll be here shortly, I assure you."

"Oh, I hope not," His Majesty said dryly. "I'm looking forward to having you all to myself for a while."

Heavenly day, what was she to say to that?

Apparently nothing, for he went on without waiting for

her answer. "I understand from her ladyship that you have a gift for me."

"Oh, yes, of course." Abby fumbled hastily in her reticule for the bottle of Heaven's Scent that Spencer had instructed her to bring. She held it out to the king, then hoped she hadn't erred. Was there some protocol for offering gifts to royalty? Had she just shown her ignorance again?

Hard to tell from the smile he gave her as he took it. He removed the stopper, sniffed, and then lifted one eyebrow. "What a delightful scent," he commented. "Though it's hard to judge scent in the bottle. If I could just smell it on the wrist—"

He hadn't even finished before four ladies had removed their gloves and thrust their bare arms in front of him, including Lady Brumley. Belatedly, Abby realized she should have done the same. Would it look stupid if she did it now?

With a laugh, he gestured to the other ladies to lower their arms. Then he held out his hand to Abby and said, "If you would be so kind as to remove your glove—"

"Oh, of course," she said quickly and did as he bade.

"I assume you are wearing the scent already." Taking her hand, he lifted her wrist to his nose and sniffed. "Exquisite," he added as he lingered over her hand.

This began to feel decidedly improper. King or no, he shouldn't be so forward.

Gently, Abby tugged her hand free. "It will please my husband to hear that Your Majesty enjoys my paltry gift."

His eyes showed amusement at her mention of Spencer. "And you, my lady? Does it please you?"

She managed a smile. "Of course."

"Then perhaps you'd honor me with a waltz."

He motioned to the orchestra, who abruptly stopped playing a quadrille and launched immediately into waltz music, which caused some momentary confusion on the dance floor.

The king didn't seem to care. He held out his arm. "Come, my dear, let us dance."

"Certainly." She laid her hand on his arm and let him lead her to the floor.

Wonderful. Just great. Nothing like going right to the top of society for a partner the first time one tested one's waltzing skills on the dance floor. Perhaps she should step on his feet now and be done with it. Thank God Spencer had been detained. At least he wouldn't have to watch her single-handedly destroy his political career.

Then she heard Spencer's voice in her head. *He's only a man after all, Abby, and no one to be afraid of.*

She stared at the king, with his elegantly embroidered waistcoat and overly pampered skin. And that's when she saw it. A flea, crawling slowly along the edge of the king's perfectly starched collar, seeking a bit of the royal blood for its supper.

It took all her control not to laugh. The king might be powerful, he might smell of the richest almond milk and the most expensive snuff, but even he could not escape the natural order of things. Spencer was right. There was indeed nothing to be afraid of.

So when the music began, she smiled at the king, lifted her heels, and danced.

The lights were ablaze at Throckmortons' when Spencer arrived, and a line of carriages still waited to get near the house. Too impatient to wait, he leaped from the hackney and walked the last few yards to the entrance. But he'd barely reached the stairs before Nathaniel emerged from the shadows.

"Why the devil are you skulking about out here?" Spencer asked. "I thought you were taking Evelina off to Gretna Green?"

"I am. She's waiting in a hackney down the street. But before we left I had to talk to you." Nat frowned. "You're here rather quickly, aren't you?"

Spencer broke into a broad grin. "You were right about Genevieve. She did use something; she just didn't tell me. So I didn't go on to the foundling hospital. I thought I'd talk to Abby first and see what she wanted to do."

Nat's low moan gave him pause.

"What's wrong?"

"I didn't mean to do it, Spence," Nat said. "It was purely an accident that she came up when I was telling Blakely—Oh, God, oh, God, you're going to kill me."

"Indeed I will, if you don't tell me what the devil you're blathering about."

Nat let out a sound of pure despair. "Abby overheard me telling Blakely that you'd gone to Genevieve's and she thought—"

"You bloody, bloody ass!" Spencer's heart nearly failed him right there. "Tell me you explained why I went there, or I swear I'll thrash you in front of God and everyone!"

"I explained, I did!" Nat stepped back, eyes wide with alarm. "I told her why, I told her about the foundling hospital, I told her you loved her—"

"Wait a minute." Spencer's eyes narrowed. "You told her about the foundling hospital? How did she react?"

"At first it seemed to please her. But then she got all cool and awful and went on and on about how she couldn't ever believe me again after all my lies and—"

"Tell me exactly what she said, Nat," Spencer put in, a cautious relief budding in his chest. "Word for word."

Nat related the entire conversation, each word lessening Spencer's panic a little more. But when Nat got to the part about Abby's leaving tomorrow, Spencer knew for sure what was going on.

Abby had already promised not to leave until after the parliamentary sessions were over. Besides, she wasn't stupid enough to run off without securing her financial future. And he couldn't believe she would ignore the significance of his going to a foundling hospital.

But she might want Nat to think she would. It was just the sort of thing she'd do.

He could barely suppress his smile. His minx of a wife had found the perfect way to get her revenge on Nat for all his manipulations. And since Abby seemed to engage in mischief only when she was happy, dare he hope that her actions signaled her return to Spencer's affections?

Whether they did or not, Spencer wasn't about to deprive her of her just revenge. Besides, he had let Nat off a little too easily. So he released an exaggerated moan for his brother's benefit.

Nat instantly reacted. "I'm so sorry, Spence. I tried to talk to her again, but she was dancing. Then I thought it might be better if I warned you before you got in there."

"Your warning is too late." Spencer injected his voice with as much despair as he could muster. "She'll leave me now for sure, and there's nothing I can do about it."

"That's not true," Nat protested. "You have to talk to her and explain."

"There's no point to it after she's made up her mind. She won't believe me."

"If you don't talk to her, I will," Nat said fiercely, turning toward the entrance.

"No!" Spencer cried. When Nat halted to gape at him, he added quickly, "Haven't you done enough? Anything you say will only make it worse."

"Damn, that's probably true." Nat sighed heavily.

Spencer shot his brother a long-suffering look. "You and Evelina just go on to Gretna Green. I'll feel better knowing at least one of us is happy." He looked back and spotted his equipage parked down the road. "No need to use a hired coach. Take my carriage. Abby came with Blakely and Clara, so they can take me home. If Abby will even let me within her sight, that is."

He almost regretted that last bit when Nat groaned and looked utterly miserable.

But in for a penny, in for a pound. "Go on then, and hurry. Lady Tyndale will start looking for Evelina any minute, and then you'll never escape." He fixed his brother with a stern look. "You've got other more important obligations now, you know."

With a nod, Nat drew himself up like the responsible young man he seemed to be becoming. Then he headed off down the road.

Once he'd disposed of Nat, Spencer could hardly keep from taking the entrance steps two at a time. His wife was dancing, was she? Well, not for long. He intended to whisk her off into a private spot where he could lay his heart at her feet.

As soon as he was announced, he ran into Blakely and Clara very near the entrance. "Have you seen my wife?" he asked them without preamble.

"She's on the dance floor," Blakely answered. "With His Majesty."

Spencer turned to look, and his heart caught in his throat. Abby was a vision of loveliness tonight. Gone was the awkward American, gone the faux Englishwoman. All that remained was his beautiful wild rose.

Somehow she managed to fit in and stand out at the same time. Her dancing was perfectly accomplished, all that any king could expect. But unlike the stiff and elegant ladies around her, she looked as if she was actually having fun. Her gown was like all of theirs, but her hair was swept up in that seductively loose coiffure, and her skin glowed richly golden under the candles. Next to the tight curls and white faces of the other young misses, she shone like a rose among daisies. He could hardly contain his pride.

"How long have they been dancing?" he asked Lady Clara.

"This is actually their second dance. They danced a waltz together first. It appears that His Majesty has taken a fancy to your wife."

Eyes narrowing, Spencer observed the adoring gaze of Abby's dance partner and then scowled. Spencer had a little surprise for His Majesty. Abigail Law, the Viscountess Ravenswood, would never be that scoundrel's conquest. "Who introduced them?"

"Lady Brumley." Clara added archly, "You weren't here, after all."

No doubt Clara remembered his behaving like an ass at the marchioness's breakfast. "I can see I'll have to have a long talk with Lady Brumley about my wife. Since they're going to be partnered in business and all."

Clara gave a small smile, but her husband looked less sanguine. "Er . . . Ravenswood . . . your brother happened to mention something in your wife's hearing—"

"I know. Nat met me outside and told me."

"You're not worried?"

"I'm not worried." Or at least he didn't think he was. "How long is this quadrille anyway?"

"It's almost over. But I'd move in quickly, if I were you. His Majesty has made his intentions fairly clear."

Spencer nodded grimly. "Then I shall have to make my intentions even clearer."

The music ended, and Spencer started off toward the other end of the room. But through the crowd that hindered any quick movement, he saw the king leading his wife out the open doors to one of the balconies.

Spencer quickened his pace. If that lecherous sot thought

he was going to lay one hand on Abby, he was in for a bloody surprise.

After he burst through the doors and onto the balcony, it took him a moment to find them. They stood at the far corner of the balcony side by side, looking up at the sky.

He overheard Abby say in a carrying voice, "Are you sure the fireworks are going to be set off now, Your Majesty? I heard earlier that it wouldn't happen before midnight."

"I do believe you're right," the king retorted. When Abby half turned as if to leave, the king laid his hand on her waist and urged her back to his side. "But the stars are so brilliant tonight, surely you don't mind keeping me company while I look at them."

With a scowl, Spencer increased his pace. Killing the king would constitute treason, but perhaps he could get away with maiming the bastard—

"I would be honored," Abby answered, though she reached back and removed the hand His Majesty had rested in the small of her back.

Spencer smiled. Until His Majesty merely returned his hand to her waist.

"Ah, there you are, my dear," Spencer said as he neared them, hoping he didn't sound as furious as he felt.

Abby's heart sank into her stomach at the sound of Spencer's voice. Swiftly she turned to find him standing nearby, feet apart, scowl in place, and a clear look of murder in his eyes.

Oh, dear, this couldn't be good. "You're here, my lord!" she exclaimed. "I'm so happy to see that you arrived safely. Your Majesty, if you would excuse me—"

"Not yet," His Majesty said, tightening his grip on her waist.

Wonderful. She'd managed to preserve Spencer's career through the waltz and the quadrille and it was now to be felled because of His Majesty's apparent death wish.

Then Spencer surprised her by inclining his head in a sketchy bow. "Your Majesty," Spencer said smoothly. "Thank you for keeping my wife company, but now I would very much like to dance with her."

The words weren't a request, no matter how courteously they were worded, and the king apparently knew it, for his hand continued to grip her with surprising strength for a man of his age and girth. "I swear, Ravenswood, you are even cooler a one than I thought. Don't you care about your wife enough to show concern when she's alone with another man?"

What a fine idea, Your Majesty. Provoke my mad husband. That will certainly help matters.

But though Spencer's eyes glittered, when he glanced to her he smiled. "It's precisely because I care that I'm not concerned. You see, I trust my wife implicitly." His gaze locked with hers. "She would never shame or betray me." *Or leave me,* his eyes seemed to say. "She's too much a woman of character for that."

Abby's heart swelled in her throat, threatening to choke off all her breath. Her love. At last he really was her love.

If not for the king's restraining hand, she would toss herself at Spencer like a shameless wanton. "Thank you, my lord." She cast the king a pleading glance. "If you will excuse me, Your Majesty, I haven't seen my husband in two days . . ."

King George eyed them both closely, then sighed. "Apparently Lady Brumley was correct in her assessment of your match, though I doubted it myself. Go on, my dear lady. Enjoy your dance with your husband." His hand left her waist. "And thank you for the bottle of scent. I'll think of you fondly whenever I smell it."

Spencer's eyes flared dangerously, so she murmured some inane response and hastened to meet him. But as he took her arm, he didn't lead her back inside. Instead he steered her toward the steps at the far end that led into the garden.

As soon as she could be sure they were out of the king's earshot, she whispered, "Heavens, you gave me a scare. I thought for sure you were going to say or do something to the king that would wreck your political future forever."

"Something like, 'Touch my wife again, you lecherous goat, and I'll personally remove your crown jewels with a carving knife?'"

A laugh bubbled up from her throat. "Something like that."

"I thought about it. And not because I don't trust you, but because I don't trust him. Bloody old sot can't keep his hands to himself—he ought to be ashamed."

"Well, I for one am glad you didn't speak your mind, even if I do find the idea of you chained in the Tower vastly appealing."

"Do you?" Spencer drew her beneath some trees, then faced her. His gaze looked uncertain as it met hers. "Is that because you want so desperately to see me receive my well-deserved punishment for all my controlling and arrogant ways?"

"That's part of it." As she tilted her face up to him, she watched him carefully. "And I like the idea of your being at my complete mercy."

"Very well." Taking her by surprise, he dropped to his knees and seized her hands. "You said I never beg. So I'm begging now. Stay with me, Abby, and be my wife."

Her pulse quickened as she stared down into his earnest and infinitely dear face. "Nat told me you went to the foundling hospital on your way here. Does that mean what I think it does?"

"That I love you? That I want you to raise our children?"

"Our foundling children?" she prodded.

"And whatever others you manage to acquire. It seems that my assumptions about my ability to sire children might have been faulty."

For a moment, her heart lurched. "What if they're not?"

He cast her a solemn look. "Whether you bear me ten or none, whether we adopt foundlings or Clara's pickpockets or the first urchin you stumble upon in the street, it is all the same to me. I want you as my wife."

"Forever?" she said, wanting to be sure.

"Until death do us part. Which I fervently pray won't be anytime soon."

Unable to control her joy a moment longer, she leaned down to kiss him hard on the lips, then murmured, "About wanting to see you chained in the Tower—did I happen to mention that I'd want you chained naked?"

A second passed during which his expression of surprise was almost comical. Then he leaped up to wrap her in his arms so tightly he lifted her right off the ground. As his mouth crashed down on hers in a stormy kiss, she thought, *At last the thunder god is mine.*

When he drew back, after plundering her mouth for what seemed like an eternity, she whispered, "What made you change your mind?"

"You're joking, right? Faced with the possibility of life without you, do you really think I'd be fool enough to let you go?"

"You said you would."

"I know. I was being my usual manipulative self, determined to have everything my way, just as you said. It's a bad habit I've developed over the years. But it's one I intend to break."

How could she not kiss him again after such a wonderful pronouncement? And this kiss lasted longer and was hotter, too. By the time they were finished, he'd pushed her against the tree and was already fumbling for the buttons at the back of her dress.

"Spencer!" she protested weakly. "Someone might see us."

"Nonsense. Why do you think they keep the gardens so dimly lit at these affairs?"

"To save on lantern oil?" She sucked in a breath as her bodice gave way.

"To reward randy husbands whose wives have just forgiven them." He drew back. "You have forgiven me, haven't you?"

"I don't know," she teased as she unbuttoned his waistcoat. Wondering if he would mention his visit to Genevieve's, she added, "I've forgiven you for everything that happened before you left. But have you done anything since that I need to forgive you for?"

"No." At her scowl, he added, "Surely you don't mean my visit to Genevieve's. Nat said he told you why I went, and I don't see anything in that to forgive."

"Don't you?" she teased, then realized what he'd said. "Wait a minute, you talked to Nathaniel after you arrived?" Suddenly, all her words came back to her, and she groaned. "Oh, no, he told you—"

"It's all right. I guessed fairly quickly what you were about. And I must say that you managed to do what I hadn't been able to—instill some guilt in my reckless brother."

Her eyes narrowed. "You didn't tell him I was bamming him, did you?"

Spencer chuckled. "And ruin your little revenge? Not on your life." He bent his head to kiss her cheek and then her neck, and the blood roared in her ears.

"So," she whispered while she still had the power of speech, "how long do you think we should wait before we tell him the truth?"

"Since he's eloping with Evelina even as we speak, we'll have to wait at least two weeks until they return." He edged her gown off her shoulders. "And after that, oh, I don't know. A while longer while we disappear."

"Why are we disappearing?"

"For our honeymoon trip, of course." He nibbled her ear. "We have to celebrate the end of our pretend marriage and the beginning of the real one. So that would be what—two more weeks? A month? Any longer, and Nat might figure out what we're up to. We wouldn't want that."

He started to kiss her, but she pulled back to stare at him. "Why, Spencer Law, I do believe you can be mischievous after all."

He grinned. "I'm learning, my love," he said as he drew her back into his arms and bent his mouth to hers. "I'm learning."

Epilogue

The arrival of children to one's employer brings additional work, it is true. But it also brings additional joy.

Suggestions for the Stoic Servant

Spencer sat in the hall, dandling Belinda on his knee and trying not to worry while Dr. Godfrey examined his wife in their bedchamber. He forced himself to focus on his baby daughter's pretty black eyes regarding him with pure adoration. She'd certainly filled out nicely since she'd left the foundling hospital last year as a scrawny and too solemn mite.

"Da," she said, wrapping one chubby fist in his cravat to tug it all askew. "Da-da."

He laughed. "Yes, my clever girl," he said, bouncing her until she giggled. "It's Da-da." Hard to believe he'd once contemplated giving this up because of some foolish fears. His little Belle, as he liked to call her, was one of the lights of his life.

Another one came barreling up the stairs. Spencer bit back a smile as a huffing Mrs. McFee followed after his other daughter and grumbled under her breath with every step. He still couldn't believe the proper McFee had married "that harridan of a servant." Or that the man was now the author—

albeit an anonymous one—of a popular instructional guide for servants.

Lily, who never walked when she could run, raced up to him, not the least out of breath. "Papa, is the doctor still with Mama?"

"Yes, poppet." A lump filled his throat at the sight of her anxious frown.

The former pickpocket was now eleven. He and Abby had scarcely been married a month when he'd suggested adopting the orphan. He'd never forgotten Lily's sad little face that day in the drawing room when she'd talked about her dead mother.

Abby had agreed more readily to it than even he had expected. Which was a good thing, because last year he'd finally accepted that he couldn't sire his own children. For a while Genevieve's claims had given him hope, but after four years of marriage and no pregnancies, they'd both acknowledged that it was not meant to be. That's when they'd adopted Belinda and started discussing how many other children they wanted and what to do about his heir.

He wasn't getting any younger, after all. And Nat was even less inclined to be the heir now that he was happily engaged in running Abby's perfume business and fathering his own two daughters. Ironically, under Evelina's guiding influence the scoundrel had finally grown up enough to be a viable heir. Yet that very taste of responsibility had made him even more adamant about going his own way.

Lily sidled close to stroke little Belinda's silky brown hair. "Is Mama . . . going to die?"

"Oh no, not at all," he hastened to reassure her. "I'm sure it's just la grippe. She'll be over it in no time once she's had some rest."

"I been telling the girl that all morning," Mrs. McFee said, folding her arms over her belly, "but she's not having a word of it. Won't rest until she hears the doctor himself say it's all right."

"I saw her throw up this morning at breakfast," Lily said. "It was awful!"

He drew his daughter close with his free hand. "I know, poppet, but I promise it will be all right." Pray God he could keep that promise.

The door suddenly opened, and Dr. Godfrey came out, smiling broadly.

"How is she?" Spencer asked as he rose.

Dr. Godfrey's eyes twinkled. "She's fine, just fine. Progressing nicely."

What the devil did that mean? Then Abby came out herself, looking a little pale but otherwise well, and he realized the doctor must be right.

"Mama!" Lily cried and ran to her. "I was so worried!"

With a wan smile, Abby hugged the girl. "Nothing to worry about, sweetheart. Now you go off with Mrs. McFee, and take your sister, too. I need to talk to Papa."

Fear made Spencer's heart hammer furiously as he handed the baby to Mrs. McFee. He could hardly wait until they were inside her bedchamber with the door shut before asking, "What did Godfrey tell you? What's wrong?"

She wouldn't look at him. "Um . . . I talked to him about your condition."

"*My* condition?"

"You know, with your . . . wounds."

"He knows about my condition," Spencer said impatiently. "What has that got to do with your condition?"

"He said," she went on, "that he's heard of cases recently where even though a man injured there was—" She waved a hand vaguely in the area of his cock, then finished weakly, "He healed after some years."

He stared at her blankly.

She met his gaze with a wary one. "I'm not ill, Spencer—I'm expecting a child. Our child."

Abby hadn't meant to be so blunt, so when Spencer paled

and jerked his stunned gaze down to her belly, she cursed her-self for her quick tongue. She'd been worrying about how to tell him ever since she'd started to suspect what was going on.

"Are . . . are you sure?" he whispered.

"Yes."

Tears welled in his eyes, and she flew to him in alarm. "It's yours, I swear it is."

He clutched her tightly to him. "Of course it's mine. Whose else would it be?" Then he stiffened and held her away from him. "Oh, Abby, surely you didn't think I would assume—"

"I was a bit worried." She smiled sheepishly. "For the past year, you've been so convinced you could never sire a child, since we'd tried for so long."

"Don't you know by now that I trust you?" he reassured her, cupping her cheek gently in his hand. "I know you would never betray me."

"Never," she vowed.

A loving smile crossed his lips before his gaze drifted back to her belly. "When are you due?" he asked, his voice hoarse with emotion.

"Dr. Godfrey says probably six months from now, seven at the most."

His eyes swung back to hers. "You've known that long?"

"I tried not to hope too much when I missed my courses the first time. But when I started feeling ill in the morning and I missed them a second time, I figured I'd better see Dr. Godfrey. I'm sorry if I gave you and Lily a scare, but I didn't want to say anything until I was absolutely sure."

"Lily." He glanced to the door. "We have to tell Lily."

"Yes." But as he turned in that direction, she held him back. "Spencer, I want to assure you that having my own baby won't affect how I feel about the girls. I'll still love them as much as I do now."

He faced her with a bemused look. "Of course you will,"

he said, enfolding her in his warm embrace. "As will I." He pressed a sweet kiss to her lips, then murmured, "Thank you."

She pulled back and arched one brow. "For what? Bearing you a child?"

"No . . . well, yes, but that's not what I meant." Growing serious, he laid his hand on her belly. "Before I met you, I was sure that having a wife and a family was an unattainable dream. So I'm grateful to the stubborn and persistent woman who showed me it was attainable after all. Thank you, darling, for convincing me to leap the chasm."

As her heart filled with joy, she laid her hand over his. "And thank you, my love, for leaping."